Tangled Up in Texas

By Katy Berritt

Edgecombe Publishing

Published by Edgecombe Publishing 2024

Cover Design by Candace Lucas

Editing by Sevannah Storm

Table of Contents

For my daughter Beret who is the only person in my family who has read my books and left me a review. I hope she'll read this one too.

Other Romantic Comedies by Katy Berritt

The Candy Capers

A Wild and Wooly Texan

Baby and the Bank Robber

Lucky's Ladies

Love & Laughter

Prologue

Texas 1886

"Don't nobody move."

The shout snapped Mac McLean out of his reverie with a jolt. The bag in which he'd stashed his wife's few possessions after her funeral rolled off his lap and landed on the floor with a soft thud. Only half awake, he bent to pick it up, his fingers skimming the needlepoint surface of the bag. He froze when a hand squeezed his shoulder, hard.

"Well, well, if it ain't my old amigo, McLean," a voice from the past said. "Just the man I bin looking for."

Mac clenched his eyes shut. If he didn't see the threat maybe it would disappear. But that, of course, was delusional. Even though it had been years since he'd heard that voice, it was like it were yesterday.

The hand gripping his shoulder tightened. "Aw, come on, Mackie, don't you want to talk with me? I sure want to talk with you."

Unable to avoid the confrontation any longer, Mac opened his eyes and allowed his gaze to slide past the scuffed boots and up the dirty pant legs to the gun pointed at him. He paused there, identifying the long barrel of the gun as a Buntline pistol before slowly sitting up until his gaze reached the face of the man holding it.

Dexter Fox. Despite the bandana covering his features, Mac would never forget his yellowish eyes and the pale blond hair poking out from under a wide-brimmed hat.

"Fox," he muttered, giving the outlaw a grim-lipped smile. "Shouldn't you still be in prison for another four or five years?"

Or better yet, hanged for murdering that poor bank teller.

The edges of the bandana tied around the outlaw's head rose when the face underneath smiled. "Well, hell, son, prison and I didn't suit, ya know. And I missed my friends..." Behind the bandana, the outlaw's yellow eyes seemed to gleam with some unnamed pleasure. He leaned forward and whispered in his ear, "Especially you, Mr. Hotshot Attorney." He snickered.

Five years and the outlaw still wanted revenge on Mac for being the prosecuting attorney at his trial.

"What do you expect me to say, Fox? I was doing my job." Anger and fear pounded through Mac's veins, but he suppressed the urge to lash out. Losing his temper would only leave his one-year-old daughter without a father after she'd already lost her mother.

"Oh, sure. I understand. We all gotta do our jobs. Even me," Fox said with another oily snicker.

Damn it. Damn his bad luck at being on this particular train on this particular day. And how unlucky to have selected a seat far from the other passengers because no one else wanted to sit directly behind the noise and dirt of the locomotive. At the time, it had seemed ideal because he'd needed the privacy to wallow in his misery. After all, it wasn't every day a man had to bury a wife who'd abandoned her baby only to die in the arms of her lover.

Not so lucky now.

He shot a quick look over his shoulder in hopes that someone was aware that he'd been cornered—and threatened—but everyone had their gazes on a second train robber who was walking slowly toward the back of the car, randomly pointing his gun at different passengers, yelling *bang*, then laughing when the person cried out.

No help there.

"So, Mackie," his nemesis said in a low voice, interrupting his thoughts. Mac jerked his gaze forward again, locking on the muzzle of the gun Fox was bouncing in the palm of his hand. "I owe you for all you done for me, and I'd just purely feel like a selfish son of a bitch if I didn't pay you back. Yeah, I think I gotta pay you back. But good. Why don't you come on outta there so's we can talk."

A ripple of dread spiraled down his spine. With his throat tight, his breath short, Mac rose and stepped into the aisle.

The outlaw threw an arm over his shoulder, pulling him close. Still desperate for help, Mac scanned the car again but like before, the passengers were watching the other bandit and ignoring Fox.

The outlaw placed his lips near Mac's ear. "Now, here's what I'm thinking. I'm thinking this here holdup ain't gonna be near as much fun without your help." He pulled a cotton bag from inside his coat and dangled it from one finger. "Sorry it ain't a more important job, but, hey, beggars can't be choosers, can they?" He chuckled. "G'wan. Take it."

Clenching his hands at his sides, Mac shook his head. Refusing might be the death of him, but he couldn't. He just couldn't.

Fox heaved a sigh. "Well, heck. I can see your gonna take some convincing." He surveyed the car. "Let's see. Hmmm." His gaze sharpened. "Aha. I got it. You see the sweet little thing sitting toward the back... the one with the straggly brown hair and the slew of freckles?"

Throwing a glance down the aisle, Mac spotted the girl Fox pointed out. He dipped his chin, a hard knot of fear forming in his stomach.

"Yep," Fox murmured, and smacked his lips. "Young. And sweet. Just the way I like 'em."

God help him. Mac cleared his throat and rasped out, "What are you getting at?"

"You do what I tell you, or I might take some unexpected company along with me when I leave." He gave Mac's shoulder a squeeze. "Comprende?"

For a split-second he considered making a grab for the gun hanging loosely in Fox's hand, but a look at the young woman, unaware of her potential fate, changed his mind. He jerked his head in a single nod.

With a chuckle, Fox thrust the sack in his hands and steered him down the aisle.

OH, MY GOODNESS GRACIOUS. They were being robbed. This was so exciting.

When Gracie boarded the train back home in Pittsburgh, she didn't imagine she'd have a real Western adventure. Of course, this was an adventure she'd never tell her parents about. They would faint dead away then order her home where she'd be doomed to do nothing but sit in their over-ornate parlor for the rest of her life, drinking tea with a bunch of insipid debutantes and old ladies.

But she was twenty-one now, an adult in charge of her own life. Argue though Hiram and Priscilla Hart did, they couldn't stop Gracie from boarding this train to travel far from home. Hopefully, to see her dream of becoming a reporter come true.

With her heart pounding with excitement, she ignored the bandit standing near the back door with his gun out to make sure the passengers stayed in their seats. Instead she watched the two bandits near the front of the car. Those two worked their way toward her, stopping at each row to collect the passengers' money, drawing ever closer. The unmasked bandit held a bag bulging with wallets while the shorter man held a gun in his hand that he didn't hesitate to point at any passenger who protested.

She inhaled sharply. Notes. She should take notes. If she intended to become a reporter, instead of a copy girl for the Dallas Daily Herald, she had to capture every detail of this important event. For certain, nobody else was writing down descriptions. She glanced at the shorter bandit, but his face was covered with a bandana and he wore a hat to cover his hair and part of his face. She snapped her attention to the taller, leaner man... the one without a mask. The man must either be brave that he wasn't afraid to show his face, or else very stupid. Whichever it was, she'd make sure she described him down to the last whisker on his face.

Ripping open the drawstring on her handbag, she rooted through the odds and ends that always cluttered her life and pulled out a small notepad and pencil. Her handbag dropped into the floor next to her.

"What are you doing?" the man next to her whispered. He sounded aghast.

"Shhh. Don't talk. I'm writing a description of the unmasked outlaw. I'm going to write an article for my newspaper."

The man grabbed her hand, yanking at it. "Are you out of your mind? You'll get us killed," he whispered.

"No, I won't. We'll be fine," she muttered, twisting so he couldn't reach her pencil. *Brown eyes. Reddish-brown hair,* she wrote on her pad of paper. *Hah. Betcha anything he had red hair when he was a boy.* She blew a wisp of her dishwater blond hair out of her eyes. *Approximately six foot two.*

Her seatmate made another grab for her pencil. Without thinking, she jabbed him with the sharp end—he yelped—and she returned to her writing.

"Oh my God," he whined. "Why are you doing this? Do you want to die?"

"No, I just want to be a reporter."

He moaned. "Right. A reporter. Well, if you're not careful, you'll be a dead one."

She threw the cowardly man a look. Why couldn't he be quiet? She was struggling to find the right words and she couldn't think with him yammering in her ear. Anyway, she didn't want the taller outlaw to hear because he might decide he wasn't that brave after all and cover his face.

The outlaws stopped a few rows away. The shorter, stockier, masked bandit growled a few words at an elderly white-haired passenger and the man meekly handed over his wallet.

As if sensing her gaze, the unmasked bandit looked in her direction. His somber brown eyes met hers. One corner of his full... luscious... oh, my... kissable mouth tightened, and a dimple flickered in his cheek.

Wow. Her pencil skidded across the page and dug a hole right through the middle of her paper.

"Better shut your mouth or you'll catch flies," her seatmate sneered.

She snapped her mouth shut. "Oh, be quiet," she ordered, still stunned by her first good view of the outlaw. She stared at her tablet. Her description didn't do him justice. Only a picture would do. Quickly flipping to a fresh page, she began to sketch, grateful for the first time for the art lessons her mother insisted she take.

A dark shadow fell over the page.

Glancing up, she gasped in alarm. The tall outlaw stood in the aisle next to her seat, his shorter, masked cohort hidden a step or two behind him, their backs to her as they robbed the poor woman sitting on the other side of the aisle. Seeing how close they were, she shoved the pad under her rear end seconds before the two bandits pivoted in her direction.

Oh my. The masked outlaw had yellow eyes. She'd include them in her written description later but for now, she was glad she'd hidden her tablet. "Good afternoon. May I help you?" she blurted, smiling like a dope. A nervous titter rippled through the car.

The unmasked outlaw rolled his eyes. *Jupiter.* His eyes were a warm chocolate with touches of bronze—*like drowning in a vat of warm maple syrup*—another detail to include in her description.

"Did you just hide your handbag?" he asked.

Shaken out of her stunned admiration, she shifted her weight, positioning more of her backside on top of the pad, and gazed up at him, widening her eyes innocently.

"No. Huh... uh... I was fidgeting because my... derrière is going to sleep from sitting so long."

The outlaw's gaze darted over his shoulder at the yellow-eyed man, then returned to her. "I don't believe you. You're sitting on your handbag. So, hand it over."

Oh dear, if he saw the picture she'd drawn, he'd take it away. She shook her head and sat more firmly on the pad, determined to hang onto it, no matter what.

At her side, the coward moaned again. "For heaven's sakes, Miss Hart. Give him your handbag."

"I won't." She blinked, scarcely able to believe her own audacity. In her chest, her heart kept time with the clacking of the train's iron wheels on the track. And her lungs had no air.

The shorter, masked outlaw stepped forward, gun in hand. He tapped it against his palm. "Come on, get the job done. Or I will."

The handsome—no, no, what she meant to say was the *unmasked*—outlaw jerked around to face his partner. "I don't need your help, Fox." Spinning toward Gracie, he leaned down till they were nose-to-nose. "You have no idea what you're doing, lady. Give me your money now, or someone's going to get hurt."

With her heart pounding harder than ever, she reached down to where her handbag had fallen, snagged the strings, and drew it off the floor. She handed it to him, her lip trembling. “Here. But don’t think I won’t remember you.”

Stuffing her handbag into his cloth sack, he grumbled, “Yeah, and I’m pretty sure I’ll remember you, too.” Abandoning her, he continued down the aisle.

His partner remained behind, staring at her with a strange look in his light eyes. “Too bad,” he murmured after a moment, and followed the other man to the next row of seats.

For a minute, she sat frozen in her seat. The spot on her arm where her handbag usually hung felt strange, unburdened, and empty. She glared at it, furious, like it was her arm’s fault but it wasn’t. It was that outlaw. He stole her money.

She swung around in her seat, searching for the outlaws in the dim light of the smoky car. They stood next to the last row where they collected a wallet and a handbag from a young couple then joined the outlaw guarding the exit door. The shorter bandit tapped the third outlaw on the shoulder, who opened the door and exited, leaving the man with the yellow eyes and the tall, lean fellow with the honey maple eyes together at the rear of the car, the sack containing all her money gripped in the masked bandit’s hand. They sat for a minute, surveying the train car, then the shorter outlaw opened the exit door leading to the platform, and they stepped outside. The door swung shut behind them.

Well, they may have taken her money, but she still had her pencil and paper, and she had an excellent memory for faces. Lifting up, she tugged the pad out from under her backside, removed her pencil from her pocket and began drawing again. When she’d said she’d remember him, he should have listened.

FOX NUDGED MAC OUT the door of the car then signaled him to halt. Outside on the platform, in spite of the fact they were somewhat sheltered between the two passenger cars, the roar of the engine and the wind were deafening.

Bracing himself on the steel railings, Mac shouted, "All right, you got what you wanted. Now what?"

Fox pulled his kerchief down and grinned, a gold tooth gleaming in the sunlight. "We wait," he stated and leaned against the car door, holding it closed with his weight while staring at the scenery whipping by.

Within minutes, a plume of dust rose in the distance. A group of riders towing riderless horses soon appeared alongside the train, whooping and waving. At the end of the second passenger car, two outlaws jumped off the train onto the horses' backs and peeled away, leaving one mounted man still riding alongside the train and towing a horse. Fox shouted something, making the mounted man spur his horse faster until he was even with the platform where Mac and his captor stood.

"There's my ride." Fox tucked the sack of purloined items into his belt. "And this here is where you and I part company."

Thank God. The whole situation could have been a disaster, in fact, he could be dead, but he'd managed to get off easier than expected.

Fox shoved the gun under Mac's nose. *Then again...*

"Jump," the outlaw ordered with a grin.

Mac stared, wide-eyed at the ground whizzing by. "Off the train? You can't be serious. The train's going thirty miles an hour. I'll break my neck."

Without warning, the gun ripped across his face. The torn flesh burned like fire, and blood dripped off his chin.

He glared at Fox, wanting to tear the man apart but knowing that any move he made would result in his death.

Fox smirked in answer and pointed the gun at his chest.

Stepping to the edge, Mac said a quick prayer. Then, curling into a ball, he jumped.

WHERE THE HELL WAS that town? Mac was positive civilization must be close because he remembered the conductor saying it was only a few minutes to the next stop. But a few minutes going thirty miles an hour, versus walking with feet shredded by tight boots, a sprained ankle, a wrenched shoulder, and a multitude of abrasions that stung like hell were two different things.

He heaved a sigh. As if having his wife abandon their one-year-old daughter to run off with another man then getting killed wasn't bad enough, somehow he'd had the bad luck to be on the same train as his old enemy, Dexter Fox.

Over the horizon, the peaked roof of a building came into view. Despite his aching body and the pain in his ankle, he picked up his pace until he reached the outskirts of the town. He hobbled down the narrow street toward a crowd gathered in front of a tall, two-story building.

Approaching the throng of people, he slowed, gazing over their heads at the confrontation going on between a harried-looking sheriff and one small woman. With a sense of fatality, he recognized his nemesis, the stubborn girl of the handbag. With her cheeks red under her freckles, she jabbed a finger in the sheriff's face, scolding him like he was a two-year-old.

"—to me. I can identify the leader of the gang better than anyone else. I have his description written right here, on this pad, and here's a picture I drew." She held the pad up and whacked it several times. "At least look at it, sheriff."

The sheriff's mouth screwed up into a tight ball, as if he'd unintentionally swallowed the worm in a bottle of tequila. Gripping the girl's arm, he marched her to the stairs. "Now, you go on inside the hotel, little lady, and we'll do our jobs just fine without you." He gave her a nudge.

"But, sheriff," the girl argued. "I can describe one of the outlaws perfectly. He's about six-foot two, with reddish brown hair and quite nice looking." She stopped, gazing out at the gathered crowd. "Actually, he looks a lot like the man there." She squinted. "In fact, it *is* the man there. Sheriff, it's the man I told you about. It's the leader of the gang. Grab him. Quick."

Mac craned his neck, searching the crowd for Dexter Fox's gloating visage. His gaze skimmed over the sea of faces, many who looked familiar—the train passengers. Oddly, their focus was on him, their stares hard and accusing.

He snapped his head to the little-bit-of-nothing girl jumping up and down and shouting, her finger extended to point at him. The people around him melted away, leaving him alone like the star on the Texas flag.

Maybe when she'd said she wouldn't forget him, he should have believed her. But it was all easily explained. Wasn't it?

The sheriff pushed his way through the angry crowd until he stood in front of Mac. The gun in the lawman's hand pointed at Mac's stomach, rooting his feet to the ground.

"Miss Hart," the sheriff shouted. "Is this the man?"

"It's him, Sheriff Beatty," she shouted back. "It's the man who robbed the train."

Chapter One

M*ay 1891*

It was late afternoon by the time he descended from the stagecoach in Los Marcos, Texas. He walked onto Broadway, a long, straight street lined with tall shade trees and a number of brick buildings housing the kind of businesses typical of many small towns.

He gazed down the street for a moment, hot and tired, wondering what his next step should be. Somewhere outside of town his daughter, Hannah, had spent the last five years living with his Aunt Martha and Uncle Jake on the small spread they'd bought after he'd moved away to go to college.

But after five long years, he was finally within a few miles of being reunited with his daughter. He should have been excited, and relieved, yet, for some reason, an uneasy sense of anxiety hammered in his mind. For more than four years, his aunt and uncle had sent him a letter every week. He'd lived for those letters but six months ago, they'd ceased. Something wasn't right. He didn't even want to think of the possibilities.

Clenching his fist around the strap of his carpetbag, he pushed away his fear. The only way to find out would be to ask. And like it or not, the sheriff's office was the most obvious place to inquire. Settling his hat more firmly on his head, he trudged down the street toward the sheriff's office.

"Hold it, McLean," someone shouted, the voice cracking in mid-sentence.

He stopped, his head jerking around to see a scared young face looming over the barrel of a gun. His heart skipped a beat. "What the hell are you doing?" he said, his gaze fixated on the gun.

The boy gawked at him; his Adam's apple bobbing as he swallowed. "Step onto the street. You and me got things to settle." He waved the gun in the direction of the street.

The gun shook, and Mac feared he'd die right there, killed by stupidity and youth. "What do you want?" he asked, not moving a muscle for fear it would be the last thing he ever did. Behind him, people scattered, darting into doorways to hide. The thud of booted feet on the boardwalk receded into the distance as someone else took flight.

The boy swiped his lips with the end of his tongue. "I told you, McLean. You and me are gonna fight it out, and only one of us is going to walk away alive."

For pity sake. Where had this fool gotten his lines? He sounded like a bad dime novel. Well, Mac refused to participate in the boy's idiocy. "Relax, son." With his free hand, he reached towards his suit coat.

At his movement, the boy jumped. The barrel of the gun rose. "Hold it, mister," he squeaked. Wispy blond hair flopped into his eyes, and he brushed it out of the way.

Mac kept his gaze locked on the boy's face. "Steady on. I'm not going for my gun. Just so you know, I don't have one. Let me pull my coat back so you can see." He waited for the boy's nod before drawing his coat open the rest of the way, letting the boy look his fill. "Satisfied?"

The youngster swallowed, eyes flitting toward the carpetbag in Mac's hand. "Then your gun must be in there. G'wan and get it out." Sweat rolled down pale cheeks still round with the softness of youth.

Mac dropped the bag on the ground. "I think you've made a mistake, son, but you're welcome to go through my bag if it makes you feel better." He toed it forward.

The boy hesitated while he considered if Mac intended to trick him. When Mac remained still, the boy used one of his feet to draw the bag closer. Kneeling, he pulled open the straps. He dug inside and tugged out the contents. When no gun appeared, he upended the bag and shook it until nothing more fell out. His gaze darted back to Mac, filled with desperation.

Mac released the breath he'd held. "All right?"

Frustration, shame, and anger skittered across the boy's face. His mouth quivered as if he wanted to weep, but masculine pride transformed it into bravado instead. Again, the gun rose.

"Johnny Lee Delray, what in the Sam Hill are you doing?"

At the loud voice, the boy scrambled to his feet. He shoved his gun into the waistband of his pants and swung to face the large man bearing down on him.

"Nothin', Sheriff Rheingold," he squeaked.

The sheriff came to a halt in front of the boy, spreading his feet wide and tucking his thumbs into the pockets of his vest. Steel gray brows lowered over tired eyes. "Doggone it, Johnny Lee. Are you playing gunslinger again?" he asked. "How many times do I have to tell you; you ain't no gunslinger, and I'm betting, neither is this fellow. If he was, you'd be dead by now."

Outraged, Johnny Lee pointed at Mac. "But, Sheriff, this here fella is Scar McLean."

The sheriff cocked his head, his gaze shifting to Mac. "You don't say. Well, well, well." He gave Johnny Lee a pat on the shoulder. "Go on home, boy. Tell yer pa I'll drop by later to have a talk with him." He gave the boy a nudge in the right direction.

The boy groaned and plodded down the street, his shoulders slumped in defeat.

Sheriff Rheingold shook his head in amazement. "Well. McLean. In the flesh. Son of a gun."

Mac opened his mouth to speak but nothing came out.

Underneath the thick gray handlebar mustache, the sheriff smiled. "I need you to come along with me, McLean," he said, tossing Mac's belongings into his bag. After picking it up, he wrapped a huge hand around a stunned and unresisting Mac's arm and towed him down the street toward the other end of town.

Mac trudged alongside the sheriff, puffs of dust from the dirt street rising under feet that seemed disconnected from his body. The hand around his arm gripped like a manacle, a grim reminder of prison. He ducked his head, that old sense of shame and embarrassment burning the back of his neck as dozens of people watched him being escorted by the law.

"Am I under arrest, sheriff?" he asked through gritted teeth.

The man chuckled. "Naw, at least not today, not unless you done something I don't know about. But until folks calm down a mite, you'll be safer in my office. I'll treat you to a cup of Arbuckle's."

Mac relaxed a little when the sheriff dropped his hand and they continued down the street toward the jail without speaking. Entering the small two-room facility, the sheriff threw his hat toward the coat rack, neatly catching a hook, and told Mac to take a seat. He dropped Mac's bag then slid behind his desk and lowered himself into a swivel chair with a sigh.

"I'm getting too danged old for this," he grumbled, his eyes crinkling in amusement. "Gotta think about retiring." He leaned back and rocked, a smile nudging up the ends of his mustache as he watched his guest. Minutes went by while he rocked and smiled. "But then, I bin saying so every day for the last five years."

Being in a jail with a lawman smiling at Mac made the skin on his scalp crawl. At last he could stand it no longer. "All right, so I'm not under arrest," he said. "Then what the heck is going on? Why did that kid challenge me to a gunfight? Why did he call me Scar McLean?"

Rheingold tipped his hat to the back of his head and scratched his ear, not answering for a few minutes while he studied Mac. "Huh. Somehow, I get the sense you don't know."

Puzzled, he frowned. "Know what?"

The other man laughed, a secretive chuckle that sent another chill through Mac. Opening his desk drawer, Rheingold rooted through it. "I don't think you're going to like this, McLean." He continued to chuckle when he tossed a frayed dime novel onto Mac's lap.

Picking it up, Mac viewed with curiosity the cover, a lurid drawing of a masked man in the middle of a gunfight, standing ankle deep in dead bodies. The book was titled *The Last Man Standing*, and the author was named Grace Hart. A long-suppressed memory tickled at the back of his mind, trying to surface, then sank into the past.

He read the short cover blurb—*The villain becomes a hero*—and snorted. "What a load of garbage."

"Maybe. But I think you ought to read it anyway. You'll probably find it real interesting."

Cracking it open, Mac began to read. It was a simple enough plot; all about a rancher whose daughter was being held captive by a gang of outlaws. Desperate to save her, he hires a gunslinger—sight unseen—to rescue the girl. The author had a nice way with words, but overall, it was crap. An unlikelier plot he'd never read. Who the heck would hire a gunslinger—a complete stranger—to rescue his virginal daughter? He looked up, an eyebrow cocked in question.

Rheingold's smile widened, making his mustache spread across his broad face. "Got to chapter two yet?"

"No."

"Keep readin'."

Mac bent his head again, turning page after page. Halfway through chapter two, the gunslinger showed up. Scar McLean. Doggone it, there was that name again. His head jerked up. "What the heck is this?"

"Turn the page," the man answered, still with a smile that began to irritate Mac.

He flipped the page and gaped at the face on the page. It was only a pen and ink drawing, but it was unmistakably his face, scar—the result of Fox's gun barrel—and all, eyes narrowed menacingly, glaring at him from the page of the book. "What the... Goddamn, what the hell is this?" he shouted.

He slapped the book closed and read the name on the cover again. Grace Hart? Grace Hart. Hmmm. Realization hit him like a fist rammed to his chest. *Goddamn it. Gracie Hart. Skinny, flat-chested, freckled-faced, 'It's the train robber' Gracie Hart.*

"Son of a... I'm going to kill her," he ranted, jumping from his seat. "I'll tear apart that skinny body of hers limb from limb. I'll remove every one of her freckles with a skinning knife. I'll... I'll kill her with my bare hands."

Shaking his head, the sheriff rose and crossed to the pot-bellied stove in the corner. He poured a cup of coffee and stuck it in Mac's hand. "Calm down, son. It's only a story. Kinda funny, when you think about it."

Fury filled him, so virulent he could hardly get the words out. "No, it's not funny. I just got out of prison. What do you think's going to happen when some yahoo who's read this garbage decides to build a reputation by killing Scar McLean? Like that idiot kid. If I defend myself, I'll be right back in prison. If I don't, I'll be dead."

The smile disappeared from Rheingold's face. "Doggone. Son, I'm sorry. I didn't realize." He sat on the edge of his desk. "You got a problem, boy."

"Tell me something I don't already know."

"No, you got a bigger problem than you think. According to what I've read, this is the fourteenth or fifteenth book this lady's written about you. And these things sell like hotcakes, all over the country."

His legs grew wobbly and the blood left his head. He slumped onto the wooden chair. The sheriff gazed at him in sympathy.

"The irony of this is," Mac said at last. "I can barely use a gun. I was a lawyer before my life went to hell. All I ever wanted was to have a nice practice to support my family." He ran his fingers through his hair. "Instead, I've got my face spread all over the country and dumb kids trying to put bullets through me thinking I'm some fancy gunslinger." *Could life get any worse?* He had no idea, but he wouldn't hang around to find out. He dragged himself to his feet. "Am I free to go now?"

Rheingold nodded. "Guess there's no reason to keep you any longer. Sure wish I could help you out of your predicament in some way, son."

With a rush of guilt, Mac remembered why he was in Los Marcos. "Well, you could give me directions to the Delaney place, if it's not too much trouble."

Concern rippled across the lawman's face. "The Delaneys folks of yours?" he asked. He grimaced in dismay when Mac said yes. "Seems like you're not having much luck, son. Jake and Martha died 'bout six months ago."

"What? What happened?"

"Doc says it was the influenza. 'Bout half the town got it. We lost a lot of folks."

His legs grew weak again. He fell into the wooden seat. "My daughter. Dear God. Where's my daughter? Aunt Martha and Uncle Jake were caring for Hannah while I was in prison." His throat closed in fear.

"Well, shoot. She ain't here no more. Far as we knew, she had no folks left, and no one wanted to take her in 'cause... well, she got a little odd after the Delaneys died."

"Odd? Odd how? What happened?" Mac swallowed the lump in his throat, pushing the fear down. At least Hannah was alive. He needed to remember that since it was the most important thing.

"You gotta understand people were real sick. Your folks lived three miles from town and by the time anyone bothered to check, Jake and Martha were dead four, maybe five days. Your daughter was sitting by Martha's side, holding her hand, when the doctor found her."

Hot prickles of sweat broke out all over Mac's body as he imagined the terror Hannah must have experienced. "Dear God." He dropped his head into his hands.

"She stayed with a family in town for a few weeks," the sheriff continued, "but they couldn't keep her. Said they couldn't deal with her 'cause she never talked after they took her in, hardly ate, and wouldn't even look at them. Said it gave them the willies."

"Where is she now?"

Opening the wooden drawer of a cabinet, Rheingold pulled out a file and sorted through the papers inside. He avoided Mac's gaze when he pulled out a sheet of paper, laying it in front of Mac, pointing to the address of an orphanage in Austin.

Picking the paper up, Mac tucked it into his pocket, wondering what else could go wrong in his life and what he had done to deserve it. He didn't understand any of it. Taking his bag, he headed for the door, the sheriff following.

"You got some place to go once you get your daughter?" Rheingold asked, his voice muted with concern.

Mac shrugged, unable to think so far ahead.

"You're going to need a place to bring yer young'un to. Your aunt and uncle's place has bin sitting empty since they died. We kinda didn't have anyone to contact... so if y'all need somewhere to stay... I'd have no objections to you settlin' here, at least until you sort things out." He held out his hand.

After eyeing the sheriff's gnarly hand for a moment, Mac gripped it. "I don't know. I'll have to see what happens."

He left the sheriff's office, anger building as he reviewed what he learned. Gracie *'It's the train robber'* Hart had a lot to answer for.

"GIVE IT UP, SCAR. YOU haven't got a chance," the marshal ordered.

"Not on your life, lawman. I'll die before I let you take me in."

"McLean, I know you're not an evil man, simply a man who's had some bad breaks. I heard what you did for that widow woman. After saving her life, you wouldn't want her or her kids to get hurt, would you? Come on. Give yourself up before something terrible happens."

Gracie wiggled in her chair, ignoring the big splotches of ink her pen dropped on her pale green skirt. *Oh, this one will be the best one yet.* And she believed it would sell the most copies as well.

She leaned back in her chair, gazing with satisfaction around her cozy library in the house paid for by her books. It was small but had everything she could want. The downstairs had a large kitchen, equipped with all the latest kitchen gadgetry, a dining room, and parlor for when she entertained, and her favorite room—her sanctuary and haven from the ordinary—the library. Upstairs were three bedrooms and an indoor water closet.

All because of the train robbery. That day was the luckiest day of her life. Being asked to cover the trial when the senior reporter got sick was the second luckiest, because it's when the idea of writing a novel based on McLean came to her. Of course, it meant it she couldn't testify at the trial, but it turned out not to matter; there were plenty of others who'd witnessed his crime and were willing to testify against him.

Being a reporter at the trial was much better. The details she learned about her hero/villain's background made her character so much more believable. And romantic. Her readers couldn't resist her stories of the successful attorney gone bad, scarred by life, both physically and emotionally.

Not for the first time, she wondered how he got the livid scar she saw at the trial. He hadn't had it on the train. But during the trial, there it was, clear as day, a thin red line slashing across his check from cheekbone to chin. But like herself, her readers didn't find the scar on his cheek distasteful. It only seemed to make him wickedly attractive.

She picked up the watch dangling on the bodice of her green dress and turned it to see the face. Four thirty, almost time to start dinner. Smoothing it into place, she stroked her hands over her chest that stuck out nicely in front. Remembering the flat-chested girl, freckle-faced girl of five years ago, she was justifiably proud of her bosom. And thankful her horrible freckles had dimmed with time—mostly. But, she acknowledged with a sigh, admiring her figure didn't get books written, so she'd better get back to work. She still had at least ten more pages to write before she finished her story, then she needed to draw the illustrations that were such a popular part of the series.

Where to go to bring the story to a satisfying conclusion? She screwed up her face, thinking about her plot. Possibilities flitted through her mind, ideas came together, and the words flowed onto the paper. Before she knew it, she became engrossed and soon reached the climax of her story.

"I still can't believe he's a bad man, Marshal. After all, look what he did for this town. Can't we do something to help him?" Penny asked, her young face hopeful.

"We paid him for the job. Now he needs to move on," Marshal Fletcher answered as he stared at McLean's steadily shrinking figure.

Penny's face fell, and her mouth drooped. "Do you think he'll ever come back?"

"No, Penny. He's like a tumbleweed who keeps rolling where the wind takes him."

Penny sighed for lost dreams. Together the lawman and the young woman watched the rider until he reached the horizon and disappeared in the blaze of the setting sun.

The End.

With a satisfied sigh, Gracie sat back and viewed the stack of papers in front of her, proof of all her hard work. Yes, definitely her best story yet. She couldn't wait to send if off to Albert, her publisher. With a sense of accomplishment, she added the last pages to her stack then slipped the bundle into a large manila envelope.

"Hammering another nail in my coffin, Miss Hart?"

She yelped. Spinning around, she froze seeing the imposing figure standing in the doorway, the brim of a Stetson shadowing his face and a long duster coat cloaking his body. The light from the fire flickered a warm gold off the barrel of the gun in his hand.

"Who are you? What do you want?" she whispered. A quick vision flitted through her mind of herself being ravished by this vile stranger. *Horrors.* Her hands trembled.

"Who am I?" the shadow asked, interrupting the dramatic scene playing out in her mind. "Do you really need to ask who I am? *You* should know. You know me intimately, in fact, apparently better than I know myself. You know my every thought, my every dream, my every move. Hell, if anyone knows me, you do."

She blinked. "I do? How could I?"

"Well, you must," the shadow answered in patient tones. Then he shouted, "Because you write about me for everyone in the Goddamned country to read."

Her heart lurched in her chest. “Oh. Oh, dear. McLean?”

“Yeah... Oh, dear,” he mimicked in a sweet falsetto. “So, Little Miss Destroyer-of-Lives, what have you got to say for yourself?” He tapped the barrel of his gun in the palm of his hand.

At the rise and fall of his deadly weapon, she nearly fainted. “Say for myself?”

“Yes. I’d like to hear your excuse about the books,” McLean growled. His silhouette seemed to expand to fill the doorway, blocking off any chance she might have to escape.

“About the books?” She cowered in her seat, hoping if she shrank herself into a tiny ball, she’d somehow disappear, and he would go away.

He shot daggers at her. “Lord, for a woman who seems pretty clever on paper, you sure don’t have much to say for yourself in person. So, let me make this easy for you. Why... did... you... use... me... in... your... books? Do... you... understand?”

“Yes,” she answered in a meek voice.

“Well?”

“I don’t know. You seemed so... colorful... romantic. And I’d met you and I'd learned all this good stuff from the trial and everything.” She ducked her head and mumbled, “And you were in, uh, p-p-p-prison so... it made you so easy to write about. She clenched her trembling hands in her lap.

At her words, his eyes seemed to blaze with a white fury. She could almost hear his teeth grind. The hand holding the gun shook, and she cringed, afraid she had seconds to live.

“I was easy to write about,” he repeated, his nostrils flaring when he took a deep breath. “Well, that’s just Jim dandy. All right, lady. Hear me and hear me good. I don’t like the way people stare at me because they’ve read your books and recognize my face from your drawings. I don’t like being the bad man of your plots. I don’t like people thinking I’m a gunfighter. I especially don’t like the idea some idiot looking to build a reputation might shoot my ass off." He paused, his eyes narrowing to slits. "I want out of your stories. Got it?"

Chastened, she whispered, "Well..."

In a blink, she was nose-to-nose with the barrel of the gun. "Yes, all right," she whispered, looking cross-eyed at the enormous black hole. "After this novel gets published, I'll create a new hero." She tapped the finished manuscript.

At those words, his gaze flew to the manila envelope sitting on her desk. His nostrils flared again. "Another one? You've finished another one?" Picking up the envelope, he opened the flap and peeked inside. "God damn it." He pulled a few pages out, and still holding the gun, perused them. His face darkened, the line of his mouth growing thinner and thinner while he read.

Observing him read her work, she couldn't help noticing again how attractive he was. He was leaner and harder than when she'd seen him last, but still amazingly handsome... for a criminal. A lock of silky hair highlighted with warm red tints flopped across his forehead from under the brim of his hat every time he dipped his head. The fire cast interesting shadows across his face, showing off his high cheekbones.

Peering at his face, she realized she hadn't gotten his mouth quite right in her drawings. She'd have to fix those details next time, she thought, her mind already busy working some of those details into future stories. It took all she had not to reach out to her drawing tablet to begin a new picture. But it was probably not a good idea.

Chapter Two

Damn her. Damn her all to hell. She'd ruined his life, and now she planned to add fuel to the fire with another one of her Goddammed books. The thought of what this latest one could do to him now he was out of prison made him see red. Before she could stop him, he picked up the envelope and flung it towards the fire. A few lose papers fluttered to the floor.

She shrieked loud enough to nearly break his eardrums. With a quickness that shocked him, she leapt from her chair, grabbed the fireplace poker and batted the bundle out of the fire. It flew across the room and landed by her chair, little flickers of fire licking at the corners. With another shriek, she threw herself on top of the smoldering envelope.

"For God's sake." McLean bounded across the room and pulled the woman up from the floor. "Are you crazy, woman? You could have lit yourself on fire."

"You beast. You've ruined my manuscript." Yanking her arm away, she knelt and gathered up the loose pages then spread them out on the floor, checking each page before setting it aside. "Oh, good, this one's all right. This one is salvageable," she mumbled. "So's this one. Good, good. This one only has a few lines missing, I can rewrite that part." She continued to leaf through the charred pages, muttering to herself.

"*I* ruined everything?" he shouted, ignoring her efforts to rescue her work and the muttering that went along with it. "Lady, you've got it backward. I spent five years in prison, doing hard labor, eating shitty food, getting the crap beaten out of me. I'd say it's more like you who ruined everything... like my life."

She sneered. "It's not my fault," she said. "You broke the law, so of course, you had to pay for your crimes."

Fury like he'd never experienced raged through him. A red haze descended, blurring his vision, blocking out all rational thought. This woman wrecked his life, and she needed to pay. He yanked her onto her tiptoes. "Yeah, I paid all right," he roared. "But I'm done paying." He grabbed the remains of the manuscript out of her hand.

"What are you doing?" she screeched.

He ignored her, instead he tucked the pages, still warm from the fire, into the large pocket of his Ulster. Then he turned to leave.

"Stop," she yelled again. "What are you doing? Give me back my manuscript."

"Not going to happen," he said in a low growl. "I'm taking it with me 'cause I want to see what I can expect from your other damned books. And if I don't like what I read, I'm coming back. Got it." To make sure he figured out who was boss, he picked up the few pages still sitting, white and pristine, on the floor and stuffed them into the pocket of his coat.

She shrieked again.

He strode out of the room, out the back door to the back yard where his horses waited. Viewing the small figure sitting hunched in front of his saddle, short little legs sticking out, eyes gazing at the nothingness of the night, a hard knot formed in his chest.

He closed his eyes for a moment, hardly able to bear the sight of this silent, still child when he remembered the toddler who had tottered after him, giggling continuously. Taking a deep breath, he moved down the stairs of the porch to his horse's side. He patted his daughter's hand. No reaction, no different from the other times he'd touched her in the twenty-four hours since he'd located her at the orphanage.

His heart seemed ready to crack open. But, instead of allowing himself to break into a thousand pieces, he mounted behind her and wrapped his arms around her waist to keep her safe. "Ready to go, sweetheart?" he whispered into her ear, and picked up the lead rope for the sorrel packhorse.

Of course, she didn't answer. She stared ahead, watching something only she could see. "Hannah, can you answer me."

"Oh, you evil man," a voice said. "You've kidnapped a child, that's on top of all your other evil deeds."

He looked down to find Gracie Hart standing in front of the horse, hands on her hips and glaring at him.

"Lady, move out of the way." He gigged the horse's sides with his heels, but she grasped the reins, stopping him.

"Where do you think you're going with that poor child?"

Leaning forward, he tried to unwind her hand from the reins, but she held onto them like glue. "I didn't kidnap her, you idiot," he said. "Now let go."

"No, I won't," she said then quickly stepped to his side and wrapped a fist around the tail of his Ulster coat. If he tried to leave now, he might drag her to her death. "I can't let you leave; you've got my manuscript. Give it back to me right now."

He gave her the same kind of look he'd give any crazy person because she was insane if she believed he would return a story that might get him killed. "No," he said. With a yank, he tugged his coat out of her hand. Not wanting to take a chance she'd seized his coat again, he reined his horse toward the road. "I'm going to make sure the damned thing never sees print. But first I want to read it. I, at least, deserve that." He clucked his horse into a trot.

From behind him came a loud screech. "No. Wait. Stop."

He kept going.

"I'll just write it again," she shouted. "And I'll write ten more just like it."

He jerked his horse to a stop. Nearly running into the back end of his horse, the pack horse also skidded to a halt. Mac took a moment to rein in his temper because if he didn't, he might kill her. His fury barely under control, he dismounted and walked back to where she stood. "What did you say?"

Her mouth pursed up, her chin rose, and her shoulders drew back. "I said... I'll just rewrite it. And ten more."

He glowered at her. Rewrite it. She could. And would. That was the problem; after today, if she rewrote it, she'd make him out to be bigger, badder, more Scar McLeanish than ever. She'd make his life hell. Maybe if he showed her another option.

"Okay, go ahead and rewrite it. That's fine. Only rewrite it without me in it."

"Rewrite my story without you? What do you mean?"

"Kill me off. Make me disappear. Create another anti-hero. Someone better, meaner, more dangerous. You're the writer." He narrowed his eyes. "Get creative."

"No," she said, her chin jutting out.

He paused before uttering, "So you won't write me out of your stories?"

She crossed her arms over her chest. "No. I won't."

"Not even if I ask nicely?" he asked.

"No."

"Do you realize your stories almost got me shot last week?" he said through gritted teeth.

She blinked.

"Because of your stories, I almost got killed. Scar McLean needs to go away. So will you kill off Scar McLean in your story?"

She blinked again, then said, "No," although her voice was less emphatic than before.

Every muscle in his body clenched in fury. "Lady, either do it or I'll... I'll..."

Her mouth lifted in a smirk. "Hah. Threats? Threats'll get you nowhere, McLean. The answer is no. I will write what I want, when I want, and nothing you can say—"

One minute he was thinking like a normal human being, and the next all rational thought vaporized, leaving a raging lunatic. He picked up Miss Smartie Pants Hart, threw her over his shoulder, carried her back to the horse and tossed her onto the pack horse's back. Quickly mounting behind his daughter, he spurred the horse into a canter, pulling the pack horse and its shrieking passenger behind him.

Miss Hart screamed bloody murder, threatening him with evisceration, hanging, and being staked on an anthill, but he didn't stop. Nor did he care. Defy him, would she? Tell him she would write another book even worse than the previous ones? Make his life a living hell, even more than it already was?

Within minutes, the lights faded as he left town in the distance.

"Stop, stop. I can't ride. I'm going to fall. I hate horses. Horses hate me. Take me home," she screamed.

Yeah, he would. Eventually. After he'd scared the pea-wadding out of her enough to make his point. After she agreed to rewrite her story so idiots like that kid in Los Marcos stopped coming after him with guns, threatening his life.

After a mile or two, his temper cooled, sanity returned, and he drew the horse to a halt. "Okay, now listen to me. I'll consider taking you back if—" he told her, twisting in the saddle, but she wasn't listening.

With a shriek, she tried to throw herself off the horse's back but got her foot tangled in one of the ropes tying down the pack and ended up hanging sideways on the animal.

Oh, for Pete's sake. Kicking his horse closer, he grabbed the back of her dress and hauled her upright. "Quiet. I said I'd take you back. On the condition you do the rewrite I asked for." They'd only traveled a few miles so, even though going back would make his journey longer, he could do it, but only after the woman promised to make the changes he wanted.

"No."

God damn it. Tightening his grip on the lead rope, he kicked his horse forward again. She squealed and threats filled the air. They rode another fifteen minutes, before he stopped again.

"Lady, I'm trying to be reasonable. All I want is for me to be out of your stories. They're ruining my life."

"Oh, piffle. How could they ruin your life?" she said, sounding breathless.

He grit his teeth. "Trust me. They are. Now, please, just write me out of your books." *Say yes.* Just say yes, and he'd take her home because the last thing he needed was this woman hanging around his neck like a hangman's noose.

"No."

God damn it. The woman was as stubborn... and stupid... as a mule.

"Last chance, lady. Write a different plot, one where I die or simply disappear, or you *will* suffer the consequences."

"Hah. Like you'll do anything," she said. "I'm not changing my story, and I dare you to make me."

His temper, already hanging by a thread, exploded. "That's it." Fury burning, he spurred the horse into a gallop. She shrieked.

"Stop. Stop, stop, stop. Please. I'm going to fall." She'd thrown herself across the horse's neck and was hanging on for dear life. Not even close to falling off. He kept going. The red haze flooding his mind kept him at a gallop until his horse heaved for breath, forcing him to slow to a walk.

Once again, his anger trickled away. *Shit.* He'd been so mad, he hadn't been thinking. He'd never lost his temper so many times in his life, even when he learned his wife had left him for another man.

But getting angry accomplished nothing. Taking her manuscript was useless. If he'd had his wits about him, he would've camped out at her house and forced her to rewrite the end of the story to suit his requirements then dropped it off for mailing so she couldn't change the story after he left.

The red faded from his brain which only reinforced the fact he was in trouble. Unfortunately, there would be no going back now, at least not for him. The minute he returned her to her home, she'd have the law on him. There would be no way he could outrun them, not with Hannah in tow. And when they caught him, it would be back to prison for him and the orphanage for Hannah.

He glanced at Hannah. Dark shadows circled her eyes. Her face was pale and the track of a tear bisected the dust on her cheeks. Austin was miles back. There was no way he was going to travel those miles simply to return this selfish, uncaring woman to her home. He wouldn't put his daughter through any more than he had to. At this point, the best option was to travel onward and find somewhere to dump her.

In the meantime, she was wiggling like she needed the facilities. Reining the horse to a halt, he dismounted, then reaching up, he pulled Hannah from the saddle and set her on the ground. "Come on, sweetie," he said.

The woman gasped. "Wait. What are you doing? Are you abandoning this child?"

He ignored her, instead, he took Hannah's hand and led her into the bushes where he helped her do her business.

"What's the matter with you? Aren't you listening to me? I want to go home. I need to get down. I need to... you know... too." Next thing he knew, the stubborn hellcat jumped down from the packhorse and was twenty feet away, running like a scalded cat.

Damn it. In a few strides, he was at the woman's side. Picking her up, he hauled her, kicking and screaming, back to the horses. "What the hell do you think you're doing? Do you think if you get away, you'll be able to find your way home? It's dangerous out there. There are snakes and coyotes. There's nothing around for miles. You'll get lost and die, you idiot."

Reaching the horse, he quickly threw her aboard. Untying one of the ropes holding the pack on, he wound it about the woman's waist, and retied it to the pack saddle.

Perfect. Until he said so, she was going nowhere. Except maybe hell.

"What did you just do? You've tied me up. Untie me, you beast, you skunk... you... you... kidnapper of women and children. I need to use the bushes," she wailed.

Since she was saying nothing he hadn't already heard, he ignored her and set Hannah back on his horse, then remounted. After wrapping his arms around her, he nudged the horse forward, despair settling over his mood.

The sky grew dark. Hannah drooped with exhaustion, and shortly thereafter, so did Miss Hart. Time to stop for the night. In the morning, he'd attempt to reach a compromise with the screeching, stubborn problem on the horse behind him. He couldn't wait to be rid of her. The trick was to find someplace with a stagecoach that could return her home slowly. He wanted to make sure he was long gone by the time she got back to Austin.

He shook his head at his idiocy. How stupid he'd been to let it get this far. If only she'd agreed to rewrite her story in the first place. Fingers crossed she'd agree to rewrite it now that he's shown her the consequences of her stubbornness. But there were no guarantees she would.

But then, riding into the darkness, an alternative wormed its way into his brain. What if...

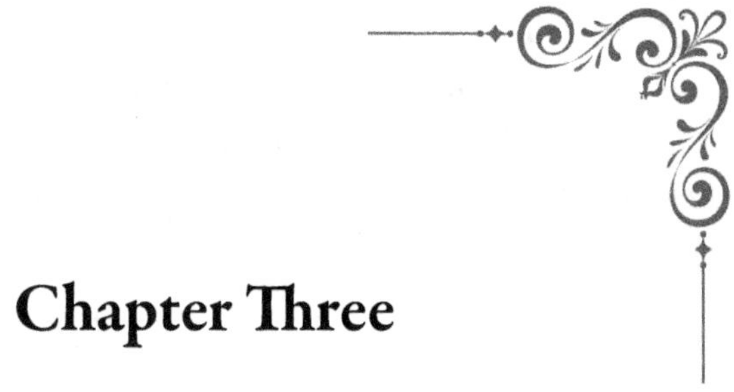

Chapter Three

The monster. The fiend. The stealer of women's careers. Oh, my God, what was she going to do? Her editor, Albert, expected a completed manuscript by the end of May so it could go to print by mid-June. Now, she had nothing to send. Albert would kill her.

Oh, she was so stupid. If she'd taken the time to think, she would have realized it might be possible to rewrite the story McLean demanded, even if it wasn't quite the story she'd intended. It might have taken time that she didn't have, but she could have done it. Or she could have lied and told him she would rewrite her story the way he wanted so he'd go away then simply not do it. Instead, she'd let her stupid stubbornness get the best of her and said no. Now, he'd kidnapped her.

Jupiter. It was like she had become one of the characters in her stories, which, when she wrote about them, sounded exciting and adventurous. It turns out adventures aren't nearly as much fun as she'd portrayed them in her books. She didn't like it at all. As far as she was concerned, she never wanted to have an adventure ever again. Even though it was a bit late, perhaps she should acquiesce and agree to his request to get rid of Scar McLean.

She considered it. No, she couldn't. Her readers demanded Scar McLean. They loved him, which meant without him, she was nothing, nobody, another failed writer. She needed McLean, or rather the fictionalized version of him.

Determined not to give him the satisfaction of complaining, she crossed her arms in front of her chest, and gazed over the horse's ears as they trotted into the darkness. They had to stop soon, and when they did, she'd order him to return to her home. She'd threaten him if she had to.

Goodness gracious, it was so quiet. And lonely. And scary. She'd never been away from civilization all by herself like this. But... so what? She was a big girl.

She could handle it. Nobody ever said Gracie Hart was a quitter. Look how she'd talked her parent into letting her move to Texas all by herself for a job. Look how she'd wangled her way into a job at the newspaper and gotten the plum assignment of covering McLean's trial. And what about how she'd parlayed that experience into a book and become a wildly successful writer. None of that would have happened if she hadn't been persistent.

Although her mother called it pig-headedness.

The sun set and black descended, in the weird way it happened in Texas, where one moment it was light and the next it wasn't. Where were they? How far had they traveled? They had ridden for hours.

The good news was, with all this time to think, she'd come up with a plan. The plan was to talk him into taking her to a nearby town where she could take a train home. Her heart thrummed with excitement. She'd pretend to accede to his demands, she'd smile and flutter her eyelashes, and use her feminine wiles, such as they were, to convince him she was just a silly weak female who would do what he wanted. She'd even sign a promissory note but once she was home, all bets were off. Yes, that could work. The minute they stopped; she'd propose her new plan.

If only McLean would stop.

Her head began to nod. The horse plodded on, but she jerked awake when it halted. Good heavens. They were in the middle of nowhere, with nothing to see but rocks and bushes and more bushes. From the looks of things, they were nowhere near civilization.

They stopped, bringing her awake.

"What are you doing?" she asked.

Rather than answering, he threw his leg over the horse's neck and jumped off then lifted the little girl to the ground. Poor kid. What would become of her with a man like McLean. She wanted to express her concern, but her mouth didn't seem to want to cooperate. Like the rest of her, it was exhausted.

The good news was she had a plan. If she wanted to convince him of her plan, she needed to start now. With her round face and dishwater-blond hair she wasn't what a man dreamed about, but she hoped she could be enticing enough to get what she wanted.

"I'm hungry. Are we going to eat?" She twirled a lock of hair around a finger and mustered up a smile.

He didn't answer right away. Instead, he walked over, untied the rope knots and lifted her down as well. Her knees almost buckled after so long on the horse.

But she desperately needed some privacy. "Gotta go," she mumbled and staggered off behind a rock where she took care of things. Returning, she asked, "Where are we?"

He shrugged. "Right now, the middle of nowhere."

She held back her curse since ladies weren't supposed to swear. "That's not what I meant and you know it. I meant how far are we from a town? How far are we from someplace I can find a train so I can return home? If you can find a town with a train, I'll just go home, and we'll forget everything. I won't tell the law what happened at all. You can just go on your merry way."

He didn't answer. Instead, his eyes slammed shut, his head tilted back, and he muttered, "God give me strength," to the sky. Then he walked to the little girl still where he'd placed her, silent and unmoving, and helped her sit down. Next he retreated into the bushes and came back with an armful of branches and dried leaves. Crouching, he arranged everything, lit a match, and set them alight. Once the flames stayed lit, he removed the small pack tied to the sorrel, pulled out a blanket, and threw it at Gracie.

"Here. It's late and it's too dark to travel. We'll talk in the morning," he ordered in a voice that didn't encourage argument. Nor did it tell her if he planned to take her home.

"But I'm hungry." Apparently agreeing with her statement, her stomach growled.

He sighed. Reaching into the bag, he pulled out a package, undid the string, and took out a long brown hunk of something. "Here, beef jerky. Eat it."

Ugh. She considered protesting, but what would be the point? Yanking it from his hand, she took a bite and chewed, glaring at him the entire time while he took care of the child, making sure she ate, then settled her, wrapped in a blanket, on the ground.

It took her three minutes to eat the jerky. She contemplated asking for more, but one look at McLean's face warned her the answer would be no. After a minute of consideration, she wrapped herself in the blanket and lay back. Okay, so her plan about the train hadn't worked out that well. The best laid plans of mice and men and all that. No matter. It was late, and she was tired. The inside of her thighs were chafed, and every bone in her body ached. Tomorrow was soon enough to tell MacLean about her plan.

Although... Well, there were a few holes in her plan, such as, how would she pay for a ticket? Highly unlikely McLean would give her any money. He most likely wouldn't return her manuscript either.

Well, she'd think about that tomorrow. She closed her eyes, and blackness fell.

The sound of McLean saddling the horse woke her. She scrambled to her feet. She needed to talk to him right now, tell him of her plan, convince him to obey before it was too late. There was no time to lose. Timidity wouldn't accomplish anything, so boldness was needed.

Steeling herself, she marched to his side and poked him in the arm. "I demand you take me to the nearest town. I can get a train there and return to Austin."

He swung around to look at her, his eyes filled with disbelief then they narrowed, a look of calculation in them. "I think you already know the answer to that. I'll give you one more chance, Miss Hart. Will you rewrite your story like I asked? Will you kill me off so your readers think I'm dead and stop looking for Scar McLean." The last sentence was nearly spat out.

She jammed her fists on her hips. "I can't. I have a contract. Iron clad. I have readers who want Scar McLean. I have a living to make." Without Scar and the income those books earned, her mother would make her return to Pittsburgh and the bosom of her family. Ugh.

His mouth tightened, his foot tapped, but his gaze wasn't on her. He was looking at the little girl, who'd she'd finally figured out was named Hannah, sitting next to the remnants of the fire from last night. The child drooped, head down, shoulders bent, staring at the ground.

Gracie returned her gaze to McLean. The fierceness usually on his face was gone. Instead, there was grief, remorse, and resignation.

Something pinched in her chest. *Probably more hunger pangs.* "You're cruel."

He shot her a look filled with fury but said nothing. Striding toward the girl, he picked her up and set her on his horse. "Come on, sweetheart. It's time to go home."

Gracie's heart jumped. What. "Hey. Wait. What are you doing? You aren't going to leave me here, are you? You can't."

His gaze traveled up and down her body, a sly smile blooming on his lips. She didn't like that smile, not at all.

"Maybe, maybe not. I figure you have two options. You can promise to eliminate me from your stories. If you do, I'll take you to the nearest train or stagecoach office or.... Option two; if you don't agree to my terms, I'll leave you here and you're free to walk to the nearest town. By my reckoning, Wallis Springs is about six or seven miles east of here. I'm sure it'll only take you half a day or so if you walk fast. In either case, I'm going to keep these pages. I want to read what you've written."

"No. No agreement. And you can't keep my book. Give it to me now."

The next thing she knew, he hustled her over to the packhorse, picked her up, and threw her aboard. Spinning around, he mounted his horse and set off at a trot, dragging the packhorse behind him. The horse jolted forward, bouncing her on the animal's back. She grabbed its mane and hung on. At least he hadn't tied her on the horse.

"Stop. What are you doing? I demand you take me to a town. I need to go home. What are you doing? Stop!"

"I changed my mind. It appears there's an option three. Now be quiet."

"I want to go home," she wailed but the horse kept trotting. And it certainly didn't appear they traveled in the direction of Austin.

OH DEAR. SHE'D TRULY been kidnapped. In spite of her demands and protesting and many tears, McLean had refused to take her to Austin. She'd gotten what she deserved, he stated, then he'd had the nerve to tell her he had plans for her, plans that didn't include returning her home.

Even after hours astride the horse, she still couldn't believe it. The last story she'd written was about a kidnapped woman, but she realized now her story hadn't done the situation justice. Being abducted was much harder than it looked. Her bones ached, and she was frightened and homesick. Her nose was sunburned, sure to turn to freckle but worst of all, her fanny—no, it was more than her fanny—was chapped and raw from sitting atop the canvas-covered pack strapped to the pack horse's back.

Would this torture never end? Hours of endless riding, sun, rolling hills. And silence, because neither McLean nor Hannah spoke a word other than the occasional order or two McLean barked.

After hearing his choices, Gracie realized no one would help her escape except herself, so she began plotting. Many of her plans relied on the fortuitous appearance of a posse, summoned by the campfire she'd somehow miraculously lit or the signal she sent with a mirror. Which she didn't have so she moved on to other, possibly, better plans. In her imagination, those plans always ended with McLean stomped into the ground by someone, she wasn't sure who, while she stood smugly over him. Although satisfying to envision, her ideas were all impractical.

With her mind distracted, the time passed quickly. Buried deep in another escape plan, she almost didn't realized they'd stopped moving. Since it wasn't yet evening, and they'd already had a noon break, the stop was a surprise.

Good heavens. In the middle of a dry, dusty yard stood a house—small, made of clapboard and fronted by a screened porch. Next to the house, a magnificent oak tree cast long shadows across a wide porch adorned with an intricate gingerbread trim. A white picket fence covered with rambling roses indicated someone once cared for the small yard. At the back of the house, huddled around the back yard, stood trees that thickened into dense woods before sloping toward a ridge looming dark and craggy to the east.

Twenty yards or so to the right of the house was a large barn, once upon a time painted red but now a motley patchwork of faded rust and tan. Behind the barn, a decent-sized pasture spread under the afternoon sun, lush and green.

The place was quiet. Other than a few skinny chickens pecking indifferently in the front yard, it seemed deserted.

"Where..." Her mouth was so dry nothing came out. She stopped and licked her lips. "Where are we?" To her embarrassment, it came out in a whine.

"Home. Such as it is," he answered, casting a look around the yard, his mouth set in a hard line. He swung down from his horse then grasped the child under the arms and set her on the ground. Turning to his horse, he flipped the saddle skirt back and loosened the girth.

When he was finished, he knelt next to the child. "This is your home, sweetie. Do you remember living here?" He stroked a wisp of fine blond hair from her face. "You'll have your room back and your bed, and lots of good food, and see..." He pointed. "There's a swing in the tree for you. You must remember the swing." The child stared at the ground, taking no notice of where he pointed.

When she didn't answer, he sighed. "Stay here. I'll be right back to take you into the house." He stood then led his horse into the barn.

Astonished at his rudeness, Gracie continued to sit on the sorrel gelding, waiting for him to help her down. The little blonde girl remained where McLean had set her, sullenly quiet. It gave Gracie the shivers. She'd given up expecting her to act like a normal child.

At last, Gracie's kidnapper returned. Still ignoring her, he picked the child up. "Come on, sweetheart. Let's get you inside and cleaned up. Then I'll fix you a warm meal. You must be tired and hungry." Holding her on his hip, he climbed the stairs to the front door and opened it, then stepped inside. It shut behind him.

Gracie blinked. Why that rude hooligan. He'd left her outside, forgotten. Well, she wouldn't give him the satisfaction of asking to come inside. He'd have to beg her first. Didn't he understand who he was dealing with? Didn't he realize she was friends with the governor of Texas and a Texas senator, not to mention many other important people, who would be delighted to throw him in jail for his dirty deeds?

She sat and waited for him to return so he could escort her inside. The sun sank lower in the sky, turning the horizon into a melting pot of colors: pinks, purples, and sunflower golds. Tufts of clouds dotted the sky like thick-carded wool. When only a fingernail of sun remained on the horizon, she realized he wasn't coming out.

Fighting the urge to weep, she painfully unstuck herself from the horse's back and slid to the ground. Her knees shook. She leaned against the horse and grabbed straps from the pack to avoid falling. When her legs steadied, she walked, bandy-legged in consideration of her chafed thighs, across the small grassy yard to the porch. Hauling herself up the three steps was the hardest thing she'd ever done.

By the time she reached the door, she reeled with pain. And anger. She hit the door with the heel of her hand. It flew open, banging against the wall. Stomping down the short hallway, she found herself in a kitchen where McLean and Hannah sat at a huge round oak table.

Gracie took one look at the dirty pans and leftover food on their plates and screamed. McLean jerked in his chair like he'd been shot. Even the child reacted, knocking over her glass and cowering. After mopping up the dribbling water with his sleeve, McLean jumped out of his chair and rushed over to Gracie.

Well, it seemed he'd finally realized what a cad he was and would apologize. But instead of doing that, he clapped a hand over her mouth and hissed in her ear, "Shut up, woman. You're scaring the bejabbers out of my daughter."

Over the edge of his hand, she eyed Hannah. His daughter? She'd believed the child was another victim of his criminal behavior. Well, it figured. A hard case like McLean sure wouldn't treat anyone else so tenderly except flesh and blood.

"Hmmmph," she said from behind his palm.

With a wary frown, the man removed his hand.

"I'm hungry, I'm tired, and my backside hurts. I need food, a bath, and a bed, in that order. And ointment."

With a disdainful look at Gracie, McLean swung around and returned to his daughter. After wiping Hannah's gravy-covered mouth with a towel, he began clearing the dishes, banging them onto the kitchen counter in anger. "There's still plenty of stew in the pot. If you want some, help yourself. The bedroom at the top of the stairs on the right is unoccupied. You can have that. As for a bath, I'm too tired to heat water. That'll have to wait till morning, but I'll see if I can find some ointment." Walking around her, he grabbed another dish off the table.

When the dishes were cleared, he helped Hannah down from her chair. Holding her hand, he plodded out of the kitchen, leaving Gracie with the unwashed dishes and cold, congealed stew.

She hobbled to the stove and grimaced at the stew pot then searched through a few drawers, eventually locating a fork stuffed into a brown crock. Too sore to sit, she stood next to the stove to pick out bites of lumpy potatoes, mushy carrots, and stringy cold beef, chewing slowly and swallowing around the tears clogging her throat.

When her hunger was satisfied, she threw the fork into the wet sink, retraced her steps to the hallway, and dragged herself up the stairs to the second floor. Thanking God her room was the first one, she pushed the door open. In the middle of the room was a neatly made bed. Two steps took her to the edge of it.

She didn't remember hitting the mattress.

MOONLIGHT CREPT THROUGH the window and slid across Hannah's cheek like the caress of death, leeching all the color from her skin. Mac leaned over and put his ear to his daughter's lips, listening, counting each breath she emitted, proof that she was alive. Reassured, he sat up and lightly stroked her hair.

How could the world be so cruel to an innocent child? He hadn't had an easy childhood, losing his parents when he was twelve. However, living with his aunt and uncle, he wasn't deprived either. They'd raised him like their own, and for the most part, he'd been happy.

But it seemed Hannah had received more than her share of tragedy in her short life. And now, she'd gone somewhere else in her mind. How could he penetrate the apathy that seemed to surround her? It seemed an impossible task, one he wasn't equipped to deal with. Prison left scars, and deep inside, he feared he was broken like his child.

He watched the gentle rise and fall of her narrow chest for a long time, trying not to think of the future.

When his eyelids drooped, he left his daughter's room and made one last detour downstairs to check on things before he climbed the stairs to his bedroom. Testing the front door to make sure it was locked for the night, he glanced outside and saw the pack horse standing, still wearing its halter and pack, in the yard. *Shit.* He'd been so distracted by Hannah, he'd forgotten. Leaving the house, he led the horse into the barn where he went through the motions of settling it for the night.

His head pounding, his back aching, and his eyes burning from lack of sleep, he closed the horse's stall and plodded to the house, locked up and headed for his room.

He closed his bedroom door, intensely thankful for the silence. Prison had created a deep primal need for quiet, for solitude. During his five years behind bars he was never alone. He worked, ate, and slept alongside men in a six-by-six cell. Even his most private functions were more or less a group activity. The sounds and smells of men were always there, invading his thoughts and dreams. He listened to their ceaseless complaints during the day and their snores at night and was privy to their tormented nightmares, like they were privy to his. He heard which men cried in the darkness for their mothers and which ones dreamt sexually explicit dreams of lovers each man hoped still waited.

Bombarded by the sheer force of so many men, any man who hoped to walk out of prison still sane built a sanctuary inside himself, a place where he could wall himself off from the oppressiveness of being constantly with others and the anger and anguish they suffered.

He slid his naked body between cool clean sheets. The seclusion was a soothing balm to his soul; something he dreamed about for five years. Yet at the same time, the silence terrified him. It gave him too much time to think, to worry, about his daughter, his lack of employment, and the unbelievable stupidity he displayed by kidnapping Gracie Hart.

God damn him. How could he have been so stupid?

His last thought before he drifted into sleep was to wonder how he would break out of his own private prison.

Chapter Four

Gracie wanted to die. Death would be preferable to the agony of raw flesh, aching joints, and cramping muscles. She didn't get out of bed—it was more that she fell, landing on her hands and knees and crawling to the chamber pot, which she desperately needed to use. Using it left her in tears when every muscle in her body protested.

Her task complete, she lay on the floor for a while, gathering the strength and the will to get up, dress, and go downstairs to eat. She would've settled for eating, but knowing McLean, Gracie figured she wouldn't receive the eating without the dressing and the going downstairs.

With hunger pains gnawing at her backbone and no excuse to linger any longer, she pulled herself to her feet with a loud groan and tugged on her dress. Using the wall of the stairway for support, she creaked downstairs.

A quiet murmur of a voice came from the kitchen so she reeled in that general direction, glad the walls caught her when she staggered. Bleary-eyed, she stood in the doorway for the second time in twenty-four hours to find McLean and his daughter finishing the last of their meal.

"Annnghhh," Gracie whined. "You've eaten."

"Yeah, people who get up at a decent hour get to eat breakfast."

"But I'm hungry," she said. Again, it was a whine, but at this point, she didn't care.

He sighed. Loudly. "There's still some bread on the counter and a little steak you can slice up. Help yourself."

She shuffled to the counter. Picking up a knife, she sliced bread and meat, slapped them together, and bit off a hunk. "Thnk ew."

"Think nothing of it," he answered in a sarcastic tone. "Come sit. I want to talk to you." He stacked his plate on top of his daughter's and pulled her napkin out of her collar.

"Nuh mmph," she mumbled, shaking her head. She swallowed. "I'd rather stand, thank you."

"Your choice. I only wanted to fill you in on how things are going to be from now on. Starting today, I expect you to get up in time to fix breakfast for all of us. I've got work to do out on the range and need to get out of here early, so I want you to have it ready by sunup. I'll shift for myself at noon, but you'll have to make something for Hannah." He wiped Hannah's mouth while he talked. "I should be back every night by sunset. Make sure you have supper waiting when I get back. I'll be hungry." He carried their dishes to the dry sink.

She chewed slower and slower while she listened until her mouth stopped working altogether and hung open in amazement. The nerve of the man. The utter gall. He thought she was going to stay? He expected her to slave in the kitchen for him? She was going to go home. Just as soon as she figured out how.

"I won't," she stated.

"What do you mean, you won't?"

"I mean, I won't cook for you. If you think I'll be your slave, you'd better think again."

Stepping closer, he loomed over her and speared her with his gaze. A muscle ticked in his jaw. "I don't expect you to be my slave, but if you want to eat, you'd better cook."

"Oh? And how are you going to make me?"

"I can damn well lock you in your room all day and give you bread and water, that's how."

If it wasn't for the fact that she considered herself indomitable, she'd be scared spitless. "You wouldn't," she challenged him even though her heart banged against her ribs like a drum. Why was she even arguing with him about this. She had no intention on staying long enough to matter.

"Try me."

She glowered. "No need. The minute we locate a train station, you're going to send me home, aren't you?"

He gave her a flat look. "No."

"What? What do you mean no?" No? How could he say no? No one ever told Gracie Hart no, at least not when she smiled at them and said pretty please. Of course, the words '*pretty please*' might be missing in this conversation.

"I mean you're staying, and since you're staying, you're going to work for your keep," he said in a growl.

"No. I won't."

"Yes, you will."

"Is that why you brought me here, to slave in the kitchen all day?" she gasped, outraged at the thought. Hands like hers weren't mean for dishwater. Her hands were reserved for holding a pen.

"It's part of why you're here, but no, not really. Since I can't leave Hannah alone all day while I'm out working the ranch, I do need someone to keep an eye on her. But I'm sure you can see, she's not a lot of trouble, so it shouldn't keep you real busy. I've got something else in mind for most of your day." He smirked. "You might even enjoy it."

At his smile, she assumed she wouldn't.

"Come with me." He led the way out of the kitchen. Too tired to argue, she followed him to a small desk tucked into a corner of the small parlor. Flipping up the lid, he extracted a sheaf of papers, then pulled out a drawer and removed an inkwell and pen. He laid it all side by side. "Here's where you'll write."

"Write?" she asked.

"Yeah, you know. String a bunch of words together to make a story."

"I know what writing is, you obnoxious oaf. I meant, what am I supposed to write?" she said.

"The same thing I wanted you to write when we were back in Austin. Bottom line, I don't care so long as the story ends with me dead or whatever else you can think to remove me permanently from your books." He slid her a glance. "Which you could have done in the comfort of your own home if you weren't so mule-headed. Understand?"

Thrusting her jaw out, she made it clear she didn't.

A muscle jumped in his cheek. "All right, let me put this in words you will understand." Holding up one hand, he ticked each item off on his fingers, speaking in a slow singsong manner. "One. I want you to write a new story. Two. I want it to convince the world Scar McLean is dead and no longer Texas's number-one most-wanted desperado. Three. I want it done quickly. Like now." He cocked an eyebrow at her. "One-two-three. Easy. Now do you understand?"

She watched him through narrowed eyes. "I won't do it."

"Wanna bet?" he growled, his nostrils flaring.

"Yeah, all right. I'll take that bet," she shot back.

"Don't make bets you can't win." He smiled, looking at her with derision. "There's no way you can win, and you might find yourself owing more than you want to pay back. Better think again."

"I don't have to think about it because you can't make me do it."

"Oh, but I can. I can keep you here, on this ranch, for the rest of your life. I don't have any friends, so I won't have any visitors to rescue you. It'll be you and me, alone, for the next twenty or thirty years. And you'll be eating bread and water." His lips curled. "On the other hand, the moment you send a completed manuscript, per my specifications, off to your publisher, I will take you home, back to your nice safe little world, and you'll never hear from me again. Got it?"

Stomping her foot, she growled in frustration. "Yes, I've got it, you skunk."

Her evil nemesis laughed. "See what happens when you make bets you can't win?" Tapping the papers stacked on the desk, he added, "I'll collect on our bet later." Turning, he left the room.

Gnashing her teeth, she mouthed a few words she didn't even realize she knew. She listened to his footsteps echoing on the floor upstairs as he moved from room to room then the sound of him clumping back downstairs to the kitchen. His voice rumbled softly to Hannah for a minute, the back door slammed, and quiet descended.

Eying the paper and pen, Gracie screwed up her face in irritation contemplating filling those pristine surfaces with the words he'd demanded. But regardless of how hard she tried, no ideas came to her. She couldn't come up with plots and stories on demand, especially one in which she'd need to create a new hero. And the whole idea of killing off Scar McLean made her sick. How could he expect her to eliminate him like her creation was nothing more than a worn-out old shoe?

And to replace him with someone else... Well, she didn't want to do it. She wasn't even sure if she could do it. But right now, it didn't matter because she was too tired to think about writing. Shutting the desktop over the writing material, she shuffled out of the parlor and dragged herself up the stairs to her room. Careful to protect her backside, she lay across the bed on her stomach and fell asleep.

THE FLOOR SLAMMED INTO her.

"Hell's bells, woman. What are you doing?" McLean roared, looming over her prone body spread across the floor.

"S—s—sleeping," she stuttered. "I was still tired."

His nostrils flared. From her supine position on the floor wedged between the 'V' of his long legs, she had a good view of said nostrils, and their admirable flaring. She'd never seen anyone do that quite so well. Maybe her stories would need to be rewritten.

"Woman, I don't care if you *are* tired. My daughter is downstairs alone. She's six years old, and she needs to have an eye kept on her when I'm gone. Now get down there, and watch her," he roared.

She thrust out her chin. No need to say the words, her chin said it all. No. She could be every bit as contrary as him.

"Do what I tell you," he growled in a threatening tone.

She glowered at him, putting every ounce of her fury into the look. "What are you going to do? Tie me to the child?"

"Oh, I don't think it will be necessary. There's a nice cold horse trough out front. What do you weigh... about a hundred and ten pounds?" He cocked a derisive eyebrow, daring her to argue.

She flushed in anger. Hmmph. According to her doctor, a hundred and five.

"Don't let me come back here and find you sleeping again, or you'll be sorry." Stomping out, his booted feet clattering on the stairs, he descended to the first floor. He left the house, slamming the door.

Well. She was already sorrier than ever in her life, but she supposed it could get worse. She couldn't determine how, but if it could be done, he was the man to do it. Picking herself up off the floor, she eased her way down the stairs to find Hannah.

THE WOMAN WAS UNBELIEVABLY aggravating. After less than three days in her company, he'd already had enough of her to last a lifetime. All she did was complain and argue. If he could write the story himself, he'd do it, but since he couldn't, he'd have to keep after her to get it done. The sooner the better because he wanted her back in Austin, where she belonged. Where she didn't present a risk of him getting arrested for kidnapping.

But in the meantime, he did need someone in the house to mind Hannah during the day while he worked. Since Miss Priss was staying to write the book, why not make herself useful and do a few wifely things?

He stopped in his tracks. Wifely things? Of course, he'd meant cooking and cleaning and taking care of Hannah—that sort of thing. Because he couldn't think of a single thing about Gracie Hart he found even the slightest bit appealing in a wifely sort of way. He didn't even like her eyes, bright blue like a Texas sky.

He shook his head, trying to shake out the image of how she looked stretched out on the bedroom floor. It was simply he required a woman to help out around the house. And any woman would do. Even Gracie Hart.

He grunted, again asking himself how he could have been stupid enough to kidnap the woman, putting his life and freedom at risk. Putting Hannah's future at risk. Regrettably, once he'd got to a certain point, it was too late to turn back. And now it was too late to change things. Taking Gracie back would only get him arrested and with nothing accomplished.

He pushed away the fear-induced nausea that had become a constant companion since the day he met Gracie Hart and strode to the barn. Taking her back might still see him arrested. He shook his head. What a fool he was.

Inside it was dark and cool, and he was glad to have something else to focus on. After brushing Horse down, he smoothed a double-thick blanket on the animal's dark brown back while mulling over his plans for making a living. Throwing the heavy stock saddle on, he tightened the girth. He had funds in his bank account from before he'd been sentenced and the money was still there. It wasn't much, but it was enough to help him start a new life as a rancher.

The nausea swirled again. A rancher. He had no idea how to be a rancher, but he'd have to learn because it was his only option. With a prison record, he'd never be an attorney again.

Fortunately, there were still a fair number head of cattle on the ranch so he planned on rounding them up to sell. With the money from their sale plus what he still had in his bank account, he'd be able to buy a few good quality horses to train, like the horses he'd worked with while in prison. A well-trained horse always brought a fair price. Raising horses wasn't what he would have chosen if he had a choice. But unfortunately, he didn't.

Chapter Five

"Damn, I hate cows," Mac growled, reining Horse to a halt outside the barn at the end of another long frustrating day. God must have looked the other way when he created bovines because sure as shooting, if the Almighty paid any attention at all, he would have given the stupid beasts some brains.

With its rolling hills and deep wooded ravines, Smith County had more places for a cow to hide than warts on a toad. He'd come to the conclusion his aunt and uncle weren't much smarter than the cows for thinking they could raise beef on this land.

After a week of effort, one thing became clear to him. A man didn't round cattle up without somewhere to pen them up. They didn't stay put. He'd managed to corral a number of cows—or possibly he'd corralled the same cows a number of times—it was hard to tell—but without a fence to hold them, they hightailed it as the minute he turned his back. So starting tomorrow, instead of chasing cattle, he'd be fixing all the fences surrounding the property. He hoped the job was easier than what he'd done for the last week.

Head pounding from the combination of sun and aggravation, he dismounted and put Horse in his stall. Throwing a couple of scoops of sweet feed and a cube of hay into both horse's stalls, he curried Horse down, then plodded to the house.

Inside, it was quieter than a graveyard. He poked his head into the parlor and found paper and pen arranged on the desktop but no hard-at-work author. Mystified at the silence, he walked down the hall to the kitchen. A plate sat on the round oak table, fork and spoon on either side. Chicken and dumplings filled the plate. Walking over to the table, he stuck a forefinger into the mess of food. Cold.

He went upstairs and opened Hannah's bedroom door. It was empty, the bed made. His heart thumped in fear. *Don't jump to conclusions.* They must be in the house somewhere. So far, Gracie had taken good care of Hannah.

He opened the door to her room. On the bed, curled around Hannah like a mother hen with her chick, lay Gracie. Both of them breathed softly in their sleep. Something red caught his eye. Peering down at them in the dim twilight, he spotted a red sash, one end tied around her wrist, the other around Hannah's.

He watched them for a long time, a butterfly of something unidentified fluttering in his chest. The sensation was so unusual, he wasn't sure whether he was angry or amused. After a while, he decided he was too tired to be either.

Closing the door, he made his way to his cold dinner. When he was finished, he returned upstairs to fall dead tired into his cold, lonely bed.

GRACIE WAS TRYING, but her life was so different before the kidnapping. With no one to please but herself, pleasing herself was what she'd done. She went to bed when she wanted, ate when and what she wanted, and got up in the morning when she felt like it. And in twenty some years, she'd never felt like getting up at five o'clock in the morning.

McLean was a sadist. He roused her before the chickens—in fact, it was she who woke the chickens when she gathered the eggs—and he expected breakfast on the table by the time the sun rose.

Then he left. Leaving her alone for twelve hours with a child who refused to speak to her and a few hundred sheets of unspoiled white paper staring at her from the desk. Every day, she sat at the desk and filled sheet after sheet with nonsense. Every day McLean came home, tired, dirty, and in a foul mood and asked to see what she'd written.

So far, she was able to wave a few pages covered with inky black scrawls under his nose without letting him get a close look at it. He seemed satisfied, but she wasn't sure how long her ploy would last.

The whole thing worried her. Like a lost ghost, the child drifted around the house on bare feet. Assuming she had some responsibility to entertain Hannah, Gracie tried everything she could think of to make friends, but nothing seemed to work. She baked cookies, read stories, sang songs, and even tried to push Hannah in the swing tied to the huge oak tree out front. Clearly, she wasn't much good with children because Hannah ignored her efforts and ghosted around like Gracie didn't exist.

Gracie was frustrated. She hated this ranch, and she was growing to dislike McLean. She wanted to go home. Within days, all she could think about was how to escape this horrible house. When she did, she would return with the law in tow. She couldn't wait to see the look on McLean's face when he was arrested. A lot of her energy that should go into writing the story McLean wanted, went towards planning how she'd make her wishes come true.

Since she had no idea where she was, she reckoned it was critical to determine the direction of the closest town, and how far it was from the ranch. She spent hours thinking up devious ways to trick McLean into telling her the information she needed. To find out, she'd have to be sneakier and more underhanded than him. Dinner, when McLean was tired, seemed like the perfect time.

She spooned green beans and onions into a serving bowl and carried it to the table while listening with one ear to McLean to him telling Hannah a funny story involving a talking bear and a sneaky lying wolf. Whatever else Gracie thought about the man, she admitted, if only to herself, he was a good father. Every time he came within reach of Hannah, he touched her head, cupping his large hand around the back of her skull and stroking her hair. Several times, Gracie surprised him in the yard, squatting to face his daughter, cradling her face with his hands while he spoke to her.

A good father he might be, but he was still a bad man, a kidnapper, and a villain, and Gracie was determined to escape. Smoothing the skirt of the cotton dress she'd found in a trunk in one of the bedrooms and altered to fit her smaller frame, she pulled a chair out and sat.

She spooned casserole onto her plate and passed the utensil to McLean. "Your supplies are getting a low," she said after eating a few bites, then daintily wiping her mouth with a napkin.

Since she hadn't volunteered a word in the seven days she'd lived in his house, McLean glanced up, his brow lifted in surprise.

When he continued to watch her without answering, she felt a spark of anger. "All right, if you're going to be that way, forget I said anything. But I'm pretty sick of green beans, pork and beans, hash and fried chicken, and I figured you probably were, too. If it makes you happy, then fine." She tossed her fork on her plate and sat back.

Eyes narrowed, he looked at their plates then at Gracie. "Are we that low on supplies?" he asked.

"Yes," she shot back. "There's no salt, no pepper, only half a bag of navy beans, a few jars of green beans, and what's left of our dried beef. After its gone, we eat eggs, kill the last of the chickens or starve. I'm not sure about you, but I'm not interested in dying."

He hesitated before answering, "I'll go into town Saturday and pick up supplies. Write out what you think we need. Just don't go crazy with the list because I don't have a lot of cash, and what I do have is going to need to last till I can sell the cattle."

Leaping from the table, she raced into the parlor and retrieved a pen and paper from inside the graceful walnut desk. Hurrying to the kitchen, she slid into her seat, uncapped the inkwell, and bent over the sheet of paper.

AS MAC FINISHED EATING, he watched the woman across the table, viewing her concentration with a degree of puzzlement. To date, he hadn't seen any signs of interest in the typical female tasks, like cleaning and cooking. In fact, she moaned and complained constantly about the few tasks he asked her to do, so he couldn't understand where this sudden enthusiasm came from. Was she thinking about poisoning him and needed a few spices to disguise it?

In spite of his lurid suspicion, he couldn't help but notice the tip of her tongue peeking out from between ripe, petal-pink lips, and that she wrinkled her little button nose. Something inside him stirred, something he'd suppressed for five years... something definitely below his belt.

Good God, it must be because of his long dry spell. Man wasn't made for celibacy, and right now he was unquestionably feeling like a man. With a shudder, he tried to pull his gaze and mind away from her.

She returned with paper and pencil. "Where do you go to buy supplies?" she asked, twirling the chunk of hair hanging from her temple like she didn't care about the answer. The sun streaming in through the kitchen window caught each strand, highlighting colors he hadn't noticed before, a rich caramel, the muted yellow of winter wheat, and the warm brown of walnut.

His gaze followed the motion, and he began to sweat. In his mind, he imagined her finger playing with the hairs on his chest, swirling around his nipples, and tracing the dark line down the center of his belly to more interesting regions.

His thoughts sank irrevocably below his belt. "Uhhh. Los Marcos," he answered after a long pause, his tongue glued with lust to the roof of his mouth.

Her pen scratched on the paper. "Los Marcos, huh? Never heard of it. How far do you have to go?" Still writing, she licked her lips.

"About... three miles," he answered, watching her pink tongue glide between her dainty white teeth. Unable to help himself, he mimicked her motion, running his tongue across his teeth. The temperature in the kitchen rose.

Pen still moving across the page, she murmured, "Three miles. It's not very far. You should go tomorrow after you get done for the day, instead of making a special trip on Saturday."

"Uh... no." He swallowed, his thoughts scattering like chicken feed. "I'm working over the ridge behind the house tomorrow. Town's the other direction, to the west. I'll go in on Saturday." Lord, it was hot in here. He tugged open the collar of his denim shirt.

"Oh. All right," she said. "Well, here's my list then." Tilting her head, she peered at him from under her bangs.

The tilt reminded Mac of a robin in the spring searching the grass for food—alert and curious. Prickles of heat spread from his neck downward to pool in the vicinity of his Levi buttons. Thinking coherently got harder and harder, along with something else. Alarmed at where his mind took him, he bolted out of his chair, tipping it over.

She squinted at him. Her gaze dropped down the length of his body before returning to his face. She frowned. "Are you finished eating?"

Grabbing his hat from the coat hook by the door, he slapped it in front of his crotch. "Yeah, gotta go," he mumbled. "Gotta feed the horses." With a perfunctory pat on Hannah's head, he sidled out the door.

Breathe, McLean, breathe. He stood on the porch. Inhaling, he focused on the bright orange sun low in the horizon, hoping he could burn the image of Gracie bent over her paper, pink tongue tangling from between her pearly teeth, right out of his brain. To his chagrin, the image persisted.

Stop this. All right, so she had lush pink lips, a cute nose, and freckles dusting her nose like specks of cinnamon, making him want to lick them off. So what? The woman was nothing more than a means to an end, and he couldn't afford to get stupid about her.

His deprived body was making itself heard, that was all. The minute it was satisfied with another woman, he was sure he wouldn't give Gracie Hart a second thought. In the meantime, he needed to throw a lasso around old Harold, his out-of-control male part.

Stepping off the porch, he made a beeline for the horse trough. Glumly, he pried his boots off, stepped into the icy water, and sat. He yelped from the cold, but it had the desired effect. Harold subsided meekly into a mere shadow of his former self.

Shivering, he sat in morose silence for a few minutes. What was he thinking—allowing his gonads to rule his head? He couldn't afford to think about anything other than getting this ranch on its feet, and his daughter. But first and foremost, his daughter. He needed to believe she would get better. He needed to spend more time with her, talk to her more, love her more.

His eyes burned. How could he love her any more than he already did?

He stayed in the icy water until he shook with chills. Then, with Harold thoroughly chastened, he heaved himself out of the trough, picked up his boots, and sloshed back to the house. Not eager to explain his soggy state, he bounded upstairs in his stocking feet and darted into his room, slamming the door behind him in relief. Peeling out of his wet shirt and Levis, he changed into a clean cotton shirt and the brown wool trousers from his suit, the only other pants he owned.

It was dark when he went back downstairs for a drink of cold water from the pump. The kitchen was empty, and so was the parlor. Returning upstairs, he inched opened the door to his daughter's bedroom. Like a kitten, she was curled up in a ball, asleep. He took a moment to listen at Gracie's door, picking up her breathing. So, everything was like it was supposed to be. Or, more importantly, the way he wished it was. Disrobing, he crawled into bed.

Chapter Six

Cupping her chin in her hand, elbow propped on the oak table, Gracie watched Hannah sitting quietly where she'd been since McLean rode out for another day's work. "Your father is a very strange man," she remarked in perplexed tones.

Hannah ignored her, choosing to look out the opened kitchen door instead. Ignored, Gracie shrugged. It didn't matter how odd he and his daughter were. Now that she'd learned how to get to town, she was leaving.

He'd be fine. Hannah would be fine. She'd handed him a list of food items he would need to feed his daughter. Everything else was up to him so why should she feel guilty? He'd promised to return for lunch so it was urgent she got the heck out of here before he showed. Yet, instead of escaping, she'd spent the last hour pacing through the house, doing nothing.

What was wrong with her? She needed to get a move on. Now. Rising, she climbed the stairs and threw into a pretty pink pillowcase the dress and undergarments she'd worn when he'd kidnapped her.

Don't go crazy with the list because I don't have a lot of cash right. The words wormed their way through her mind while she packed.

She'd never considered what it was like to not have money. Having a father who was a successful manufacturer meant she was could buy anything she wanted. Even being a self-employed woman, she lived very comfortably.

In her entire life, it hadn't occurred to her to wonder where her next meal would come from.

Looking at her surroundings, it struck her for the first time how shabby the house was. The walls were dingy and desperate in need of a coat of paint. Although of good quality, the furniture showed signs of wear and tear.

She'd assumed, being a successful attorney and train robber, McLean would have funds stashed somewhere, but it appeared he didn't. Surely he'd received his share of the robbery so why didn't he have any? It was a mystery.

Well, it didn't matter, because she was leaving. She threw in the hairbrush she'd found in the bathroom and tied the neck of the pillowcase. An eerie tingle ran up the back of her neck. Whirling around, she found Hannah standing in the open doorway of her bedroom, staring gravely at her.

"Hannah," she croaked, searching the girl's still face. "Hi. What are you doing here?"

As usual, Hannah didn't answer, making Gracie wonder, not for the first time, why the girl was so rude to her. "I'm busy right now," she said. "What do you want?" The little girl continued to watch her.

When no answer came, Gracie grabbed the pillowcase from the bed, brushed pass Hannah and stomped downstairs, stopping for a moment to view the tiny desk in the parlor. Her gaze sought the small pile of papers covered with the reams of nonsense she'd written in the last few weeks. Thank the Lord this was the last time she would have to see all those pages, the last time she'd have to feel remorseful about her refusal to do what he wanted.

She looked around, intending to say a brief goodbye to Hannah, but she was nowhere in sight. Well, fine. It was better this way. Better not to see Hannah's accusing look. Getting a firmer grip on the pillowcase, Gracie walked out onto the porch and bounded down the three stairs to the ground. With a last look at the frame house, she strode down the tree-lined road.

She gave a brief thought to Hannah, wondering where she'd gone to, feeling terrible that she hadn't said goodbye. But as soon as she stepped past the trees at the end of the drive, thoughts of Hannah receded to the background.

She was free. And more cunning than any of her heroines she wrote about. In fact, when she got back, she would write her own story. Although, maybe she wouldn't, because, for some reason, she had this strange feeling she'd done something wrong. It seemed almost like guilt, although she had no idea why she should be feel bad about anything. She stopped for a minute and looked back in the direction of the house. It was still sad and depressing. Sort of like Hannah. Where was she? Was she all right? Gracie nibbled on a fingernail. Maybe she should return. Hannah was too young to be by herself for any length of time.

No, Gracie couldn't do that. McLean might catch her. The best solution was to walk to town then ask someone to ride to the ranch and take care of the child. It was a mere three miles to the town, and she would hurry.

Yes, there was the solution. Still, her conscience pricked at her.

The sun warming her shoulders through the leaves of the broad trees, she hurried down the narrow road, singing under her breath. Her mind swiveled between writing her memoirs in her mind and worrying about Hannah, while she admired the lush woods surrounding her.

A strange tickle squiggled on the back of her neck. She whirled around, scanning the road behind her, searching. The trees huddled close to the edge of the road, dense and impenetrable, preventing her from seeing farther than a few feet through the leaves. Was someone there, hiding, watching her? Shifting from foot to foot, she strained her ears, trying to separate the rustle of wind in the leaves from noises that didn't belong.

But there was nothing. Reluctantly, peering over her shoulder, she continued on. Rather than abating, the strange tickle worsened. She spun around again.

"Who's there?" she called.

Nothing moved in the depths of the gloomy forest. Even the birds were quiet, as if something large and evil frightened them into silence. With that chilling idea in her mind, she didn't wait. Hiking up her skirts, she bolted down. Her pillowcase bumped her leg, tangling in her skirts as she ran until she came to a fork in the road.

Oh dear, oh dear. Which way? She danced from foot to foot, her head swiveling to view both routes. To the left, the heavy summer foliage hung low over the rutted road, throwing dark shadows on the lane. The gloom made her shudder.

The other way opened into a sunny meadow blanketed in blue bonnets.

A twig snapped. She screamed and raced down the right fork, toward the sun and the blue bonnets. A scuffling noise followed, telling her whoever—or whatever—it was, still chased her. Fear pounded in her chest. Tripping in a hole, she dropped her pillowcase but didn't take the time to pick it up. Without its weight, she could run much faster.

Leaping over the deep ditch that ran alongside the road, she scrambled up the other side, crashing through a dense thicket of dried weeds. Her corset pinched, making it hard for her to catch her breath. How could she be so stupid, to wear a corset when she was supposed to be escaping from a kidnapper? How many other heroines would be so dumb? She leaped over a dead tree.

But at last, scared witless or not, she had to stop. Bent over, hands on knees, she panted. Whoever was following her would have to kill her because she couldn't take another step.

Finally catching her breath, she straightened and looked around. The meadow was far behind and the road, too, it seemed. She scanned the surrounding area for any sign of which way to go, but everywhere she looked, there was nothing. No road, no meadow—nothing except thick trees. She looked around again, hoping the view would improve the second time.

It didn't.

She couldn't figure out how this happened. Granted she was a city girl and never had much of a sense of direction unless the streets were marked east, west, north, or south, but even so, the way seemed clear, a nice wide road which should be easy to follow. Now what?

Behind her, the bushes rustled. She shrieked and whirled around.

"Hannah!" Knees already weak from her flight, she collapsed in a heap. "Hannah, I may kill you."

SO COWS WEREN'T AS stupid as Mac had thought. Last Saturday, with no fences and no way to corral the beasts, he saw cattle all over the open pasture, like fleas on a dog's back. But now, five days later, with a small section of his fences repaired and waiting for something to hold, the damned cows had disappeared into the woods.

The blazing heat radiated in waves off the drying grass, and all he'd gained for his efforts was a chapped ass and a chafed temper. He'd spent the morning crisscrossing the northern section, and he was hungry, tired, and discouraged. At the rate he was going, Hannah and he would starve to death.

He punched a hole in a can of tomatoes with his pocketknife, then bit off a hunk of bread and chewed. Taking a sip of juice to wash down the stale bread he'd brought along to replace the breakfast he hadn't eaten, he closed his eyes for a minute and laid his head back against the tree trunk, too exhausted to care that the morning was passing and he'd accomplished nothing. Within seconds, he drifted into a hazy nothingness.

Horse whuffed, snapping Mac awake. He opened his eyes, and there, no more than thirty feet away, stood a magnificent bull, his speckled hide shining in the sun, looking fat and sassy. A gleam shone from the big animal's eyes, one of delight, as if he had nothing better to do than service as many heifers as possible.

Looking at the bull, he realized this animal could be the answer to his prayers. He rose to his feet, easing quietly over to Horse and mounted. Setting himself deep in the saddle, he nudged his mount forward, shaking out his riata.

The bull's head came up. Ears alert, he followed the horse and rider with his eyes, his nostrils flaring to show the pink inner lining. When the horse and rider got closer, the bull's tail rose, and he quivered. His ears swiveled.

In an explosion of energy, the animal darted left. Horse sprang after him, easily cutting the bull off from his intended path upstream. The animal shifted his massive weight, spinning on his cloven feet, and cut to the right. Clods of dirt shot into the air. Horse followed, again blocking the route.

Digging his feet into the stirrups, Mac gripped the horn and wrapped his legs around Horse's barrel. Another sharp turn and shift in weight, they inched closer to cornering the bull against the rocky ledge overlooking the stream.

Snorting in frustration, the bull stopped, sides heaving. Sweat darkened his smooth hide. Mac shook out his noose, eyeing the impressive spread of the bull's horns.

Then he tossed the loop, praying his long hours of practice would pay off.

The bull burst into motion, uncoiling like a spring. For a split second in time—an infinite moment filled with all his hopes—the riata floated in the air. Then, miraculously, the noose landed neatly over the horns.

Triumph flooded through Mac. He rocked back in his saddle and wrapped the riata around his saddle horn. The bull hit the end of the rope, and it snapped taut with a loud whine, flipping the captured animal around in a flurry of legs and tail.

The sudden jerk lifted the rear of the saddle off Horse's back, straining the girth. The saddle shifted sideways. With a whine, the riata unwound.

The saddle tipped further and the ground rushed up to meet Mac. It had only gotten harder since the time he'd jumped from the train.

Picking himself up, he watched the tail end of his riata snake over the top of the hill and vanish. Watching his best hope for a future disappear, he cursed, using every word he had in his arsenal—and he'd learned some good ones in Huntsville—until he was out of breath.

The saddle hung around Horse's belly, whose liquid brown eyes stared reproachfully at Mac as if to say, "How could you be so stupid?"

"I'm sorry. I forgot to tighten the cinch," he yelled, then flushed in embarrassment. Life hit a new low when he was reduced to making excuses to his horse. "Come on, I've had enough for the day. I told Miss Priss I'd go into town for supplies. May as well do it now."

Undoing the girth, he removed the saddle which was now hanging under Horse's belly and re-placed it properly on his back. This time, he made sure the girth was tight around the animal's barrel before mounting.

It was a long, discouraging ride home. At least he was home while it was still daylight. He pulled the horse to a stop and dismounted, led him into the barn and got him settled. Done, he walked to the house.

It wasn't that he expected someone to come rushing out with his slippers and a pipe, but the house did seem quiet for barely past eleven, especially since he'd told Gracie to have Hannah ready to go into town with him.

The front door was closed—unusual in itself because his reluctant author never seemed to shut anything—but even more significant was the silence that seemed to permeate the interior when he entered. In only a few weeks, he'd become used to the sounds of a woman swearing, and the crinkle of crumpling paper with dozens of those balls of paper all over the parlor floor.

Today, no swearing came from the parlor. And no paper littered the floor.

His heart whacked the inside of his sternum like a ball peen hammer. Where was the hell was she? And where was Hannah? He raced upstairs, two steps at a time, hoping he'd find them taking a nap like before. Slamming his hand against Hannah's bedroom door, he peered inside. Her bed was neatly made, a habit she must have learned in the orphanage. It only took a glance in Miss Hart's room to see they weren't there, either.

Fear choked him. He raced downstairs, leather heels skidding on the bare wooden steps as he rounded the landing and ran into the kitchen. Nothing. The panic became so intense, his chest seemed ready to explode. Christ, he had only just turned thirty-three. Too young to have a heart seizure. But he might if he didn't get a grip.

He stopped. One hand against the wall, the other clutching his chest, he inhaled deeply to steady himself.

All right, now. Think. Other than the fact Gracie and Hannah weren't in the house, there were no signs of anything wrong. Everything was tidy, even the parlor that usually bore witness to a day of writing. Possibly the desk held a clue. A pile of papers sat aligned precisely on the desktop, row after row of neat copperplate crawling across the white surface.

He picked up a sheet. *These are the times that try men's souls,* he read. Frowning, he read the next line. *Four score and seven years ago, our Fathers brought forth a new nation.*

What the hell. *Well done is better than well said.* Incensed, he read on. *A horse, a horse, my kingdom for a horse. The pen is mightier than the sword.* His jaw clenched.

Tyger, Tyger, burning bright.

He moved to the next paragraph, the scribbled lines making him swear aloud. *But, soft! What light through yonder window breaks.* Shakespeare, for God's sake. His nostrils flared. Son of a bitch. He'd been had.

But there was much more. Turning the page, he caught his name, and it sent him from a slow boil into a raging flame. *Pack bag. Get directions to civilization. Find sheriff. Have McLean arrested.* The last line was underlined and punctuated with several black dots that perforated the paper.

Cursing, he ripped the list into tiny pieces then stomped out of the house, mounted poor Horse, and spurred him down the road toward town.

The thump of hooves beat in his ears, and hot anger coursed through him. Where was his daughter? Was she safe? Had that woman abducted her? Were they halfway to town by now?

Dear God, if Gracie and Hannah reached Los Marcos, he was in trouble.

He imagined himself walking nonchalantly up to one of Los Marcos's leading citizens and asking, *"By the way, you haven't seen a crazy lady raving about being kidnapped and a kid who doesn't talk, have you? I seemed to have misplaced them."* Or worse, *"I was keeping this woman prisoner in my house so she'd write a book about me. She seems to have escaped. Any idea where she might be?"*

But getting in trouble was the least of his problems. More concerning was his daughter's safety. He yanked Horse to a skidding halt. *Shit.* Going off half-cocked was what got him into this mess in the first place, and now he was about to do it again. He needed to stop and think.

Relaxing in his saddle, he took a deep breath until he could think rationally. The woman was on foot. A young child—an uncooperative, unwilling young child—also hampered her. Rather than panicking, he needed to slow down and look for signs the two females had passed. And if she made it to town—well, he'd deal with it when he had to.

Calmer now that he had a definite plan of action, he nudged Horse into a trot, keeping his gaze peeled for any sign of either of them. He wasn't a frontiersman by any shot, but he'd done all right following cows this last week, so he figured he could manage.

A mile from the house, he came to a fork in the road. Reining to the left, he started down the road toward town when a flash of pink towards the right caught his eye. He stopped and squinted.

He glanced left again, tapping his fingers on his saddle horn. That fork led toward town and logic told him to go that way. But when was Gracie Hart ever logical? If he put himself into the crazy woman's mind—the idea sent a shudder through him—then the only possible direction would be in the wrong direction, away from town.

With a disgusted sigh, he turned Horse down the right fork.

It took less than a minute to reach the pink item buried in a thick growth of weeds. Dismounting, he moved the weeds aside and saw one of his aunt's pink pillowcases. Alarm raged through him, jangling an anxious tattoo along his nerves. What could have happened to make her abandon her belongings on the side of the road?

He picked it up and tied it to his saddle. After a quick search, he discovered a break in the foliage edging the road. Coiling his reins in a fist, he pulled Horse behind him and forced his way through the shrubbery to follow her trail.

Bushes got trampled underfoot, their stems broken, and green leaves smashed flat. An occasional thread from her clothing had caught in the brambles, swaying in the breeze like a semaphore flag shouting her direction. With a momentary flash of humor, he acknowledged even he, with his minimal knowledge of tracking, could follow her. She'd left a trail a buffalo would envy.

He threaded his way through a flower-studded meadow, the path of the wreckage meandering aimlessly. The foolish woman was lost. Of course. Following her, he became aware her path moved in a gentle arc, taking her back in the direction of the road he'd recently left.

Calculating the degree of the arc, he figured she would come out on the road about a hundred yards from where she'd left it. Abandoning his chase, he cut through the woods to where he'd started.

He saw them long before she spotted him. Head down, Hannah in her arms, she was trudging along, talking in a low, whiny voice.

"Hannah, can't you walk? My arms, back, and legs are killing me."

His daughter simply nuzzled her nose into Gracie's neck in response.

"I wish you'd say something. I can't be so horrible you're afraid to talk to me."

Mac frowned. It sounded like the woman had no idea Hannah didn't speak. After all this time, how could she not know? Mystifying. Wanting to hear more, he took a careful step backward and hid behind the trunk of a large oak tree.

"Hmph. I'm the one doing all the work here. I'm the one who should be out of breath and too tired to talk. I don't see how your father can stand the way you mope around, sulking until you get your own way."

He grit his teeth. The woman was insulting his daughter.

"He robbed my train. He stole my handbag, and that's criminal." She stopped for a moment and hiked Hannah up in her arms. "Just like it's criminal how good looking he is. It's not fair. It distracts me into thinking there's a possibility he's not such a bad man, after all."

Now that was interesting. She thought he was good looking?

He shook his head. What did it matter? It didn't change the fact she was supposed to write a story that got him out of the mess she'd created, and she hadn't. Instead, she'd tried to escape. The idea she could have reached town sent a cold shiver up his spine.

"I have to keep reminding myself he's an outlaw. He robs trains. He kidnaps innocent women. He threatens them. He makes them slave in the kitchen."

Anger burned in the pit of his stomach. She wasn't a slave. And he hadn't threatened her. Well, he had, but for a good reason.

"This is all your father's fault. He drove me to it. Now I'm going to die."

Oh, for Pete's sake. That was too much. When she was a few feet away, he stepped out and growled, "Lady, you'd better have a world-class excuse for what you did today."

He expected her to scream, but she didn't. Instead, she looked up at him with red-rimmed eyes. "Thank God you found us," she said, her voice quivering.

He was prepared to ream the hell out of her, but her words took the wind right out of his sails. Deprived of his tirade, he rubbed his aching temples in frustration. "Are you both all right?" he asked gruffly.

She nodded, her lower lip shaking.

Righteous words still simmered in his brain, dying to be released, but she looked like she'd had enough for the day. Right now, the most important thing was to get them home. He'd deal with the rest later.

Keeping those words to himself, he boosted Gracie up onto Horse's back behind the saddle and set Hannah in her lap. He awkwardly pulled himself aboard and headed back home.

Chapter Seven

"Stop lying to me," McLean said.

"I'm not," Gracie exclaimed. "How many times do I have to say it? I didn't take your precious daughter. She followed me." Why couldn't he believe that?

Slamming a hand down on the kitchen table, McLean shouted, "You're lying. Hannah would never have followed you."

"Stop being such a stubborn jackass," she shouted back. "She did follow me. Why would I want to take her with me? I don't want to have anything to do with either of you." She shook a fist at Mac. "I'd hoped to never see either one of you again," she shouted. "You've ruined my life. How will I ever be able to go back to Austin? Someone is sure to find out about my kidnapping. If anyone learns I was alone in this house with you all this time, it will ruin my reputation. And I didn't deliver my manuscript on time. I broke my contract, and my editor is going to fire me. My career will be over. I won't be able to support myself, and I'll have to go home to Pittsburgh to live with my parents again. I'll be a failure." Tears etched shiny tracks on her cheeks, and her voice came out hoarse. "You've ruined everything, and I hate you."

Rage whipped through Mac at her words. All the frustration he had ruthlessly suppressed over the last five years blinded him to everything except the need to vent his anger. Picking up a plate filled with leftover breakfast food, he hurled it against a wall. It shattered. She shrieked and covered her head with her arms as food flew. He picked up another plate and hurled that as well, half of his brain shocked he'd caused her face to turn white with fear. The other half—the low-down, mean half—was filled with intense satisfaction.

"You selfish brat, you don't understand what you're talking about," he raged. Fury burned through his veins. "All you do is whine and moan about your stupid reputation and your idiotic books. You have no idea what a ruined life is. Ruined is your mother dying when you're only a year old. Or having your father sent to prison for a crime he didn't commit, leaving you without any parents. Ruined is having the people who were caring for you, who you love, die so you're left alone with their dead bodies for five days. Ruined is having people label you crazy and dumping you in an orphanage where everyone treats you like an idiot because you can't speak."

Panting with rage, he yelled, "When you've had all that happen to you, then you can talk about your life being ruined."

Gracie reached a hand out to him but he slapped it away, white hot rage burning in his brain.

Her eyes wide, she stumbled backward, one hand covering her mouth to muffle the sounds of her sobs.

Anger blazed through his body. Then, watching her futile efforts to pull herself together, the anger turned to horror. Dear Lord, what had he done? Prison had turned him into an animal. He had become a beast, an out-of-control beast who abused women. As angry as Valerie made him—and she had infuriated him at times—he'd never touched her in anger. He was bigger and stronger than a woman, and he didn't believe in using force against females.

But, God help him, now he had.

Shame filled him. What was the matter with him? He swallowed several times, trying to push back the nausea welling in his throat. Feeling lower than a snake's belly, conscious that he wasn't any better than the felons he'd shared a cell with, he dashed through the door into the backyard, anxious to escape her accusing eyes.

He paced under the spread of the maples, his hands trembling, panting in agitation. What was happening to him? He'd managed to survive the humiliation of a public trial and endured prison for five years. *Oh God. God help me.* He slammed his hand into the trunk of a tree. Knuckles split, and blood spurted. He'd been freed, only to become a kidnapper and an abuser of women. His life was unraveling.

Cursing, he thrust his injured hand under his armpit, stomping his feet to alleviate the throbbing, but the physical pain didn't make him forget the nagging pain of shame.

The agony kept him walking around the small yard. He mourned for his daughter who deserved a better father than he was, and for himself for not being that father. He was failing at his one hope of earning a living because he was behaving like a mean son-of-a-bitch to Gracie. But he couldn't seem to stop.

Trapped by the close environment of the backyard, he bolted toward the barn. It was where he belonged, with the other animals. Racing around the corner, he found Hannah sitting alone under the oak tree, staring at his gelding grazing in the pasture and shredding a piece of grass between her fingers.

Seeing her, he lurched to a halt. What was she doing? Was she getting better like Gracie said. Mac hadn't believed her when she'd said so, but what if she hadn't lied? What if Hannah was improving and had truly followed Gracie?

Kneeling by her side, he cupped the back of her head in his hand. "Hannah? Hi, sweetie. Did you get enough to eat today?" He tucked an errant wisp of hair behind her ear. "Gracie says you followed her. Did you? Hmmm?" Touching her shoulder, he became aware of the fragility of her small bones, and the frailty of her mind. Inhaling, he breathed in her sweet innocence. "Can you look at me? Please, Hannah, look at me. Tell me you see me, that you hear me. I need to know you're in there somewhere."

A hawk flew up from inside a clump of bushes in the field, wings spread to catch the breeze. Its feathers glittered in the warm, buttercup sunlight. The gelding squealed and kicked out, racing back and forth across the grass in equine delight.

Distracted, he followed the gelding's progress with his eyes then turned to his daughter, who hadn't noticed anything.

GRACIE'S PALM STUNG from his slap. But worse than the sting was her sense of ill-usage. She hated him. She wanted to go home. Succumbing to her pain and misery, she crouched on the floor and wailed. It was all too much. She wanted her old life back, but it didn't appear that would ever happen.

Gradually her distress subsided and with it, her sobs. Loath to give up the one thing she'd enjoyed in the last two weeks—wallowing in her misery—she gave a last shaky whimper, hiccupped then reluctantly stopped.

Pulling herself to her feet, she wiped her runny nose on the sleeve of her dress and proceed to think evil, vengeful thoughts.

More than anything, right now she wanted to hurt McLean the way he hurt her. She would march out there right now and tell him she refused to write one word for him unless he released her. Once he understood she refused to do things his way any longer, she would whack him over the head for being such a jackass.

Digging through the cupboards, she pulled out several frying pans and hefted them. She needed one heavy enough to make a dent in his stubborn skull. The third pan she tested seemed perfect, delivering a satisfying 'bong' when she bounced it off the top of the table.

Pan in hand, she strode out of the kitchen and down the hallway to the front door. Her quick search found him kneeling under the oak tree, stooping over his daughter with his back turned.

The heck with fair play and promises. This was too good an opportunity to pass up. Wiping the sweat on her palms onto her skirt, she crept down off the porch and inched across the lawn.

She raised the skillet and mentally painted a big red bull's eye on the back of his head.

"Please, baby," he said. "Look at me. It's all I'll ever ask. Just look at me."

She hesitated, her arm pulled back, the skillet hovering over her head.

His finger stroked Hannah's cheek, causing a grudging sense of sympathy to rise in her chest. It must be difficult to be a father to such a sullen child. Gracie got that his daughter might be too shy to talk to her, but why couldn't the child make her father happy and say a few words to him?

She frowned, trying to recall the words he'd shouted while shaking her. Something about Hannah. What was it he'd said? Something about dead bodies and being crazy. No, that wasn't it.

Lowering the pan, she rubbed her forehead.

His voice interrupted her musing. "Damn it, Hannah. Stop this. Stop it right now." A protest leapt to her lips when he gripped his daughter's chin in one hand, forcing her face up, but the words died on her lips when he cried, "Why won't you talk? Why won't you look at me?" Raw anguish shook his voice. "Is it because I deserted you? It wasn't my fault, sweetie. I didn't want to go away. I missed you every day I was gone."

Then his voice softened, became less demanding and more supplicating. "Do you hate me for leaving you? If I hadn't gone away, you wouldn't have had to live with Aunt Martha and Uncle Jake. None of those horrible things would have happened to you if I hadn't left and if they hadn't, maybe you would still be able to talk. Talk, please talk. Say anything."

Shocked at the revelation, Gracie lowered the frying pan to her side.

"If you hated me, I wouldn't blame you a bit. Tell me you hate me, Hannah. Please, even hearing that would make me happy."

His words hung in the air for a moment, then his shoulders slumped. Folding his daughter's unresponsive form in his arms, he buried his face in the crook of her neck and held her tight. Uncomfortable with her unintentional voyeurism, Gracie edged away.

Then something stopped her in her tracks.

Even thinking himself alone with only his daughter, he tried to stifle his sobs, so the one that escaped was harsh and painful sounding, rasping out of his chest in a brief sharp burst, the sound of a man who had no practice weeping.

It made her cringe. She had an impulse to stroke his beautiful hair; at the same time she experienced a coward's impulse to flee. She couldn't deal with his pain. Nor would he want her to witness it.

She wavered for a moment before cowardice won. Backing away until she reached the porch, she tiptoed up the stairs and across the dusty wooden porch. With one last peek, she slipped into the house and eased the door shut.

Whenever she was upset about something, writing always was her refuge, so her feet automatically took her to the small, lidded desk she had avoided for the last weeks. Seating herself, she opened the lid and surveyed the pile of papers, sheet after sheet covered with spidery black lines. She randomly picked one to read.

'A little neglect may breed mischief. For want of a nail, the shoe was lost; for want of a shoe the horse was lost; and for want of a horse the rider was lost.' Benjamin Franklin was one of her favorite authors so she'd memorized most of his quotes. In fact, she had filled several pages with his wisdom. Skipping a few lines, she read, *'A penny saved*

is a penny earned.' Well, her healthy bank account could certainly attest to that..

'Early to bed, early to rise makes a man healthy, wealthy, and wise.' All right, so she didn't follow all of his principles exactly. Surely a woman could be excused one or two indulgences.

She turned the page, her gaze leaping to the first line. Unease stirred when she read, *'Any fool can criticize, condemn, and complain, and most fools do.'* It was if Franklin had written about her. She criticized and complained, just the way McLean had said, and in more than one way, she condemned him.

Not that she would defend his behavior, after all, he was convicted of robbing the train, a deed he swore he was innocent of. But didn't everyone protest their innocence? And the fact was, he was definitely guilty of kidnapping her by refusing to take her home.

But still. Despite his conviction, so many things about him didn't add up. He didn't seem like a bad man, not like the two other men who'd robbed the train, who the law had later caught and tried.

Perhaps he was merely misguided or desperate.

No, something didn't make sense, and she suspected, just maybe, she'd made a few mistakes.

Shame filled her, because regardless of whether or not he was guilty, perhaps it wasn't fair to use his life for the basis of her plots. He seemed to be trying to live an honest life, and unintentionally, she had made it harder for him.

On the horizon, the sun slipped into late afternoon. Inside the house, shadows crept through the curtains in a lacy mantilla of darkness, draping over Gracie in heavy folds matching her guilt. She wished it would go away, but guilt had a habit of clinging.

Drumming her fingers on the desk, she admitted the possibility he deserved some kind of compensation. Picking up her pen, she dipped it into the inkwell. She pulled a clean sheet of paper from the drawer and reflected for a moment before scrawling a few words across the page.

Sitting back in her chair, she read what she had written. *The End of a Legend.* Yes, it would do, she decided, and pulled out another clean sheet.

REGARDLESS OF THE HAVOC that woman had wreaked over the last few days, life needed to go on, which meant going into town today. The problem was, what to do with the woman while he was gone. He couldn't risk her running away again.

Padding up the stairs in his stocking feet, he opened her bedroom door and peeked inside, finding her still asleep even though the sun had risen several hours ago. She slept curled into a little ball like a kitten, the bedclothes pulled loose and wadded around her body, her face buried under one arm. Holding his breath, he checked the door for a key. He didn't find one. Well, so much for his idle threats to lock her in her room.

Scratching the end of his nose, he reviewed his options, then retraced his steps down the stairs, and walked out to the barn.

After rooting through a few storage bins, he found what he sought. Making a few adjustments with some blacksmith tools, he took his discovery to the house. Walking to the kitchen, he found her sitting slouched and sleepy-eyed in a kitchen chair. He cleared his throat.

With a loud yawn, she lazily raised her head to view him. A tired smile lit up her face. "Oh, good. You're still here. It was so quiet, I was afraid you'd left already." She reached for the small stack of papers sitting next to her plate.

He cleared his throat. "I'm going into town to get food like I promised. I'm taking Hannah with me to see a doctor," he said, fighting to keep his voice from cracking. Finding her in his kitchen, in a frilly nightgown, still rosy and rumpled from sleep, incited an urge in him to stretch her out on the braided rug under his feet.

She faced Mac, an expression of apprehension settling on her face.

"I can't take you into town, and I can't take the chance you'll run off again if I leave you here alone." Her eyes widened with fear, but he steeled himself against it. "I can't risk you going into town on your own."

"What are you saying?"

Bringing his hand from behind his back, he held out silver handcuffs held together with a chain. "My uncle used to be a part-time deputy in Los Marcos," he explained. Nausea swirled in his stomach when her eyes deadened.

"So you're going to chain me?"

He squirmed. "I'm sorry. I don't have a choice. You didn't leave me one." Stepping around the table, he knelt in front of her. "Give me your foot," he ordered, holding his hand out.

She stared at him, her brown eyes big and sad. "You're going to be sorry if you do this," she said.

Reaching under the edge of her gown, he pulled out a bare foot. Her small heel nestled in the palm of his hand, her toes dainty and tipped with small pink nails. The soft skin and fragile bones of her foot were as enticing as the near-naked breasts of the most practiced whore. Holding it, his hand trembled.

"I already am," he mumbled. Pulling out the roll of gauze he'd stuffed in his back pocket, he wrapped the fabric around and around one ankle, then the other. Done, he snapped on the cuff. Then the other. Once both were in place, he turned and walked away.

"STOP. COME BACK. UNSHACKLE me," Gracie yelled, but Mac didn't.

Surely he wouldn't leave her like this? The murmur of his voice speaking to the child reached her ears. She strained to hear the words. Footsteps sounded, the heavy tread of a man, and the lighter steps of the child, then the front door opened and shut. Hobbling to the window, she watched him lead both horses out of the barn and hitch them to the small buckboard beside the barn. Hoping he'd return and unchain her, she waited, but he didn't. Instead, he lifted Hannah onto the seat of the wagon and drove off.

The beast. That horrible, horrible man. He'd left her.

Due to her weeping and wailing, she had no idea how much time passed. Now she had a scratchy throat, swollen eyes, and a nose that ran like a leaky pump but being engrossed in her misery, she'd ignored the more intense urges of her body. And the situation was desperate.

Legs stiff from sitting with them folded so long, she creaked off her chair. The chain clanked with a metallic sound. She hobbled toward the hallway, her gait hampered by the short chain stretched between the cuffs. When she reached the stairs, she stopped to catch her breath, staring peevishly up the stairwell.

Lifting a foot, she stretched for the first step. One inch from the surface of the step, her foot came to an abrupt halt, stopped by the length of the chain. Well, shoot, she'd never be able to climb those stairs in the normal fashion. After mulling it over, she figured out how to boost herself up, one step at a time on her bottom—a long, embarrassing process. By the time she reached the top, her ankles were chafed from the shackles in spite of the fact McLean had wrapped her ankles with gauze.

Her short-term needs satisfied, she planted her bruised backside and equally bruised ego on her bed to consider what she should do next. Fury filled her. And hurt. She'd stayed up until after midnight the last several days to write, just to help the ungrateful beast out of his predicament. He didn't deserve her help, but after due consideration, she decided she would finish the story anyway, if for no other reason than the satisfaction of making him feel like an obnoxious ass when she demonstrated how a truly magnanimous woman behaved.

More importantly, if she wrote something, anything, no matter how awful, then he'd have to let her go. Escaping from this nightmare was far more essential than revenge.

She slid back down the stairs and entered the parlor. Picking up her pen, she dipped it into the inkwell and began writing. Under normal circumstances she could write three thousand words a day. Her stories were usually around forty-five thousand words. Calculating her usual rate of writing, it would take over two weeks, which was a lot longer than she wanted. So she'd have to write faster, even if it meant staying up nights to accomplish it.

This nightmare would be behind her, and she could return home to her lovely house and her predictable life and her previous writing career. The career where she wrote stories about Scar McLean.

She'd show him.

Chapter Eight

Dr. Lentz dropped the steel instrument onto the metal tray with an impatient clank. "I'm going to tell you the same thing I told Clark and Jane Braddon, the couple that took little Hannah in when your folks died. There's nothing wrong with this child's ears. Since she could talk fine until your aunt and uncle died, I'm pretty sure there's nothing wrong with her tongue, either." He peered at Mac over the top of his spectacles while he put away his medical instruments.

"Are you saying she refuses to talk?" Mac asked, doubt creeping into his voice.

The doctor sighed and rubbed the back of his neck. "No, I'm not saying that at all," he answered in a gentler tone. "I'm saying, for some reason, she can't talk. I've read of two cases like this in medical journals, both times involving a trauma of some sort. Up in Kansas, there was a boy whose family was massacred by rebel guerillas during the war, with him the only survivor. Also, a few years back, I read about a woman who lost her husband in a fire. Both stopped speaking after the incident."

"Did either of them speak again?"

Doctor Lentz removed his spectacles, pulled out a handkerchief from his breast pocket, and cleaned the lenses, all the while avoiding Mac's gaze. Holding them up to the light, Lentz checked them for spots, folded and slipped them into his pocket. "I only read about these cases, you understand, so my information is years old and may not include all the facts."

Tapping his hand on his knee, Mac gritted, "Did either of them ever speak again?"

"The woman did eventually, after a couple of years," the doctor answered with a sigh.

That tightness burgeoned in Mac's chest. "What about the boy, Doctor Lentz? Did he recover?"

"Last I heard, he hadn't," Lentz responded.

Mac rubbed the pain under his breastbone, his hand trembling. "Is there anything else I can do? Any place I could take her where they might have better treatments?"

"I read there's a doctor in Europe somewhere, France, I think, who's had some success with these kinds of cases. You could take her there and see if they can help."

"France. I could as easy take her to the moon. I can hardly afford to bring her here, much less France," he said, watching Hannah who was staring out the window, her face showing no emotion.

Lentz grimaced. "I understand. And there's no guarantee those doctors would be able to help anyway. My advice is to keep doing what you're doing, loving her, talking to her, and she might surprise us. Your daughter's young, and the young have remarkable recuperative powers."

"The boy in the Indian massacre—he was young—and he never did. Right?"

"No, he didn't," the doctor answered.

Mac arched a brow. *I told you so.*

Picking Hannah up, Lentz set her on the floor. He reached into a glass jar on his desk and pulled out a licorice whip, handing it to her. After studying it for a moment, she slipped it into her mouth and sucked.

"Each case is different, Mr. McLean," Doctor Lentz said. "Every child is different. You're doing the right things for her, and you have every reason to hope. You told me yourself when you first brought her home that she didn't react to anything or look anyone in the eye." He poked a finger into Hannah's soft tummy. Her eyes widened a fraction, and she blinked at him in surprise then cocked her head, her expression puzzled. "See. From what you've said, this isn't the same child you brought home a few weeks ago. Don't give up hope." He stroked the back of Hannah's head, nudging her toward her father. "And don't stop trying. It could make all the difference."

Unable to answer, Mac pulled a coin from his pocket, paid the doctor the dollar he owed and picked Hannah up. Mumbling a good-bye, he fumbled the door open and left.

He walked to the general store carrying Hannah on his hip. His mind numb, he ignored the condemning stares and averted faces that greeted him when he stepped inside the gloomy interior. Anxious to get his business done and get home, he set Hannah on her feet and threaded his way through the congested aisles until he found a clerk.

Seeing a customer approach, the clerk beamed automatically. Recognition flickered in the man's eyes, and the smile slipped. "What do you want?"

Mac blinked, taken aback by the hostility in the chubby man's face. "I have a list of supplies I need; meat, salt, a few vegetables."

"Take your business elsewhere. We don't need the likes of you in this town," the man answered. All three of his chins wobbled in outrage.

Son of a bitch. Mac leaned over the counter, looming over the man. "First of all, there is nowhere else to take my business. Like it or not, you're the only game in town."

The storekeeper's pasty face screwed up into a tight ball of spiteful pleasure, looking like a bloated dumpling. "Then I suggest you leave town to make your purchases. Tyler is only twenty miles away."

"Damn it," Mac spit out, resisting the urge to plant a fist sized dimple to the man's face. "I need supplies, and I'm not traveling miles to another town to get them. Are you going to wait on me, or do I have to get your boss?" Curling a hand around the back of Hannah's neck, he pulled her close. Her little body trembled against his leg. Behind his back, the other customers muttered when they became aware of the argument.

A blood vessel throbbed in the clerk's forehead. "I *am* the boss, McLean, and I can choose who I serve. And I don't choose to serve you. I heard about the trouble you caused with Johnny Lee Delray and I don't want any kind of trouble in my store. Get out."

At the mention of his name, the muttering of the other shoppers became an indignant roar. A few comments like "*jailbird*", and "*thieving scum*" reached Mac's ears, and his face burned. Damn it, he needed those supplies and this town had nowhere else to buy them. So even though it galled him, he would have to beg.

Squeezing Hannah's shoulder, he pushed her forward. "This is my daughter, Hannah. We're living out at the Delaney place." Digging a hand into his jacket pocket, he pulled out the list Gracie wrote and a ten-dollar bill. He held them out to the proprietor. "We only need a few things. The place was pretty bare when we arrived, and we're down to scraping the bottom of the barrel." He tried to smile. "Hannah needs fattening up."

A sneer spreading across his face, the storekeeper ignored the outstretched hand. With a sinking heart, Mac realized begging would do no good with a man who derived pleasure from others' misery. He swore under his breath. All right, there were other methods.

Releasing Hannah, he lay a heavy hand on the man's shoulder. He squeezed. Hard. The man winced and flushed.

"I'm a paying customer," he growled under his breath, "but if you don't want to take my money voluntarily, I'm more than happy to help myself."

The doughy man trembled, big drops of sweat landing on his shirtfront. "I told you to get out," he squeaked. "Get out now, or I'll send for the sheriff."

"I don't think that'll be necessary, Hiram. I'm already here." The low voice startled Mac, and he swung around to mee Sheriff Rheingold's gaze.

"Hello, McLean," the sheriff greeted Mac, tipping his hat back off his forehead. "I heard you were in town."

Mac dropped his gaze to the list clenched in his hand. "I came in for supplies."

One side of Rheingold's mouth crooked wryly. "So I hear." He glanced at Hannah standing beside her father. "I see you found your daughter. Good." Reaching out, he took the list and money from Mac's hand.

"Why don't you and your little girl come on over to my office for a while," Rheingold suggested.

Hiram grunted in triumph.

"Is that an order, sheriff?" Mac gritted from between teeth beginning to ache from all the clenching they'd done today.

Chuckling, the sheriff picked up Hannah. "Nope, it's an invitation. I got Arbuckle on the stove I can heat up. Your daughter and I can get to be friends while Hiram here fills your order." While speaking, he thrust the list and the money at the shopkeeper. "Shouldn't take you longer than—what, Hiram—half an hour to fill this order, wouldn't ya' think?" He stared at the shopkeeper.

With a dark flush staining his face and neck, Hiram reached out with sausage fingers and grasped the paper between his fingernails. "Half an hour," he muttered and stomped into the stock room.

The sheriff and Mac didn't talk until they entered the small jailhouse. Pulling out a chair, Rheingold set Hannah on it and wandered over to the potbellied stove in the corner. He wet a finger and touched it to the coffeepot with a sizzle and a muted yelp. He glanced over his shoulder at Mac.

"Hot," he admitted sheepishly while pouring coffee into two ceramic mugs. He handed one to Mac and lowered himself into his chair with a hefty sigh. "I'm getting too old for this. Gotta think about retiring."

His comment surprised a laugh out of Mac. It reminded him some people didn't change.

"You think I'm not serious, McLean?" the sheriff asked, cocking an eyebrow while sipping his coffee with a slurp.

Mac shook his head. "What? Do you think if you convince me you're too old for the job, I won't make trouble for you?"

Rocking back in his chair, Rheingold tapped his finger on the rim of the cup. "To be honest, it's exactly what I'm hoping. Y'all got enough trouble on your plate, without antagonizing the local citizenry. How long you been back, anyhow?" He leveled a steady look on Mac.

Heat rose up from under Mac's shirt collar. Those sharp eyes made him feel young as green grass. He dared a glance toward his feet to make sure he wasn't scuffing his toes in the dirt like a five-year old. "About two weeks," he shrugged.

"Two weeks," Rheingold exclaimed. "And you've already royally teed off one of the most important men in town. I guess nobody told you Hiram Potter is the mayor here in Los Marcos? Within one minute of you walking into his store, I heard about your argument from five separate sources. The way I heard tell, you planned to shoot up the store and Hiram with it, never mind the fact you scared the pee-waddin' out of Mabel Hastings and Gertrude Muller—the two biggest gossips in town. Geez Louise, McLean. How dumb can you get?" With a quick thrust of a foot, he set his chair to rocking, staring at Mac with disgust written all over his face.

The heat creeping up Mac's neck now spread over his cheekbones, setting them on fire. He tried to return that glare but couldn't. His gaze wavered, then fell. Hell. This morning when he awakened, he'd looked in his mirror and seen a man—not necessarily a nice or a good man—but definitely a man, complete with all the obligatory male parts. Now he was tempted to reach between his legs to see if he still had both balls.

For a long time, Rheingold studied Mac. Mac looked everywhere but at Rheingold. Hannah ignored them both in favor of the foot-long licorice whip she was still sucking on.

It was a relief when the silence ended. "So how are things out at your place?" the sheriff asked in a kinder tone, taking a sip of his coffee.

Mac snapped his gaze to meet the sheriff's. "Fine. Why?" Damn, did Rheingold find out about Gracie somehow?

At his suspicious tone, the older man's eyes narrowed. He swished the coffee around in his cup. "It was purely a neighborly question, McLean. Is there something going on out there I should know about?"

Shit. Even after five years of prison, surrounded by hardened criminals, Mac hadn't learned how to think like one. "No. No, everything's fine out at the ranch. I'm on edge with everything that's happened this morning. We're doing fine." Sweat trickled down his temple. Hopefully, Rheingold would attribute it to the heat.

"Mmmm." A world of skepticism resonated in the sheriff's answer. After a pause, he asked, "What'd you decide about staying on here in town?" He turned his head, watching Hannah when she slid down from her perch on the straight-back chair and wandered over to look into a box in the corner of the office.

"We're going to stay. Not much choice for now."

"Sounds like a plan," Rheingold murmured, his gaze still on Hannah as she stooped and peeked into the box. Heaving himself to his feet, he sauntered to the box and reached inside.

"Here, liebchen. Want to see?" he asked. Without waiting for an answer, he pulled out a sleepy yellow puppy by the scruff of its neck. Wrapping an arm around Hannah's shoulder, he cupped her hands, showing her how to hold the tiny puppy and folded it into her arms.

Over his shoulder, he continued to talk to Mac. "You working the ranch?"

Distracted by the sight of his daughter holding the puppy in her arms, Mac was slow in answering, "Yeah, but I plan on selling the cattle and raising horses instead."

Rheingold crooked a finger under the puppy's chin and tickled. It's tongue flopped out and lapped the sheriff's hand. He grumbled in disgust at the trail of gooey saliva left behind. A tiny, inarticulate gurgle emanated from Hannah, and her mouth twitched.

Mac couldn't take his eyes off his daughter, barely paying attention to Rheingold, who was flicking his hand and shaking the drool off.

"Horses, huh? There's good beef stock on your land, worth a fair amount of money if you can catch it. Seems like it'd be easier to raise those cows rather than go to all the work of rounding them up and selling them."

Jerked away from the sight of his daughter's smile, Mac shrugged. "I like horses. I know horses. On the other hand, I don't know much of anything about cows. Except they're dumb." He kept to himself the fact that he didn't know diddly about breeding horses either.

A dry chuckle from the sheriff filled the room. "Yeah, gotta agree. The only critter stupider than a cow is a sheep. And I oughta know since I grew up on a farm. That's why I became a sheriff. I'd rather die from a bullet than spend another minute babysitting cows that starve to death because they're too stupid to dig through the snow in winter, or even worse, that walk into a bog to cool off but drown."

Frowning, Mac asked, "Cows do that?"

"Oh, yeah. Horses ain't too bright, but they're smarter than cows," Rheingold rolled his eyes. "There are several ranchers in the area raising some fine horses. This seems to be good land for that, and there's a market for them right now. Especially a well-trained cow-horse." He raised his eyebrow, implicitly asking about Mac's experience with horses.

Propping his chin on the closed fist that he rested on the back of his chair, Mac said, "I have some experience training horses. Huntsville had a contract to break and train mounts for the army. They brought in wild horses from the range, and anyone who wanted to volunteer to work with them was welcome to try. Most of the fellows didn't want to—the horses could be mean at times and you could get pretty banged up—but I thought it was better than swinging a pick and shovel."

Picking Hannah and the puppy up in his arms, the sheriff returned to his chair and sat, settling her on his knee. He took the puppy, that was almost being crushed in Hannah's arms and dropped it on her lap. It bounced in the drape of her navy-blue dress and yipped, sounding like a shrill tin whistle.

Her eyes never leaving the puppy, Hannah laid a tentative hand on the dog's back. It rolled over, waving four stubby feet in the air. Enthralled, she pressed a finger into the furry belly. The muscles in her face, usually tense and wary, relaxed with pleasure.

Neither Mac nor Rheingold spoke for a minute while watching her stroke the little dog but observing her, the sheriff had a revelation. "What are you doing with your daughter while you're out rounding up cows?"

Shit, shit, and double shit. "Well. Ummm..." Mac stumbled. "I don't go far from the house, and I take her with me. Usually, I leave her sitting under a tree while I work nearby." Pathetic, but the best he could do on short notice.

Those bushy brows drew together, and the sheriff stroked his mustache. "Lord, McLean, I don't think it's a good idea what with rattlesnakes and spiders and all kinds of things a kid could get into."

Mac compressed his lips. "I don't go far, and I watch her carefully."

Shaking his head, the sheriff muttered, "However you look at it, not a good idea. Y'all ought to get someone to watch her. Why don't I ask around, and see if there's a lady in town who's interested in keeping house for you?"

His face stiff to hide his panic, Mac answered, "I don't need some sanctimonious old biddy in my house, judging my child. The women of this town didn't want anything to do with her before, and I won't have them near her now."

Rheingold blinked, concern reflected on his face, but he wasn't a man to push too hard. "Well," he said, "if you change your mind, I'm always here to help out." He glanced at Hannah. "Wouldn't want anything to happen to this sweetheart. Give me a holler any time you need help."

Mac stood, thankful their coffee break was at an end. He wasn't sure how much longer he could have endured it. "I'm sure Potter has our order ready by now. We'd best be going."

Standing, the sheriff set Hannah on her feet and stooped to talk to her. "It was nice seeing you again, young lady. You come back and visit again." He tucked his enormous hand under the puppy's belly to take him back from Hannah. She didn't let go.

"Come on, liebchen. Let me take the puppy. He needs to go back to his bed." Rheingold tugged again. A mulish expression flitted across Hannah's face, so faint Mac wasn't sure if he'd imagined it. He frowned.

Sitting back on his heels, the sheriff scratched his cheek. "I don't think she's gonna give that puppy up without a fight."

Observing his daughter's tiny hands gripping the puppy to her chest, Mac swallowed against the lump in his throat. "She hasn't shown this much interest in anything since she's been with me." It took a mere second to make his decision. "Would you be willing to sell me the dog?"

Rolling his eyes, the sheriff patted the puppy. "Heck, you can have it for free. I ended up with it 'cause Mitchell Crapper over at the funeral parlor was gonna drown it otherwise. Take it. Take the fleas too, while you're at it." He laughed and stood, his knees cracking.

Something released inside Mac's chest. He picked up Hannah, puppy and all, and set her on his hip. "Thanks for the Arbuckle, Sheriff," he said. *And everything else.*

"It's Oskar," the sheriff responded, walking with Mac to the door. "See y'all around, McLean."

With a wave of his hand, he left. His head ached, and he was exhausted from the stress. He wanted to take Hannah home and forget about the humiliations of the day, but he still needed to pick up their supplies. But Rheingold had, at least, made one task a little easier.

Unfortunately, the difficult part of the day was yet to come. Facing Gracie.

Potter wasn't much nicer when he and Hannah collected his groceries but if he got what he needed, he didn't care whether Potter was polite or not. Nice manners didn't feed himself or his daughter. Or his recalcitrant author. Holding the puppy in his arms, he took the cloth bag of groceries Potter held out, led Hannah outside then boosted her onto the seat of the wagon. Handing her the puppy to hold, he climbed up to sit next to her.

Clucking to the horses, they left town. The team ambled along the shady lane leading to home, their instincts telling them a long drink of cool water and a manger filled with sweet alfalfa awaited them.

Hannah clutched the puppy, an expression on her face that was almost a smile. The puppy wiggled, and she let out a gasp, then a giggle.

Mac's heart stopped. Laughter. His daughter laughed. Tears pricked his eyes, but he forced them away. Tears might upset her, set her back. With trembling hands, he shook the reins, pressing the horses on. Now that his tasks were complete, worry urged him to get home.

He'd left Gracie shackled—hobbled—like a horse.

He couldn't forget the horror on her face when he'd snapped the cuffs on. Almost the moment he'd done it, he'd realized he'd made a mistake. Even thinking about it made shame burn through him. But she hadn't left him any choice.

Entering the barnyard, he pulled the wagon around to the back. Hopping to the ground, he lifted Hannah down and led her into the barn. She looked up at him, the puppy still in her arms.

"Until the puppy is housebroken, he needs to stay out here."

Her lip trembled.

"I'm sorry, sweetheart, but he can't stay in the house until he learns to do his business outside, but he'll be fine here. We'll make him a comfy bed, and you can visit him whenever you like." Having delivered his ultimatum, he found a wooden box and lined it with several gunny sacks then placed the puppy inside. "You can bring him food later."

With a sigh, his daughter nodded, and Mac's heart expanded in his chest with elation. A simple nod, and his world changed. "Tell the puppy goodbye then let's go inside."

She patted the puppy on the head then taking Mac's hand, followed him into the house. No one was in the kitchen when they entered. After sending Hannah upstairs to change her clothes, he checked the parlor, but that too was empty. Surely Gracie wouldn't have tried to escape while wearing the shackles. He climbed the stairs. Her bedroom door was closed.

"Gracie."

No answer. He knocked. Still no answer, so he tried the knob. The door was locked. He banged on the door a few times, demanding she come out, but her response was a stony silence.

Fine. He'd come back later. Maybe she'd answer then. But she didn't. Dusk fell, then night. Closing up the house, he put Hannah to bed then did the same.

But he'd gone to bed feeling guiltier than ever.

He slept, but his sleep was restless, so he got up and walked down the hall to Gracie's door. Tentatively, he twisted the knob. The door swung wide to reveal her sprawled on top of her mattress, fully clothed, her arms flung wide, both legs hanging over the edge of the bed. Her pink lips were parted, revealing the edges of her small white teeth.

Something hot shifted inside his chest. He recognized shame—and guilt, because it was ever present—but something else was mixed in he couldn't—or didn't want to—identify. Her chest rose, the cloth of her bodice tightening over her breasts, outlining the buttons of her nipples, and the heat in his chest dropped to his groin. His cock hardened and pointed eagerly—like a goddamned Irish setter—at what it wanted.

Though no one was there to see the tent in his underdrawers, he clapped a hand over it. "Damn it, Harold, not now," he whispered. Disregarding his discomfort, he crept up to the edge of the bed, bending his head to get a better look at her ankles.

Damn it. Her skin was pink from the chafing.

Going down the stairs to the pantry, he retrieved the supplies he needed and returned to her room with the key to the shackles. He sat on the end of the bed and carefully removed them. Grasping her foot, he propped it on his knee, scooped some salve from the jar and spread it on her slim ankles.

The abrasions were rough and hot, the skin above smooth like silk, and cool. Without meaning to, he found his hand straying, his fingers lightly caressing the slim bone on the outside of her ankle, amazed at how tiny and dainty it was. Withdrawing his hand back to her foot, he cradled it in his hand.

Don't. But his hand didn't listen. Blood thrummed hotly through his veins, and the bed vibrated with his trembling. The tips of her toes brushed the thin cotton of his drawers, making his hands shake. *Ah, God.* He inhaled sharply, shaking with desire.

Harsh breathing echoed in the dark room, and he realized it was him. Fuck, what an idiot he was. God forbid she wake up and find him in her room, holding her foot. But she slept on, her lips slightly parted, her breath soft.

In her sleep, she moaned and flung an arm over her head.

He jerked. Flushing, he pushed her foot off his lap and tucked his hands into his armpits. Trying to master the urge to touch her again, he took a deep breath. *Behave yourselves*, he told his hands. In the pockets of his armpits, they twitched longingly.

When he was sure his hands would behave, he returned to wrapping her ankles, using strips of linen he'd torn from some old sheets, moving carefully so he didn't touch bare skin.

By the time he was done, his body shuddered with tension, and a thin sheen of sweat coated his chest. With a last shaky breath, he gathered all the bits and pieces of torn cloth and draped the cuffs over an arm. He left the jar of salve sitting on the floor when he left.

Chapter Nine

Mac pulled bread and bacon out of the pantry and held both up. "What do you think, Hannah? Toast?" His daughter didn't respond, simply watched him from her spot at the kitchen table. "And look here, I got bacon to go with our eggs. How's that sound, sweetheart?" Tossing the slices of bread onto a rack in the oven, he next sliced the bacon and laid the strips in a frying pan.

Although she didn't answer any of his queries, her gaze followed him moving back and forth between the table and the stove, setting the table. Hope coiled in his chest, almost painful in its intensity. "Did you give the puppy the milk I set out, Hannah?"

She blinked, and his heart swelled. Another good sign.

He flipped the bacon over. "You know, sweetheart, we can't call him Puppy forever. He'll need a name. You should think about it and tell me what you've decided to call him." He smiled at her over his shoulder, elated to find her staring out the kitchen door to the path leading to the barn, where they'd housed the puppy.

The bacon crisping up, he cracked a few eggs and added those to the pan. The pungent aroma of frying filled the air as fat cooked out of the meat, popping and sizzling in the pan.

When the bacon was crisp, the edges of the egg whites brown and lacy, he took the pan off the stove. He picked up a rag to wipe up the greasy mess his cooking made.

Footsteps thudded behind him, and he turned.

"Chain me up, will you, you skunk."

He got a quick impression of a mouth pursed in anger, brows meeting over snapping brown eyes, and clenched fists. Instinct made him step back, but he wasn't fast enough. Her foot—shod in hard-heeled shoes—came down on his bare toes. He howled, hopping on one foot. His foot slid on the greasy floor. He flailed, trying to catch his balance.

His hand caught the handle of the frying pan on the way down. It flipped with a clang, flinging five eggs, sunny side up across the kitchen to splat against the opposite wall. The yolks slid down, leaving a yellow snail trail on the wallpaper.

Blinking up at Gracie from his position at her feet, he cradled his throbbing toes. "God da...da...darn, woman," he roared. "What the... he... fu... darn it..." At least three of his toes were probably broken, or at least they felt like it. He bit his lip, furious because he was unable to vent the string of curse words ringing in his head.

By way of an answer, she threw her shoulders back, drawing herself up to her full five feet nothing, and stuck her nose in the air. "See how you like hobbling around for a while," she snarled. With a swish of fabric, she turned on her heel and exited through the kitchen door.

His toes throbbing, he stayed on the floor after she left. Hannah cocked her head, gazing at him with a puzzled look, then slid down from her chair and came to join him on the floor. He wrapped his arms around her and pulled her into his lap.

Her warm body relaxed into his, and her head nestled against his chest. Then a tiny hand rose and patted his arm. Toes aching, surrounded by grease, shriveled bacon, and runny eggs, he hugged his daughter. "Guess what, baby? I deserved that. Your father's an idiot, and Gracie should have broken my head instead." He chuckled. Then thinking how Gracie—a woman about half his weight—had sent him toppling, he roared with laughter.

SEVERAL HOURS HAD PASSED since Gracie had gone downstairs and stomped on McLean's toes—the highlight of her week. But doing that had left her without breakfast, so now she was starving. Surely McLean had gone to work by now, and she could sneak down and get a bit of food. Holding her breath, she tiptoed down the stairs and sped into the kitchen, flinging herself over the threshold in her haste.

A dark shadow moved by the stove.

She skidded to a halt. "What are you doing here?" she squealed.

McLean looked up, knife in one hand, a slice of bread in the other. "Making sandwiches?"

Stamping her foot, she shouted, "That's not what I meant. Why are you still here? You aren't supposed to be here. Why aren't you out catching cows or... or... something?"

His eyes narrowed. "Well, first of all, it's Sunday, a day of rest. And second, I can't get a boot on over my toes." Sticking his foot out from behind the table, he showed her the floppy felt slippers he wore.

A tiny twinge of guilt poked at Gracie—probably the guilt she hadn't experienced earlier—but as hungry as she was, she refused to devote more than a second to it. "I'm starving. I didn't get anything to eat earlier."

A wide grin with a hint of malice spread across his face. "Whose fault is that?" He handed the sandwich he'd finished to Hannah sitting at the table with a wicker basket in front of her. The little girl wrapped it in a cloth napkin then stowed it in the basket.

"Yours," Gracie shrieked. How dare he smile. She stamped her foot again.

Cutting another slice off the loaf of bread, McLean slapped it on the table and slathered butter on it. He picked up a slice of tomato, laid it on the bread, and added a slab of meat. "Well, I can't say I agree with you, but it's Sunday, and I don't want to argue."

Her mouth opened, ready with a rebuttal. He held up his hand, knife still in it, and she shut it. "I thought since I can't do any work, Hannah and I would go out to this stream a few miles from here and have lunch. Like a picnic. Come with us?" he asked.

"Lunch," she squeaked. "You want me to go with you on a picnic lunch?"

McLean grinned a lopsided, off-center smile. "That's about the size of it. Want to come?" He cut another sandwich in half then gave it to Hannah to wrap and stow in the basket.

Gracie blinked, stammered, then scratched her head. It wasn't like him to be nice. She didn't trust him any farther than she could throw him. Since that wasn't very far, it might be best to go along with him so she could keep an eye on him and find out what he was after. "All right. I'll go with you," she responded in a suspicious tone.

"But you won't have fun. Right?" He packed the last sandwich into the basket.

Her back straightened like a flagpole. "I never said that."

Grasping Hannah under the arms, McLean set her on the floor. "If you're going to come with us, get whatever you need—bonnet or whatever—while I hitch up the wagon." Hooking his thumbs into his belt loops, he smiled at Gracie.

Ooooh. With a tiny huff of irritation, she spun and raced upstairs, got her bonnet then stomped outside to find him standing in front of the buckboard with Hannah sitting on the bench seat.

During the fifteen-minute trip, McLean's conversation was peppered with comments, all designed to give the appearance of solicitude, all delivered to positively infuriate Gracie. By the time the wagon arrived at the spot he'd picked out, she was so irritated she wanted to stomp on his toes again.

Pulling the horses to a stop under the shade of the lush oak tree, McLean helped Hannah down and held his arms out for Gracie.

Viewing his outstretched arms, her eyes narrowed. "I don't need your help, thank you very much," she snarled. Why was he being so nice to her?

"Sure, whatever you say." He turned away to unhitch the horses.

She eyed the distance to the ground. It hadn't seemed so far when McLean's hands were there to catch her, but now, faced with getting down on her own, she realized the wagon lacked anything adequate to hold onto. The ground seemed miles away.

McLean unhitched the horses and put hobbles on them to keep them from wandering away. He and Hannah circled to the back of the wagon and began unpacking things, pulling out several blankets and the basket of food.

Still Gracie sat.

Arms loaded with picnic equipment, he found a shady spot under a tree and set everything down. He picked up a red plaid blanket and shook it out. "Come on, Hannah, help me spread this." He held out one side to his daughter, and after a moment, she took it. Together, he and Hannah spread it onto the grass.

Gracie stayed on her perch on the wagon, irrationally angry he hadn't helped her down, even though she'd rejected his offer.

He looked up, his eyebrows raised in question. "Want some help?" he said.

"No," she snapped.

"All right. Tell me if you do."

She scowled at the two of them as they settled on the blanket. He took out the sandwiches and laid them on a napkin, then unpacking some jars, he pried them open. Unwrapping a sandwich, he handed it to Hannah, selected one for himself and waved the sandwich in her direction with a fiendish grin. "Nice day for a picnic."

She growled. She could easily learn to hate the man. But she wasn't about to give in. So she waited.

He continued eating with intense pleasure. Biting into his sandwich, he chewed, then swallowed. "Hmmm. Yummy," he said.

Oh, drat. How stupid. Holding onto the back of the seat, she turned around, stuck one foot down and groped for the top of the iron-hooped wagon wheel with her toe. She lowered the other foot to join the first. The wheel shifted. Her foot slipped. She screamed and tumbled backward off the wagon.

The ground slammed into her back.

Can't breathe. Dying. Eyes wide, she stared at the sky, her paralyzed lungs fighting for air. Her head buzzed. Her vision frayed at the edges.

Someone yanked her upright and whacked her back. With a loud wheeze, her chest expanded and air filled her chest. She coughed, loud rasping hacks.

"Lord, woman. What are you trying to do, kill yourself?" McLean ripped her bonnet off her head and tossed it aside. Running his hands all over her body, he poked and prodded and patted her back, and her front, yet for some reason she didn't mind. His touch was warm and comforting, so maybe she wouldn't die after all.

Closing her eyes, she leaned across the solid thigh supporting her, her head hanging between his knees as she drew a deep breath, then another, then another. Once she was sure she would live, she opened her eyes. And saw an eye-popping view of brown wool stretched tight over long, muscular thighs and the bulge of male parts.

A sharp thrill zipped through her.

"Like what you see?" a sly voice whispered.

She shrieked and sat up. Her head hit something hard, stunning her. McLean howled and fell backwards, holding his nose.

"Jeeezus Christ od a crudch, lady." Blood seeping between his fingers, he glared at Gracie from tear-filled eyes.

"You're crying," she said stupidly.

"Imb nod crying," he barked, his masculine pride apparently insulted. "Id stings like a sum-ob-a-bitch. By eyes are watering." He tipped his head back, pulled a handkerchief from his pocket, and wadded it over his nose.

He is too crying. She crossed her arms over her chest and observed his efforts to stanch the bleeding.

Satisfied with her conclusion, she rose to her feet. She gave the tender spot on her scalp a rub. "I'm hungry, Hannah, aren't you? Let's eat." Daintily gathering her skirts in one hand, she stepped over McLean's legs and strolled over to the blanket, throwing him a glance over her shoulder. His face was contorted in a combination of anger and confusion. She smiled. Good, she accomplished exactly what she wanted.

THEY ATE IN SILENCE. McLean kept a careful eye on the Gracie, brushing aside her offers to help even though his nose burned. Undeterred by his rejection, she smiled and finished her lunch then pulled out a sticky bun, peeling the paper away carefully so she didn't remove all the frosting.

"What do you do out here all day?" she asked with a quirk of an eyebrow.

He wasn't sure he wanted to have this conversation. "I fix fences and round up cattle," he muttered while saying to himself, *or I try to.*

"Is cattle ranching profitable?" She took another big bite of sticky bun, shaking the gooey paper from her fingers.

Now what was she after? "I guess," he answered grudgingly. "If you know what you're doing."

"I see," she said, nodding. "And do you?"

He winced. Damn, trust the pernicious woman to get right to the painful point. "I'm learning."

She tore another large hunk off her sweet roll and popped it into her mouth. Hannah's eyes widened, watching the bun disappear into Gracie's mouth, then made a small sound, almost a groan.

Mac snapped his gaze to his daughter, seeing the yearning on the child's face. He reached behind him to retrieve another sticky bun from the basket, but Gracie tore a chunk off her own bun and handed it to the child. Hannah crammed it into her mouth, hummed in satisfaction then licked her lips, her tongue going round and round her mouth, making sure she got every sweet drip of icing.

"So you're going to raise cattle?" Gracie continued and slipped another chunk of sweet roll into Hannah's hand.

"What's it to you?" His gaze was fixed on his daughter watching her take a bite of bun.

Gracie huffed in anger. "You don't need to be so suspicious every time I ask a question. It's that it seems like you work very hard. I can see you're a good father to Hannah, so you must have some kind of plan to make a living." She snorted. "Especially since you can't go back to robbing trains."

God damn. He opened his mouth to retort then snapped it shut when he caught her sly smile. The woman was purposely goading him. Well, he wasn't about to let her win this game. He grinned just to piss her off.

"I guess being a cattle rancher seems like a pretty good way to make a living," she said next, her tones sweet as sugar.

He considered his answer, still wary of her motives. "No, I'm not interested in being in the cattle business. I plan on breeding and training horses."

She screwed up her mouth. "Hmm, that's nice. I like horses." Her gaze darted to where Horse grazed contentedly next to the sorrel gelding. "He looks like he'll make nice babies."

Mac snorted, lemonade coming out through his nostrils. He could sense her gaze on him when he hacked and coughed. "Honey, that horse will never be a daddy."

"Why not? He looks young and healthy enough." She turned her gaze to Horse again.

"He's a gelding, is why not."

"A gelding? What's that got to do with it?" Gracie asked.

He goggled at her in amusement. What kind of innocent didn't know what a gelding was? *City-girl.* "He hasn't got the right equipment to make babies."

She looked for a long moment at the grazing horse before turning a puzzled look towards Mac. "Equipment? What equipment? He looks fully equipped to me. Four legs, a tail, big yellow teeth."

Faced with having to verbalize male anatomy to a young woman uninitiated to the facts of life, he began to sweat. "He hasn't got... uh.... you know."

Pulling up her legs, she propped her chin on her knees. "No, I don't. Otherwise, I wouldn't ask, now would I?"

He stared back, wondering how anyone who looked like Gracie could cause so much trouble. If it weren't for her... ripe... delicious... perky... bosom, she wouldn't look any older than Hannah. And although her cheeks were round and shiny, her mouth was pink, lush, and eminently kissable.

His tongue tingled, anticipating what it would taste like, to put his lips on hers and run his tongue around the satiny lining of her mouth. His head buzzed. He stifled a moan.

"Well," she demanded, waking him out of his lust-induced stupor.

"He hasn't got, um... the parts, that... uh..."

She cocked an eyebrow at him.

Grimacing, he struggled on. "...that part you were so interested in looking at... Before... when you... were..." He gave up.

She watched Horse. As luck would have it, Horse chose that moment to spread his legs and drop the part of equipment under discussion from inside its sheath. With a horsy groan of relief, he watered the grass.

She watched until the horse was done, then her gaze swiveled to Mac. "It looks to me like he has everything he needs. In fact, he looks extremely well-equipped," she murmured.

Dropping his head into his hand, Mac dug his fingernails into his scalp. "Damn it, woman," he groaned. "It's not my job to teach you all the finer points of the male physique. Don't you have anything better to do than to pester me?"

Silence fell in response to his question. He shot a glance at her from the corner of his eye just in time to catch a knowing twinkle shining from her eyes. One side of her mouth ticked up in amusement.

Damn it. She'd played him for a fool. And he deserved it. "You... You..."

Her smile growing broader, she scrambled to her feet and held out her hand to Hannah. "Yes, I have plenty of things I'd rather do," she laughed. "Come on, Hannah. Let's go find something that doesn't pester your father."

Cocking her head, Hannah looked between Gracie and her father, then rose and took the proffered hand. Ignoring his beleaguered expression, the two marched off downstream, their backs identical ramrods of female indignation.

The minute she and Hannah moved out of sight, Mac lurched to his feet and hobbled in the other direction. A few hundred feet upstream, he found a quiet inlet where the rushing stream carved a deep pool lined with small stones. Tiny fish darted back and forth in the crystal-clear water. Shaking off his felt slippers, he waded in and sat with a tired sigh. The water was icy cold, raising goose bumps all over his body. Damn. He closed his eyes in resignation. Another good pair of pants ruined.

Chapter Ten

"Hannah, come look at this. I've found a huge salamander," Gracie called. Her toes burned from the cold water, and the muscles in her calves cramped, but it felt good on her chafed ankles. She turned her head to find the girl standing on the bank of the stream.

"Come in, Hannah, and see what I've found."

Hannah stared at her, her face pinched.

"Are you afraid?" Gracie asked, noting the timid expression on the child's face. "Would you come in if I helped you?"

Hope flared in Hannah's eyes in answer.

Treading carefully, Gracie made her way to shore and held her arms out for Hannah. The girl took a small step back.

"It's all right, sweetheart. I promise I'll take good care of you, and I won't drop you, or anything. Please? I'd like it if you trusted me."

Hannah hesitated, then held her arms out to be picked up.

Gracie scooped Hannah up, settling her on her hip. "Hang on tight, honey."

She waded to the log mired in the muddy bottom and pointed at the salamander, dark brown with big bulging eyes, clinging to a submerged limb, its knobby toes flexing on the slippery bark.

"See it? See how it can sit under water without breathing?" she asked.

Hannah buried her face in her shoulder and shook her head, her nose scraping across her collarbone.

"All right, then I'll sit so you can see better." Gracie squatted onto the log. The ice-cold water soaked into her skirt and undergarments. She kicked her feet in the water.

Peering over her shoulder, Hannah watched the water spin in a lazy circle, creating smooth swirls and eddies. Seeing the child's interest, Gracie kicked again, harder this time. Crystalline drops sprayed over the pool, sending a faint rainbow arching across the water.

The little girl shrieked, pointing.

With a frown, Gracie watched her. "Why won't you talk? You certainly scream well enough," she asked.

Hannah's head swiveled to look at Gracie, a question in her eyes.

"What happened to make you stop talking?" When Hannah didn't answer, Gracie sighed. "I wonder what you would say if you could talk. Would you tell me your father was innocent?" Scooping water into her cupped hand, she splashed a few drops onto Hannah's legs. The child gasped.

"No, you were too young to understand what happened. You probably don't even understand what's happening now. Well, it doesn't matter anyway, because he's guilty. Everyone said he was guilty, and it's what I wrote in my newspaper report." Why didn't her conclusion sound right? Why did she continue to have doubts that grew stronger the more time she spent with McLean?

Hannah dipped her fingers into the water and splashed Gracie with a tentative motion.

Gracie screamed in mock surprise. "Oh, you silly girl. Look what you've done. Brrr, I'm freezing. I'm going to get you for that so you'd better run. Quick, quick. Jump down and run." She waited until Hannah jumped off her lap and splashed her way to the bank, then pursued her.

Hannah shrieked with glee as Gracie chased her in and out of the water.

It was late afternoon and Hannah's lips looked blue with cold by the time they waded to shore and dried off. After picking up their shoes, they walked back to join McLean.

He lay on the blanket, sleeping in the warm afternoon sun.

"Shhh," she cautioned Hannah. "Your daddy's asleep. Let's not wake him up." Sitting next to him, she put Hannah's shoes on. "I think your daddy's got the right idea. Not sure about you, but I'm exhausted. Why don't we take a nap too."

Tired after such an active afternoon, Hannah didn't protest. She waited until Gracie got herself settled comfortably on her back before lying down and cradling her still damp head in her lap. Gently untangled the knots in Hannah's hair, Gracie stroked her curls until they both drifted to sleep.

THE LOW HUM OF GRASSHOPPERS rubbing their legs together woke Gracie. A slight breeze sprang up, ruffling her hair across her face. Eyes still closed, she twitched her nose; too lazy to raise her arm and remove the strand of hair bothering her. The wind picked up, and the strand of hair slithered over her cheek into her mouth.

She opened her eyes. McLean lay on his side with his head propped on his arm, staring at her and Hannah, his eyes dark with some emotion she couldn't identify.

A muscle in his cheek twitched, and he took a deep breath. "All I ever wanted to be was a good husband and father," he said. "I wanted my family to have a decent life. I didn't need to be rich, just happy. I wanted to be a good attorney, to send bad men to prison where they belonged and to make it possible for the innocent to prove their innocence."

Startled at his sudden, unsolicited, disclosure, she licked her lips uneasily.

He closed his eyes, his mouth a thin line. "I failed." He picked Hannah's hand up and caressed her small fingers, running the pad of his thumb over her grimy knuckles up to the childish dimples on the back of her hand. His thumb rotated around and around the soft indention.

"I failed her... And I'm afraid I'm going to fail her again."

Gracie was silent, having no idea what to say.

When she remained quiet, something shifted in the depths of his eyes. He looked away, a slight flush staining his cheekbones.

"McLean, we all have mistakes in our lives, things we regret," Gracie murmured. She certainly did.

His nostrils flared with anger.

"Sometimes things happen," she tried once more. "We make bad decisions—"

"You have no idea what the hell you're talking about, lady," he growled.

"You're right, I don't. So why don't you tell me?"

He paused so long, she was sure he'd decided to ignore her. Then his gaze jerked away from hers. "I was so goddamned proud the day I passed my bar. It meant I could marry Valerie. I was crazy in love with her, and I couldn't wait to get married. I wanted to make a home for her, because she was raised by a crotchety old uncle and never had a home of her own. I wanted to give her a family... Someone to love." He swallowed, his throat working. "But things weren't... good... in Baton Rouge where we lived. She had friends... people I... I didn't like... So I decided we had to move. I got a job in Lockhart, Texas, thinking things would be better there, away..."

He stopped, his jaw flexing. "But I'd had dealings with Dexter Fox in Baton Rouge. This was before we moved to Lockhart. From when Fox held up the bank Baton Rouge—did an unbelievably bad job of it—and got caught. I was the prosecuting attorney at the trial, and I got him ten years in prison."

He rubbed a hand across his face. "But the town should have hung the son-of-a—" He paused, his jaw tensing. "A man was killed during the holdup. Everyone but Fox got away. The law never found the money—over thirty thousand dollars. A fortune. For some people, it was almost every penny they had, their entire life savings. I couldn't prove he'd killed the teller—some witnesses said it was a different man—so I tried for armed robbery instead. I figured, if nothing else, there was a chance we could get the money back. Because once he was hanged, the money was gone forever. I thought, with time, Fox would tell someone where it was. It was so much money..."

Gracie snorted and McLean faced her, a puzzled look on his face. "What?"

"Is that how all criminals excuse their crimes?" she sneered. "If it's enough money, it's excusable?"

"What are you insinuating?"

"I'm saying, how convenient for you, to be the attorney on a case where thirty thousand dollars was stolen, a fortune, then a short time later the two of you are on the same train where there's another holdup." She flinched when McLean sucked in an angry breath. Why had she said that? Why was she being so cruel when she was no longer sure her accusations were true?

"Let's not beat around the bush, lady. I've always believed in plain speaking. Say what you mean."

For some reason, she couldn't stop the words. They popped out, horrible words that cut, shredded, and weren't what she truly believed yet she said them anyway. "All right. I think when you realized how much money was at stake, you went for a lesser sentence then joined forces with Fox so you could find the hidden loot. And I think you got in on the train robbery as part of the deal." Her pulse throbbed in her ears, muting the curse he emitted.

Standing, he grabbed her wrist and yanked her to her feet. "Come on. I've got something to say to you, and I don't want Hannah to hear it." He dragged her, kicking and protesting upstream. When they reached a grove of trees, he stopped.

Turning, he flung her hand away. "The reason I was on the train was because I was coming back from New Orleans where I had buried my darling wife two days before that."

Oh God.

"We—my wife and I—lived in Baton Rouge, but I decided we had to leave because she was having an affair. I thought getting her away from her lover would fix things. But it didn't." He paced, running his hands through his hair in agitation.

"Everyone knew except me. I was too stupid to figure it out. Too stupid, or too much in love. So when I finally woke up, I moved us to Texas, hoping to save our marriage. But it didn't work. She wanted things I couldn't give her—money, power, status. Within six months of leaving Louisiana, she left me. To be with a wealthy man." He glared at Gracie, his face working with suppressed rage.

She glared back. "All the more reason for what you did. Money would bring her back. Lots of money would bring her back faster." *No, no. Stop, Gracie. Don't say another word.* But she couldn't stop. It was all the horrible mean things she'd thought about him in the last weeks, all her frustration and anger at what he'd done to her life, and she had to let it out.

"Damn it. Dexter Fox was in jail in Louisiana over two hundred miles away and had been for over a year. So how would I have managed to make any kind of deal with him? Huh? Huh?"

"I don't know," she whispered.

"I couldn't. And I didn't need his goddamned money anyway," he snarled. "Not by the time Fox robbed the train. I told you. Valerie was dead. I'd just buried her. She left me for another man who killed her. I didn't need the money. I never needed it. I wanted a mother for my twelve-month-old daughter and money can't buy that." He was panting in anger, his throat working.

Gracie stared at him, stricken by the painful sincerity in his voice.

"You destroyed my life," he whispered. "You and your stories ruined me. The holdup? It was all Fox and his gang. It was a coincidence I was on that train, so your stories were not only stupid but inaccurate. But you plastered my name and my face all over the newspapers until there wasn't an unbiased person in the whole state of Texas." He took a shaky breath. "You didn't check the facts, instead you just made up a bunch of lies. And now you're still ruining my life with your damned books." His eyes gleaming wildly, he turned away.

The afternoon had waned, and the temperature had dropped. She, still in her clammy dress, shivered, partly from the chill but more from the growing realization she may have made a mistake. She didn't understand. All the evidence pointed at him. Thirty witnesses testified McLean was part of the gang, that Fox treated him like a partner. Could she have been wrong all this time?

He'd been tried and found guilty. She didn't know what to believe, but right now, he sounded so innocent and convincing.

She swallowed the lump in her throat. "I'm sorry." He faced her, scorn wrenching his face into harsh lines. "Truly. I was nineteen. And stupid. And only thinking of myself. It seemed romantic to write about the bad man, then once I got started, I couldn't stop. I'm so sorry. You were guilty, but it didn't make it right to use you for my stories."

He clenched his eyes shut for a brief second then opened them. "It's time to leave." Turning, he started back to the blanket.

She grabbed his hand, stopping him. "You're a good father," she said in a whisper. "You are, and you shouldn't assume you've failed."

"Yeah, well, it doesn't change anything. You still think I'm guilty, and my life's still shit."

"It does make a difference to Hannah. She's aware that you love her, and she's getting better all the time."

He frowned at Gracie, the hope in his eyes so blatant it hurt her to see it.

"Do you know what she did today?" she asked. "She played in the water with me. And she laughed."

He pushed his hair off his forehead. The muscles in his throat worked. "Sure. Come on, it's getting late."

Because it was what he wanted, she walked back with him to the blanket and helped him pack up the remnants of their picnic. Hannah slept on the way home, snuggled up against her father's lap. McLean was silent, staring over the horses' backs.

Gracie huddled on her side of the wagon seat, lost and unsure. Was she responsible for sending an innocent man to prison? But how could she have been wrong?

Taking a deep breath, she turned her face away, tears pricking the back of her eyes. God help her, she had a feeling she perpetrated a horrible injustice.

Chapter Eleven

Her new story was easy to write. All she needed to do was imagine it was McLean talking, and the words flowed onto the paper. After hours hunched over the desk, her neck burned with tension and her head ached—a sign she had worked too long. By necessity, this story would be shorter than her usual lengths but now that she was writing for so many hours, it would be complete in the next few days. If she mailed the story on an express train, her agent would receive it in less than a week.

She stopped, putting her pen down, and stretched to work out some of the kinks. Rubbing tired eyes, she sorted through the pages, beginning to end, and began to read, comparing the twenty pages she wrote that evening with stories she'd written in the past.

When she finished reading, she returned to the beginning and reread it. Done, she gazed out the window, not wanting to think about her new story. It left her with an odd sense of... discomfort. Or unease? She—the consummate master of words—wasn't sure how to describe her emotions. What she did know was that the writing she'd done in the past suffered by comparison. It seemed shallow and immature to her now compared to this current work.

Feet padded on the bare floor, and Hannah appeared at her side. "Hannah, what are you doing out of bed. It's the middle of the night."

Hannah leaned her elbows on the desk and peeked up at Gracie with solemn eyes.

"Go back to bed, sweetheart. I don't have time for you right now because I'm working on this story for your father."

Hannah frowned.

Gracie rolled her eyes. "Well, I'm sorry but he's driving me crazy. My life was all set until he barged into it. I was completely happy writing my stories the way they were, making him the perfect villain." Wadding a page up in her hand, she tossed it into the waste basket. "Then he doesn't even have the decency to be guilty. Or maybe he is. I don't know anymore." She sighed. "I wish I did."

Holding onto the arm of the chair, Hannah crawled into Gracie's lap and rested her head against her shoulder.

Gracie wrapped her arm around the little girl. "Darn it. He was convicted. And I wasn't the only reporter writing about the trial. Other journalists attended, and they were all convinced he was guilty too. But he blames me for everything." She considered her work. "And he's even changed my writing style."

A small hand slipped into Gracie's.

"Don't go getting cozy with me, Hannah. I'm not in sympathy with either of you right now. If your father has his way, my whole life will be destroyed." She heaved a sigh.

Hannah tilted her head.

"Yeah, yeah. He's your father, so of course you think he's innocent." Gracie rubbed a finger between her brows in an effort to erase her headache. "But you know what? I guess it doesn't makes sense he would rob a train. I mean, why would he? He was an attorney. He probably made a good living. And if he was going to rob something expecting to get a lot of money, he'd probably rob a bank, not a train, right?"

The little girl didn't say anything.

"I'm sorry, Hannah. I think I jumped to conclusions. I do that sometimes."

She stopped. Thought. "Okay, I do that a lot. So maybe he is innocent? Oh, God, that would make me a terrible person. I not only accused him, but I wrote all those books. And I made all that money from his misfortune. Did I do that, Hannah? Did I help convict an innocent man?" Her lip trembling, she glanced down at the little girl.

Hannah looked back, her gray eyes trusting.

"I can't decide what to think anymore. If he's innocent, I owe it to him to fix things. Even if he's not, I think I owe him. But how do I fix it?"

The little girl snuggled closer.

Gracie grimaced. "Well, I suppose I could take the facts and bend them a bit for the sake of the story. I don't think it would damage my integrity. The other fellow, that Dexter Fox...? Your father said he was the one. I guess it wouldn't hurt to write a story and make him the villain. He seemed pretty villainous to me during the robbery. What do you think, Hannah? If I wrote a story with Fox as the real villain, do you think it would make up for everything?" She glanced down.

The child let out a quiet breath, her head nestled against Gracie's breast while she slept. Carefully, Gracie jotted a few notes on a piece of paper and then carried Hannah to bed.

FOR SOME STRANGE REASON, Mac looked forward to getting up this morning and seeing Gracie's face glowering at him—as usual—from across the kitchen table. He'd tugged on the too-small brown worsted trousers he'd shrunk in the stream and pulled a sleepy-eyed Hannah from bed. Rushing her into one of her two navy blue dresses, he dragged her downstairs, expecting Gracie would already be hard at work in the kitchen.

He entered the deserted kitchen and came to a halt, disappointment settling in his stomach like a batch of bad eggs. Well, what had he expected? The woman had made it clear she considered him nothing more than a criminal.

A hot flush burning his ears, he stomped to the pantry to fetch eggs and bread to make battered toast. Forcing himself to throw off his misery, he smiled at Hannah, hoping his smile didn't mirror the pain he felt.

"All right, honey. Let's you and me get to work. I'll rustle up some breakfast. In the meantime," he said and handed her a bowl of scraps. "Take this out to the barn and feed the puppy." Hannah left, heading toward the barn.

He returned to the pantry to retrieve a slab of bacon. After lighting the stove, he set to work slicing things up. The thump, thump, thump of his knife on the wooden cutting block was the only sound in the kitchen as he worked. A soft breeze drifted in through the open back door, cooling the kitchen, carrying the sweet aroma of honeysuckle, the acrid smell of grass and moist dirt. Finishing with the chopping, he laid the strips of bacon into the skillet. Beating eggs in a bowl, he dipped the bread into the mixture until each piece was saturated and laid them in the skillet with the bacon.

Although he was still disappointed his suppose-to-be author wasn't downstairs yet, he found himself humming and smiling to himself while he tended to breakfast. It made no sense to be gloomy when his daughter had progressed in the last week. She'd gone from an impassive marionette into a child who smiled and seemed to connect with other people even though she still wasn't speaking.

Going to the cupboard, he pulled out clean dishes and arranged them on the table. As he worked, a picture of Hannah danced in his head—a laughing, talking Hannah—holding out hope for the future. In the meantime, dozens of mundane, day-to-day tasks needed to be done.

He focused his attention on flipping the frying bread in the pan. Hearing the sound of someone in the doorway, he turned.

Leaning dreamily against the doorframe, still dressed in a faded blue nightgown and a robe from his aunt's closet, Gracie smiled a sweet sleepy smile, her eyelids blinking. The sight of her candy-pink mouth, still swollen and slack from sleep, made his toes curl and his manhood protest the too-tight confines of his shrunken pants. Jerking around to face the stove, he grunted a good morning.

She mumbled a response, pulled a kitchen chair away from the table with a scrape and plopped into it. He turned in time to see a yawn and her nose wrinkling while her eyelids blinked over slumberous eyes. A jolt of lust shook his frame, starting at his groin and spreading to the extremities of his body. Squeezing his eyes shut, he pivoted to face the stove again.

"I thought you were supposed to cook the meals around here," he grumbled when he was able to force his tongue to function. He pulled the frying bread from the pan and stacked the slices on a plate, then broke a couple of eggs into the skillet.

A contented sound, like a sleepy kitten, filled the room. His shoulders tensed.

"I'm sorry," she slurred in a languid voice. "I was so tired. I'll try to do better, all right?"

He peered over his shoulder in time to see her lay her head on top of her crossed arms, her hair a mess of uncombed curls while an innocently seductive smile lifted the corners of her mouth. To Mac, she looked like she just rose from a man's bed after being well and truly loved.

He groaned, and picking up another egg, he smashed it against the rim of the skillet. The egg shattered and the yolk plopped into the pan. Bits and pieces of shell floated in the soft yellow centers. He glowered at the shards, not bothering to fish them out. The eggs sizzled and popped.

Too impatient to wait any longer, he yanked it off the stove. He stuck his head out the kitchen door and yelled, "Hannah, come eat."

Then he slammed the skillet on the table. Grabbing a big serving spoon, he slapped eggs on all three plates.

Head still cradled in her arms, the barely awake woman gave him a foolish smile. "That smells good. I like the things you cook."

He threw himself into his chair, his weight making the rungs protest. Hannah appeared in the open door, the puppy draped over her arms.

Gracie's head popped up. "Oh, a puppy. Where did it come from? I always wanted a puppy." With an impatient gesture, she waved Hannah over. "Let me see him. Oh, he's so adorable. My father would never let me have a dog. It is a boy, isn't it?" she asked.

Mac grunted an affirmative.

She returned to admiring the puppy, burying her face in his fuzzy stomach. "Oh, look how cute he is. Look at his darling floppy ears and those big brown eyes. What's his name, Hannah?"

Her brows puckered, Hannah frowned at the dog, then at Gracie.

Somehow she understood the look. "You want me to guess? All right, let me see." She tapped her chin with a finger. "Would it be Droopy, for his ears?" An exasperated expression crossed the child's face.

"Not Droopy, huh? How about Stubby?" Taking the lopped-off tail between two fingers, she wagged it for the puppy. The puppy yipped and slobbered all over Gracie's hand with his pink tongue. "Or Pinky."

Violently opposed to both names, Hannah shook her head. She narrowed her eyes.

"Well, this certainly is a very hard decision, isn't it, Hannah?" Gracie threw out a few more names, all silly, and Hannah reacted by shaking her head wildly, causing her hair to swing in a pale fan around her shoulders.

His heart lurched, and he stopped breathing. For a moment, he wondered if he was having a heart attack after all. Hannah's delight and Gracie in her nightclothes were almost too much for a man to handle first thing in the morning.

She wrinkled her nose. "So, Hannah, a name is a very important thing. It tells the world who you are. If we do something good, people remember our names and say we have a good reputation." She turned her focus to Mac. "If we do something bad, it blackens our name." She watched Mac, her expression expectant.

He looked back with shuttered eyes.

She shrugged. "All this time I've was thinking of silly dog names, but I'll bet you picked a good, strong name for your puppy, like..." She paused a moment, idly tugging on the puppy's ears. "My father was born Augustus, but everyone calls him Gus. I always thought Gus was such a nice strong name. Would that be his name, Hannah?"

Hannah blinked for a moment, then she grinned.

"This has been a lot of excitement for Gus. Why don't you put him in his box so we can eat?" she said and placed the puppy in his daughter's arms.

Hannah pouted at the idea of relinquishing the dog. Her arms tightened around his fat little tummy until he protested with a squirm.

"His box is outside on the porch where I moved it this morning," Mac said. "He's a baby, Hannah, and needs his sleep. And I'm hungry so I want some food." After a moment's hesitation, Hannah carried him outside. She quickly returned and scrambled into her seat.

Mac took a bite of eggs. They were perfectly seasoned, perfectly cooked. "Good," he said, striving for some normality.

Rather than responding, she jabbed at her eggs with her fork.

"The potatoes are good too," he said, trying again for a reaction.

Another nod was his answer.

Perplexed by Gracie's preoccupation, Mac watched her fiddle with her bacon and eggs, wincing at the thoughtless mutilation of food as it was stirred, mashed, and dissected by her fork. He wondered what was going through her head, convinced if he lived to be a thousand years old, he'd never understand women.

He retreated to the stove, his bastion of masculine safety these days. Surveying the glutinous mass of cooling eggs and bacon still in the pan, he sighed. What the hell happened to his life that he felt safer in front of a stove than dealing with a short, irritating, but definitely feminine—and why couldn't he get her lips out of his mind—woman?

A chair scraped, followed by the soft thud of tiny feet hitting the wooden floor. A plate, scraped clean of food appeared at his side, silently held out by a tiny hand.

"Thanks, sweetie," he murmured, taking it from her and setting it in the wet sink. "Go on out and play now." She disappeared from his side.

He picked up a soapy rag, aware of Gracie's gaze drilling into his back. The heat of her gaze sent his pulse racing. He shifted as his cock hardened against the front of his trousers.

"What's wrong with your pants?" she blurted out.

He leaped a foot off the ground. Slapping the dishrag across his front, he swung around to face her. "What? What's wrong with my pants?" he yelped.

She blinked at him, her soft pink lips falling open. "Well, look at them. Those pants are four inches too short in the legs. What did you do to them?" She did the head-cocking thing that drove him crazy.

He took a deep breath. Seconds passed while he wracked his brain, but the most he could manage was a weak smile and the word 'water' in a low mumble. She looked at him oddly.

Hell, what an idiot.

"Don't you have another pair of pants? Besides being too short, they're too tight in the...uh seat." She paused for a moment. Her gaze roved up and down his body, and poor, hungry Harold grew restless.

"Those must be awfully uncomfortable..." she muttered. "Don't you have other pants?"

Bracing his hands on the range top, he let his head drop to his chest. *How did she do it?*. How did she manage to *always* find his weak spot?

But he had no answer to her question.

She frowned. "Hmm, I read somewhere pants that are too tight can cause your brain to swell. If you like, I can lengthen the hems and let out the seat. That way you'd be more comfortable."

His head swiveled so fast his neck popped. "What did you say?"

"I said I'd let your pants out for you."

"You'll fix my pants?" he asked, facing her. "Are you sure?"

"Yes," she growled. "I said I would. Take them off, and I'll fix them."

Any remnants of control he had over Harold disappeared in an instant. His manhood hardened. He dropped his hands, hoping to hide the evidence.

Fortunately, her gaze stayed on his face, instead of roving over dangerous territory. "Come on. I don't have all day. If you want to me take care of your problem, take those pants off now."

His knees nearly gave way at the mention of his *problem.* He cocked an eyebrow, trying for a nonchalant air that would put him back in control. "Lady, I don't take my pants off in the kitchen for just anyone. If you want me out of my clothes, you'd have to come upstairs." He smirked at her.

She sneered back, freezing the smile on his face.

His face burned red. "My bedroom. And I'll pass you my pants through the door," he mumbled. Hands in pockets, he trudged upstairs. Stripping out of his trousers, he opened the door a crack and handed them out to Gracie.

He paced to the window, paced back to the door. Damn, he felt naked. More pacing. Grabbing the quilt off the bed, he wrapped it around himself. Better. He returned to pacing. Time passed. Where the hell was she? What was taking so long, he grumbled to himself, kicking the end of the ragged wedding-ring quilt out of his way for the umpteenth time. Was she deliberately trying to torment him? He'd been here for what seemed like hours. She could have sheared a sheep, spun the wool, and woven the material, never mind sewn the pants, all in the time he was cooped up in his bedroom. If he was able to get even one of his legs into his shrunken Levi's, he would have already marched down there and given her what-for.

But without pants, he was stuck.

What was she doing? There hadn't been a peep out of her or Hannah in ages. In fact, it was too darn quiet, and that worried him. She could be doing anything, even running away again. Pants or no pants, he decided, he was going downstairs to find out what was happening.

Yanking the end of the quilt around his waist, he swung open the door and marched out of his bedroom. He slipped down the stairs, listening for noises, anything to tell him where she might be, but it was quieter than a graveyard. Creeping up to the parlor door, he poked his head around the edge of the jamb.

The sight greeting him made him catch his breath. Gracie sat in his uncle's big easy chair holding Hannah, who was clad in her thin cotton shift, asleep with her head resting against Gracie's shoulder. Her arms were wrapped around Hannah. In her hands was Hannah's severe navy-blue dress, which she was slowly and carefully stitching so she didn't disturb his daughter.

Hearing the noise at the doorway, she looked up at Mac. She smiled and laying the dress down, ran her hand up and down

Hannah's bare arm. "She saw me sewing," she whispered, "and she wanted me to fix her dress. It had a little tear. You could hardly see it, but it seemed important to her. She has so few clothes, and I wanted her to have something pretty, so I got some lace from one of the dresses I found in the closet, and I'm sewing it on her collar." She smiled at the sleeping child then gestured to the pants she'd left draped over the arm of the easy chair in the corner, indicating they were done.

Inside his chest, something shifted. It hurt when it did, leaving him breathless and light-headed. He couldn't take his gaze off his daughter cuddled close to Gracie, the woman he'd believed to be callow and selfish and the woman he was prepared to hate. Gracie Hart, the woman who'd turned out to be not at all what he'd expected.

Chapter Twelve

It was going much slower tonight than in the past few nights, and Gracie was growing frustrated with the lack of progress. The first few chapters wrote themselves because she liberally borrowed ideas and entire paragraphs from what she remembered of her most recently written book, the one that would never be published because McLean had hidden it from her. But she was in fresh territory now, and her thoughts weren't coming together on paper.

She'd completed four chapters and her new plot was well established but she wasn't sure where to go next. When she'd been so angry with him and plotted revenge, her story kept him alive and continuing with his usual exploits, thereby doing the opposite of what he'd wanted when he kidnapped her.

Now, instead, she had to find a way to introduce Fox into the story while killing off McLean, but not too soon. The biggest problem was that her readers would be devastated by his death. One way or another, she required a new hero as a central character for her future publications. She'd considered using Fox even though he wasn't the handsome, romantic figure McLean presented. In fact, if memory served, he was sort of ugly, and definitely creepy, but she could change all that. It's what writers were good at, after all, bending the truth to suit the narrative.

No, now that she thought about it, better to invent her hero.

She sighed then realized she'd sat, staring idly at the wall, for at least ten minutes. Gripping her pen tighter, she bent her head over her paper then wrote a few words before her hand slowed and stopped altogether. Really, the problem was she'd grown to love Hannah and didn't want to leave her, which was what would happen once her story was done. As to McLean, she'd started to believe... well, that she could tolerate him... or respect him? Admire?

Maybe what she meant was she liked him? Like him? Or...

The pen fell from her hand, splattering large blobs of ink across the page. *Oh, my gosh. No.* She couldn't feel anything stronger for that man than liking? It wouldn't do. He was hard-headed, stubborn, obnoxious, hateful... Jupiter, he'd chained her up.

Then he'd spread balm on her chafed skin and bandaged her ankles.

She tried to put a halt to the suspicion rioting through her mind, but the word forced its way into her mind anyway. Love? God forbid, she couldn't love McLean. Why, she didn't even know his first name.

No, she didn't love him. She had a job to do that she hoped in some small way would atone for her mistake and vindicate McLean to her reading public. Of course, the reason she wanted to stay was simply because she wanted to complete her work. She'd create a new hero, someone who could lead the way to dozens of future books, someone who'd be even better than Scar McLean. How happy he'd be when he learned she'd killed off his alter-ego.

So, a new hero. Surely she could create a hero that would out-hero McLean. After all, she was a writer so, of course, she could invent someone handsomer and more heroic. Someone different. Someone who didn't remind her of the man who was the basis for Scar.

An idea struck her. Of course. That was the answer. Picking up her pen again, she bent over the paper, words flowing from her mind like water over a dam.

IT WAS DARK SO INTENSE, it was tangible. And damp, the chill from the stone seeping up through the floor, invading tired bodies with icy fingers until bones and muscle burned fiercely. The sonorous clank, clank, clank of chains banging on stone filled the air. Steel doors slammed. Men wept, eerie cries of despair. The sounds made him sick to his stomach, wondering whether next time it would be him making those hideous noises. If only he could see. He needed the light because bad things happened in the dark.

And something lurked in the shadows, something he didn't want to think about, that made his heart pound.

With a jolt, Mac awakened, his heart pounding in his chest so hard it hurt. The corners of his bedroom were blacker than the inside of an undertaker's hat. He blinked and shook his head, trying to shake away the last vestiges of the nightmare lingering in his mind. His gaze sought the comfortable glow of the lamp he kept lit even during the night.

He didn't want to think about the dark or prison. *Think about something else.* Think about Gracie and what he was going to do about their situation.

He'd gone to sleep telling himself he was wrong, that his emotions were merely a reaction from seeing the sweet picture the two of them made. After all, what man wouldn't be moved by the sight of his daughter in the comforting arms of a lovely woman?

Especially one half dressed. That must explain his reaction. It was nothing more than lust... passion... desire... or just plain horniness.

That had to be it. He was horny. After all, he'd gone five years without a woman. He needed to get laid. Any woman would do; it didn't have to be Gracie.

Of course, he'd enjoy it a lot more if it *was* Gracie. He banged a fist on the bed in frustration. Was it possible he was obsessed with Gracie, like he'd been with Valerie? He took a moment to roll the idea over in his mind before he decided, nah, he couldn't possibly be infatuated with that snub-nosed termagant. Valerie was ice; all snow-white skin, pale blond hair, and calculating coldness. Gracie was nothing like her. She wasn't the type to incite obsession; fury, yes, frustration, indubitably but certainly not love.

No one in their right mind would love a woman like Gracie. Inflexible, and stubborn, in addition to cranky, argumentative, and unreasonable.

She could also be quirky and funny, which made him laugh, but it wasn't enough to make a man fall in love. Nor were her occasional bursts of thoughtfulness enough to make up for her more consistent pig-headedness. Nor was it the fact she seemed able to communicate with Hannah when he couldn't. They were both females, so it made sense.

Then how did he explain the odd clenching in the region of his heart?

He swore, disgusted with himself. God damn it all. He'd never even kissed her, so all his mental meandering meant nothing. No way he was in love with Gracie Hart. Attracted, yes. Horny as hell. Absolutely. But not in love.

Apparently he'd let his emotions get the better of him, and it caused him to make some stupid decisions. He was an attorney, for Pete's sake, or at least an ex-attorney, and weren't attorneys supposed to be logical human beings?

So. Number one, she wanted one thing from him which was a quick trip back to Austin. Like Valerie, she had other ambitions that didn't include Mac. Two, let's face it, no matter how he tried to dress it up in clean linen, he wasn't good enough for her. No decent woman would be interested in marrying an ex-convict who might be one step from going back to prison for kidnapping, a man who could barely make a living, and who came encumbered with a child with serious problems.

Now he thought about it, those were also reasons three, four, and five. So, there you had it. Five good, logical reasons why there was no possibility she could be part of his life.

Even if he did want her so much he ached.

But if he couldn't have her, she would have to return to Austin. And it would be better if she left before Hannah got too attached. He couldn't bear it if he... rather she... Hannah... grew to love Gracie then the woman left—and she would leave—like everyone else in his life had. Tomorrow. He'd tell her tomorrow then everything would return to normal.

The muted drumming of rain hitting the roof could be heard over the rustle of leaves as the wind blew through the trees. Rain. It hadn't rained in several weeks, but it was welcome. Although, if it continued during the day, gathering the cattle might become impossible.

And being stuck in the house with Gracie would be torture.

He closed his eyes, trying to go back to sleep, but it wouldn't come. Eventually, the darkness changed from pitch black to charcoal gray then misty gray as the sun made an appearance on the horizon.

Depressed and gritty eyed from another nearly sleepless night, he dragged himself out of bed, stumbled to his washstand, and stared blearily at the haggard visage that greeted him in the mirror. Shit, he looked like hell. His nose was still a bit swollen, the bridge mottled with a purplish bruise. Reddish brown hair stood in spikes all over his head, bright red stubble peppered his face, and his eyes appeared to be a road map of crimson veins.

Groaning, he leaned his hands on the washstand; wanting to do nothing more than stagger back to bed and sleep the day away, but it wasn't possible. He had a job to do. In truth, he had several, starting with telling Gracie she was going back to Austin. He couldn't keep her here any longer. It would be disastrous.

Squinting at his image, he poured a little tepid water into the stoneware bowl sitting on a stand and wet his shaving brush, then swished it around in his soap mug. He slapped lather on his face and picked up his straight edge. His hand trembled. Oh Lord, he was going to cut his throat... which might be for the best.

Taking a deep breath to steady himself, he laid the razor's sharp edge against his cheek. He drew it downward, leaving a bare path surrounded by soapsuds. He repeated the motion, holding his breath each time his hand trembled, until he'd removed all the stubble.

Wiping the last of the soap from his face, he dragged himself to his bed, where his newly hemmed pants hung on the bedpost, and stepped into them. He pulled a clean shirt out of his drawer, slipped it on, and buttoned it with fumbling fingers. Tucking the tails into the waistband of his trousers, he forced the large buttons down the front of his fly through the buttonholes. Clean socks—both with holes in the toes—came next then his well-worn, down-at-the-heel boots.

Checking out the window, the rain had stopped, and the sun was out. Good. It meant he'd be able to work. He looked at his pocket watch to check the time. Nine o'clock, a considerably later start than usual, and if the noise from downstairs was any indication, he was the last one out of bed.

He hesitated at the closed door.

Loosening the top button of his pants, he re-tucked his shirt. Then he re-checked the buttons on his fly to make sure each was done up. He ran his hands through his hair again. Patting both pants pockets, he checked for his watch. He brushed a thread off the sleeve of his shirt and unbuttoned his collar.

Idiot. He was just delaying the inevitable. Tugging his watch out of his pocket again, he flipped it open. Nine oh five. Oh, hell. He sighed and left the room.

The tang of onions and lilac-scented female assaulted his nostrils when he walked into the kitchen. His jaw locked, he moved to the cupboard for a cup, and poured himself some coffee. He nervously took a sip and waited for Gracie to remove the pan from the burner.

Her task completed, she looked at him with a raised eyebrow.

"I need to talk to you," he mumbled, setting his cup on the counter and stepping toward the back door.

She gave him a long, level look while she spooned eggs onto Hannah's plate then, setting the pan down, she followed him onto the back porch.

He shut the door behind him. Striding to the end of the porch, he gazed at the ridge that sloped away from the house. Damn it. He paced, still not sure what to say.

Why was he having so much trouble saying what he needed to say? It shouldn't be so hard. He'd bet everything he owned—not that he had a lot—she'd be happy when he told her she was going home. He darted a glance at Gracie. She looked puzzled and a little put out.

He licked his dry lips. "I'm sending you home."

Her mouth fell open then her eyes narrowed, and she jammed her fists on her hips. "What. Now?"

"The minute I can get someone out here to watch Hannah, I'll take you to Beaumont to catch the train."

"No, I can't go right now," she said.

"What do you mean, you can't go? Of course you can. It's what you wanted."

She blinked. He could almost see the wheels turning in her head as she groped for an answer. What finally came out was, "All my clothes are in the wash."

What? She barely had any clothes, having been kidnapped in what she wore that day, and what clothes she did have weren't even hers, they were dresses she'd found in a closet that had belonged to his Aunt Martha. Her illogical argument wasn't even worth discussing.

Staring at her, he tried to ignore the amber streaked tendrils of her fly-away hair brushing against her full lower lip and the freckles dotting her nose, begging for his tongue to lick them off. He ruthlessly suppressed the heat filling his loins, making him ache with longing.

Pressing a finger to his aching temple, he started over. "It might take me a day or two to find someone to replace you—"

"I can't go yet. I'm still working on that... thing... you know, um, Hannah's dress. I still have to sew the trim on the cuffs and repair the tear," she said.

He inhaled, irritated, hurting, and wanting to get this over with. "As I said—" He bit off each word. "It might take me a few days to find someone to... Oof." A small—unexpected—fist drove into his stomach. "What the heck's the matter with you, lady?" he mumbled, rubbing his abdomen.

"Nothing," she said primly. She walked to the edge of the porch and watched Horse frolicking in the pasture, enjoying his unanticipated vacation. "Don't you have work to do?" she said.

His stomach aching—her fist was small but powerful—he took a second to catch his breath then stepped out of her reach. "I'm trying to tell you I'm ready to send you back to Austin."

She stamped her foot and faced him. "I understand what you're telling me. I'm not stupid. I'm simply not ready to go."

"What?" he asked, bewildered. This was the last thing he'd expected to hear from Gracie Hart, the woman who'd whined so much about leaving, she'd made his life a misery.

"You heard me. I'm not ready to go."

"What are you talking about? Of course you're going." Of course she was. He was up all night making the decision, and he wouldn't change his mind now, not after all those sleepless hours. Stupidly, he made the mistake of telling her. "I thought about it, and I decided it's time for you to leave."

"You decided," she growled. "You decided. Who made you God? Who made you the decider of my life? Who do you think you are?" She stomped her foot. "I'm not going."

"God damn it, you are too," he yelled back, nearly losing track of what they were arguing about because he was so distracted by her fit of temper. Her face was rosy with anger, sending a hard jolt of lust to his groin. All he could think about was kissing her.

Well, in reality, he wanted to do a lot more than that, but he figured he'd start by kissing her.

So he did.

He pulled her to his chest and covered her open—still yelling—mouth with his. She stiffened, and a muffled *hmmmff* slipped out when he slanted his lips over hers. Her warm heat invaded his senses, starting a fire that sizzled along his nerves. Everything faded into the background, and his entire world became her hot mouth.

She tasted smoky, like bacon. Under his assault, her jaw slackened and allowed him into the warm recesses of her mouth. He thrust his tongue inside, running the tip over the smooth surfaces of her teeth as he'd longed to do. Soft breasts pushed against his chest, the nipples hard and pointy, sending little jolts of sexual lightning through him.

Shaking with desire, he gripped her hips, and tugged her closer.

A jolt of desire ratcheted through him when her arms wrapped around his neck. Encouraged, he let his hand creep up her side and touch her breast. He stroked his thumb across her sensitive nipple.

She gasped, her lips pulling away from his then she stepped away. "Oh, my," she whispered. She touched her breast, wonder in her eyes.

"Hell's fire," he whispered. He backed away from her, running a shaky hand through his hair. Damn it. What was he doing? Making love with Gracie would mean he'd be obligated to offer marriage. But marriage wasn't possible. He wasn't any better a man today than yesterday. Still an ex-convict, broke, and an idiot who'd kidnapped this woman.

His mind went numb. How could he have allowed himself to steal that kiss? He'd been married. He was completely capable of controlling his lust or at least he thought he was, but this was something else, something more than he'd ever suffered before.

That kiss was the most dangerous thing that ever happened to him. He had to find a way to make her go back to Austin. For her own good, which meant he had to ignore the ache.

GRACIE WAVERED ON HER feet, her body on fire, her thoughts scattered. McLean looked lost, desperate, and uncertain. She'd seen the minute regret replaced desire. Hmm. The next thing that happened would be him telling her again to go home.

And she was determined to stay. She didn't understand why, but she was. At least she had to stay until the story was complete. And sent off to Albert. And published. And distributed to all the bookstores and newsstands in the country. Then maybe she'd be ready to leave.

The question was, given the guilty look McLean wore, how was she going to accomplish her goal? She ran through her options. He'd kissed her. Did it mean he loved her? No, everyone knew men liked to kiss for the sake of kissing.

So using his desire for her probably wouldn't work.

Should she tell him she loved him? Hah. Why not give the poor man heart failure while she was at it. Anyway, was it love? Hard to say. Only time would tell. But she needed to say something soon.

"You can't send me away right now," she burst out. He cocked his head in wary inquiry. "I've already got six chapters of the book done.

It would be silly to send me home now, when if you would give me a few more weeks, I'll be done. Then you'll get you want, and I'll get what I want, and everyone will be happy."

"The book," he repeated woodenly. He watched her, his eyes hooded. "I guess... if you're that far along, naturally you'd want to finish it." He frowned at her from under the lock of hair falling across his forehead.

She clasped her hands together to stop herself from tucking the tendril of hair behind his ear. "Absolutely. I could never leave such an important piece of work half finished. I *always* finish what I start."

He rubbed his chest, his face grim. "How long, do you think, before you're done?"

"Oh, at least another three or four weeks," she responded, crossing her fingers behind her back, and hoping God would forgive her for the lie. And why wouldn't He? He'd forgiven much worse.

Besides, all things were fair in love and war, and this was love.

Maybe.

Possibly.

Who knew?

Oh God, it was, she knew it was. It was there in her body and in her heart.

McLean stroked his finger across his lower lip. He didn't look happy. But he wasn't unhappy either. In fact, she couldn't tell what he was thinking, she only hoped he was thinking he'd let her stay.

She waited on pins and needles before he said, "All right. Four weeks. To finish the book? That's the agreement?"

Her heart turned a few cartwheels. "Four weeks," she agreed, holding out a hand. "I'll finish the book, and everyone's happy. Then we can go back to our lives, like none of this ever happened. I'll go to Austin, I'll tell everyone I've been back east visiting my parents so my reputation is saved, and you'll have your reputation restored."

After a pause, McLean wrapped his much larger hand around hers. His was warm and callused, a very masculine grip that sent a shiver through her.

They looked at each other awkwardly for a moment, their hands locked then she withdrew her hand and returned to the kitchen while MacLean retreated to the barn. A short while later he exited, mounted on Horse. While she watched him from the porch, he reined him out of the yard and headed toward the back pasture on his way to resume his eternal quest for cows.

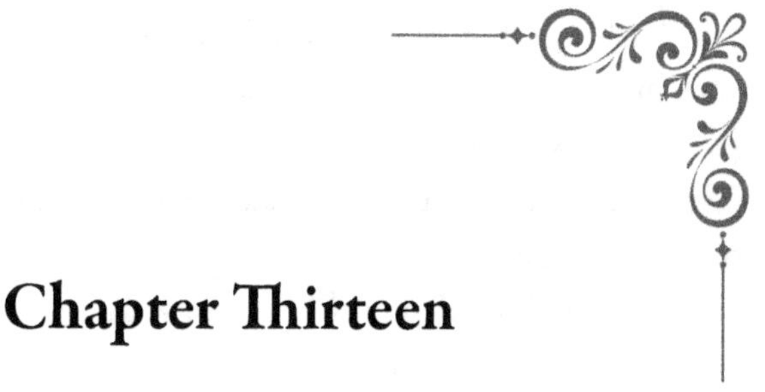

Chapter Thirteen

The house seemed normal after McLean left, big and echoing with the usual reminders of everything Gracie still had to do. Reluctant to think about what happened on the porch, she wandered around the house for a while, Hannah sticking to her heels like a cocklebur. Hoping that keeping busy would occupy her mind, Gracie cleaned the mess left from breakfast and climbed upstairs to make the beds. Hannah helped, tugging on the spreads to straighten them and patting the sheets smooth.

Finished with making the beds, Gracie searched for another chore to keep her busy. A pile of discarded shirts and underclothes littered the floor of McLean's bedroom. After hesitating a moment, she opened the drawers of his dresser. The first drawer held a worn gray shirt, the second one was empty.

She looked at the empty drawer, then at the small pile of laundry on the floor. She opened a third drawer to a single handkerchief and a pair of socks. Frowning, she slid it shut. Somehow, the idea of Mac making an easy living robbing trains didn't jibe with what she saw.

Smiling wryly at Hannah, she said, "I think today is laundry day, Hannah. Why don't you get your dirty clothes so I can wash them?"

Hannah raced off to her bedroom, leaving Gracie alone. She gathered the pile of clothes from the floor. A white collarless shirt was on top, the cloth dingy and thin in spots from wear. The heavy stench of sweat—and McLean—permeated the clothing.

Holding a shirt to her face, she inhaled deeply. She could almost taste his lips again. The place between her legs throbbed the same way it had when he'd kissed her. The tips of her breasts tingled, tightening into hard beads. What came next, she wondered, after the kiss? Surely there was more.

Footsteps sounded in the doorway, and she jerked her nose away from the shirt. Hannah peeked around the jamb, looking at her oddly. Embarrassed, she picked up the rest of McLean's clothing. "I sure wish you could talk," she murmured, rolling everything into a tight ball.

Hannah pulled on one of her pigtails.

"Because then you could tell me what to do about your father." She tied the sleeves of a shirt into knots, using it for a laundry bag.

Suspicion seemed to flood Hannah's expressive eyes.

"Or maybe it's better you don't talk. Come on. Let's go do laundry."

Several hot, sweaty hours later, with the laundry hanging on the line to dry, Gracie took time to relax for a few minutes. Although she'd never had much of an interest in all the housewifely chores, today she enjoyed her hours outside. The sun was warm on her back; a slight breeze whispered through the trees. The serenity of the day made it easy to complete the laundry, write inside her head, and keep an eye on Hannah while she played under the nearby oak tree with her puppy.

Now, with the housework done, a pressing urge to get her story ideas written down rose. Sitting at her desk, she pulled out pen and paper. Hannah stood next to her, her arms crossed on the desktop, her chin propped on her hands. Gracie frowned at her.

"I have to write. Can I get you something before I start?"

A long pause ensued before Hannah shook her head.

Tweaking a braid, Gracie said, "Well, if you don't want anything, I'm going to spend some time writing. All right?"

Hannah frowned and shook her head.

Gracie crossed her arms, exasperated. Maybe it wasn't such a good thing the little girl was getting better. The child seemed to have definite opinions of her own that Gracie didn't always agree with.

"I'm busy writing. See, I already have almost seven chapters written." She held up the pages for Hannah to see. The child peered at them then at Gracie, her face puzzled.

"Look, why don't you practice your reading while I work?" She thrust a few randomly chosen pages at her. The child peered at them for a few seconds before laying them carefully on the desk.

"Don't you want to read it?" Gracie asked. "It's about your daddy. Sort of."

Hannah frowned.

Slowly suspicion blossomed in Gracie's mind. "Hannah. Can you read?"

Hannah's mouth pursed into a tight bud.

Sitting back in her chair, Gracie stared in stunned silence at the child. Good heavens, she couldn't read. To Gracie, who'd learned to read at four and devoured everything worthwhile in her house by the time she was seven, this was unfathomable. Hadn't the child gone to school?

But thinking about it, she realized she'd probably had no opportunity to learn. At only six years old, she would have lived in an orphanage during the time when most children learned to read. And given her mental state, why would the teachers have bothered teaching her? They probably believed her an idiot or insane.

Saying goodbye to her plans to write with an inner sigh, Gracie hoisted the child up onto her lap. "Come on. It's time you learned how to read." She picked up her pen. "All right," she explained patiently. "This is an A, like for apple." She drew an A then an apple on the paper.

"Here's a B, for ball." She sketched a ball beside the apple. "Here's a C." She wrote the letter on the paper and showed it to Hannah. "This letter has two sounds. It makes a sound like kay, like in corn. Sometimes it makes a sound like ess, like in city," she continued, drawing the letters out to stress the sound. "This is a T, as in Texas, where you live. Now if I put the letter C and A and T together it says—" She paused while she drew something underneath the letters. "—Cat," she exclaimed triumphantly and held up a picture of a funny, furry, fat cat lying on his back, all four feet in the air.

Hannah squeaked in pleasure and bounced on her lap, her shod heels banging on Gracie's shins. The girl smacked her hand on the paper with excitement, indicating she wanted more.

Well, this was progress. Next Gracie wrote the letters for dog and drew a picture of Hannah's puppy with his nose in his food bowl, fat tummy dragging the ground. Hannah laughed and clutched the picture to her chest, her face alight with pleasure.

The rest of the afternoon passed with blinding speed. Maybe Gracie had missed her calling and should have become a teacher instead of a writer because, by the end of the day, Gracie had taught Hannah to match up the words 'cat', 'dog', 'snake' and 'horse' with the appropriate pictures. She could also identify the letter sounds Gracie said with the correct letter written down, all except 'Y'. She couldn't remember the last time she'd gotten that much pleasure from her skills of writing and drawing.

McLean riding into the yard captured her attention, so she gathered up the paper and pens and put them away. She helped Hannah off her lap, enjoying the sight of the child's round face alight with joy, her eyes sparkling with life.

Tweaking the child's button nose, she smiled conspiratorially. "Let's not tell your father what we've been up to today, all right. Let's surprise him later when you've learned lots of words."

After frowning for a minute, Hannah tapped the paper then her chest, indicating she agreed. When McLean entered the house thirty minutes later, they sat together in the parlor with Gracie sewing a lace cuff on one of Hannah's dresses, and Hannah playing with a rag doll on the floor.

POST-KISS DINNERS WERE definitely strange. Several days had passed since The Kiss and every evening, after putting Horse out to pasture and cleaning himself up, Mac sat in his chair at the kitchen table for dinner. Other than the typical one-sided conversations he always had with Hannah, he ate in silence. The rest of the time, he kept his head down and his gaze on his plate while he tried to eat the maximum amount of food in the shortest time possible. All to escape from the table before he burst into flames. But it was getting harder and harder to do. No matter how he tried to ignore Gracie's presence, she was a tangible force at the table.

She spent meals talking about her day with Hannah and the puppy, telling him all the small, intimate details of her life, details so feminine, they made him ache. She usually had news about her progress on her story and how excited it made her. Her excitement was a sharp reminder of her coming absence in his life, but he told himself her leaving was the ultimate goal.

So he tried to block out her conversation. But she made it damned hard to do. Most nights he could sense her eyes on him while he ate, which had the definite tendency to derail his determination. He tried to catch her at it so she'd stop but the second he would look up, her gaze slid away, glancing out the window.

Deep down, he admitted he kind of liked it. All her funny enthusiasms and her contradictory feminine softness were what was missing in his life for so long, and he craved everything she was. But the fact they had an agreement and he couldn't respond the way he wanted—which was to bend her over the kitchen table and kiss her until she couldn't breathe—were driving him crazy. Every time he sensed her gaze on him, old Harold got his balls in a twist and started demanding Mac act on those urges.

For Mac, his dinner normally ended with him bolting out of his chair to seek refuge in the barn. Which meant he was missing a lot of desert. Sadly, his determination to stick with his plan was getting shakier by the day.

That was why, a week later when she broached the subject of him going to town again, he sat up and listened. The night's dinner started like any other. He came home, washed up, and showed up in the kitchen for dinner full of nervous anticipation. Hannah smiled at him and patted his hand hello when he dropped a kiss on top of her head and slid into his chair.

Gracie brought a large platter, filled with ham, carrots, and potatoes cooked in red gravy till everything was glazed a honey brown, to the table.

He groaned inwardly. His favorite meal, and he wasn't sure if he'd manage to stay long enough to eat his fill. She served up a plate for Hannah, poured her some water, and cut up her meat before helping herself. Grabbing his fork, he speared a slice of ham onto his plate, added some vegetables, and dug in, shoveling the food into his mouth. Rude behavior, but what was a man to do in his condition?

As he ate, her gaze was on him. She cleared her throat. Damn. With a sigh, he looked up.

"I need you to go to town for me," she started while fiddling with her knife and fork.

"Huh?" he mumbled around a mouthful of potatoes. He sounded like an idiot, but under the table, he was more than half erect, a reaction to her staring that was both painful and distracting. She plain brought out the dumb in him.

Her face scrunched up, and her nose wrinkled. "You have to go into town," she uttered, enunciating each word carefully like he truly was an idiot.

He stopped chewing. "I do?"

"Yes, you do. I want you to send a telegram."

"You do?" he asked.

She huffed in anger. "Would you stop."

"Stop what?" he asked, confused. What was the matter with the woman?

"That... that... Oh, never mind. I can't explain. Just listen to me." She crossed her arms over her chest. "I want you to send a telegram."

He set his fork down and sat back in his chair and tried to ignore all the fundamental demands his body was making on him so he could focus on what she was saying. "All right. Why do you want me to send a telegram?"

"You might not remember, but my publisher expected a finished manuscript three weeks ago. He didn't get one."

"So?" It was irritating how stupid he sounded, but he kept getting distracted by the tiny gap between her front teeth her talking exposed. It reminded him of how he'd reacted when he probed her mouth with his tongue. The memory led him to other, more explicit thoughts, ones about her thighs and how comfortable Harold was nestled in the warm crevasse between them.

He started to sweat.

"If you expect me to get this thing published, I need to communicate with my publisher. More than likely, he's furious with me for missing my deadline. I've got to inform him I've got a new story with a different plot in the works, and it will be arriving soon." She waited for a nod from Mac. "Plus I have to let him know about the new direction I'm going with the hero. I can't, willy-nilly, send him a completely different story weeks late and expect he'll be happy. Without his agreement to all this, I'll be lucky to get this thing published at all." She paused. "Then my entire time here would be wasted, and I may as well go home now."

He forced himself to focus over the ache in his groin. What she said made sense. She was doing what he asked so, yes, contacting her publisher to get the book printed would be required, which would certainly solve the problem of being the target of lunatics like that kid Johnny Ray. But once the telegram was sent, she would be gone.

Something inside his chest pinched. Of course, he could just not send the telegram.

He shook himself. No, not sending the telegram meant living with the possibility another snot-nosed kid seeking to make a name for himself might come hunting for Mac. Did he want to take the chance? Probably not.

"All right, write down what you want to say, and I'll send it tomorrow."

Setting a piece of paper on her desk, she wrote out her message, folded it, slipped it into an envelope, then handed it to him. "Thank you." She smiled.

He glowered and slipped the envelope into his pocket.

Chapter Fourteen

"Three dollars and ninety cents," Mac yelped, his voice rising in astonishment. "Lord almighty, are you charging by the letter?" He scowled at the clerk.

Sticking his long pointy nose in the air, the clerk pursed his lemon-sucking lips and raised a supercilious brow. "No, we charger per word. There were thirty-nine words in the telegram, sir," he said, stressing the word sir so Mac understood he wasn't worthy of the term. "At ten cents a word, it comes to three dollars and ninety cents. To be paid in advance." He held his hand out for the money.

Mac growled. He wondered if that honestly was the charge or if this was one more way this town showed its disdain for him. Leaning both hands on the counter, he glared at the clerk.

The man's supercilious eyebrow rose higher in response, indicating he was not intimidated in the slightest. With another growl, Mac reached into his pocket, pulled out a worn wallet, and counted out four tattered one-dollar bills. A tight-lipped smirk gracing his face, the clerk made change and turned away to send the telegram.

"Good lord," Mac muttered, thrusting his hands into his armpits so he wouldn't strangle the telegraph operator. "And they call me a thief."

"I heard that," the clerk shouted over his shoulder, still tapping away on his telegraph key. "I can always refund your money and give you back the message."

Gritting his teeth, Mac put a smile in his voice. "No thanks, just keep doing what you're doing."

The clerk snorted, tapped a few more times and rose. "Done," he uttered in a snotty voice. He tugged the ends of his too short sleeves down over his bony wrists in a prissy manner.

"Good," Mac barked back and walked out the door, forgetting to retrieve both Gracie's note and her receipt.

His shoulders in knots, he strode across the street to the general store. Money problems or not, new trousers were a must. And he had to pick up the spool of barbed wire he'd ordered last time he was in town. The small amount he'd found stored in the barn was used up last week, so if he was going to round up any more of the fifty or so cows still roaming the back section and make them stay put long enough to sell them, a bigger enclosure to keep them in was necessary.

Which meant, even though he hated dealing with Potter, he would have to have to bite the bullet and visit the general store. Taking a deep breath to prepare himself for the certain abuse, he opened the door.

OSKAR RHEINGOLD LIKED Thursdays. Thursdays were quiet. The previous Friday, payday for most folks, was six days in the past, so the young fellows who spent their pay on wine, women, and song were out of the necessary funds for any more wine, women, or song, and tomorrow, another payday, was yet to come. So Thursdays were a day of calm and relaxation for Oskar, a day when he mostly sat on the front porch of the jailhouse and rocked and smoked and watched the goings-on of the town.

This Thursday was turning out to be an interesting one. McLean was back in town, after an absence of almost two weeks. Buried in the shadowy overhang of his porch, Rheingold had plenty of opportunity to watch the convicted train robber crisscross the street several times, going about his business.

Two weeks having passed since the man's last trip to town, Oskar understood the stop at Hiram Potter's, which made the sheriff steel himself for trouble when he saw McLean enter. But McLean's initial stop at the telegraph office puzzled him. The way McLean told it, he had no family. So who would he send a telegram to? Feeling fat and lazy in his comfortable chair on a warm afternoon, the sheriff was in no hurry to jump up and investigate but promised himself he'd get to it real soon.

When he observed McLean leave the general store and cross over to the closest saloon, the one that had girls available for a few dollars, he had to smile. Personally, he was long past the age where getting his desires taken care of by a prostitute appealed to him, but for a young man in his prime like McLean, especially one who'd gone without, so to speak, for five years, well, who could blame him? After a brief hesitation at the swinging doors, McLean pushed the doors open and entered.

Oskar half closed his eyes, setting his chair to rocking with a gentle push of a toe and kept an eye on the saloon door. McLean was entitled to his fun but not if it resulted in a ruckus in Oskar's town. After a few minutes passed with no shouting, shooting, or broken windows, Oskar figured everything was under control, rolled a cigarette and lit it with a Lucifer match he struck on the sole of his boot. Then he sat back and smoked and waited.

It wasn't nearly long enough for much fun to have occurred when McLean banged through the swinging doors of the saloon looking madder than fire. Oskar took a deep calming breath of tobacco and watched Mac march back to the general store. He exit soon after, rolling a heavy spool of barbed wire towards the edge of the boardwalk where his wagon waited. For a minute Oskar was tempted to go over and help the man load his supplies into the back of his wagon, particularly when one of Potter's clerks came out to stand on the boardwalk. Oskar prepared for trouble, but McLean and the clerk exchanged a word or two before, together, they picked up the two-hundred-pound spool and set it on the floor of the wagon.

With a grudging nod, McLean climbed up onto his wagon seat and gathered up the reins. Oskar relaxed back into his seat and watched McLean drive out of town, a single lonely figure on the seat of the buckboard.

Rheingold tapped his fingers on the arm of his chair. Something odd was going on, something wrong he couldn't quite put his finger on. He tapped some more, retracing McLean's progress through town in his mind, trying to put his finger on what was bothering him. Then he had it. The man came into town alone. So where was McLean's cute little girl?

Staring hard at the receding figure of McLean, Oskar put his mind to work on the problem and came up with no answer. With an exasperated sigh, he heaved his bulk out of his comfortable chair and plodded over to the telegraph office, his arthritic bones protesting. Damn, he was getting too old for this. He needed to seriously consider retiring.

WHY DID NOTHING SEEM to go the way he planned. Mac glowered at the horses' butts as the team plodded along the road towards home. Hah. How appropriate. Because that's what he was—a horse's butt. His visit to the saloon cost him five dollars, five dollars he could ill afford, and what did he get for it? Nothing except a bellyful of embarrassment. Thinking about the whore's sympathy still made the tips of his ears burn and his insides squirm sickly.

"Honey," she'd said sincerely, "Don't feel bad. It happens to the best of 'em, right?"

He gnashed his teeth, remembering. The best of them? He didn't want to be the best of them—he'd never considered himself a great lover—he only wanted to be in the running, for God's sakes.

He'd selected... Phyllis? Mabel?... a tall, slender and brunette... out of all the other girls because she looked nothing at all like Gracie. But when push came to shove... well, let's just say, he didn't have what it took to do the pushing... or the shoving. Because all he could see in his mind was Gracie's face and all he could think about was how he'd rather be making love to her, not some five-dollar whore while still wearing his socks and shirt.

So, having failed to bring either himself or the whore to any kind of satisfaction, he was mortified to the core. You'd think after five years without even the smell of a woman and he'd be popping his cork.

But he didn't.

Holy hell, what if something was wrong? What if lack of use had caused it to atrophy or something and he'd turned into a limp dick, a molly-coddle, a wet noodle? Then what kind of man would he be? He squirmed.

Trying to wipe those humiliating thoughts from his mind, he pulled up the memory of his kiss with Gracie. He'd sure had no trouble getting hard when his lips were locked on hers, in fact he couldn't remember ever feeling so hot, so ready to explode like when he'd kissed Gracie.

Remembering the sweet taste of her mouth, the plumpness of her hips and breasts pressed against his front, made him tingle. Thinking about touching her again, rolling her sweet nipples with his fingers while rubbing the length of his cock against her femininity, made heat spread from his face, down his chest and arms, traveling like electricity straight to his crotch. The tingle settled between his legs, tightening his scrotum, waking up good old reliable Harold.

Hitting a deep rut in the road the wagon dropped, then lurched back up to whack Mac in the backside. Yanking on the reins, he pulled the wagon to a stop and laid his head down on his knees. Ouch. Well, at least now it was obvious nothing was wrong with his working parts. He simply had a bad case of the hots for the bane of his existence. He'd get over it. Eventually.

Unfortunately, eventually wasn't soon enough, not with Gracie—tempting, tantalizing Gracie—waiting for him at home. He needed to do something about his problem right now. Glancing around, he recognized territory he was familiar with.

Tying the reins to the brake to keep the team from wandering off, he climbed down off the wagon seat and headed through the trees towards where he could hear the cool sound of running water. Within a few yards of the road he found what he'd looked for, a narrow rivulet of clear cold water.

He stood and studied it for a few minutes. The cold water would cure what ailed him below the belt. He wished it was this easy to find a cure for the painful ache in his heart. With a sigh, he prepared to step into the water. At least this time he remembered to take off his new pants.

It took twenty minutes for things to return to normal. Shivering from sitting in cold water, he returned to the buckboard and clucked the horses on. They traveled the rest of the way at a walk while Mac stewed over his visit to town, his problem with Gracie and worry over Hannah. Pulling into the yard, he unhitched the team and put them away for the evening. Gathering up the sack of supplies, he walked into the house. It was quiet.

"Gracie? Hannah?"

"In here," came the response.

Nodding to himself, he made his way to the kitchen. "Here's the things you asked for."

She pointed to the pantry. Taking that to mean he should put things away, he did.

"How was your trip into town?" she asked, her back to him as she stirred something on the stove.

His heart gave a little leap. "Uh, fine," he said. The words caught in his throat, making him cough. He cleared his throat, not sure what to say. He sure as hell wasn't about to tell her about his visit to the saloon, nor would he mention his stop at the creek. The very idea sent creepy-crawly fingers of disgust up his spine and froze his tongue in his mouth. Even the idea that she might ask more questions about his trip made him want to flee the house.

"Time to eat. Hannah's in the back yard, can you call her in?" she said and set a dish filled with beef stew on the table.

"Sure." Going to the backdoor, he called Hannah, who raced inside and held her arms up for Mac to help her onto her seat. Once she was settled, he sat, the events of the afternoon buzzing in his brain, yet unable to be said.

The itching feeling crawling along his nerves grew more intense. He wanted her—no, it was more than want, it was a craving like addicts had for opium. But he couldn't have her. He'd tried to take care of it by going to the saloon but that was a bust. So here he was, sitting across the table from the woman who had invaded his brain, and taken over his heart, destined to hunger forever.

"My telegram? Did you send it?" she said, her eyes alight with eagerness.

Damn it, he couldn't take it another second. His tongue was in knots and his body was burning up. "I'm not really hungry. I'm going to go check on the horses," he blurted out, and fled to the one place Gracie never went, the barn.

Of course the horses were fine, and he'd known that when he said it. Bypassing the stalls, he climbed the ladder to the loft, and threw himself onto a pile of hay. God, the woman was going to kill him, her with her pert bosom and her sweet-smelling hair that he wanted to nuzzle until he died from ecstasy.

But right now he was the farthest from ecstasy that a man could get. There was always his hand but somehow he sensed the relief would only be momentary. Because he wanted Gracie, not his cold, calloused hand. Rolling over onto his stomach, he closed his eyes and tried to ignore his burning desire. The barn grew dark as the sun set and eventually he dozed.

The creak of the barn door opening woke him.

"McLean?" Gracie called, her voice getting lost in the depths of the barn.

Mac struggled to sit up. Damn. What the hell was she doing here? She never came into the barn. This was his place, his refuge, the only place he could go to get away from her and the itch that plagued him. "Go away," he growled.

"McLean, what are you doing? You've been out here for hours, and I'm worried about you. You didn't even eat your dinner."

"Go away," he shouted, but his mind said, *are you here for me? Will you join me?*

"Why should I? You haven't even told me if you sent my telegram."

Oh, for crying out loud. "I sent it, all right? Cost me almost four bucks. Now go away." *Or stay. Yes, please stay.*

He waited. Below, it was quiet. What was she doing? What was she thinking? Was she thinking of him, or was she thinking about that damned book that he'd wanted written and now could care less about? He held his breath, wondering.

Her head popped up at the top of the ladder and scared the ever-loving starch out of him.

"God damn it, woman, are you trying to give me a heart seizure?" he yelled once he caught his breath.

Climbing the rest of the way up to stand knee deep in straw, she brushed herself off. "No, are you trying to give *me* one?"

"What the hell are you talking about?"

Cocking her hands on her hips, she said, "You have no idea what kinds of things I've imagined, have you? I wanted to talk to you, and instead of granting me that courtesy, you run away and sit out here for hours at a time. I've been worried sick. Glory, you could be bleeding to death or dying of some horrible disease and I wouldn't know until days later when I found your desiccated dead body."

"Little do you know," he muttered. "I may as well be dead."

Damn it, he was in a bad mood. All day he was unable to think about anything but how much he wanted to make love to Gracie, how he had weeks' worth of unspent passion backing up in his plumbing he hadn't been able to vent with a whore. The mere sight and smell of Gracie left him aching, but damn it, he had nothing to offer her and being an honorable man, or at least a man who was trying to hang onto what was left of his honor, he was trying like hell to stay away from her.

"What's that? What did you say?"

He shot her a glance but didn't answer. Up till now he'd been pretty successful at it. Staying out in the pastures until it was time for supper helped. Gulping down his food, which wasn't doing a damned thing for his digestion, then bolting for the barn, where he stayed until after bedtime also helped. And now she'd gone and spoiled it by showing up in the one place she normally avoided. He'd never be able to come into the barn again without thinking of her. Which meant he'd be hurting a lot.

Trapped, defeated, he moaned.

"No, you tell me," she ordered, walking over to stand next to the reclining McLean. "You said you may as well be dead. What did you mean?"

Sorry he'd said anything at all, he backed away. He didn't want to talk about his feelings for Gracie—especially *to* Gracie.

Hell, he didn't even want to think about it. In a year or so, he'd be able to say with a laugh, *Oh yeah, there was this woman I once loved... but I got over it.*

But he couldn't say it right now, not with Gracie standing right in front of him in a frilly pink night robe gaping open just enough to give him a hint of her unbound breasts underneath.

"Well?" she asked again.

Damn it. What was wrong with this woman? Didn't she understand there were things a man didn't discuss with a woman?

Her foot started to tap against the wooden floor of the loft. The silence dragged on so he figured she'd gotten the hint and the topic was closed. Until she drew her foot back and kicked him in the knee. He yelped, even though it didn't hurt because she was wearing slippers. It was more that fact that he expected it to hurt since this wasn't the first time she'd kicked him and last time it had hurt like hell.

"Damn it, what was that for?" he said.

"Tell me what you meant when you said you may as well be dead?"

"Mind your own business, you little witch," he gritted. He grunted when her foot connected with his leg again even though it didn't hurt any more than before. He simply enjoyed complaining. "God damn it, woman. What is the matter with you?"

But damn, she made him mad. And hot. Kicking him caused her breasts to bob enticingly under her gown. Blood started to collect in his penis, thickening it to the point of painfulness.

"Tell me or I'll kick you again. And I'll keep kicking you till you do." She drew her slippered foot back to carry out her promise.

His ego bruised, and his manhood primed to do all the manly things God intended, he had enough. Roaring up out of the pile of hay, he tackled Gracie, knocking her flat on her back. He threw his body across hers and pinned her shoulders to the ground with his hands.

"Leave me alone," he snarled in her face.

"I would—" she whispered. "Except you're on top of me. That's going to make it hard to leave." Then her arms wound around his neck and pulled him tight. The part of him he'd given up on mere hours ago leapt, the hot blood roaring out of control through the rest of his body.

Underneath his body, her curves molded to his angles in all the right places and his cock instinctively nestled into the 'V' of her legs.

He flexed his hips. The heat of her womanhood seeped through the cloth barriers separating them. Though he was sure he couldn't get any harder, he did. Closing his eyes, he thrust against her again. One hand crawled up to cover her breast. A rosy-hued nipple rose up to greet him, surrounded by the puckered flesh of her aureole.

Sweet, so sweet. He fingered the nipple, and it sharpened, tightening into a tiny bud that drew him irresistibly. Bending his head, he sucked it into his mouth through the cloth.

SHE HISSED, HER BACK lifting straight up out of the hay. Oh my stars. Desire zipped through her body, ricocheting from her breast to her fingers, then racing back to her breasts. The tiny bolts turned south and lit the area between her legs on fire.

"Gracie, ahh, sweet heavens," MacLean groaned. "I want you," he muttered into her neck. His hands flexed, biting into her flesh.

He wants me. He doesn't hate me, he wants me, she thought, unsure if she was confusing wanting with loving and not sure if she cared. Because, right now, wanting was enough for her.

She let her hand drift down over McLean's shoulder, following the line of his collar till it reached his chest. His chest was the perfect size to fill her palm with lots of hard muscles. Tentatively, she swirled her hand over his chest, imitating his actions, fingering the firm bulge covered by taut skin and the hard bead of his masculine nipple tickling her palm.

Yum. She remembered how much she liked it when he tantalized her breast. Using her thumb, she flicked his nipple.

He flinched at her touch and hissed. "Sweet Jesus. Don't do that."

"Why? Doesn't it feel good?"

McLean laughed nervously. Taking a deep breath, he laid his forehead on hers. "Yes, it feels good. Too good."

"Isn't that the point," she murmured.

"Yes. No. God, yes." He sounded like he was in pain.

"Well, which is it? Yes or no?" Not a lick of space existed between her body and his, and the place where McLean was wedged was reaching furnace-like temperatures. Unable to help herself, she opened her legs wider.

With a grimace and a noise that might be a laugh, he answered, "Yes. Yes, it's supposed to feel good. And it does. But I can't stand it when it feels too good."

Now she was confused. How could anything feel *too* good? Wasn't that the whole point? "That makes no sense at all."

Another noise rumbled out of McLean's chest, a definite groan this time. "Woman, I'm trying to do the right thing here. I'm on fire for wanting you, it's like my skin is too tight for my body and my... my..." Here he stumbled, his voice growing raspy. He cleared his throat.

"Your what," she asked, consumed with curiosity.

"Gracie," he barked. "I'm trying to stop things before they get too far."

Suddenly, she *knew* what he was talking about. She had no idea how she figured it out, she simply did. Everything clicked into place;

the kisses, the tingling, pulling sensation in her breast that leapfrogged into her loins, the hot, hard length nestled between her slack legs. The things he said that day by the stream.

With a smug smile, she removed her other hand from around her nervous partner's neck and thrust it between their bodies. Wrapping her hand around his length through his trousers, she squeezed lightly.

"Do you mean this?" she whispered.

He yelped, jumped a foot and came back down, panting like a steam engine. "You little vixen," he growled, laughter burbling from his throat. Flexing his hips, he pressed his heat against her softness.

"Yes, damn it, I meant that. *That...*" He flexed his hips again. "...wants *this...*" he continued, his finger working its way under her gown and stroking the soft tissue of her womanhood.

Moisture followed the path of his finger. "Ohhh," she expressed in wonder. "I see. Well, what does it want to do?"

"Do you really want to know," he said. With a gentle pat, he removed his hand from underneath her nightgown.

She gazed up at him, barely able to see anything in the dim light. But she could see his eyes, and his eyes were warm and filled with tenderness.

"Yes. I really want to know. Show me."

Chapter Fifteen

Pressure built inside Mac, like steam in a kettle without a valve and he wanted, no, needed—desperately—to put himself inside this fey, funny, sexy woman. And he needed it now.

He rucked up the hem of her gown, exposing her hips and stroked the feathery-light hair covering her femininity before dipping the tip of a finger into her core again.

"It wants in." He pressed with his finger. "Here." She shivered when he pressed inside her. He could smell the aroma of rising excitement. His skin twitched and jumped everywhere it made contact with Gracie, but somewhere in the dim recesses of his feeble mind, there was still a small kernel of common sense that wanted to give Gracie one last chance to save herself.

"I want to put myself inside you... right here." He slid his finger in to the first knuckle for emphasis, "And make love to you until you die of pleasure, or *it* falls off, whichever comes first."

He took a deep breath, calling himself ten times a fool. "But I shouldn't make love to you. It wouldn't be right." Removing his finger from her body, he let the breath out. Shit.

In typical Gracie fashion, she cut right to the heart of what mattered most to her, herself. "Why not, if I want you to. And I do."

"Gracie, you... I... we..."

"What?"

He closed his eyes with a sigh. "I'm no good for you. I have nothing to offer a woman like you."

She remained quiet for a long time before saying, "You have you. And all I want is you. Please. Everything else doesn't matter right now. Everything else can be figured out later."

Tears of frustration and suppressed pain stung his eyes. "Damn," he muttered. "Is nothing ever easy with you?"

She smiled her funny little smile. "No, why should it be? What would be the fun in that? So..." She smacked her lips. "What are you going to do about it?"

"Gracie..."

"Oh stop." She giggled. "Actually, I mean, don't stop. I meant go."

With a huff of laughter, he yanked at the buttons of his fly, popping the top two open, and sending another flying. "If that's what you want, I'm going to make love to you."

Small feminine hands worked their way inside the back of his trousers, cupped his buttocks and gave a light squeeze.

"Well, good. It's about time," she murmured.

Trailing a hand up the inside of her thigh, McLean stroked his thumb over the small nub buried in the damp folds of her body. She shivered, her legs flexing and tightening around his thighs.

"Are you still sure?" he asked in a hushed whisper.

She couldn't help that her answer came out a shaky sigh. "Oh yes."

Keeping his thumb where it was, McLean slid the length of his finger downward and swirled it around her opening. Then parting the folds, he slipped his finger inside again. "You can tell me to stop, okay?" His voice was husky, unsure.

Her hands gripped McLean's shoulders. She was the violin and he was the bow as he stroked her and coaxed sweet, sweet music from her body.

"No, don't stop," she breathed.

With his free hand, he widened the opening of his trousers and pulled them lower on his hips, releasing the hard, hot length of himself. With the same hand, he held his cock and rubbed himself over her slippery femininity. A spasm shook her when he inserted the tip inside her body.

"I'm asking you one last time—for your own good—while I can still stop. Do you want me? Do you want this—and what it'll mean?"

She didn't answer.

"Don't answer until you think about it. I want you, my God, do I want you, but I'm no good for you and I don't want to hurt you." He rested his forehead on hers. "Don't let me hurt you. Say no."

"No," she said.

His breath escaped in a hard whoosh from disappointment.

"No—" she whispered, kissing the lobe of his ear. "No, I don't want you to stop." Her tongue made little circles inside the whorls of his ear. "No, I'm not going to deny us what we both want. No, you're not going to hurt me because I want you, McLean, in all the ways you described."

"What? What did you say?" he said, shocked.

She laughed. "I said, stop wasting time. You said you were going to make love to me, so do it. I'm dying to find out what comes next, after the kissing and the touching. Do something, otherwise I'll think you're nothing but a tease."

A tease? When he was trying his damnedest to allow her to decide what she wanted. But it seemed she had decided. Tilting his head, he covered her mouth with his, nibbling on her lower lip, running the tip of his tongue across her teeth. One hand swept her nightgown up to her ribs, baring her belly and above that, the ridges of her rib cage.

He smoothed his hands along the curved indention of her waist then cupped his hands around her breasts. Sitting her up, he grabbed the hem of her gown, yanking it over her head and leaving her buck-naked. The gown flew over his shoulder to land in the corner.

Then he laid her back into the hay.

He caressed her body, each stroke a whisper as he kissed her gently. Returning his finger to the slick folds between her legs, he stroked the tip of his finger across her opening, dipping inside and spreading the moisture until she was wet and slippery.

But he wasn't done. Slipping his forefinger inside her again, he flicked his thumb across the tiny nub buried in her folds. She gasped, bucked, and gripped him tighter, her muscles spasming.

"Do you like this?" he murmured, giving her another flick.

"Don't stop. Don't you dare stop," she gasped. "Oh my, I can't stand it."

"It gets better," he muttered in her ear. "Do you want better?" He replaced his hand with his eager shaft.

"Oh, better," she groaned. "Definitely better."

The smell of her arousal burned through him, the lure of her plump lips called. He kissed her, a long slow, lingering kiss. Then he slowly pushed inside her soft, hot body.

"Ooohhhh." The sound was a low drawn-out sigh of pure pleasure. "More."

He laughed. "My pleasure." He pushed in a little farther, and then partially withdrew. Slow and easy. He pressed forward, further this time, until he reached the barrier separating the innocent Gracie from the woman she was about to become. It gave slightly under the pressure. She gave a muffled protest.

"Ssshhh," McLean soothed again and gave a sudden, hard thrust, breaking through.

"Oh. Ouch," she said, sounding surprised. "Is that the better part?"

He burst out laughing. "No, now comes the better." Clamping his mouth over hers, he kissed her, using tongue and lips and teeth to excite her. He continued to move in a slow, steady friction that soon made both of them pant.

Cradling the back of her head with a hand, he kissed her while the other hand caressed her breasts, stroking across her nipples, making her gasp. She dug her fingers into the muscles of his back, driving him to move harder, faster, rougher, until her breath rasped harshly. She moaned, a long tremulous groan then her thighs clenched shut and she tightened on him and he felt her completion. At the last second, he pulled out and exploded onto her stomach.

He lay over her, replete. The sound of breathing filled the loft, his heavy and raspy, hers light and fast. It was a long time before he had the strength to lift himself up off her soft body—and he didn't want to because she felt so good—but after a moment, he slid to the side and flopped over on his back, still panting.

"Oh my," she gasped in amazement.

He chuckled, patting her still sweat-slicked stomach, and rolled over to lie beside her. "Yeah, oh my."

The silence stretched out, while their breathing slowed and the rustle of the horses shifting in their stalls drifted up from below. The hum of cicadas whirring filled the night overlaid by the eerie hoot of an owl outside the loft door. A slight breeze wafted through the opening, drying the sweat on their bodies, and cooling them pleasantly.

IN THE DARK, GRACIE blinked in awe. She loved what she and McLean did together. Her body still hummed, although the humming was receding like a train whistle fading into the night. And yet already she wanted to do it again—in fact, now would be best—so she could recapture the glow.

But their lovemaking had crystallized the other feelings eddying inside her for days. Love—it had to be love—filled her, like an enormous soap bubble, growing bigger and bigger, glistening and filled with subtle colors that shifted and changed with the light.

It was lighter than air, so delicate the sunshine filtered through it, lighting it from the inside out.

Her soul soared with the bubble, shining with a thousand hues in the light of McLean's lovemaking. Filled to bursting, she wanted to tell him she loved him but she felt awkward and shy and afraid.

Instead she asked, "Um. Are we... done?"

"For now." He smiled lazily. "Harold will need to catch his breath before he can do it again."

"Who's Harold?" she demanded. She rolled onto her side to look at his face. Even in the dark she could see his face flush.

"Who's Harold?" she demanded again when he didn't answer.

He grimaced. Grabbing her hand, he placed it over his male part. "Gracie, meet Harold. Harold," he choked out. "You've already met Gracie."

She said nothing, only left her hand where he'd placed it, on his semi-erect... sticky... Harold. He... it... Harold... was warm and intriguing and had two soft hairy things below that she hadn't noticed before. She moved her hand, two fingers tentatively caressing the length and breadth of him, up and down from the base to the head.

He tensed at her touch. It made her smile. And think evil thoughts. Girding him with her fingers, she gently shook Harold up and down.

"I'm pleased to meet you, Harold," she murmured. "I hope we get to know each much better in the future."

He exploded into laughter. Grabbing her around the waist, he hugged her, laughter still shaking his body. "God above, woman. I can never tell what you're going to say."

"Me either," she responded with a giggle. "I'm the utter despair of my family. Growing up, I was always saying or doing exactly the wrong thing and embarrassing my mother in front of all her snooty society friends. I think she was secretly glad when I said I was moving to Texas. And now that we've done this." Heat rushed to her face. "I'm glad I did, too. I wouldn't have had this much fun if I stayed in Pittsburgh. I would have been stuck sitting in my mother's parlor acting like the good little virgin she wants me to be, either that, or married to some stuffy banker."

Pulling away, he abruptly sat up. "Christ," he muttered, and buried his face in one hand. "God, I'm such a..." His voice trailed off without completing the sentence.

Unease stirring low in her stomach, she sat up. "What's the matter?"

His jaw tensed. "Nothing's the matter," he muttered. "Everything's fine."

No, it wasn't. She could see it wasn't. "Did I do something wrong?" she asked, a chill that had nothing to do with the night air sliding down her spine.

"No," he answered gruffly. He swiped a hand down his face.

"What? Something's wrong. I can see something's wrong. Was it something I said? Tell me."

"For God's sake, Gracie, leave it alone. It was nothing you said. You didn't do anything wrong. It's me. I shouldn't have... I'm..." He stopped, swallowed. "Listen, never mind. It's fine. Everything's fine. Today was fun, but it's late and I've got a lot of work to take care of tomorrow."

Her heart, the one she'd just laid at McLean's feet, wrenched in her chest. "Fun?" she asked in a tiny voice. "You thought it was fun?" Well, it was, but it was so much more. But apparently she was the only one who thought so.

"You and I both understand that you have to get back to Austin soon. You might even want to go back to Philadelphia after this. I mean, maybe you don't feel safe in Texas anymore so returning back East might be better."

Nausea roiled in her stomach. "Back East?"

"Sure, you know. That's the life you really belong in, not this hard scrabble barely subsisting ranch that I may never make a living from. But I've got to try so we can't afford to take any of this too seriously. But it was fun, don't you think?"

Tears pricked the back of her eyes but she held them back. No way would she allow this... this... stupid man see that he made her cry.

"Oh, yes, it *was* fun. In fact, I'd say it was about the most fun I've had in years," she jeered. "Why, it ranks right up there with taffy pulls and hayrides." She heard the bitterness in her voice but it was impossible not to feel bitter.

He folded back into the hay. "So why don't you go back to the house? It's late, and Hannah is alone. Don't wait for me. I've got a few things to take care of." Folding his arms under his head, he looked up at the rafters like he had nothing better to do.

She studied his face, once again admiring the firm jaw and the lean cheeks softened by the floppy curl of mahogany hair hanging in his eyes. She loved him so much. She loved how he could laugh even in the middle of his anger, even when she did her best to make him mad. She loved his tenderness with Hannah and how hard he tried to make a success of this ranch.

Tonight was a whirlwind of emotion for her. The sudden realization that she loved McLean frightened her when she thought something had happened to him. And made her angry that he was behaving like a first-rate jackass. But her anger became yearning when he kissed her. Her varied emotions left her wildly spinning, riding the wind like a paper pinwheel.

But the heat of their lovemaking had faded and so had McLean's desire. Apparently, since his momentary desires were satisfied, he didn't want her anymore.

But she wanted it all, love, family, fidelity, and she wanted it with McLean. And, for a short while, she'd thought McLean wanted that too.

But now she was at a loss. She didn't know why he said what he said. She didn't know if he really didn't want her or if, in some stupid, male logic, he thought he was protecting her.

So she said nothing. Instead, she gathered her nightgown and stood, using it to shield a body she was self-conscious of. Spinning around, she slipped her nightgown over her head and buttoned it all the way to the top. She retrieved her robe and drew it on over her gown, cinching the belt around her waist.

The entire time she dressed she was aware of the brooding presence of McLean behind her, staring holes in her back. When she was fully clothed, her body and her emotions protected by layers of opaque cloth, she faced McLean, her arms crossed over her arms over her chest.

"Will you be leaving the house at the usual time tomorrow?" she asked. As long as he still needed her help, she wouldn't give up hope he would grow to love her. There was never a time in her life when her optimism and energy wasn't enough to conquer any goal she set her mind to.

He nodded, not looking at her.

She looked at him for a minute, searching for something she didn't find. "All right. I'll have your breakfast ready for you."

Stepping over to the ladder leading to the lower floor, she didn't wait for his murmured acknowledgement. An odd thought flashed through her mind as she put a shod foot on the first rung. She'd made love for the first time tonight—lost her virginity—and never took her shoes off. Very peculiar but something she hoped to tell her grandchildren—not her children, God forbid, for fear they would copy her behavior—but definitely she would tell her grandchildren someday. The idea brought hope to her heart. Determined to unravel the mystery of what just happened, she climbed down the ladder.

Chapter Sixteen

The sun was blistering hot. The back of his neck burned, the fabric of his cotton shirt adhering to his body, searing his skin like hot oil. Despite the heat, he didn't take it off because he needed the protection both from the sun and the sharp barbs of wire he was working with. Leaning against the post for leverage, he tautened the strand of wire and hammered a brad over it to nail it in place.

Sweat dripped in his eyes, blinding him, and he cursed under his breath. He hated this work. The only thing making it bearable was the knowledge these fences would someday contain horses instead of cattle.

Giving the brad a final tap, he stepped back, breathing hard, wiping the sweat from his forehead with a dirty handkerchief. He surveyed the long line of poles stretched out into the distance, all strung together with gleaming strands of new barbed wire. It was backbreaking, grueling work with hours spent digging post holes eighteen inches into the rock-hard ground that left his shoulders tied in knots and his legs and arms trembling from exertion. Even then, the work wasn't done; there was always the additional dangerous time spent stretching the wire that insisted on curling and twisting and springing back into its original coiled shape.

His body ached and under his gloves, his hands were blistered. Barbs gouged deep scratches into his arms and chest and face when he lost his grip and the wire recoiled.

He checked his watch, aware even before he looked, that it was still only two o'clock, hours before he had to return to the house and spend another evening sitting at the table with Gracie, watching her eat, remembering the feel of her body under his, around his.

Feeling regret and shame and unrelenting hot desire.

How stupid could he get? Stupid, stupid, stupid, to make love to Gracie Hart when he'd already decided being involved with him would do nothing but ruin her life. Closing his eyes, he groaned. He told himself he should feel guiltier than he did, but memories of making love to Gracie kept intruding. How could he feel remorseful about something so perfect?

His life was a mess. He returned to the wagon to uncoil enough wire from the spool lying on the wagon bed to reach the next post. Gripping the end of the wire, he tugged it, trying to free a few feet of wire, but the wire refused to come loose from the spool. He leaned into the wagon, examining the coils.

To make his job easier, he'd set the bottom of the wooden spool on a stack of gunny sacks in the bed of the wagon. The soft, slippery surface of the sacks so that the spool would spin and the wire would unwind when he pulled. But now the wire refused to unwind when he pulled.

Seeing no reason for it, he yanked harder. But instead of unwinding the way it should, the spool slid off the gunny sacks, lurched across the wagon bed and stopped. His heart jump in his chest.

Damn it. The spool now hung precariously over the edge of the wagon bed. Not good. He put his shoulder to it, trying to shove it further back into the wagon but it refused to move since it no longer sat on the gunny sacks. He tried one more time, still no movement. One more time, and it didn't budge an inch. Hell, he could do this all damned day and accomplish nothing. He gave up. It would be fine. He could work with it the way it was.

Now to the bigger problem. Why was the wire not unraveling? He studied the front side of the spool where everything seemed fine, then craned his neck to look around to the backside.

Shit. The backside was an unnatural mess of crisscrossed wires, overlapping each other from top to bottom. Given the extent of the mess, the best option was to climb up in the wagon and manually uncoil the ten or so rows of wire. What a waste of time.

Grabbing the side of the wagon, he leaped up next to the spool and knelt. He gingerly began unsnarling the wire, one lethal barb at a time. The wire was stiff and reluctant to unwind, fighting him for every inch that came loose. The barbs speared through the thin leather of his gloves, poking holes and scratches into his skin so hot blood collected under the leather. Slowly, a little at a time, the wire came undone and lay in stiff, spine-laden curls on the wooden wagon floor. When about ten feet was loose, he came to a particularly stubborn snag and no matter how he twisted or moved the wire, the layer remained firmly stuck.

Unlike the law, where he could easily spend hours searching through legal journals for obscure facts, he had little patience with this kind of task and today he had less than usual.

"Dammit," he swore, tugging at the wire. "Dammit, dammit, dammit." Out of patience, he gave the wire a hard yank. The wire laying across the floor in lazy, seemingly innocent coils, snapped tight, sprang towards Mac in a mass of deadly spears that cut its way through the heavy wool of his pants, scoring long deep gashes in his leg and waist.

Gasping in pain, he closed his eyes. God damn it. It felt like a thousand razor blades cutting into him. A shiver ran through his body. He gritted his teeth and clenched his fists, trying to control the pain. His stomach rolled over, nausea burning inside.

When the intensity ebbed, he opened his eyes again to survey the damage. What he saw made another shiver run up his spine. The end of the coil had wrapped around his waist, every barb digging into the soft flesh of his sides. From there it flipped around, reversing into a lazy S so the next loop curled between his legs, hanging up in the nubby wool covering his crotch before reversing directions again to snag into his thigh.

He took a deep breath to steady himself.

All right. All right. It wasn't an impossible situation. If he was careful and moved slowly, he could untangle himself from all this. It would take time—and more patience than he usually exhibited. With a grimace and a muttered oath, he removed his gloves and patiently picked each barb out of his clothing.

His fingers trembled from the tension, but eventually he undid a few feet, a tricky maneuver at best since he didn't dare let go of the wire he'd pulled loose. The work was exhausting, tedious and painful. His shaking hands caused him to stab himself several times and soon his hands were slippery with blood, making it harder than ever to work carefully. His breath shuddered in and out in short gasps. He tried to ignore the pain, but he was aware of time slipping away.

The sun dipped towards the horizon, signaling dinnertime for the horses hitched to the wagon. Horse and the sorrel moved restlessly in their traces, shifting and stomping their feet.

He glanced over his shoulder at the team. The sorrel was angrily bobbing his head and looking thoroughly disgruntled because of the delay in his supper. He stomped his foot again, then losing patience, he leaned into the traces, causing the wagon to roll forward a foot or so. The spool shifted, pulling the barbed wire tighter.

"Shit," he yelled, while cursing himself for forgetting to tie the brake down. He twisted around and called in a low voice designed to calm the animals, "Whoa, Horse. Steady, steady boy." Horse turned his head to gaze serenely at Mac. He nickered softly but the sorrel, his team mate, hunched his back, signaling his dissatisfaction.

"Good boy," he called. "Steady, Horse. Stand. Stand." He bit his lip, panic beginning to filter through him in short, sharp stabs that flipped his stomach upside down.

The sorrel gelding stomped his feet again and nickered, then bobbed his head up and down, an expression on his horsey face that said, *I've had it. I'm hungry, and I'm going home.* Leaning into the leathers, he stepped forward, pushing hard off his hindquarters.

Everything happened at once. The wagon jerked forward, the wooden spool shifted, and the wire tightened around his waist.

Shit!

The wagon jolted forward again. The spool tilted. A whinny, the wagon bounced. The spool canted sideways.

Mac lunged towards it, digging his fingers into the top of the spool and leaning back. The barbs bit savagely into his flesh, but he was either too late or not heavy enough to stop the momentum. The spool of wire tipped the rest of the way out of the wagon, pulling Mac with it.

Time slowed. He twisted his body in an effort to save himself, and for a moment, he believed he'd succeeded. But an instant later, he hit the ground with a bone-crushing. The spool landed on top of him with all the force of a speeding locomotive, driving the air from his lungs in a hard whoosh. Dozens of needle-sharp daggers rammed into his chest, tearing through skin and muscle like knives through butter. He screamed in agony.

It was another short fall into unconsciousness.

The pain brought him awake. The air was cooler. The coolness indicated evening was approaching, but he couldn't be sure without opening his eyes. And he was afraid to open his eyes. Even the tiniest movement seemed to trigger unbearable pain. Breathing expanded his chest and forced the barbs deeper into his body, dragging the tips sideways through tender muscle and scoring gouges into bone. It made him light-headed. The falling temperature made him shiver.

Steeling himself, he forced himself to open his eyes. He couldn't see much. The spool filled the majority of his field of vision and what he could see he didn't like. The spool had fallen at a slant across his body, one side of the spool resting on the ground, the rest covering most of his chest in addition to his left arm, pinning him to the ground and leaving him with one hand to free himself.

Shit, he was in trouble now. Even half empty, the spool weighed over fifty pounds and with all the barbs buried in his flesh he couldn't roll it off. It had to be lifted, but how could he do that with one hand?

Hardly able to breathe, he contemplated his situation for a while, liking the odds less and less. He slanted a look down his body again. Blood covered his shirtfront, responsible in part for his growing weakness, he was sure; the trapped arm jutted out from under the rim of the spool at an unnatural angle. Possibly broken. And unlikely to be of much use in lifting the weight off his body.

The sun dipped towards the horizon and the shadows lengthened. He would have to make an effort at removing the spool sometime. But he wished it didn't have to be now. Because it would hurt. A lot. It made him want to give up before he even started.

Come on. Be a man. Handle the pain. Handle the pain or die trying. Dying wasn't an alternative. Dying now would be a miserable waste. He wasn't done raising Hannah, who didn't need to lose any more people in her life. And then there was Gracie. Funny, fiery, unpredictable Gracie, with whom he hadn't had a chance to explore what might be. Who he'd let believe he didn't love her.

And God help him, he wanted the chance to change that.

Gritting his teeth, he grabbed the rim of the spool and pushed. His muscles bunched as he strained. He pushed, biting his lip against the agony, the barbs digging deeper, tearing open the already existing wounds in his chest, the metal barbs grating against bone with an audible sound. His arm trembled from the weight, but for all his pushing, the spool didn't move an inch.

Oh God, he cried silently, it's no good. His grip slipped and the heavy wooden spool settled back onto his chest. He screamed and passed out.

When he woke again the sun was rimming the top of the trees. It was cold. Colder than late June should be. He shivered, which brought a twinge of pain. Sound. Light, fast breathing. And moaning, a moaning that went on continuously, monotonously, irritating him. He wished the noise would stop, then realized it was him.

His legs were numb, his hands and fingers no longer a part of his body. There was no air in his chest. He sensed himself detaching from his body, from his mind. Dying.

His last thought was one of regret. Gracie.

Chapter Seventeen

It was a long time since Oskar was out to the Delaney place, so the sheriff had forgotten what a pretty ride it was. Most of the road was tree-lined, with huge ancient oaks and sycamores spreading like giant toadstools over the road, casting inky shadows on the ground that were interrupted by lemon yellow sunlight working its way through the gaps in the leaves. Bluebonnets, daisies and golden poppies bobbed their heads in the gentle breeze and whispered through the grass.

Yep, a real pretty ride, but it didn't make no never mind when he was feeling foolish for making the ride at all. Of course, he was going to let on it was a social visit and all, but McLean was a smart man and probably wouldn't buy it for a minute, even though Oskar timed his visit to coincide with dinner.

No dummy, McLean would realize he was being checked up on and not very subtly either. But foolish or not, Oskar couldn't let go of the idea there was something not quite right going on out at the Delaney place—to him, a telegraph signed with the name Grace Hart was a sure sign of not right—so he wouldn't be doing his job if he didn't at least check it out.

The problem was he didn't want to be right 'cause—contrary cuss that he was—Oskar kind of liked McLean and he didn't want to have to go arresting him or anything. On the other hand, if he was wrong.... well, he'd admit then, to being plain foolish.

Being rather conflicted, Oskar developed a heavy hand on the reins, and approaching McLean's house, his horse walked slower and slower.

The woods ended, to be replaced by wide grassy fields spread out like the gentle rolls of a calm sea. At the end of the road the white clapboard house Oskar remembered from his last visit sat pretty and pristine, framed by the protective branches of several large old trees.

With a small tug, he pulled his bay to a halt. Tipping his hat back on his head, he scratched his nose and contemplated the house. Everything looked quiet and orderly, the barn door shut tight, the front gate leading into the flower-filled yard also latched. He pulled his hat back down over his forehead and gigged his horse forward.

It didn't take long to ride into the yard. From his position halfway between the barn and the house, everything looked deserted and shut down, possibly because McLean was out in the pastures with his daughter. But it was getting close to dinner time and it seemed reasonable that the man would return for his evening meal, so Oskar swung a leg over the cantle of his saddle, his aging bones creaking, and stepped down off his horse. He'd wait.

He led his tired horse over to the water trough for a drink. The bay gelding plunged his nose in, darkening his muzzle till it was almost black, and sucked up the cool water with long slurping gulps while Rheingold relaxed by his side and enjoyed the faint call of bobwhites in the distance.

The faint sloughing of the wind in the trees filled his ears, lulling him. A sharp yip, followed by a high-pitched giggle, snapped him to attention. What the heck? Leaving the sorrel's reins trailing in the dirt, he strode around the corner of the house to the back yard. Sheets white as fair weather clouds billowed on a clothesline, along with several men's shirts hung by the shoulders, and rows of dainty feminine undergarments edged in lace.

Hannah raced into view, followed by a yellow puppy Oskar recognized. The dog yelped in excitement and tackled the back of the little girl's heel. She squealed and fell into the grass, giggling. The puppy threw himself on her chest.

"Hannah?" called a disembodied voice from somewhere behind the clothes. "Are you all right?" A female head poked out, the round face puckered into a worried frown. Wide brown eyes found Hannah in the grass then traveled on to meet Oskar's eyes.

A look of horror passed over the woman's face. The baby-soft pink mouth opened, then closed, like a carp stranded in the grass.

"Oh, shoot," Oskar grumped, allowing his body to sag in despair. "I purely hate being right."

"MA'AM, TELL ME AGAIN that part about why you're here?" the sheriff asked for the third time. He scratched his head, looking perplexed.

How dense was this man, anyway? Under the table Gracie clenched her fists, fists that wanted to reach out and whack the obtuse man sitting across the tablecloth from her. She took a deep breath, reining in her temper.

"As I said, it's very simple," she explained patiently. "I'm writing a book to help clear McLean's name, or at least make the public believe he was cleared so he won't have to worry about someone trying to gun him down again. He's got Hannah to worry about." She sat back in her chair, arms folded across her chest.

The sheriff peered at her from underneath his bushy gray eyebrows, eyes full of suspicion. "And who are you again?" he asked.

"Grace Hart. I've already told you that." My stars, the man was dumber than a stump.

"Grace Hart. The same Grace Hart who wrote all those books about McLean."

She took another deep breath. It was getting harder and harder to control her temper, but it never paid to lose your temper with the law—dumb or not—so she hung on to it. But only by the skin of her teeth. "Yes, that's right. That's what I said before. I'm the author of those books."

"Hmm. Seems to me I heard tell Grace Hart was from up Austin-way. How'd y'all get to Los Marcos?" he inquired, leaning forward, his steely gaze drilling holes into Gracie.

Oops. It was a good question, one she wasn't prepared to answer, at least not honestly. She smiled, aware her smile spread sickly across her face, a sure sign, her father would have said, she was about to tell a lie.

"McLean wrote to me, asking... no, begging for my help and I couldn't ignore him. After all, a lot of his troubles are my fault. I felt like I had to do something to atone." Wanting the sheriff to stop badgering her and go away, she glanced down, folding her hands meekly in her lap. Her mother always said, *appearance equals good manners,* and in this case, appearance meant getting rid of this nosy sheriff.

But evidently the sheriff wasn't dumb or else appearances meant nothing to him because he snorted—how rude—and growled, "Ma'am, now I can tell you're flat out lyin' to me. I'm aware within half an hour when every person comes into my town. I know what they were wearing, what time they arrived and how they got there, whether by wagon, horse, or stagecoach... and you didn't arrive by wagon or stagecoach. That leaves by horse and I don't see a pretty young thing like you makin' the trip alone." He shook his head at Gracie, his silver mustache drooping in disapproval.

Her smile got sicklier.

"Now, are you going to tell me the truth or am I going to have to arrest you?"

She squeaked, alarmed. Arrest her. Arrest a Hart? In a hundred and twenty years not one single Hart had ever done anything to warrant arrest. She couldn't be the first. Her mother would simply die. Her father would be furious and would surely force her back to Pittsburgh.

And worst of all, she would lose any hope she had of staying here. She'd lose Hannah. She'd lose any chance of finding love with the contentious, stubborn, wrong-headed... handsome and adorable McLean. Panic squeezed a fist around her heart, making it hard to breathe. She blinked her eyes against the tears threatening to give her away.

The sheriff winced.

Hah. Inside, a smile blossomed because what good was being a woman, if you couldn't use an occasional feminine wile?

"Honest. "I wouldn't lie to you, Sheriff Rheingold," she said in her most earnest voice and she dabbed at her eyes with the hem of her sleeve.

Under his mustache, the line of Rheingold's mouth flattened. Shaking his head, he said, "Doggone it. I sure do hate to do this but you've left me no choice." Heaving his bulk out of the uncomfortable kitchen chair, he reached behind his waist and pulled out a set of cuffs.

Jupiter. Jumping up from her chair, she threw herself at the sheriff, grabbing the collar of his open shirt in her two hands and hung on. "No, no, you can't. You can't arrest me. That would spoil everything. Please don't take me away."

"Come on, now," he muttered, ducking and dodging her efforts to climb up his body. "Just tell me the truth and everything will be fine."

"McLean kidnapped me," she wailed, letting loose a fresh torrent of tears.

The sheriff sat down, which had the felicitous effect of releasing Gracie, leaving her unsupported and teetering in the middle of the kitchen floor.

"Gee-hosaphat," the lawman exclaimed. "He kidnapped you. I'm going to kill the bastard."

Then his face flushed red. "Sorry, ma'am. No offense intended." His long jaw thrusting out, he muttered, "I thought better of the boy. Doggone it. Now I'm going to have to arrest him and he'll go back to prison. Doggone it," he repeated.

She lost the battle to stay upright. Fear weakened her knees and she found herself crouched at the sheriff's feet, holding his hands in hers and pleaded. "Oh, please, please, please, don't arrest him. It's all my fault. I identified him as one of the train robbers when it turns out he wasn't and I wrote those horrible stories which ruined his life and then I refused to help him even when he begged me and begged me to write a different story so he threw me over his saddle just to scare me and carried me just a short way and offered me a chance to do what he asked but I yelled and screamed and told him I wouldn't and so he went a bit further and said the same thing again and I still wouldn't do it and by that time it was too late to take me back so..."

A tear dripped down her check. "So here we are. He wouldn't have kidnapped me if I hadn't made him so mad. Or just done what he asked."

She gulped in a breath and glanced up at the sheriff, hoping her act had swayed him. It didn't look promising. The sheriff's mouth twisted with doubt, definitely unconvinced.

Laying her head on his knees, she gave up and gave in. "Please," she pleaded. "I love him. I couldn't bear it if another bad thing happened to him because of me." A tiny sob escaped her. The sheriff couldn't take McLean away now. She wouldn't allow it, not after what they'd done together. McLean made love to her last night and darn it, that made him hers and she wasn't giving him up without a fight.

Sheriff Rheingold sighed. "Aw, shoot, now stop crying." Gingerly, he patted her head. "It's going to be fine, honey, honest. We'll work something out." He patted again, not touching her, only the fluffy puff of hair pinned to the back of her head.

"Really?" she gulped. "Everything will be all right? You won't arrest McLean?"

"Well now," he back-pedaled. "There's a few conditions attached to that."

"Conditions?" She yanked herself upright. "What kind of conditions?"

He blinked at the sudden change in her demeanor. "Umm," he stalled. "Like not staying here any longer. You'll need to leave and come on into town."

What? "I can't leave now," she exclaimed. "That would ruin everything."

"It would?"

"Well, of course it would." Men. They could be so stupid. She shook her head in disgust.

The sheriff scratched his head, looking more puzzled than ever before. "How would it ruin everything? Didn't you say the two of you were in love? You can court as easily from town as from here. And—" He hesitated, clearing his throat uncomfortably. "—it would preserve your reputation. It's not fitting for you to be out here alone with him."

"Phssst." Apparently, men didn't listen either. Squaring her shoulders, she looked the sheriff directly in the eye and addressed him the same way she usually addressed her brother Seth's two-year old son. "I said I loved him. I never said he loved me."

She shivered thinking about last night. "I think he could get to love me. But not if you force me to move into town, for heaven's sake."

"All right," the lawman said, the words dragged out of him, obviously still not getting it. "And why would that be?"

Arrggghh. She put her head down, figuratively beating herself over the head with her fists. When she was done, she raised her head and said in a singsong fashion, "*Out of sight, out of mind? The way to a man's heart is through his stomach? Absence sharpens love, but presence strengthens it? Come live with me, and be my love, And we will some new pleasures prove?* Get it?"

The man ran a hand down his face, flattening his nose and mustache, then ran his hand back up again, ending by digging it through his hair. "Good golly, Miss Hart. So what you're saying is if you leave the ranch and go into town, McLean won't love you?"

Beaming, she bounced up and down where she knelt, excited he'd understood at last. "Yes, that's exactly what I'm saying. It's important to be here, every day, where he can get to know me better, see me, eat my cooking and get to depend on it. Because if I'm here, he'll..." she paused, her face flushing bright red. "...so he'll..." The sheriff raised his eyebrows. "...he'll... he'll..."

Rheingold growled. "You're not saying what I think you're saying, are you?"

With a surge of relief (he'd made it easy by not making her say the words), she nodded her head. "Well, maybe. Or maybe not. I'm not sure. At least I don't think I'm saying that, it's just that, if he sees me and I, you know..." She fell back when he glowered at her.

"Oh no, young woman. I'm not leaving you out here for McLean to... to..." He seemed to struggle for words, the color surging to his face strangely at odds with his normal tan. "...to take your young womanhood. I won't be responsible for you being despoiled. And it would be kind of a dirty trick to play on McLean, using... ahem ... to trap him, doncha think?"

Little did he realize it was too late to be worrying about her innocence, however, she declined to use sex to trap McLean. Lying down in order to win the man she loved would be cheating. She'd win him standing on her own two feet. So to speak.

The idea this old geezer believed she would stoop so low made her pretty mad. Well, the heck with him. "It's not what I meant at all."

"Well, what did you mean," he growled, sounding irritated.

"I would never use... uh... s... s..." She grimaced at the sheriff. "Well, you know, to trap him into marriage," she completed. She crossed her fingers behind her back and added to herself, maybe I wouldn't *use* sex but no one said anything about not *having* it.

Shrugging her shoulders, she gazed at the sheriff helplessly. "How else can I get him to fall in love. If I go off to town, he'll close himself up in the shell he was in before, when he was mad at the world all the time. Right now he doesn't want anyone else in his life because, for him, love is only a responsibility, and he's got enough worries for two men. But I make him feel things, good things. I make him laugh. I make him care. I even make him lose his temper and enjoy it. He needs me in his life." Tears filled her eyes, and already sensing what a softie the sheriff was, she let one fall. "...and so does Hannah."

He sighed. "All right, honey. You can stay for a while. But you got to stay out of town because it sure wouldn't do McLean's reputation any good if folks figure out he's livin' out here with you all alone and the man doesn't need any more enemies than he's already got. I expect he'd like to stay in Los Marcos, and for that, he has to start making friends." Idly rubbing a finger across his mustache and looked at Gracie, a challenge in his eyes. "How long did y'all say it would take you to finish your book?"

Euphoria filled Gracie at his question. She'd won—not that she'd viewed it as a contest—but the alternative to winning was losing McLean and Hannah, and she couldn't have born that.

Trying to temper her smug elation, she answered, "The manuscript is nearly finished now, only another chapter..." A complete lie, she was only about half way through. "...but I want to be here when it's published and hits the stores. Will you let me? It normally takes about two months to get it published, but I asked Albert, my editor, to rush the job so maybe a month. It wouldn't be a first quality printing, but at least it would be on the bookshelves and the newsstands."

Stroking his upper lip, he mulled this around. "Why do you have to be here until the book hits the shelves? Seems just getting it to your editor ought to be more than adequate."

She watched her fingers twisting and fidgeting in her lap. This was so hard. She'd always been a person who was sure of who she was and where she was going. Part of her sureness meant she didn't doubt whether her actions were right or wrong. She did what had to be done, confident it was the right thing so it was hard to admit her way of doing things might have a few flaws in it.

With a little grimace, she muttered, "Right now McLean likes me. And he also..." She forced the word out, "...lusts... for me. But until I fix what I did to him, he won't forgive me and if he can't forgive me, he can't love me." After thinking last night about everything that had happened, she came to the conclusion that must be what bothered McLean. "I have to prove that I love him. Until he sees the book in print, on sale, he'll always have doubts. And if I'm somewhere far away, how will I know he's even seen it? Do you understand?" she asked, putting her heart in her eyes.

He sighed and then stood. "All right. Until the book comes out, but no longer. After that, I don't think it would be fair or right to have you stay on if he's not willing to marry you. Got it?" He waited for Gracie to acknowledge his instruction, then picked his hat up off the table and clapped it on his head.

"I'll leave it to you to explain all this to McLean. Don't let me down, now." Again, she nodded. "Is there anything else I can do for you?"

She started to say no, then changed her mind. "Could you take a package with you and mail it for me? It's the first half of my manuscript. I don't want to ask McLean to do it." She flushed. "I don't want him finding out I've sent it off."

His eyebrow rose up into his hairline and she hastened to add, "I promise I'll explain all this to McLean... eventually... but I want the fact that the new story is out to be a surprise. I haven't really been keeping him up to date with my progress." She shrugged.

The lawman shook his head with a sigh but gave in, waiting while she retrieved the chapters. With a final pat on her shoulder, carrying her envelope like precious cargo, he exited through the kitchen door and walked to his horse.

After waving the sheriff off, she returned to the kitchen. "Go outside and play with Gus for a while, Hannah."

Tapping Gus on the head to alert the puppy, Hannah and the dog went outside. Gracie finished chopping the vegetables and braising the beef for the stew and, once she'd set it on the stove to simmer, she followed them outside to watch them play.

Time passed, the sun hung on the western horizon and McLean hadn't returned. Standing, she checked the watch pinned to her bodice. Five thirty. Supper time, and he wasn't home. Something must have delayed him but Hannah should eat regardless. She called her in and set a bowl of stew in front of her. More time passed, Hannah finished her meal and McLean still wasn't home.

"He's only a bit late. He'll be here soon. I'm sure he got busy and lost track of time." She wished she was as confident as she sounded but, for the child's sake, she had to keep up the charade. She nudged her out the back door.

Where was he? He most likely lost track of time, but in spite of what she told Hannah, she was worried and the more time that passed, the more it seemed she had reason to be concerned. This wasn't like McLean. He always made a point to be home in time to eat with Hannah and then spend some time with her afterwards.

Scraping the food scraps from Hannah's meal into Gus's bowl, she wiped her greasy hands on a towel and then walked outside to stand on the back porch. From there she could see most of the back pastures and the road leading to the south section where McLean said he was working. She wrung her hands, her eyes on the horizon, searching for a dark silhouette.

With June reaching its end, it didn't get dark until almost eight o'clock. She supposed McLean could be taking advantage of the long daylight hours to get some extra work finished. But a tiny part of her worried he hadn't returned because he was avoiding her, that this was his way of informing her that last night meant nothing to him.

She told herself her doubts were illogical, that last night was wonderful for them both. She believed he was honorable so she didn't believe he would betray last night's fragile beginning so callously, no matter what he'd said at the end.

But still she doubted. And worried about her doubts.

Her questions wouldn't get answered standing on the porch, so she wandered back indoors, thinking she would spend the time with some mending. Pulling out the wooden box of sewing equipment, she settled herself in the parlor with a gray shirt of McLean's requiring a new button. She threaded a needle, centered a button over the still visible thread holes in the material, and poked it through one of the holes in the button, her mind barely on her task.

Instead, her mind drifted to last night and what she did in the hay with McLean. Even hours later, she remembered his hands on her body, how the rough workman's calluses on his hands scraped across her sensitive nipples, catching on her skin with a slight tug that made her short of breath. The memories were almost more potent than the actual event. Her breasts drew tight under her chemise, the nipples touching the fine cotton close enough to send a tingling jolt through her. A sudden throbbing pressure erupted between her legs, reminiscent of the ache McLean's hand created.

A bead of sweat dripped onto the cotton, leaving a widening dark spot. She blinked herself back to awareness, realizing she'd sat for several minutes doing nothing but reliving making love with McLean. No more of that. With a shake of her head, she forced the sensual haze she'd fallen into out of her mind. Dark shadows covered the floor of the parlor, telling her at least a half an hour had passed.

Oh, my stars. What was she doing, sitting here dreaming in the parlor when McLean still wasn't back, and it was almost dark. Something wasn't right. Jumping up, she raced outside to survey the landscape again, hoping she'd simply missed him; that he'd come in unnoticed. It was possible he was in the barn right now, putting the horses away.

"Hannah," she called. "Hannah, come here, quick." Within seconds Hannah appeared at the foot of the porch stairs, Gus barking at her heels. "Did your father come home?" she asked. Hannah shook her head no, her brows meeting over worried eyes.

Fear clenched her stomach, causing the little bit of dinner she'd choked down to roil uncomfortably. Wringing her hands, she stared again at the horizon, straining her eyes to penetrate the growing darkness. A small black smudge near the tree line moved, catching her attention, so she swung her head in that direction and peered through the gloom. The smudge approached, moving towards the house. Her heart thumped. She stepped down off the porch, watching the smudge grow larger until she could see the outline of horses silhouetted against the setting sun.

Thank the Lord. Grabbing up her skirts, she ran towards the wagon. Her legs ate up the ground, leaping over a bush or two in her hurry. The muted metallic jingle of harness and the dull thud of shod hooves on hard packed ground reached her as she neared the wagon. Far behind, she could hear Hannah's small feet.

"McLean," she shouted. No answer came, so she kept running, until at last she reached Horse's head, gasping and out of breath.

"McLean?" Still panting, she jogged past the horses who had halted, until she was saw the buckboard seat. Empty. She thrust her foot through the spokes of the wheel and hiked herself up to search the back of the wagon.

"McLean, answer me. Where are you?" she called, but it was obvious that nothing was in the wagon but a few small items. A hard fist slammed into her chest, leaving her breathless.

The horses had come back without McLean.

Chapter Eighteen

It was blind luck they found him, that or possibly Horse's instincts and determination. Having no real idea where McLean was, after lifting Hannah into the bed of the wagon and climbing up to the buckboard seat herself, Gracie steered the wagon around and drove it back in the direction it came from. The sorrel, intent on returning to the barn for his supper, fought against returning to the pastures by dragging his feet and yanking on the bit but Horse walked on, his feet steady and determined.

The sun sank lower, and the light faded. Terrified, Hannah clung to Gracie's arm, whimpering in fear as the wagon jolted over the rough terrain. Gracie tried to soothe her and manage the horses at the same time. A ball of fear pressed so hard inside her chest, her breastbone ached. Although the air still held the afternoon's warmth, she shivered.

When they found the fence line, she said a heartfelt prayer of thanksgiving. He'd told her he would be stringing fence today so she hoped by following the line, they would find him. She hoped when they did, it was soon enough. She wasn't a praying sort of person, but now she pleaded with God for all she was worth that she was headed in the correct direction.

The team abruptly stopped. She flicked the reins over the horses' backs, but the team refused to move. She lifted the reins to snap them again when a sound, barely discernable above the jingling of harness and the whirring of crickets in the brush, reached her ears.

She stood to listen. Her heart stopped, then raced when she heard it again. "Stay here," she ordered Hannah, tying the reins to the brake. Until she understood what the sound was, she didn't want to put Hannah in danger. Climbing down off the wagon, she rushed forward.

At first, she was sure she was mistaken, that the reason the horses stopped was because there was a big rock in the way. Then she heard it again, a definite moan and definitely human. Running towards the dark shape, she could see, rather than a rock, it was the spool of barbed wire McLean kept in the back of the wagon. It was tipped to the side. And underneath was McLean.

She threw herself to her knees beside it. "McLean?" She ran her fingers over his face. His skin was cold and clammy, sweat beading his upper lip. "McLean, say something." The fact no answer came horrified her. She could tell from the occasional low groan and his shallow erratic breathing that he was still alive, but she had no way of telling how badly he was hurt without being able to see him.

Cursing herself for not preparing better with supplies or at least a lantern, she reached under the spool and ran her hand over his body. A barb caught the back of her hand and she hissed in pain, yanking it back to suck on it before returning to McLean's chest again. Her hand met material, wet and sticky with what she believed was sweat before realizing it was blood.

Dear God in heaven. He was covered in blood, trapped and unconscious and she had no idea what to do. Tears filled her eyes. Never was the limitations of her upper-class upbringing more apparent. A ranch wife would know what to do, but faced with such a monumental task, her brain ceased to function. She pressed her fingers to her lips, trying to hold back the sobs that threatened to erupt.

A light touch on her shoulder made her turn. Hannah stood in front of Gracie, her pale face gleaming in the moonlight.

"Hannah, oh Hannah." She threw her arms around the child's waist and hugged her. "He's hurt, and I don't know what to do." The sob she'd suppressed escaped, followed by another. She laid her head on Hannah's chest and shivered.

Hannah held still for a moment, and then pulled herself free. Walking over to the other side of her father's limp body, she put her hands on the rim of the spool and pushed, grunting with the effort.

"Hannah, stop. You'll hurt yourself. There are sharp barbs of metal and you'll get cut," Gracie said. Hannah grunted and pushed against the spool again.

Heat burned in Gracie's face. Coward. *The man you love needs your help, and you've given up. Even a six-year-old has more courage than you do.* Watching Hannah struggle to lift something that weighed twice her weight, she felt ashamed of herself.

"Hannah, stop," she said again. "You're too small to lift that. We have to figure out something else, find a way to get it off your daddy without hurting him." Hannah stopped straining and straightened up to listen to Gracie. "Come on. Let's go to the wagon and see if there's something there."

The two of them ran to the back of the wagon. She climbed in and pulled Hannah up beside her. They rooted around the few tools lying on the bottom. A post hole digger, wire snippers, a clamp, a shovel, several short logs, and several boxes of brads. In the other corner, lying in a tangled heap was a rope and several mud-covered horse halters and rope lead lines. Not much to work with. Once again, she wished she were one of those handy ranch wives. What was she supposed to do with a few things to dig holes with, a couple of small hand tools, and some rope? If only she could simply lift the spool—but to do it, she'd have to be strong as an ox.

Or a horse.

She didn't have much to work with, but she did have the horses. And a rope. And, thinking about it, the logs. It would have to be enough.

Grabbing Hannah's hands in hers, she turned her until they were nose to nose. "Hannah, help me. Do you think you can handle Horse? Lead him forward?" After a small hesitation, Hannah nodded yes. "All right, come on. We have to get to work."

She grabbed the rope and the two logs and hopped down from the wagon. Grabbing the horses' bridles, she tugged them so the wagon was in front of McLean, its side to him. She helped Hannah out of the wagon then began unharnessing Horse, leaving the sorrel still harnessed. Snapping a lead onto Horse's bridle, she handed it to Hannah.

"Hold him still, Hannah, while I get everything else set up." She ran back to McLean and knelt down, studying the spool in the dim light, using her hands to search out all the holes and crevasses she might use. Unless she attached the rope just right, it could roll over rather than lifting, and fall back on top of McLean.

The top had several large holes in it. If she could thread the rope through both holes, it would help control the direction it rose. Grasping the end of the rope, she threaded it through hole near the center of the spool then through the one on the edge of the rim, hoping that would keep the weight balanced properly and allow the spool to tip upright on its side.

Out of breath from her exertions, she stood and wiped the sweat off her forehead then picked up the other end of the rope and threw it over the side of the wagon. Then she ran around to the other side and retrieved the rope she'd thrown. She could only hope the sides of the wagon was high enough, and strong enough, to provide the necessary leverage.

"Hannah, bring Horse over here, quickly." She could hear the metallic clop of hooves when Hannah led the horse around. Backing him up, she tied the rope to his collar, checking her knots to make sure they were secure. If the knots came loose at any time while the spool was being lifted, it would fall back on McLean and likely kill him.

Finishing, she knelt next to Hannah. "Hannah, it's very important you lead the horse real straight. And you have to go slowly, one step at a time. Don't start until I tell you. Can you do it?" Fear radiated from Hannah, but nonetheless, she nodded.

Having done all she could there, Gracie raced back to McLean's side. She checked him one more time, placing her fingers on his neck, looking for a pulse. He groaned a muted groan, and a breathy word.

"McLean?" She bent her head down, placing her ear next to his mouth. "McLean?"

This time she heard a distinct moan. "Uhhmm." Panting, shallow and pained. "Gra..." The word trailed off and he groaned.

"McLean, can you hear me?" she asked urgently, hoping for some kind of reply. It would be easier if he could help, even if only to roll himself out from underneath when the weight lifted.

His head tipped a few degrees in her direction. "Mmmmm. Go...d. Hurt."

Her stomach lurched. Dear Lord, now she realized it would be better if he was unconscious while they lifted the weight. But he was awake, and she was committed to doing what must be done.

"Lie still," she whispered in his ear, "and it will be over in a jiffy." She patted his shoulder, her fear so intense she pressed a fist against her breastbone, hoping to ease it.

"Wha...t?" McLean asked. His breathing grew harsher.

"I'm going to get you out," she gritted, clenching her jaw to control the shaking of her voice.

"No," he gasped. "Hurt... you." The effort to speak made him groan in pain. "N...oo."

His voice was feebler this time, which meant there was no time to lose. Placing the heels of her hands under the rim of the spool, she called, "Now, Hannah. Slowly, very slowly, lead the horse forward."

At first, she imagined Hannah didn't hear her or that she wasn't able to get the horse to move because nothing happened. Then the rope tightened, stretching taut from the wire spool over the sides of the wagon to the horse. The horse grunted, but nothing else happened. Her heart pounding, she willed the spool to move. Then it did. With a raspy protest, the heavy wire spool lifted a few inches.

McLean cried out.

"Hannah, stop. Stop." The spool stopped moving, the rope still stretched tight. Her body quivering with tension, Gracie shoved one of the logs under the edge of the spool, holding it in place. She removed one shaking hand from her grip on the spool rim and ran her hands along McLean's body. Her fingers caught on sharp barbs, barbs also caught in his shirt and probably underneath his skin, pulling out and causing him unbearable pain when the weight lifted.

Oh, dear Lord. She couldn't do this. Her hands shook, her insides quivered like pudding, her stomach seriously threatening to expel her dinner. Emergencies were not her forte and she was even worse when it involved pain and blood. Tears burned her eyes. She leaned her forehead against the rough wood rim next to her hand and a sob erupted.

"Gracie." The word was a whisper. "Do... it. Please. Please," he begged.

Another sob escaped with a shaky breath. She closed her eyes, praying for strength and put her hand back under the spool. "Now, Hannah. Pull," she shouted, and threw her weight against the heavy weight. With a jerk, it rose. McLean screamed but she kept pushing, using her foot to shove the log further under the spool so it wouldn't fall back on him. The spool rose, teetered for a moment and settled abruptly on its rim beside McLean's limp body.

"Stop. Stop," she screamed at Hannah. "Don't pull anymore." The rope went limp and so did Gracie. Her legs gave out and she fell to the ground with a sob. Covering her face with her hands, she wept.

THE REST OF THE NIGHT was worse than any night of her life. After his brief moment of lucidity, McLean fell into unconsciousness and was no help at all getting his long, lanky body into the wagon. Sweating rivers, she dragged and pushed and pulled him until she got him to the tailgate of the wagon where she pushed and pulled and boosted with Hannah's help to get him onto the bed of the wagon.

She grunted. Trying to maneuver him into the wagon was like dealing with a straw-filled scarecrow whose limbs were loaded down with rocks. She'd no more get one part of his body in the wagon and begin working on the next, when the first part would flop out. But with Hannah's help, eventually he was in the wagon. That done, she put Horse back into the traces and clucked the team towards home.

He was deathly quiet on the way back, and she stopped often to make sure he still breathed. Nightmares filled her mind of arriving at the house to find he'd died during the journey. When they drove into the yard, she pulled the wagon close to the back porch and repeated the previous process, this time in reverse, until he was inside, lying on the floor of the kitchen. Racing upstairs, she pulled the small mattress off Hannah's bed, trundled it into the kitchen where she laid it next to McLean's inert body and rolled him onto it.

Seeing the fear in Hannah's pale face, she put her to work in hopes being able to help would take the little girl's mind off her fears. "Hannah, bring me some lamps." She raced off to return a minute later balancing a hand-painted lamp between her two small hands. She set it on the floor and ran back for another.

Digging through the pantry, Gracie found matches and lit the lamp. Then she knelt and looked at McLean for the first time. She drew back in horror. His cotton shirt hung in ribbons exposing flesh lacerated with dozens of large and small cuts oozing blood. Long rips ran the length of his trouser legs, gapping open to expose the deep gouges in his thighs. So much blood covered his clothes she didn't see how there could be any left in his body. Sick at the sight, she put her hands over her mouth and swallowed several times.

A noise behind her made her whip around to see Hannah, standing in the doorway holding another lamp. To prevent Hannah from seeing her father in such a state, Gracie spread her skirts over his body. Taking a breath to calm herself, she said, "Hannah, put the lamp down right there and go upstairs and get sheets. Lots of sheets."

Hannah bit her lip.

"Go," Gracie yelled. Hannah started, set the lamp down with a rattle of glass, and ran out of the room again, her blond hair flying.

The next few hours were a blur. She stripped McLean to the skin, appalled at the gruesome cuts covering his body. Bruises were beginning to form on his abdomen, arms, and chest. She boiled water, tore sheets, and carefully cleaned the dozens of wounds. Her hands shook when McLean groaned and writhed when she scrubbed the dirt and blood from his body with water so hot her hands were bright red from the scalding. Numerous times she ran to the back door for fresh air before she passed out. And all the while she worked, Hannah hovered in the doorway, her face white, her small body shaking. At some point, Gracie realized she needed to take care of the horses so she rushed outside, unharnessed them and led them into their stalls, leaving alfalfa and water.

Night passed and the sun rose without notice and would have continued to remain unnoticed if she hadn't looked up to find Hannah curled up in a ball in a corner of the kitchen, sound asleep, her tired face tinted yellow by the sunshine streaming through the window. She twitched and moaned in her sleep, reminding Gracie she herself hadn't slept in over twenty-four hours. Her eyes burned, her body ached as if pummeled and her mind felt fuzzy. And she hadn't yet visited the outhouse.

Lurching to her feet, she staggered outside to answer nature's call, before rushing back inside to find Hannah standing over her father, stark fear on her face. She fell to her knees beside Hannah and wrapping her arms around the slight body, pulled the child against her chest. The girl was stiff in her arms, her arms hanging by her side. Gasps of breath rattled in and out of her lungs.

"Hannah, Hannah," she soothed. "Shhh, hush, baby. He's going to be fine." Hannah shook her head no, her chin rubbing across Gracie's shoulder.

Tears stung the back of her eyelids. God in heaven, she forgot how many people the poor child had lost in her short life. How many more people could the child lose before she lost her feeble grip on the world altogether?

McLean *had* to get better. Pulling away, she sat on her heels and took Hannah's face between her hands, gazing into her eyes. "Listen to me. I promise you," she swore, "I won't let anything happen to your father. Do you understand?"

A tear trickled down the girl's cheek.

"He's very sick but I'm going to make him better. I promise," she repeated, emphasizing the word. "Trust me, Hannah," she ordered, and stroked her hands over the sleek blond hair. For a very long time Hannah was silent, staring out the kitchen door with the blank soulless look she used to have. She feared her promise was too late, that Hannah was retreating from the real world again. Then Hannah blinked and re-focused on Gracie, dipping her chin in a tiny nod.

"Good. Now go feed Gus," she ordered and sent Hannah outside.

Over the next twenty-four hours Gracie had cause to bitterly regret her words. McLean got sicker and sicker, his temperature rising until his skin was tight and dry. She tried to keep him cool, but it was almost impossible. She found no ice in the basement icehouse, and the water from the well in which she soaked cloth after cloth was tepid at best and the cloths lost their coolness almost immediately after she laid them on McLean. In between swabbing him down, she snatched brief moments of sleep.

Although he never fully woke, at first he had enough strength to protest fitfully and push her away when she scrubbed at the wounds to remove the dirt and grime. But by the second morning he was blazing hot and had sunk into a stupor nothing roused him from.

Pacing back and forth in the crowded confines of the kitchen, she wrung her hands. Tears of helplessness tightened her throat but she refused to shed them; why bother since crying didn't help. Somewhere in the back of her mind she was aware her back ached brutally, that she was filthy, her hair hanging in strings down her back, and that she'd barely slept in almost two days. But her thoughts about herself were overshadowed by her terror. She'd done everything she could think of and McLean was still in a raging fever.

Thinking about the endless days when she volunteered her time for the hospital in Pittsburgh, doing nothing but wrapping bandages while sitting in her mother's parlor eating petit fours with her society friends, made her want to scream in fury. How useless. How stupid. What a waste of time. All the things she learned growing up, the attention to art and writing and dancing classes, the lessons in how to pour tea properly and how to flirt with the right man. Of what use were social mores' now?

Round and round the kitchen she walked, muttering to herself, the pressure inside getting tighter and tighter, harder and harder, till she was sure she'd choke on the ball of fear jammed in her throat. There was no one to help, no one who could give her advice, and she felt small and helpless and alone in her fear.

She needed to do something but what? What? What? Jupiter, she was losing her mind with worry and fear.

She stopped. Staring at McLean, she clenched her fists. She couldn't do this alone. She didn't have the knowledge, she didn't have the skills, and she didn't even have any medicine. There was no choice but to find someone to help.

Her decision made, she ran from the room and up the stairs to get Hannah. She pulled the sleepy child from her bed. Grabbing the navy-blue dress hanging from the bedpost, she tossed it to the girl. "Quick. Get dressed, Hannah. We're going into town."

Hannah blinked, still groggy and confused from sleep. Pulling her shoes and socks out from under the bed, Gracie quickly slipped them on Hannah's feet and ran back to the door.

"Hurry, Hannah," she called, racing down the stairs.

Her next stop was the barn, where she pulled Horse out and slipped a bridle on him, thanking her lucky stars he was cooperative and opened his mouth for her rather than fighting the bit. Admitting she couldn't manage the heavy stock saddle, she decided she and Hannah would have to ride bareback. She led him from the barn to find Hannah waiting on the front porch, still looking tired and confused.

"Here." She thrust the reins in Hannah's hand. "Hold him. I'll be right back." Out of breath from the running she had done, she trotted back into the kitchen. Using a metal pitcher, she filled it with cool, fresh water from the kitchen pump and set it next to McLean in case he woke up; then she soaked several clothes and laid them all over his body.

Returning to the porch, she hoisted Hannah onto Horse's broad back and then clambered up herself, using an upended flowerpot as a stool. Taking up the reins, she kicked Horse into a lope they maintained until they reached town.

DOCTOR FRANKS RETURNED with them. Together, they managed to get McLean up the stairs and into his own bed but still, the doctor couldn't assure her McLean would live even though he employed every cure in his medical journal. Quinine for fever, scrubbing the wounds with carbolic acid—the doctor subscribed to the old biblical adage; cleanliness is next to Godliness—opening up each wound to let the infection drain then applying honey for healing.

Sometimes she was scared her right down to the soles of her feet, making her acknowledge she loved him with every fiber of her being. After another a long day, the fever finally receded, giving her hope he wouldn't die.

The next morning her patient lapsed into a deep, restful sleep, and the doctor returned home, confident McLean would survive.

Now that the danger was past, Gracie could admit that she never wanted to leave him, no matter how stubborn and difficult he could be. But three days had gone by in which she'd not had time to complete her story and foot-dragging, whether her fault or not, might well have cost him the right to see his name cleared. With him lying sick in bed, aware he could have died with that stain on his name still hanging over him, she experienced an overwhelming urgency to have the world told of his innocence.

She realized she didn't want to take the time for the lengthy editing, printing, and shipping process her books usually went through. Instead of the full-length book she originally planned on, she decided on a much shorter version. She spent the quiet hours rewriting the remainder of her chapters, bringing the story to a rousing and satisfying close. It was forty pages shorter than she'd planned but how it ended was the important part.

It had to be sent off now.

As if he'd read her mind, the sheriff stopped by again—having heard from the doctor of the accident—and she asked him to send another wire to Albert, begging him to publish her story in the next month's edition of *The Westerner*, a wildly popular magazine that carried short stories of Western adventures that Albert's publishing house also published. *The End of a Legend* was not exactly a short story but, with Albert's help, she knew her status as Grace Hart, famous author of the Scar McLean series, would mean the editors of *The Westerner* would jump at the chance to publish the entire story in their next publication.

She handed the finished pages to Rheingold which he promised to send by special express messenger when he returned to town.

A WARM BREEZE WAFTED through the window, fluttering the curtains and cooling the nervous sweat beaded on his forehead. Steeling himself against the pain he anticipated, Mac wiggled his toes again, testing the achy-ness of his body and a soreness he couldn't account for. Fuzz clogged his brain as he crawled through his memories, trying to dredge up some explanation for his soreness, but nothing came to him.

He had a vague recollection of pain, intense pain. All right. Deal with that. Trying to control his thoughts, which persisted in scattering in a dozen different directions, he culled through them one at a time. He remembered working the fence line. It was late in the day. And hot. And he'd been tired and irritable. Then something happened. What? Hmmmm. His mind was a blank.

Dammit. Why couldn't he remember? Frustrated, he tried to raise his arm, only to find it tied to his side. Pain knifed through him, and a muted scream erupted from him.

His eyes flew open to find Gracie bent over him, her face puckered with concern. She laid a hand lightly on his chest, holding him down. "Shhh. Everything's fine. Just be still." She pulled the covers he had dislodged back up over his chest.

He gaped at her in stupefaction. What the heck? Why was she was talking to him like he was a child? He tried to speak but a croak came out. He tried again. "Wha...?" His voice cracked and trailed off.

She grinned. "Oh, you're really awake this time. Good. I didn't think you'd ever wake up." Plopping down next to him on the bed, she patted his hand in excitement. "You've been asleep forever, almost a week in fact. At first, it looked like you were going to die. You had such a fever and you'd lost so much blood it was amazing you had any left in your body, but then it looked like you would live, but I got worried because you slept and slept and slept. But the doctor said you would be all right. I'm so relieved he was right."

She smiled brightly at him. He blinked back, his head spinning from the flood of words she threw at him. But despite her deluge, he was no clearer on what happened than before.

He frowned and opened his mouth to ask a question.

"Don't talk," she interrupted him. "The doctor said you needed to save your strength to get well. Just let me take care of you." She jumped up and trotted to the washstand where a pitcher of fresh water sat. "Water? You want water?" she asked but didn't wait for his answer. Instead she poured some into a glass and sat next to Mac again. Reaching an arm under the pillow, she hoisted him up and held the glass to his lips.

He stifled a groan of pain when she pulled him up. The glass was shoved between his lips and tilted. Forced to swallow, he took several big gulps. Like a damned baby. He glowered at her but soon the water soothed his mouth and throat, loosening up enough saliva so he could talk.

"What... happen?" The effort to produce those few words and to sit up for the water left him exhausted. He slumped down on the pillow and watched Gracie replace the glass on the nightstand and pull a chair over to sit by him.

"Don't you remember?"

He shook his head no, his brain too tired and achy to think so hard. She tucked her legs up under her in the chair, pulling the hem of her dress over her feet.

"You were gone forever, and I was frantic. I didn't know what to think when the wagon came home without you. I was scared to death." She took a deep shaky breath and chattered on, something to do with barbed wire and the wagon and Horse but his brain couldn't absorb the flow of words.

"Of course you're concerned about the book getting done but I wanted to tell you I've already sent out a draft of the book," she said. "You don't need to worry. I told you it would be four weeks and then I'd be out of your hair. I still have..."

His eyes drifted closed, and he missed the rest.

Chapter Nineteen

It was hot. The sheets were wadded up in a sweaty ball under his hips. His mouth had a dirty sock taste again. And he needed to piss.

"Now you do it, Hannah."

God, his back ached. Slept too long. Voices brought him closer to being awake.

"That's right, sweetie. H-O-R-S-E spells horse. You're getting very good at this. Now you spell something, all right?"

He had to pee *now*. He opened his eyes and blinked.

"That's good, honey. Except the word 'daddy' has two 'Ds' in the middle, like this."

He turned his head towards her voice. She sat at a table with Hannah in her lap. Hannah jabbed at something on the paper.

"Di? What's Di? I don't understand," Gracie said in a low voice.

Hannah let out a whine of frustration and pointed to something on the paper.

Gracie wrinkled her brow in a frown. "Daddy? What about your daddy?"

Using her index finger, Hannah traced something on the page.

"No," Gracie exclaimed. "Oh, my. No, honey. Your daddy's not going to die. I promised I wouldn't let your daddy die, and I won't. He's almost all better now."

Hannah shook her head, a tear trickling down her cheek.

Taking Hannah's face in her hands, Gracie said, "Listen to me, Hannah. I understand that you're afraid. Sometimes, no matter how much we love someone, bad things happen to them, and we don't know why. But love is a wonderful healer, so if we love your daddy lots and lots, he'll be up and around in no time. All right?"

Worry shining from her eyes, Hannah pressed her lips together.

"But he's getting better. The fever is gone and he's woken up a couple of times. We just need to be patient. In the meantime, we can surprise you daddy by practicing your reading. You're getting so good I might let you be my editor."

Her face alight with happiness, Hannah patted Gracie's face between her two small hands.

Mac blinked back his own tears. His daughter was reading, a form of communication, just not with her voice. Did that mean she was getting better?

"Gracie?" His voice came out in a husky rasp. He was shocked at how weak he sounded.

"McLean. You're awake again," Gracie said. Lifting Hannah off her lap, she nudged the little girl towards Mac.

He reached towards his daughter. "Hannah. Sweetheart." He stroked her face with trembling fingers. "Hi." His head swam.

She grinned back and patted his hand. Twining his fingers through her smaller ones, he turned her hand in his and kissed her palm. The effort exhausted him so he released her hand, wanting to close his eyes and sleep some more but he forced them to stay open. He had questions. What had happened while he was ill? Apparently he'd slept for days and the world had moved on. He focused his attention on Gracie. She would know the answers.

He turned his attention to Gracie. "Hannah..." he whispered, his voice croaky like a frog's. "Reading? Why... you... teach...?"

"Because she deserves it. Because I love her."

His heart flared. She loved Hannah. What about him? He closed his eyes for a moment so the room would stop spinning. When his head settled, he opened them again. "Gra—" His voice failed. Damn it. So much to say, so much to ask. And he was as capable as a newborn baby.

Gracie squeezed Hannah's shoulder. "Your daddy's tired, honey. Go outside and play with Gus so he can sleep." She nudged her towards the door.

"Don't..." he mumbled, wanting to ask her to allow Hannah to stay but everything hurt, his throat, his ribs, every inch of muscle and skin. Steeling himself, he took a deep breath. A sharp pain stabbed under his heart. "Ahh, God. Hurt... Don't... Hannah..."

Gracie flashed him a look. Her lips tightened in anger. "Don't worry, McLean. I'm not going to hurt your daughter." Swinging the door open, she left, slamming it after her.

That wasn't what he'd meant. But he'd gotten an answer anyhow.

HE WAS SICK OF BEING sick. For four days, he'd lain in this bed, stewing and fretting about everything from the quality of the food she served him (oatmeal and broth, for Pete's sake.) to the amount of time flying by with nothing getting done. Secretly he tried getting out of bed, but the first time she caught him, she pushed him back into bed moments before his legs gave out. Although he'd never tell her, he admitted to himself he was grateful to her for saving his ass. If only she weren't so smug about it.

With his legs unsteady as a newborn foal, unable to stay on his feet for longer than a few seconds, he had nothing to occupy himself except sleeping, eating, and scratching at the million and one still-healing gashes covering his body.

To distract himself, he asked for some books to read, but it seemed every other word reminded him of Gracie. A poem describing a walk through a garden and the long-stemmed sunflowers reminded him of the glint of gold in her hair. A description of a starlit night brought to mind their unforgettable night in the barn. Even the mention of a rose reminded him of her sweet scent. Saliva pooled in his mouth when he recalled the taste of her on his tongue.

Every day, she was in and out of his room a hundred times, driving him to the point of insanity with wanting. In his heated mind, he construed her solicitude as love for him, but he told himself it wasn't possible. She had other plans for her life.

Then he would remember the cataclysmic joining in the hayloft, and he'd have to ask himself how a properly brought up woman could make love with a man and *not* love him. Of course, the answer was, she couldn't, not unless she'd gotten carried away like him.

Yes, that was the answer. It was an unfortunate mistake. She was innocent and hadn't understood the ramifications of her act. She hadn't meant it to happen, he'd overwhelmed her, and it didn't change anything.

With his head aching from his constant indecision and his relentless state of lust forcing him to swelter under the heavy blankets whenever she entered the room, he got surlier and surlier each day that passed. Even his visits with Hannah didn't soothe him.

Day five. He stared moodily out the window at the purple haze of dusk smudging across the sky. Hours ago, she'd brought his dinner, thick stew with big chunks of beef, carrots, potatoes, and onions.

Setting the tray down on his lap, she'd patted his check, reminded him to be careful of his arm, which fortunately wasn't broken but was severely sprained, and left him alone to eat his meal. She rattled around downstairs for a while, the murmur of her voice talking to Hannah filtering up through the floorboards.

Later their feet thudded on the uncarpeted steps when Gracie and his daughter came upstairs. His door opened, and Hannah rushed in like a whirlwind, skidding to a halt at his side, a smile of delight on her face. She patted his hand and held her face up for a kiss goodnight. Gazing into her sweet face, eyes closed, and pink lips pursed, his heart swelled with love. He silently apologized to God for all his whining about his problems.

All too soon, Gracie pulled Hannah away, taking her off to bed, leaving Mac alone with nothing to do but looked glumly out the window at the falling night and contemplate his contrary thoughts and mending body. His sprained arm ached like a son-of-a-gun and he shifted, trying to get more comfortable.

The smell of congealing grease from his unfinished dinner sitting on the tray straddling his lap was making him queasy, and he wished Gracie would come retrieve the tray since he couldn't remove it himself with one hand.

Reaching under the tray across his legs, his good hand delved down below the covers to scratch and gouge at the scabs covering his thighs and lower stomach. Even though she threatened to tie his good hand to the headboard if he didn't stop scratching them, the barely healed wounds were driving him so crazy he was compelled to rake his nails up and down his body.

He winced when his nail caught on a long deep scab on his thigh, pulling it painfully. Moving upward towards the dozens of pesky itches on his abdomen, he stopped and gave the half-aroused Harold—a fairly constant state these days—a consoling pat. Down boy, he muttered, and moved on to a particularly troublesome scab near his navel. He picked idly at the spot.

He wished he could change the things he'd done.

With a vengeance, he wished his body wasn't one massive itch but since it was, he wished Gracie would come help him scratch it. And he wished he wasn't such an idiot, wishing for things he couldn't have.

The long gash on his thigh flared up and his leg spasmed, upsetting the tray over his lap. His half-empty glass tipped over onto the blankets, leaving a huge spreading wet spot.

"Damn it," he roared.

SHE HEARD THE SHOUT from across the hall, noting the frustrated, pathetic masculine sense of helplessness it carried. Smiling, Gracie continued to remove her dress, stripping off her chemise and underdrawers and folding them away into her dresser. She slipped a fresh nightgown on over her head and thrust her feet into the slippers she'd found in the closet. Then, thinking about that shout, she walked to her dresser and took her hair down, placing the pins into a little tin box. Picking up her brush, she ran it through her hair, smiling at her reflection in the mirror.

Being here with Mac, taking care of him and his needs seemed very much like being a wife. She cooked and cleaned for McLean and took care of his child. She tended his wounds, soothed his fever and alleviated his discomfort, all wifely duties. Sometimes she saw him at his best, but these days she mostly saw him at his worst; surly, belligerent and quarrelsome, traits men tended to save for their wives.

Yes, it was very much like being his wife, which meant it hadn't taken her long to figure out the reason for his bad temper. If he believed his raised knees, heaped bed covers and hands crossed over his lap were fooling her, then he must have forgotten about their night in the barn. There was no way she would ever forget her first sight of McLean's ready body, how his... uh... uh... Harold—she giggled, remembering his embarrassment—stuck straight up from the base of his belly, long and thick and hard. It was a sight difficult to forget and unmistakable even under the layer of blankets.

Well, now she had learned the best and the worst of McLean and despite everything, she loved him and wanted to marry him. If, that is, he wanted to marry her. But so far the stubborn muleheaded man was determined to play the self-sacrificing hero. Well, that didn't work for her at all. She would simply have to show him that he loved her in the only remaining way she could think of. Of course, she'd promised Sheriff Rheingold she wouldn't, but, as her mother always said, promises were meant to be broken when necessary.

Her hair brushed into a glossy cloud on her shoulders, she put the brush down and left her room, leaving her robe behind. She approached his door, hand out to knock and to ask permission to enter but before she could, he yelled, "Gracie," his voice more a whine than a shout.

Hold your horses, she thought and grinned to herself.

Pushing the door open, she swept in. "Did you call me?" she asked and smiled brightly. He growled, looking down at the spilled tray. Then his eyes bobbed up, and flared with a strange light when he realized she was half dressed. He visibly gulped.

"Oh, you poor man," she purred and hustled over to his side, all the while thinking, *perfect, perfect, perfect*. Picking up the tray, she set it on the floor out of the way. "Here, let me take care of everything." Turning back to McLean, she grabbed the top edge of the wet blankets and yanked them off the bed onto the floor, leaving him lying in bed covered only by his cotton drawers and his bandages.

He yelped. Face flaming, his knees jerked up to hide his erection.

Surveying his long, lanky body, a surge of desire swept through her. She noted the white bandages around his thigh and a second bandage strapping his injured arm to his body. Her eyes zeroed in on his cotton drawers and the tent his erection created no amount of knee raising could hide.

It also didn't hide the red lines his fingernails left all over his body.

"You've been scratching," she declared, her eyes narrowing in dire warning.

"Damn it," he blustered. "I itch. I itch like a son of a gun. I can't help it."

Tapping a finger on her chin, she considered the idea for moment and then she smiled, an evil, wicked smile. "I warned you what I would do if you didn't stop scratching those scabs." Reaching up, she pulled out the drawstring holding the neck of her nightgown closed. Then she descended on McLean, grabbing his one good hand before he realized what she was doing and tying it to the bedpost over his head.

"Hey. Hey, what the hell are you doing?" Yanking on his arm, he attempted to get loose, tugging several times before apparently realizing his tugs only tightened the knot. Sagging onto his back, he gazed at the ceiling, his desire for her evident. He waited, his face showing his unease.

A surge of feminine power swept through Gracie followed by a hot tingle of desire. Even scarred, she loved everything about his body; the strong muscles of his legs, the swell of his masculine chest and the bulge of blue veins rising under the thin skin of his arms. She loved his graceful feet and hands and the cords standing out in his neck when he was angry.

Bending over him, she grabbed the string tying his drawers closed and yanked. He grunted, a muffled sound of surprise but with his sprained arm strapped down and the other tied to the bedpost, he was defenseless.

Hooking her thumbs under the edge of his drawers, she pulled them down to his knees. He winced, his body stiffening, and groaned. It was the first time she saw his erect manhood in the light and open to her perusal. It rose, straight, heavy and throbbing from a thicket of hair at the joining of his legs. She cocked her head, studying the way it widened at the head, noticing with avid curiosity the pearly bead of moisture gracing the tip. It took her breath away. And she wanted to touch it.

But she didn't. Instead, she asked, "Did I hurt you?" with a sly smile. "I hope not. I just want to take care of all those itchy spots for you, okay? I don't want you to suffer, after all."

All she got in response to her comment was a moan.

"All right. So long as I'm not hurting you." With a single motion, she stripped the drawers the rest of the way off, leaving him bare except for the bandages. Walking to the commode by the window, she picked up a small jar of balm and carried it back to the bed.

"This is going to make you feel all better." Sitting on the side of the mattress, she dipped a finger into the jar, scooped out a dollop of thick white cream and spread it onto the scabs on his legs. Round and round her fingers twirled, slowly, slowly rubbing, slowly spreading the cream into every nook and cranny of his leg. He moaned under his breath. The skin on his thigh twitched. His face twisted into an expression that was half ecstasy, half agony.

She hid her smile and scooped up another blob of cream for his chest. More rubbing, more spreading... more groaning. Lots of trembling and shaking.

His breath was whooshing in and out of his chest like he'd run five miles. More cream was spread on to his poor scabby arm, the one tied to the bedpost. She'd save the other arm for later when she changed the bandages.

One last dip into the jar and the cream was gone. She sat back, staring at her handiwork, staring at the magnificent body spread out in front of her. "Better?"

He squinched his eyes shut and bit his lip.

She tapped her chin. "Well, that's all I can do to make those itches go away. Now, the question is, what should I do about the other itch?"

His eyes popped open. "Jesus, Gracie, stop torturing me."

"Since you asked..." Leaning down, she laid her lips on Harold and kissed it... him.

His whole body leapt up off the mattress. "Jeeezus." His breath gusted out in great explosions of sound. "What are you doing?" he asked in a strangled whisper.

Looking up the length of his body, she answered, "I'm getting re-acquainted with Harold."

He groaned. Recognizing what his groan meant, a thrill jolted through her. Staring at his erect manhood, a heavy beat throbbed in her veins which made her breasts tingle and throb. The tender feminine flesh between her legs softened and slicked with moisture, preparing itself for his invasion. She ached for him.

She paused, staring at McLean lying flat on his back, hands tied in one fashion or another. Something was wrong with this picture. Shouldn't she be the one on her back?

"Hmmm," she murmured.

His eyes popped open. "What? What's wrong?"

Her gaze came up to meet his, a little abashed. She rolled her eyes. "I don't know what to do next," she admitted.

His head falling back onto his pillow, he laughed weakly. "Ride me," he rasped.

"Huh?" She frowned.

"Ride me," he gritted. "Straddle me like a horse and put me inside you." His cock twitched once, almost like it was beckoning her.

Her face flamed red. "Put you inside me?"

"Yes," he barked. "Get on. Mount up. Now." He sounded like he was in pain. And desperate.

Well, when you put it that way. Drawing her gown off over her head, she tossed it on the floor. She climbed onto the bed and threw a leg over his hips. Tight-lipped, he growled, "Take me in your hand and put me inside."

A little embarrassed, she took his manhood in one hand. He was hot, and velvety soft and hard at the same time and suddenly it didn't seem so difficult to do what he asked. She placed him at her entrance and lowered herself. She stretched. And burned. A good burning, an eager burning. Closing her eyes, she swiveled her hips.

He thrust upwards. She moved her hips in response, lightly moving the tip of him around her entrance. His head rolled back and the veins in his neck bulged.

Bending his knees, bracing his feet on the mattress, he surged into her, seating himself to the hilt. He gasped. "Move," he begged. "Please move."

She hesitated, sending him a questioning look.

"It's all you, Gracie. You're the one in control here. Do whatever you want. Whatever feels good." He thrust a bit with his hips, demonstrating his lack of mobility.

I'm in control. Me. Gracie Hart. I can do whatever I want. The idea made her nipples tighten and something deep inside spasm in total pleasure. She reached and placed her hand on McLean's furry chest. Spreading her fingers, she combed the dark hair. From his breastbone she stroked outward until she reached the deep rust of his nipples peeking out from the hair. The nipples were large and turgid, like hers when she was cold. She stroked a finger across one several times.

He shivered, his skin twitching, and moaned. "Gracie. Oh, God. Don't."

"You said I was in control." She smiled wickedly.

Closing his eyes, he swore, "God dammit all to hell." He took a deep breath. "Dammit, dammit, dammit." His hips bucked, touching a spot deep inside Gracie, and she lit up like a Roman rocket. Under her closed eyelids she saw oranges and reds and yellows and purples. Rising up on her knees, she sat down on McLean, hard.

He groaned. She groaned herself and rose up again.

It was warm in the room. Sweat ran down her sides and between her breasts. It shone on McLean's muscular torso. She could hear the sound of her rhythmic movements each time she came down on McLean's hard body, slapping in the quiet of the night, accompanied by their mutual moans of pleasure. Each thrust of his manhood stroked the sensitive lining of her core, sending pulses through her body in waves, each wave harder, tighter, more electric than the last. The skin on her face tightened.

Opening her eyes a crack, she studied her partner—her lover—with avid attention. His eyes were screwed shut, his lips stretched in a grimace, his head thrown back with the tendons of his neck tight ropes. His left hand gripped the cord tying him to the bed.

He bit his lip, panting, his chest rising and falling, a gleam of sweat highlighting his sculpted cheekbones. It was beautiful to watch. A beautiful man—her beautiful man—in the midst of passion. He opened his eyes a slit and gazed at her through his lashes, his eyes warm and a slight smile on his face as he labored in her body. The look sent sparks along her veins and the mainspring coiled inside her released, sending endless hot waves through her body.

She took a moment to enjoy the feeling, then leaned forward and untied his hand from the bedpost. "Now you're in control."

THE SUDDEN FLUSH OF Gracie's breasts, the widening of her pupils, the arch of her body as she eked out every moment of her release sent a surge of heat through him. His release awaited him, pressing at the base of his cock, but first Gracie. Gracie of the cinnamon dusted body. Gracie, of the slim, lithe limbs and a generosity pure and unadulterated. Gracie, the woman he loved. With his arm now free, he touched her everywhere, her belly, her breasts, her lovely face. He pushed into her, withholding his own release, and enjoyed the bliss of her emotions on her face as her body pushed into that final ecstasy.

With a sigh, she relaxed and fell limply on top of his chest.

The need to come burned. Thrusting up into her one last time inside her, he rolled her off and quickly withdrew. He came in seconds, wave after wave of ecstasy as he spilled onto the bedcovers with a long, low shout of completion.

She lay next to him, her body warm and moist, her breasts pressed against his stomach, her knee draped on his hip. Warmth flooded through him, unlike anything he'd ever experienced before, wonderful and painful in its intensity, and he realized he would never be the same.

Sliding to his side, he settled her head on his arm. The tension left her body, her breathing slow, and soon she was asleep. He kissed the top of her head then spent most of the night wondering what he did to deserve her.

Wondering how, after tonight, he would ever give her up.

The next day he was on his feet, creaking and groaning like an arthritic old man, but still, he was vertical rather than horizontal. Hannah was delighted to have her father back at last and dogged his footsteps during the day while he took care of a few light chores like putting a fresh coat of whitewash on the barn.

He worried about the amount of time elapsing but in a way, he was glad. Within a few days, he was able to go outside and start working on a few projects to fix up the house. He spent hours with his daughter, getting to know her better, deepening the bonds between them. She delighted in handing him nails and hammers and holding up fence slats while he nailed them to the crossbars. A frown of concentration on her small face, she wielded a small paintbrush, mimicking her father's motions as he stroked paint up and down the weathered boards of the barn.

The August heat was intense, and it was hot, sweaty work but he found he enjoyed it. Every day Hannah laughed a bit more, played a little longer, and became a bit more affectionate. He could see the walls she built around her emotions crumbling each day, bit by bit.

And he could sense himself changing from the man he'd become while in prison back to the man he'd been before.

In prison, fear and the misery and the despair had invaded his soul, poisoning his mind, and leeching his soul of lightness, infecting his days with bitterness and his nights with dark terrors. Now, day by day, the bitterness drained away as he spent time in the clear yellow Texas sun with his daughter. And with Gracie sleeping at his side, warm and naked, the night terrors disappeared. For the first time in years, he slept deeply and dreamlessly and awoke refreshed.

Of course, sleep was not all they did in his bed. While daytime meant discovering the depths of his daughter, the nights were astounding hours of uncovering the many layers of Gracie Hart. A creative writer, she was also innovative in bed, astonishing Mac with her imagination. Who could believe two people could do so many titillating things with a few pink hair ribbons.

Overall, the first few days after leaving his sickbed was ones filled with happiness. The sole fly in the ointment was the still unclear relationship between them. Every day, while he and Hannah worked together around the ranch, Gracie retreated to the parlor and wrote, filling reams of paper with her small, slanted script.

At the end of each day, while Gracie was in the kitchen cooking dinner, he would sneak into the parlor and stand, staring at the white sheets littering the desk, looking but never reading them. He'd run a finger over the surface of the paper, tracing her words, wondering what she was writing, and a sense of sadness and futility would overwhelm him. Was she writing the story that would set him free from the past she'd saddled him with? Or was she simply writing another Scar book that would ensure her future was guaranteed to continue, a future that didn't include him.

He wouldn't betray her trust by reading what she'd written but the question burned within; did she mean to leave him once she no longer needed him as her inspiration? He couldn't believe she would walk away from him now, not after all they had shared but he wasn't reassured when he remembered Valerie, who'd made passionate love to him the night before she'd run away with her lover.

Better than anyone, he was aware that ambition could be stronger than love, and that sex could be used to hide secret desires. In the end, it seemed easier to let things drift along, unchanged.

The day came when it was time to get back to real work. "I'm going to the south pasture to finish off the fence today," he told Gracie. Using his toast, he swabbed up the last of the sticky yellow egg yolk on his plate and stuck it into his mouth.

She frowned. "Oh. Do you have to? Do you think you should?"

He lifted one corner of his mouth in a wry grin. "I was almost done with it before the accident. It'll take me another day or two to finish. And I'm not likely to be that stupid or that clumsy again."

"But still..." Her voice trailed off.

"Gracie, I've got to do it. Unless I can afford to hire men to help, those fences are the only way I have of gathering a herd." He paused, gazing at his daughter. "And I need that herd."

Her lips tightened. A shadow darkened her brown eyes. He could see her anxiety, her reluctance to let him go but instead of protesting, she pasted on a smile. "Of course. I understand." Standing, she cleared the plates from the table and carried them to the sink. The rattle and clink of the stoneware plates filled the air.

Standing, Mac shoved a last piece of toast into his mouth and walked into the hallway where he gathered his hat. He hated the idea that he was distressing her but without those cows, there wouldn't be enough money to buy the horses he wanted. Without the horses, his long-term prospects for success were dismal.

He walked out the door without a word, hoping this was not the day she decided to leave him.

Chapter Twenty

Spreading her legs wide, Gracie lifted the hem of her dress. Ugh. It was too hot, and she couldn't bear it. She flapped her skirt, trying to create a draft under her clothing and cool off her legs, but it was a futile effort. There was no denying it. August in Texas was August in Texas, which meant it was hellishly hot. She should be in the parlor, working on the second installment of her new series starring her new hero Pecos Smith but it was simply too hot to be indoors.

Her eyes burning, she rested the back of her head against the decorative railing surrounding the front porch and let her mind drift while watching Hannah and Gus race around the yard, both of them streaked in mud from their soaking in the horse trough. If only she were still childish enough to climb into the cooling water with them.

She checked the watch pinned to her bodice, aware without looking it was getting close to suppertime and soon McLean would be home. Even tired, a thrill of excitement sizzled through her. He'd ride back in, hot, sweaty and exhausted, as he had for the last week, pretending there was nothing special about his homecoming.

As she did every day now, Hannah would run to greet him, help him put Horse away and, while Gracie put the finishing touches on their meal, the two of them would sit together on the kitchen porch reading.

After setting the last of the dishes on the table, she would instruct Hannah to run and bring up the jug of lemonade kept in the coolness of the root cellar. Hannah's feet would clatter on the wooden stairs leading down into the cellar.

In the kitchen, McLean always used the time to reach for Gracie, pulling her hungry body towards his, wrapping a strong arm around her back to fit her curves against his lean body to take advantage of Hannah's brief absence. Then he would put his lips on hers, tasting her mouth, tugging on her lower lip with his teeth before moving down her neck to her breasts. The heat of his mouth, wetting her through the cotton of her dress always sent a thrill through her.

Thinking about it excited Gracie, and she sat up, flushed and bothered by her daydreams, to find McLean standing in front of her, back from his hard day in the pastures. His eyes smoldered, his pupils reflecting the orange fire of the early evening sun and smiled knowingly.

"Fall asleep?" he asked, his voice low, his eyelids sliding down to hide his burning gaze.

Something deep inside Gracie responded, igniting into flames at the sensuality in his voice. Licking her lips, she arched her back, thrusting the tips of her aroused nipples into prominence through the thin cotton of her dress and stared at his crotch to see his trousers ballooning out in front.

"You witch," he marveled, his mouth twitching in amusement. "I'll get you for this."

Rising to her feet on the porch step so they were on the same level, she peered at him from under her lashes. "I certainly hope so. I've counted the hours."

He shook his head. "Hannah," he called over his shoulder, still holding her gaze with his eyes. "Come on, suppertime." Narrowing his eyes, he whispered for her ears alone. "And later, you and I will have our own meal, mm?"

She blushed, heat spreading in waves over her body, embarrassing moisture gathering between her legs. Turning, she marched up the stairs. "Only if I'm still hungry," she snipped.

"You will be," he murmured. "I'll make sure of it."

She counted on it.

He winked. "Oh, by the way, I'm going into town for the day tomorrow. I have some business to attend to. If we need any supplies give me a list of what I should get."

She raised her eyebrows in surprise. "Tomorrow? Tomorrow's a Thursday."

Swallowing a mouthful of hash browned potatoes, he answered, "I think I've rounded up whatever cattle I'm going to be able to." He sat back, smiling with satisfaction. "I've got over forty head in the north pasture so time to start looking for a buyer."

She laid her fork down to gape at him in surprise. "Over forty? That's wonderful." A flush of pleasure for Mac and his success filled her. He'd worked his rearend off this summer with very little going right for him and he deserved his success.

They spent the next few minutes discussing how he planned to find a buyer and the price he hoped he'd get while she cleared the dirty dishes off the table and carried them to the sink. Afterwards, he and Hannah walked back out onto the front porch to finish the book he'd read to her for the last week. After stopping in the kitchen to steal a kiss, McLean took his daughter upstairs to put her to bed then returned downstairs again to join Gracie in the kitchen.

His arm snaked around her waist. She leaned back against the warm, hard body of the man she loved, closing her eyes in contentment. The ridge of his erection nudged her backside, making it clear where his mind was. A gust of hot breath warned her moments before his tongue traced the line of her jaw.

"Mmmmm. You smell good. You taste good," he murmured.

Her knees weak, she relaxed against his body. "Roast chicken and green beans," she muttered back.

"No. Definitely Gracie," he stated and turned her to face him. Lowering his head, he pressed his mouth to hers, running his tongue along the seam of her lips, sipping and biting, arousing them both until they were sweaty and panting.

He raised his head, a gleam in his eyes. "I've got you where I want you now, wench. You're in my power." With a chuckle, he hoisted her up to sit on the edge of the kitchen table. He locked his hand around her wrist and placed her hand on the firm bulge between his legs.

"Hmmm..." Her head lolled back. "McLean? Uh, Hannah? Are you sure she's asleep?"

He sighed. "Right." Pulling away, he strode to the door, dragging a chair with him. With a screech, he wedged it under the doorknob.

Within seconds, he was back between her legs. "Now, where was I?"

She undid a button on the front of his trousers and slipped her hand inside, stroking the soft skin of his penis. "Here, I think."

His hips jerked in reaction. "Right. How could I forget. He pulled her skirt up around her hips and spent a moment delving under her petticoats looking for the opening in her drawers. He unfastened the rest of his buttons.

"All right, woman. It's time to pay the piper," he growled and drove into her.

Wrapping her legs around his hips, locking him into her body, she drew his head down for a kiss and whispered in his ear. "Oh, yes," she said in a husky voice, running the tip of her tongue around the whorls of his ear. "I sincerely hope so."

At her words, a shiver shook McLean's body and his thrusts strengthened, pounding into Gracie with a driving force that wiped out any thoughts of further discussion.

Even though he pulled out at the last minute, the climax was better than any story she'd ever read.

HEAT RADIATED IN WAVES from the ground, mingling with the dust horses and men kicked up in the street. The sun glinted off the windows of the telegraph office as McLean pushed open the door and entered, his shoulders hunched, anticipating another unpleasant confrontation with the nasty, pinch-faced clerk.

"Mr. McLean," the clerk exclaimed when he saw who entered. "How are you today, sir? What can I do for you?"

Mac tipped his hat back, staring at the man. "Uh... I need to send a few telegrams."

"Of course, of course, whatever you say," the man said in obsequious tones, an oily toad-eating smile on his face.

Mac's suspicions deepened. What was the little toad-licker up to, he wondered. Why was the man being so polite? Even though he didn't trust him, Mac handed over his hand-written messages, albeit reluctantly. Taking them, the clerk sat at his desk and began tapping on his key, sending Mac's telegrams to their destinations. When he was done, he stood and handed back the notes. "There you are, Mr. McLean. All done, right and tight."

"Mmm," he grunted. "What's it going to cost me?"

The clerk beamed. "Oh, consider this one on the house."

"On the house? I don't think so." He pulled a bill from his wallet and slapped it on the counter. The clerk frowned, picked it up, and tried to shove it back into Mac's hand. Mac raised his hands to shoulder level, putting his hands out of reach.

"But sir," the man whined. Leaning over the counter, the clerk tried to push the bill into Mac's shirt pocket.

"Dammit. Stop." Mac shoved the hand away.

The skinny clerk got a mulish expression on his face. "No. It's on the house, like I said."

Mac slammed the man's hand down on the counter, money still clenched in his knobby fist. "Keep the goddamned money," he yelled, and walked out, fuming. What the hell was the matter with the man, acting like they were best friends or something all of a sudden? He and the weasel weren't friends, never were and never would be.

He stomped across the street to finish the rest of his errands. He was still fretting when he arrived at the general store. Facing the wooden double doors leading into the store, thinking about Mayor Potter waiting on the other side, his shoulders tensed, and his belly clenched into a knot.

After taking a breath to steady his nerves, he stepped through. The dimness hid his entrance for a moment; then heads spun around, eyes focused on him, and a hum of whispering rose from the customers inside the store.

Hell, you'd think in a town this size people would find something else to talk about besides him. Narrowing his eyes in preparation for the confrontation he anticipated, he strode up to the counter where he saw Potter talking to another man. All his chubby chins wobbled like pudding when Potter's head swung around to face Mac.

"Mr. McLean," the storekeeper beamed. "Welcome. Welcome to Potter's Mercantile Store. What can we do for you today?" He spread his arms wide, hypothetically offering up his whole store.

Mac's chin practically hit his chest. He blinked, tempted to lay the back of his hand under his chin and close his mouth. How...? Why...? What was going on?

"What are you up to, Potter?" he growled, suspicious of the man's motives.

Potter's piggy little eyes widened, and he jerked back in affront, his chins bouncing. "Why, Mr. McLean, I have no idea what you mean."

"See. That's what I'm talking about," Mac growled, jabbing a forefinger at Potter's spongy chest. "You're being nice to me."

The storekeeper's eyes narrowed into tiny shotgun pellets, shining out from within the puffy creases around his eyes. "Nothing is going on, McLean. I only wanted to offer you my help." His face reddened, a sign he was struggling with his obvious temper.

"Right."

"Hmph, well, Mr. McLean, if you're going to be like that. Do your shopping..."

Mac curled his lip in a burst of self-satisfaction. This was more like it.

Potter harrumphed, "... and... and have one of my clerks total it up when you're done." He waddled away, his rear end jiggling like a bowl of aspic jelly.

A husband and wife approached. The man tipped his Stetson. "McLean," he acknowledged, the corner of his mouth tilted up in a slight smile. The wife ducked her head shyly and murmured a good morning before they exited. Mac scratched his head and frowned. What in the hell...

Something odd was going on, he just couldn't figure out what. He tried to force this morning's strange events from his mind and walked towards the shelves holding a variety of cans, startling every time someone greeted him. At his side, someone—he had no idea who—handed him a wicker basket to put his purchases in. He blinked and accepted it before he had time to think.

"Thanks," he muttered, and dropped a few items into the basket before moving on to the next shelf.

A pretty young blonde dressed in yellow dimity smiled at him. Raising a hand, she tapped a well-manicured finger on a sack of flour.

"This one," she said in low tones, batting her long eyelashes at him. "It's the best quality."

He reached for the flour but stopped when the young woman sent him an enticing glance and did a two-fingered walk up his arm to his shoulder with her hand. His heart thumping, he took a step back.

"My, my, Mr. McLean, you look just the way you're described in those stories, tall and handsome and heroic-looking," she purred and flicked a finger along his jaw. "My name's Sarah Hacker. And anytime you want help shopping, just know that I'm available."

He dropped the basket on the floor with a thud, his fingers having lost all feeling, staring at the women as if she were a rattlesnake. Good God almighty, had the world lost its mind? Spinning on his heels, he sped out the door of the general store and practically ran down the street to Rheingold's office.

With a bang, he threw open the door. "What the hell is going on in this town?"

Oskar jerked awake, almost tumbling out of the rocking chair he'd fallen asleep in. When he recovered himself, he settled back and cocked his head.

"Hello to you, too," the man chuckled, his eyes crinkling in amusement.

Mac threw himself into an empty chair and ran his hands through his hair, leaving it standing on end all over his head.

"Yeah, yeah. Hello," he muttered in distraction. "Now tell me what the hell is going on here?" he repeated.

"Going on, how?"

Furious—and completely confused—by the morning's events, he growled, "Everybody's being *nice* to me. That tight-assed weasel at the telegraph office didn't want me to pay, a damned fine-looking blonde flirted with me, and Potter... Potter... welcomed me to his store... well, he sort of did, but I got kind of snitty about it and he took it back. What the hell is going on?" he said in frustration.

The smirk on Oskar's face widened, lifting the ends of his mustache till the tips almost touched his sideburns. He reached into a drawer and pulled something out. "I guess you haven't seen this." He threw the object into Mac's lap.

"GRACIE." THE BELLOW echoed through the house.

She jumped, splattering cake batter down the front of her dress. She swiped at it, leaving little chocolate prints smeared across her chest. *This is what I get for not wearing an apron. I wonder if McLean will lick it off.* Grinning, she turned to face him when he entered. Uh oh, he looked mad. Her grin faded.

"Where's Hannah?" he demanded, his eyes sweeping the kitchen.

Puzzled at the angry tone in his voice, she answered, "I put her to bed early. She had a sunburn and didn't feel well."

He gritted, "Why didn't you tell me?"

Immediately her mind replayed the last week, trying to recall anything she hadn't told him. Stumped, she grimaced and shrugged her shoulders. "I forgot?" she answered, stalling for time.

"How could you forget." McLean demanded. "I understood that we had an agreement, and I can't figure out how you could forget to tell me about something this important." Reaching inside his shirt, he pulled out a magazine. He held it out to Gracie.

Craning her neck, she peered at the cover. "Oh," she squealed, grabbing the magazine with both hands. "Look, McLean. There's your story." She held it under his nose and punched the cover-blurb with a forefinger. "See. *The End of a Legend.*"

Thrilled, she gazed at the image of McLean she drew for the cover. "It's published. I'm so excited. Aren't you excited?" Clasping it to her chest, she danced around the kitchen then, throwing her arms around his neck, she stretched up on her tiptoes and kissed him.

He didn't kiss her back. Settling back on her heels, she tapped her chin, puzzled. "Why aren't you excited? This is what you wanted." She didn't understand his attitude. Wasn't she the one who should be depressed since the completion of the book meant she met the terms of their agreement which meant—hypothetically—it was time to go home? Not that she had any intention of going. Still, if anyone should be depressed it was her. He looked away.

"I guess I am excited," he explained slowly. "I just... I don't... I thought... I'd get to read it before you sent it in... approve it, sort of. I guess." He shrugged.

She eyed him. How like a man. Give them what they want, and they don't want it anymore. "Have you read it yet?"

He shook his head.

Hands on hips, she snorted. "Well, read it before you say anything." Irritated, she slapped the magazine into his middle. He grabbed it before it could fall. Putting her back on him, she walked away and left him standing flat-footed in the middle of the kitchen. After a moment of uncertainty, he left the room and retreated to the parlor to read.

Halfway through the story, it got too dark in the room to see the words on the page. Still reading, he rose and lit a lamp. Sitting again, he finished the story by its flickering yellow light, then leaning back in the chair, he slowly leafed through the magazine again, rereading a passage here and there before closing the pages to sit back in his chair, unconsciously rubbing his hand across the cover of the magazine. Her story was beautiful, filled with insight, compassion, and a patent belief in his innocence. She hadn't even killed him off, instead she had him changing his name and traveling west to live another life.

He didn't dare think it, but love seemed to leap off the pages of her story. A swell of emotion filled his chest, closing his throat. His eyes burned, and he blinked. Then a sound made him spin around. She stood framed in the doorway, shifting from foot to foot, twisting her hands in her skirt. She watched him, pleading in her eyes.

"Come here," he said gruffly. One slow step at a time, she approached until she stood in front of him, their knees touching. Taking her hand in his, he pulled her down onto his lap and wrapped one arm around her. With his free hand, he unpinned her hair, letting it flow down her back and stroked the long strands.

"It wasn't what I expected."

She tensed at his words. He tipped her head against his shoulder, swallowing against the lump in his throat. "Why did you write this? How did you write this?"

She bit her lip. "That's what I do... I write. It's who I am."

Who she was. A writer. A woman with a career.

The memory of how much he had loved Valerie filled his mind, and fear filled his heart. Just like Gracie, Valerie wanted other things, things he couldn't give her. How long before Gracie's ambitions outweighed her affection for him? How long would she wait before she, too, left him?

Other men seemed to possess something that made their women stick to them like glue, faithful for all their lives. Whatever it was, he didn't seem to have it. Sadly for him, it would be only a matter of time before, like Valerie, Gracie realized it.

Wearily, he closed his eyes. "I have to go out of town for a few days," he said, his voice rough.

She sat up. "Why? Where are you going? Why do you have to go?"

"I found a buyer, one who raises both horses and cattle. It's possible we can work out a trade, my forty head of cattle for ten or twelve horses, but I've got to go talk to him and see what we can work out. If we come to an agreement, I'll pick out my stock, and he and some of his hands will return with me to drive the cattle back." One corner of his mouth lifted in mute apology.

"All right," she murmured. "I think I understand."

"Will you be all right while I'm gone?"

"Of course. Why wouldn't I be?" she responded. She lifted herself off his lap and walked upstairs.

"I'M DEPENDING ON YOU to take good care of Gracie, sweet pea, 'cause you know how she is. Us McLeans have to keep her out of trouble, right?" Picking Hannah up in his arms, he gave her a kiss on the tip of her chin. Hannah beamed, nodding and patting his cheeks with her palms. He grinned back, touching his forehead to hers. Looking at her smiling and laughing, so different from how she was at the beginning of the summer, his heart was near to bursting.

"Do your chores and help Gracie out and there might be a surprise for you when I get back." Hannah gasped in delight and bounced in his arms. He gave her another hug and transferred her to Gracie's arms.

"I shouldn't be gone any longer than three or four days," he told the woman he loved. He searched the warm depths of her eyes, hoping to see some sign she returned his love.

She ducked her head, playing with a thread on the cuff of her dress.

"Sheriff Rheingold is going to come out in a day or so to see how you're doing. If you need anything, tell him, all right?"

She grimaced, worry leaving deep creases in her forehead. He wanted to grab her and kiss her senseless, but her crossed arms and frown warned him away. They stood in awkward silence, waiting for the other to speak, to say what was in their hearts, but neither did.

With a self-conscious laugh, he turned away and mounted Horse.

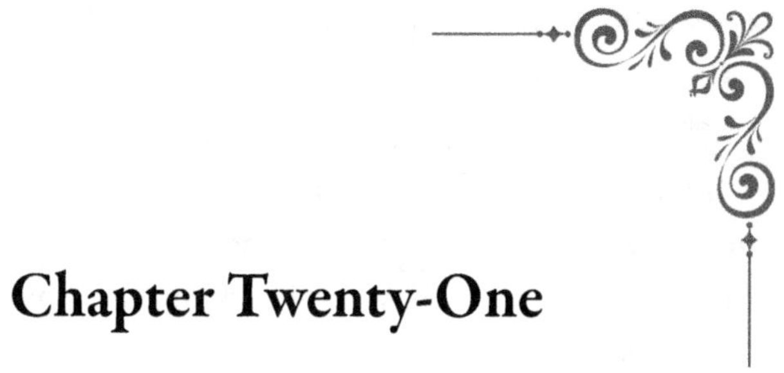

Chapter Twenty-One

"Don't nobody move. This is a stickup." The threatening words echoed in the dim recesses of the general store. Chaos erupted. A woman screamed and fell to the floor in a faint, knocking an entire shelf of cans over with a clatter. Men cursed, more shelves fell over, a child wailed.

Cletus smirked. He loved this part of his job, terrifying people, making them shit their pants with fear. The fact his puny frame—barely a hundred pounds when soaking wet—and his narrow face with its weak chin and round, lash-less eyes wouldn't scare a duck never occurred to him. He'd had more fun and made more money in the last year since hooking up with Dexter Fox than ever in his life.

Eyes narrowed over the top of his bandana, he let his gaze shift around the store, keeping his pistol aimed at the cowering crowd gathered near the back counter while Dexter paced back and forth in front of them.

"Now, y'all are gonna do like I say and everyone's gonna be all right," Dexter snarled, jabbing the barrel of his gun into the neck of a tall, blond cowboy who looked ready to challenge him. His Adam's apple bobbing, the cowboy backed down.

Hot diggity dog, Cletus thought in admiration, that Dexter was one mean sumbitch. Proud to be part of the team, he stood taller, stretching up to his full five feet and shared a gleeful glance with the third member of their trio, Buck Pardue. Lifting his bandana with the tip of his pistol to expose the lower half of his face, Buck grinned and raised a thumbs-up gesture.

Cletus thrust out a thumb in response.

From inside his vest, Dexter pulled out a red bag made from quilted satin. "All right, folks. Let me tell ya how this is gonna work. I'm gonna pass the pretty little sack around, the one my sainted mama made special for me, and you folks is gonna fill it up with goodies."

One of the women in the group whimpered, leaning against her husband for support. A burly man dressed like a farmer looked angry, leaning forward on the balls of his feet, waiting for an opportunity to attack. Another man in a dark suit leaned to the side and whispered—loud enough for the entire world to hear, "Don't do anything foolish, Jeff. Someone will get hurt," into the farmer's ear.

After a moment, the farmer gave a curt nod, but continued to look daggers at the three men with guns.

The rest of the group, two men, three young women, and a young boy huddled towards the back, the women shivering and whimpering.

"Buck, get to work," Dexter barked, scaring the shit out of Cletus it was so sudden. He jumped, banging his head on the counter he'd stooped under while trying to steal a couple of soggy crackers from a wooden crate stored under the tablecloth. Rubbing his head, he watched Buck dart forward, panting like an over-eager mutt wanting to please his master.

Cletus curled his lip. Buck just didn't have no class, not like him and Dexter. Called back to duty, he retrained his pistol on their victims, forgotten in his efforts to swipe a cracker, and screwed his face up, trying for that Dexter Fox mean look. As ordered, Buck walked around taking wallets, emptying pockets of loose cash and watches, and cutting the strings off the ladies' hand bags. The holdup victims gave over their valuables without a word.

Bored that no one was fighting back, Cletus's eyed the shelves for anything portable enough to steal without too much trouble and without alerting Dexter since Dexter didn't like it when his gang did things without his say-so. So he meandered up and down the rows, until he saw a glass case with lots of good stuff inside. He opened it and selected a pocketknife with a carved bone casing.

Not bad. Pulling the blade out, he tested it sharpness. Damn! He stuck his bleeding thumb in his mouth, catching the attention of the cowboy, who sneered. Closing the knife, he stuck it in his pocket before going back to browsing. Next a gold pocket watch caught his eye. Shee-it. This was real nice. Darting a glance at Dexter to make sure he was unobserved; Cletus hooked the chain to his belt and dropped the watch down his pants. It landed in his drawers. He kept walking, liking the coolness of real gold against his balls.

A shelf with books and magazines caught his eye. Hot damn. Maybe his favorite serial, *The Abeline Kid*, had a new episode. He liked that series a lot. It had lots of gun fights so's he could pick up good ideas, and great stories where the Kid—a tough hombre Cletus aspired to be like—always won, but most especially he liked the fact there were lots of pictures, seeing as he didn't read so good and Dexter wasn't mostly willing to read to him.

Bending down, he studied the titles, trying to pick out the words. He scanned the rows, moving past the ladies' magazines, the farmer's magazines—stupid sodbusters, what for did they need a magazine about dirt—before finding what he was looking for.

The Westerner. He picked it up, sounding out the words on the cover, disappointed to find no mention of *The Abilene Kid*. He turned to the table of contents inside. Nope, not there neither. Well, shit on a shingle. Now he was madder than hell. They'd said in last month's issue the next installment would be out in the August issue, and it said right on the cover August and they'd outright lied, those egg-sucking varmints.

Slamming the cover closed, Cletus stretched to put it back on the shelf when he found his attention caught by the drawing on the cover. He cocked his head to the right, then cocked it to the left. Well, hell, if that didn't look like that there Scar McLean, the one books was written about which he didn't read them 'cause there were too many words. What was Scar's pitcher doing on a magazine? That lady author always wrote about Scar McLean in books.

Picking the magazine back up, he read aloud, slowly and laboriously, "The End—of—a—Legend. The Vin—dee—ca—shun of Scar McLean." Wow. Quickly turning to the page indicated, he skimmed a few pages, picking out words here and there he recognized.

A name leaped off the page at him. Dexter Fox. Wait a minute. Dexter was in a magazine? Backing up a few words to get a running start at it, so to speak, he read, "*and the bad man, Dexter Fox, was shot down in the streets like he*...uh...uh," Cletus had to sound out the last word, "...uh...*dee-served.*"

An outraged squawk erupted from his mouth. Son of a bitch. They done kilt Dexter in this here story. "Dex," he hollered, waving the magazine. Dexter threw a quick, irate glance over his shoulder. "Dex. Dex. You gotta come look," he yelled and rushed forward to thrust the magazine into Dexter's hand.

"God damn son of a bitch. You stoopid maroon. Are you trying to get us kilt?" Dexter ranted, grabbing Cletus by the collar and shaking him.

His eyes bulging, Cletus shook the magazine in Dexter's face and gurgled, "Bud look, Dexter. Y'all is dead...in dish here story." He coughed, gasping for breath when Dexter dropped him to grab up the magazine.

Dexter's eyes swiftly scanned the cover titles, ignoring the victims muttering in the corner and then turned to the story inside. After a moment a bellow of rage filled the air.

He slapped Cletus over the head with the magazine. "Why the hell didn't you show me this earlier?" he demanded, again whacking Cletus, this time on the ear. Cletus ducked, trying to evade the blows.

Shoving the magazine into the front of his shirt, Dexter snatched the sack filled with loot from Buck's hand. "Come on, you stoopid assholes, let's ride. Someone's going to pay for this."

He charged out of the store with Cletus and Buck scratching their heads and trailing behind.

AS PROMISED, SHERIFF Rheingold dropped by the days after McLean's departure. Gracie invited him into the kitchen for a glass of lemonade, delighted to have speaking company. The sheriff pursed his mouth, an accusatory look in his eyes.

"Well, shoot, Miss Hart, I guess I can tell from looking at your face you didn't listen a lick to what I said, did you?" He pulled his earlobe in disgust.

It was obvious what he was talking about although it didn't stop Gracie from batting her eyes at the sheriff like she had no idea what he meant. She'd discovered that the topic of sex and women seemed to top the list of men's not-open-for-discussion topics but, glory, woman had to have some fun somehow, so she smiled and said, "I have no idea what you mean."

Rheingold's salt and pepper mustache twitched. "So you're going to play the game that way, are you?"

Dipping her head to hide the amusement in her eyes, Gracie took a sip of her lemonade and changed the subject. "So how are things in town, Sheriff? McLean said a few people spoke to him last week."

Heaving a gusty sigh, Oskar shook his head and surrendered. He answered her questions about the doings in town, pausing long enough to greet Hannah, who'd entered looking for a drink and stayed to crawl up on the Sheriff's lap. After a few minutes Gracie switched topics again, wanting to see what the reaction of the town was to her story and was pleased to hear it was primarily responsible for the greetings McLean experienced on his last visit. She hadn't heard, however, about his reaction to that change, how it disconcerted and angered him, so she got a chuckle out of hearing the story.

"Would you like some more lemonade?" she asked, noticing the sheriff's glass was empty.

He held his glass up for more.

"Hannah, honey, would you run down into the cellar and bring up some more sugar and a lemon for me?" Hannah slid off the sheriff's lap, and flinging open the cellar door, bounded down the stairs. A few minutes passed while she and the sheriff talked; then Hannah marched in through the front door, carrying a cloth bag and dragging Gus along behind her on a rope.

Oskar frowned, glancing with a puzzled expression at the still open cellar door and at the front door where Hannah re-entered. "What? How...? She went...?"

Laughing, Gracie explained, "There are a set of storm doors on the side wall of the house in urgent need of repair. She wiggles through the cracks in the doors and then runs around to the front porch to scare me. It's a game she likes to play." With a nod and a grin of mischief, Hannah picked up Gus and dumped the struggling half-grown dog into Oskar's lap.

"Well now, will you lookie here," Oskar exclaimed to Hannah, picking up the squirming dog with a feigned look of astonishment on his face. "Why, he's nearly grown. And look how healthy and happy he is. You've done a fine job taking care of him, missy." Leaning against his denim-clad knee, Hannah beamed up at her friend while she stroked one of Gus's long furry ears.

They chatted for a few more minutes about this and that until Oskar stood, putting his hat back on. "Well, it's getting kinda late, and I've got to be heading back." Together, they all walked outside to where his horse waited, where he said, "I don't want to interfere in your business, ma'am, but I do want to remind you of our deal." He stared down at her from his great height, one hand resting atop Hannah's head.

Chewing on her lip, Gracie took one of his large hands in hers and shook it. "Of course. I made a promise and I never break my promises. When McLean comes back, we'll either get married or I'll go home to Austin," she vowed.

After studying her face for a minute, Rheingold said, "All right, I'll trust you. And I hope you get what you want, young lady. In the meantime, if you need anything at all, you know where to find me." With a final chuck under the chin for Hannah, he mounted his horse and rode off.

SOMEONE KNOCKED AT the door. She lifted her eyes from the torn shirt she was repairing. She frowned. It was two days since the sheriff visited and since McLean should be home tomorrow, she wondered why the sheriff was back.

Well, it didn't matter. Good company was always welcome. Standing, she walked to the front door and opened it. A beefy hand hit her in the chest, shoving her backwards. She fell with a bone-rattling thud.

"Where's McLean?" the man snarled, pinning her to the floor with one worn boot planted on her chest. Staring up at the man's pale, mean eyes and the hard eyes of the two other men who stood on either side of him, her throat dried up in fear.

The heel jammed harder onto her abdomen, forcing the air from her lungs. "I asked you a question. Where's McLean?

Her heart pounding, she wheezed, "He... he... he's gone. Why?"

Removing his foot, the man leaned down, grabbed Gracie by the hair and yanked her to her feet. She screamed with pain.

The man thrust his face into hers, his mouth a cruel sneer, his eyes cold and dead. "I want the goddammed bitch what wrote that story in that there magazine and made me the laughin' stock of Texas. I already done went to Austin, and she ain't there no more so McLean's gotta know where she is." The other two men, obviously members of his gang, grinned in agreement.

At his words, ice congealed in her veins. Dear heavens, did he mean her? Why? What had she done? What was he talking about? And what was she going to do? McLean was gone, and she was here alone... except for Hannah. Remembering the child playing out back, her fear tripled. Dear God, she had to protect Hannah.

Twisting his hand tighter into her hair, the leader dragged her into the kitchen and looked around, even opening the pantry door to search. "Cletus, go on down to the basement and see if he's hidin' out there." Cletus, an elf of a man with dirty dishwater blond hair, clattered downstairs into the basement.

"He's not home, I tell you," she whispered, terrified. Her answer was an agonizing jerk on her hair. She gasped in pain.

A hollow sounding voice echoed up the stairwell. "Ain't no one down here, Dexter."

Dexter. Her eyes widened. Jupiter. Dexter Fox. The real Dexter Fox, not her fictional Dexter Fox. Her jaw sagging, she gaped at him in horrified fascination. How had she not recognized those yellow eyes? The only explanation was, five years had passed, and somehow, the image of her fictious Dexter Fox had replace the memory of the real man.

Five years in which she'd written about bad men or least men she believed were bad. She'd believed McLean was a bad man but now, staring into the soulless eyes of the man gripping her hair, she realized she'd never truly seen bad before. This man was worse than bad—he was evil. He would kill her and Hannah and McLean—when he came home—and give it no more thought than if he'd stepped on a scorpion. Her stomach lurched like she was about to be ill.

Her mind in a sick haze, she almost didn't feel the pain when he dragged her from the kitchen and back into the hallway. He gestured for one of his men—the non-Cletus one—to go upstairs and search the bedrooms. It didn't take him long to accomplish and he soon returned.

"Nobody there, boss," he said, his small eyes sliding up and down her body.

Dexter threw her against a wall. "Goddammit, bitch. Where the hell is he?"

Her shoulder throbbing from where it hit the wall, she sobbed, "I told you, he's gone. Check the barn. You'll see. His horse is gone." She hoped and prayed that if the outlaws realized McLean was away, out of their reach, they would grow impatient and leave.

A nod of Fox's head sent the same outlaw—the one with the creepy-crawly eyes—out the door at a run. Like the last time, he returned within minutes with a negative shake of his head. "She's right, boss. Only one horse in the barn but there's bedding for two horses. The second stall ain't been cleaned, and the manure's a couple days old."

Backing her up against the wall, Fox wrapped his fingers around her neck, forcing her up onto her tiptoes. "Let's you and me start over, lady. First off, who the hell are you?"

Her mind recoiled. Her mother accused her of not having any common sense but in this case, she didn't need any common sense. She knew for a fact that if she told this man she was Gracie Hart, she'd be dead in a heartbeat. If there was ever a time to lie, this was it.

"I'm M-m-mr. McLean's housekeeper." She started to volunteer her name but stopped. For once in her life she decided to shut her mouth while she was ahead.

Fox watched her, searching her face for signs she was lying and then decided to let it go for the moment. He was more concerned right now about McLean.

"Where'd he go?" he snarled.

She shrugged. She honestly had no idea where he was. He hadn't given her any details other than he was going west towards Austin. The fingers tightened, and she choked, gasping for air. "T—t—to b-b-b-buy horses," she squeaked. Lack of air was making her vision dim and dark clouds swirl around in her head. Stretching higher on her toes to ease the grip of Fox's hand, she glanced to the side and her heart dropped into her stomach.

Hannah stood framed in the kitchen doorway, holding her rag doll squished against her chest, an expression of concern on her face. Gracie gasped before she could stop herself. All three men swung around.

"Son of a bitch." Dexter swore. "Grab the kid before she gets away." It was a moment's work for one of his men to scoop up a startled Hannah and carry her back into the kitchen. Fox dragged Gracie into the kitchen as well and pushed Gracie into a seat and leaned over her, his mouth pulled up in an evil sneer. "Whose kid is that?" he gritted through his teeth, his pale gaze burning through Gracie like acid.

"Mine," she answered quickly. "Hannah's mine. McLean allows me to bring her while I clean." She held her breath in fear, praying he would believe her.

She could see doubt still smoldering in the back of his mind, but he put it aside, again focused on McLean. "How long till McLean comes back?" he asked in his one-track fashion, baring his teeth.

"T—t—two, three days," she lied and prayed she'd think of some plan before tomorrow.

Fox sat in one of the other chairs and fixed his colorless eyes on Gracie's chest. "No problem. We'll just wait." He smiled.

TEARS HOVERED AT THE back of her throat, always ready to spring from her eyes unbidden. Exhaustion swamped her. A day had passed and she'd gone hours without sleep, too terrified to shut her eyes for more than a few seconds. The first time she did, she jerked awake to find Dexter's hand on her knee, under her skirt.

She'd screamed, and he walked away with a laugh, leering over his shoulder, "Later, housekeeper. When I've got nothin' else on my mind."

The next time she'd slept, she'd opened her eyes to see Hannah sitting on one of the other men's lap—the one everyone called Buck—who was smiling down at her.

Gracie shrieked, "Hannah. Get over here right now," startling Buck enough he let Hannah go. Hannah jumped off the man's lap and rushed to join Gracie.

Hannah clung to Gracie, the two of them protecting each other, although being together was slim protection. The looks thrown their way by the three outlaws told her if one on them wanted either her or Hannah, nothing she did would stop them.

When dinnertime came, Fox ordered her to fix food, which she prepared with Hannah hanging onto her skirt while she moved back and forth in the kitchen. Shaking, she got up enough nerve to ask if one of them could take Gus some table scraps. Cletus left for a few minutes. Night fell, Buck and Dexter went upstairs to sleep, and left her and Hannah alone with Cletus.

She stayed awake most of the night, leaning against the wall, holding a shivering Hannah in her arms, trying to calm her with words of comfort while whispering her father would save them, that he wouldn't let anything bad happen to them, and everything would be all right. Once when their guard's back was to her, she whispered in Hannah's ear, "If you get a chance to escape, run. Run fast like the wind and get Sheriff Rheingold." Hannah didn't react to the message, and Gracie couldn't tell if she'd heard or understood.

Morning came—the day McLean was due to return home—and she still didn't have a plan. Her terror increased.

"MR. GRUBER, I WANT to thank you for your help. And the good deal." Mac shook the older man's hand with a self-deprecating grin, aware he'd gotten a better bargain than he probably deserved. Ten top quality quarter horses that, when trained, were worth fifty dollars a head—easy—for forty head of cattle.

The older man grinned back, his bushy sideburns standing out from his jaws like squirrels' tails, revealing a few tobacco-stained teeth. "Oh, twarn't nothin', son. I bin where you are onst and someone give me a helpin' hand so I always said if I could return the favor, I sure 'nough would." He hawked and spat a hunk of chewing tobacco to the side. "Wouldn'ta made it without that helpin' hand."

Setting his hat on the back of his head, Mac watched Gruber's ranch hands pushing and prodding the cattle he'd sold to the rancher, hi-yaying and whacking the cows' butts to get them moving out of the fenced pasture. He shifted his gaze to the ten fine quarter horses he'd already turned loose, his chest swelling with pride at what he'd accomplished. Facing the ranch owner, he smiled again and said, "So I guess you want me to pass the favor along someday if I can."

Gruber stuck another chaw in his mouth and chewed. After masticating the chaw for a minute, he spat it onto the ground. "Well, I ain't sayin' you hafta. But ya' know, no matter how often life stomps on ya', there's always a body what's been stomped on worse. I bin blessed. In spite of rustlers, flood and drought, I got my place. But mostly I got my Rosie."

"Your wife seems like a nice lady," Mac said. "Probably everything a man could want in a wife." A twinge of jealousy pinched inside his chest.

Gruber chortled. "Haw. If Rosie heard you say that, she'd laugh herself plumb to death. That woman is the contrariest, most stubborn, ball-bustin' woman God ever created. If I say left, she says right. When I say it's mornin', she insists it's evenin'. When I tell her she's the best thing what ever happened to me, she tells me to go soak my old thang..." He blushed before continuing, "...ahem, in the water trough."

"Yeah, but that's just talk. She's stuck by you all these years, so she must love you."

The old rancher roared with laughter. "Son, that woman has left me more times than I can shake a stick at. Says she's got better things to do with her life than hang around some dried-up old piece o' shit like me."

Mac blinked in confusion.

A smile spread across Gruber's face, reveling his stained teeth, and lighting up his eyes. "But she never gits farther than her sister's house in town, and she's always back to cook supper."

"I don't understand. Why does she leave you so often?"

"Son, it's the nature of the beast." Gruber shook his head. "Jist like cows is stupid, women are naturally contrary and skittish. Don't mean they don't love ya', jist means sometimes they're scared or just plain feelin' ornery. 'Course they always gotta blame it on us men."

He bit off another chaw. "Naw, Rosie may be tough to live with, but I wouldn't want to try livin' without her." He gathered up his reins. "So, that bein' said, gotta get on back to my Rosie," he grinned, settling himself into his saddle. "And y'all oughta git back to your Gracie ya bin tellin' me about."

Mac smiled at Tom Gruber, an ugly little man missing most of his teeth and hair, whose fingers were gnarled from arthritis and who limped. But the old man considered himself blessed because he was going home to his wife, a plump woman closing in on sixty with gray hair and wrinkles, who apparently cussed him out on a regular basis, had no compunction about saying she was leaving him, and had less than complimentary things to say about his... well, best leave that one alone.

And yet, it was obvious she loved him. And Gruber loved her back.

Something fragile shivered inside him. Gracie was probably afraid, like he was. She told him she loved him in the only way she could, through her writing and her lovemaking. For a well-bred young woman, it was the only way. The rest was up to him. It was his job to say he loved her first, and if she rejected him, well, as a man, it was his job to handle it.

But somehow, after hearing Gruber's story, he didn't think she would turn him away. "That's good advice, and I thank you for it." He shook hands one more time, and watched, with relief and ill-concealed glee, the ass ends of his cows being driven away by Gruber and his hands. Gathering up his reins, he headed home, determined to tell Gracie about the blessings he had received—and that he loved her. Not even putting Horse away in his stall because he was so anxious to see Gracie and tell her of his success, he headed straight for the house.

"Gracie," he yelled and bounded up the stairs of the front porch. Impatient to see the joy and pride in her eyes when she heard about the ten new horses he'd negotiated for, he banged open the front door and rushed in.

"Run," she screamed. "Run, McLean, run." Pain exploded in his head when something hit his skull and then blackness.

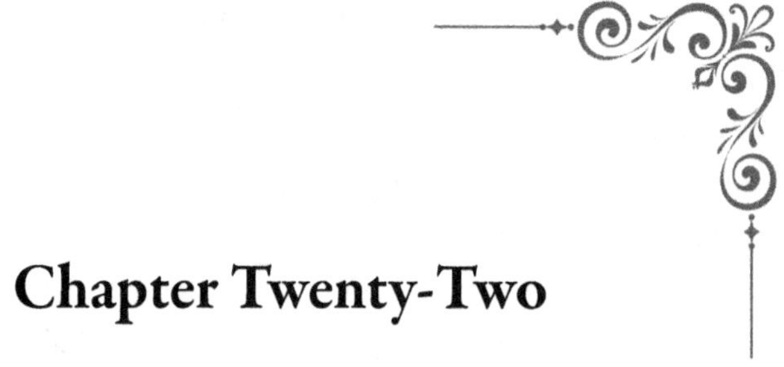

Chapter Twenty-Two

Water hit him in the face, almost drowning him. He coughed, gagging when it ran into his nose and throat. Raising his head, he blinked the water out of his eyes.

"Well, mornin', sunshine," a smarmy voice whispered in his ear. "How nice of y'all to join us." A hand locked into his hair and slammed his head against the wall.

He stared Fox in the eyes but behind his back, he pulled at the ropes binding him, testing the knots, careful not to let the outlaws see his movements. "Fox. What the hell do you want?" He pulled and tugged on the ropes to no avail. *Damn it, tighter than a virgin's thighs.*

His hand still twined in Mac's hair, Fox gave another hard yank and laughed. "Now, is that any way to greet an old friend?" he said with a sneer.

"You're no friend of mine," Mac spat. A slap spun his head to the left, giving him the opportunity to get a quick look around the kitchen. Gracie stood against the far wall, her face bleached white and her eyes big as half dollars, holding Hannah's shoulders with her hands.

With a glance, he assessed their condition. Gracie seemed fine. So did Hannah. Scared but uninjured, thank God.

He turned back to face Fox. "What do you want?" he repeated, swallowing his fear, recognizing that, like all animals, fear would make Fox more vicious.

Pulling a long Bowie knife from his boot, Fox began paring his fingernails, letting the clippings fall into Mac's lap. "Well, to say I'm a might peeved at you would be understatin' the situation a tad," Fox said. "I read that there story that Hart woman wrote," he continued and used the tip of his knife to push up the brim of his hat. "...can't say I much care for the manner in which it pro-trays me." Leaning over, he put his hands on the arms of Mac's chair, putting his face level with Mac's.

"In fact, it makes me look like a damn fool," he roared. "And I ain't gonna stand for it. I figure you put her up to it so for that I owe you." Running the blade of his knife down Mac's cheek, he left a thin red line of blood parallel to the scar he'd given Mac five years before. "But first... yer goin' to tell me where that bitch woman, Grace Hart is, 'cause I owe her even more."

Surprised Fox that didn't recognize the woman he was searching for stood ten feet away from him, Mac forced himself to keep his eyes from sliding in her direction. "I didn't put her up to it, and I'm not aware of her location." His reward was another slap, harder than the first that left his head ringing and his eyes watering from the sting.

He let his head hang down for a while, buying time.

"Wrong answer, McLean," Fox snarled.

"It's the only one I've got," he sneered in return. This time a fist met his face. A few stars twinkled against the blackness eddying at the edge of his mind. After a moment, the stars blinked and blinked out.

MAC SLOWLY BECAME AWARE that he was still tied to a chair, still aching in every joint, every muscle. His head spinning, he wondered how much pain a body could take before it grew numb altogether. It seemed like if anyone should have the answer to the question, he would be the one—given his little incident with the barbed wire and all—but since he'd been unconscious for a good bit of that pain part, he probably wasn't a good judge of pain. But he guessed he would find out.

A fist hit his already swollen eye with a squishy sound. He groaned, having ceased long ago to care about how much noise he made. It made him feel better to groan, and it seemed to make Dexter feel better too, because he didn't hit Mac nearly so hard when Mac made lots of pained noises.

In fact, now that he contemplated it, he was getting kind of used to the constant bludgeoning. It had a comforting familiarity to it, almost like an old friend. In his head, he could time the event. Fox would yank back his head. Splat. A sharp, burning pain wherever the fist landed. A pause. A bit of panting on his part. Fox would sneer and survey with pleasure the damage he inflicted. "Where is she?" was growled in his ear after each blow. There would be another pause while Fox waited for Mac to answer. Mac would say nothing and then it started all over again.

It hurt like hell, but fists were much preferable to the knife tucked in Fox's belt. It was hard to be sanguine about having parts of his body carved off, but lucky for him, Fox wasn't a very subtle person and seemed to get much more satisfaction out of beating Mac to a pulp than carving him up. Thus far, the outlaw limited himself to quick jabs that left him hurting, but he was afraid even Fox's dim mind would realize sooner or later how much more effective the knife would be.

He was tired, and the temptation to give in was strong but he only had to look at Gracie, her arm protectively around Hannah, terror whitening her, to determine he wouldn't—couldn't ever tell. Fox was occupied with beating him now, but the minute he told them what they wanted to hear, he was dead, which he could live with—he chuckled to himself at the irony—but so were Gracie and Hannah which was a thought not to be born.

Gritting his teeth, he prepared himself for the next punch.

THE ONE THING KEEPING Gracie on her feet was an incomprehensible belief that if she stayed, the outlaws wouldn't kill McLean, that and an overwhelming urge to keep Hannah safe. Watching McLean taking punch after punch, her heart twisted with guilt each time a blow fell, understanding that each blow was to save her. Yet she could do nothing to save him.

But possibly she could do something to save Hannah. For a long time an idea had wafted in and out of her mind, a dangerous idea she'd discarded several times already but it resurfaced again and again.

She looked down at Hannah, precious Hannah. No, she couldn't. It was too dangerous. She'd never forgive herself if something happened to the child she loved because Gracie hadn't made the right decision. She glanced back at the three outlaws, seeing the brutality in their faces, the cruelty they took no pains to hide.

But she had to do something. Otherwise, they all were dead anyway.

She coughed and glanced at McLean, bowing her head to peer out from underneath her bangs. He lifted his head and blinked at her. She rolled her eyes towards the partially opened basement door for a moment then glanced down at Hannah before looking back at McLean, a question in her eyes. For a split second he looked back, indecision on his face.

Then he nodded, an infinitesimal movement of his head.

She settled back against the wall, waiting. The wait seemed endless. Fox hit McLean again, then stepped back, shaking his hand, his face a combination of fury and pain from his hand.

"Tell me where she is," he demanded, probably for the hundredth time.

Mac didn't even bother to shake his head.

Buck sighed. "This is getting boring and I gotta pee. I'm going upstairs to find a pot so's I can take a piss," he said. "Be right back." Exiting the kitchen, he pounded up the stairs.

"He ain't looking for no pot," the elfish man said, the one called Cletus. "He's up there going through the drawers and closets looking for loot."

Fist already raised to strike McLean again, Fox rounded on Cletus. "Get him. Now," he snarled.

Cletus scuttled out of the kitchen and trotted upstairs.

Now. Now was the time. Only Fox remained in the kitchen, and his attention was all on McLean. Gracie nudged Hannah and jerked her chin towards the basement door. Hannah's eyes opened wide, looking back and forth between Gracie and the door several times, disbelief in her face.

Gracie gave Hannah another nudge. "Yes. Your daddy said yes. Rheingold," she whispered, and after a brief hesitation the child's expression changed from doubt to resolution. Slowly, an inch at a time, she edged toward the door until she reached it. Without a sound, she slipped through the gap and was gone. Gracie heaved a silent sigh of relief and glanced at McLean.

He was staring at her, his eyes blazing with something which caught her breath. He whipped his gaze away from her face, careful not to give away their secret, but in the brief second before he did, she saw pride and approval and—God, please let her not be mistaken—love. Her heart leap-frogged in her chest and the words *I love you* hovered on her lips in response.

Cletus slithered back into the kitchen, a sour-looking Buck on his heels. "Couldn't find no pot," Buck said, staring at Fox with a challenge in his eyes. "But we ain't eaten in hours and I'm hungry."

"So get some food, asshole."

Buck smiled and strolled to the pantry with Cletus following him. After surveying the shelves, Buck pulled bread and a jar of jelly off the shelf and took their finds to the table. They sat down to eat.

Fox took another swing at Mac, so half-hearted it didn't even make a sound when it landed.

Fuck," the outlaw snapped. "This ain't working, the hero here will die before he tells us anything." Obviously frustrated, he leveled a malignant stare at Mac who glared defiantly back, albeit from bloodshot swollen eyes. "I got to think of something else."

STARING OPEN-MOUTHED at Fox's frustration with his captive, Cletus wiped the snot dribbling from his nose and rubbed it off on the seat of his pants.

Gol-damn that McLean. He was making Fox look real bad and that made Cletus madder than spit. If Cletus done had his way, he'da already cut McLean up good and had him by-God singin' like a prairie dog. Wastin' time was all they was doin'—fartin' around tryin' to get that there McLean to talk. He sure wished he could figger a way to help Dexter.

Kicking at the floor in anger, his gaze wandered to the rag doll abandoned when he'd grabbed up the little girl. Huh. Why would a kid want to play with a stupid stuffed doll what didn't even look like a real baby when there was more fun things like slingshots and popguns and stuff like that? Girls sure was dumb, 'specially girls what lost their dumb dolls. Dumb girl oughta hang onto her stuff better.

Kids was nothing but trouble, howsomever people like McLean seemed to dote on them, even if they wasn't even their own. Thinking about the kid, something tickled the back of his mind.

Oh. Yeah. The kid. There was an idea. They should use the kid to get McLean to talk. Hot damn, Dexter was gonna to be so proud of him.

Intent on carrying out his plan, he scanned the room, looking for the strange, silent kid. Not locating her the first time, thinking he was mistaken, he took another sweep. Puzzled, he picked his nose and examined the booger he'd pulled out while he cogitated on it.

She was here a while ago. He musta missed her, her being so tiny and quiet and all. Moving back a step to get a better view, he looked again. Nope. No kid, big or little. Oh, dad-gum it. Dexter was gonna be madder than a skillet full of rattlesnakes.

His insides shaking, Cletus whispered in a shaky voice, "Dex?" No answer. "Dex," he said louder, but still not loud enough. Oh shee-it, Cletus cringed, his stomach doing flip-flops of terror. Dexter was sure as shootin' gonna have a hissy fit.

"Dexter," he hollered, his voice cracking.

"What the fuck do you want," Dexter roared, swinging around.

Wrapping his arms around his head, Cletus cowered. "That there kid?" he whimpered, fear turning his face white. "She ain't here no more."

Fox spun on his heel, viewing the room in a matter of seconds. Striding to Gracie, he leaned over until they were nose to nose. "Where's the kid?" he roared.

Gracie gathered her courage and lied like hell. Normally she was a terrible liar but today she lied like Hannah's life depended on it. Because it did. "I think she went upstairs to sleep."

"Check upstairs," Fox ordered. Cletus hurried up the stairs then clattered back down.

"Nope."

"Son of a bitch!" Fox swelled with fury, stomping his feet like a two-year-old. Then his eyes got mean and he yelled, "You two lame-brained, mule-eared sons-a-bitches, get your asses out there and find that kid."

IF THE SITUATION WASN'T so serious, she would have laughed. Buck and Cletus looked ready to expire from fright they were so unnerved by the angry Fox. Their fear was probably justified by the fact that, in his rage, Fox leaped on Cletus and used his Bowie knife to lop off the tip of Cletus's ear, saying if he was so goddammed deaf he couldn't hear one measly kid sneaking off he didn't need the goddammed ear anyhow. He was goddammed lucky it weren't his eye instead.

Looking more scared than a gobbler at a turkey shoot, Cletus bolted from the kitchen followed by Buck, who was running with both hands over his head, clearly anxious to keep his own ears. Silence descended on the room after the pair left, a silence broken by the sound of Fox's pacing and swearing. She exchanged looks with McLean, wincing at the sight of his broken face, but cheered when he sort of winked at her with his swollen eye.

Down but not out, thank God.

They both jumped when Fox pulled a chair around to face McLean and plunked himself down in it. Glaring, he growled, "Y'all may think yur purty smart, McLean, but them two fellers is gonna catch that kid." Sucking on his gold tooth, he affirmed, "And then we'll finish this. But until then...we'll wait." Raising the Bowie knife, he bared his teeth in a smile that didn't quite reach his eyes and proceeded to pare his nails.

BUCK TRAMPED THROUGH the damn fields for hours. Thinking they'd find the kid faster, he and Cletus split up and went in different directions. But Buck could tell, no matter how much he'd like to get his hands on the kid, it wasn't going to happen. Too bad. She kinda reminded him of his little sister, Mary, the one who died last year of diphtheria. 'Bout killed his mama. For a while there, seeing the resemblance, he thought maybe he'd bring the kid home to her to replace Mary. Oh well. Maybe he could find another kid.

The sun had set several hours ago, making it darker than the bottom of an outhouse hole. He'd long ago lost sight of the house and now he was wandering and wondering what the hell he'd gotten himself into.

Clenching his fist, he punched a tree, and swore at the pain. This whole idea was stupid. What did he care about some lady writer and Fox's beef with her? He'd come, thinking there might be some money in it, but it was obvious to him McLean didn't have a goddammed dime and now the kid was out there maybe blabbing to the law. No, there was nothing here for him except for a prison sentence, so the minute he could retrieve his horse, he planned on mounting up and heading out for parts unknown.

Cursing and sweating, he wandered for a while more before finally stumbling into a line of split rail fences. With smug satisfaction, he recognized the pasture where they'd hidden their mounts. Huh. He musta walked in a circle but that was fine by him. Climbing over the fence, he moved around the perimeter, whistling quietly for his horse, Jack. A low knicker came from his left and he changed directions. Seeing the black and white form of his paint, he approached him with care, talking to calm the animal.

The dark silhouette drew closer. He reached a hand out and touched warm furry hide. Wrapping his hand in the horse's mane, he led Jack to where they hung the bridles on a fence post then slipped the bridle in the horse's mouth and swung up onto his bare back, thinking with a twinge of regret about his hand-tooled saddle stashed under some straw in the barn. Well, the hell with it—he'd steal another one. Kneeing the horse over to the fence, he opened the gate and reined Jack outside. He shut it behind him.

Without a backward glance, Buck spurred the horse into a rolling canter, heading west towards bright lights and soft women.

"GOL-DARN IT," CLETUS muttered to himself, "I sure do hate the dark." It purely gave him the trots, the way the shadows snuck up on a man, and all the creepy noises emanating from the bushes, which explained the reason he was talking to himself. No telling what kind of long-toothed, saber-clawed critters made them noises. If he weren't even more scared of Dexter's long knife, he'd have guv up the search for the brat long ago. But he was sure if he didn't come back toting that kid, he better not come back a-tall.

Come to think, the woods weren't so terrifying after all. "Nosirree," Cletus whispered into the darkness. "I kin handle it jist fine."

To the left something large rustled in the bushes. Cletus shrieked and jumped, his heart hammering. Well shit. Maybe he *was* safer with Dexter, knife or not.

Swiping at the sweat running down his face, Cletus turned to walk a bit further. "No, better just run," he muttered, breaking into a trot. "Runnin'll git me there faster." Something crashed in the bushes, and he heard the sound of tree limbs breaking and lots of leaves falling, the sign of something big.

His heart now in his throat, Cletus tore down the gloomy road. Something leaped out of the bushes in front of him, something dark and big like a bear. He screamed, a long, shrill tremolo of terror. His heart jerked against his ribs once, his eyes rolled back in his head and he collapsed.

"Oh, hell," Cletus said, right before his head hit the ground. He wuz gonna die.

"WAKE UP, BOOMER," SAID a low, gravelly voice in his ear. The bear shook him. Cletus wailed and wet his pants.

"Doggone it," someone rumbled in a disgusted voice. "Would you look at that, Oskar. You scared the piss right out of him."

Cletus's eyes popped open when Oskar answered, "That's not all I'm going scare out of this piece of dog turd if he doesn't answer my questions, Murphy."

His eyes wide, Cletus gawked at a giant of a man who was glaring down at him, in his fear hardly aware of the six or seven other men standing in a ring around him. He clambered to his feet, hoping that standing upright would put him on a level playing field. But, dang, like usual, they was all taller than him. And it kinda looked like they were all meaner'n him too.

He whimpered. "I didn't do nothing. I wuz jist takin' a evening stroll."

Oskar gave a snort of laughter. "Do you believe that, Murphy? He was taking a stroll. Eight o'clock at night, the sun's down, miles from anywhere, and he's taking a stroll." He clucked in disbelief, the sound sending chills up Cletus's back. The chills got worse when light from a lantern glinted off the silver star attached to the bear's vest.

Cletus moaned. The law. Oh damn.

"Hey, mayor, did you hear the lie this piece of dung said?" the lawman asked a middle-aged man who so far kept to the back of the group of men surrounding Cletus. "What do we usually do in Los Marcos with liars like Cletus Boomer, mayor?"

His lips quivering uncontrollably, his eyes almost popping out of his head, Cletus craned his skinny neck to look over the bear's shoulder at the heavy-set man the sheriff was addressing.

The mayor stepped forward and said in a self-righteous voice, "Why, we don't generally have to worry too much about his type around these parts. The last low life we caught, instead of putting the county to the expense of hanging him, we strung him up by his balls till they ripped off."

Belly shaking with laughter, Potter continued, "I'm not sure if he ever lied again but I can tell you this, if he did, he lied in a falsetto." He grinned, his chins wobbling. "Course this one's so puny it might not happen. He might hafta hang there till his nuts rot and fall off."

Grabbing his crotch, Cletus blubbered, "No, no, that's inhuman. Y'all cain't do that to a man."

Oskar studied the buttons on the front of Cletus's trousers as if assessing his next move. "Mayor? Is our hanging post still up or did we take it down after the last fellow?" Someone snickered, a sleazy laugh, and the men edged a step closer towards Cletus.

"Aright, aright," Cletus screeched. "Tell me what you want. Whatever ya' want, tell me and I'll do it."

His eyes hardening to blue agate, the law yanked Cletus up to his tiptoes. "That's what I wanted to hear, Boomer."

Still with a chokehold on Cletus, Oskar said to the man standing at his shoulder, "Larkin, go fetch McLean's little girl and bring her here." He faced Cletus, narrowing his eyes while twisting his fist into Cletus's dirty collar.

"Now," he growled. "Tell me everything going on at the McLean place."

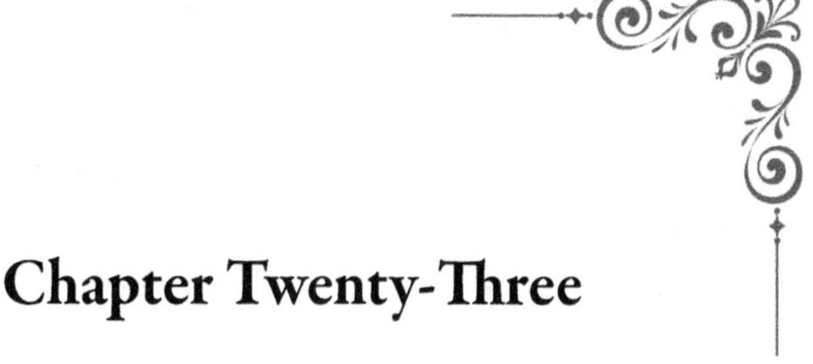

Chapter Twenty-Three

"I don't think your men are coming back."

"Shut yer mouth, woman. They'll come back," Dexter snarled, glaring at Gracie, his pupils narrowed to pinpoints in his yellowish eyes.

She lifted her nose in the air. "Hmmph." The more time that passed since those horrible men left, the more positive she was Hannah escaped which naturally delighted Gracie. After all, how often did a female manage to pull one over on a genuine outlaw? Jupiter, she could write a terrific book about this experience.

But her smugness deflated when she saw Mac glaring at her and making frantic jerking motions with his chin, so against her own—better—inclinations, she bit her tongue.

"For Pete's, Gracie, stop. Don't make him angry," he hissed.

All right, maybe it wasn't a good idea to make the outlaw angry. She shouldn't have said what she said but sometimes she couldn't help herself. Knuckling under to mean-spirited bullies was something she just couldn't do, but there was no point in giving McLean a heart attack and killing him quite yet. Dexter Fox might do that soon enough without any help from her.

Fox drummed his fingers on the back of the chair he straddled. After nearly driving Gracie crazy with his nervous tapping, the outlaw grew restless and wandered to the window. He moved the curtains aside to peer outside into the darkness, all the while muttering virulent threats involving knives and branding irons and what he was going to do with his two henchmen when he got his hands on them.

With Dexter's back turned, Gracie took the opportunity to kneel down and test the ropes behind Mac's back. "Do they hurt much?" she whispered.

He shook his head and chuckled, a low rusty sound. "I can't feel my hands anymore, so no, I guess you could say they don't hurt." Checking over his shoulder, he whispered, "Do you think she's all right?" They both understood his question.

The fear she tried to ignore resurfaced and she bit her lip. "I don't know," she answered back in a low voice and pulled herself upright, her knees popping. The long day and night without sleep were beginning to tell on her but she was trying to stay alert and positive for McLean's sake. She pressed up against his side, letting his heat warm her, wishing it would absorb all the way inside where icy fear still lurked.

"But I think it's a good sign they haven't come back with her. It must mean she got away, don't you think?" she whispered.

Mac smiled with one side of his mouth (the other side was too banged up for smiling) and muttered, "If nothing else, at least I'll know she's safe until this is all over."

"Don't talk like that," she hissed, keeping one eye on Fox still standing tensely at the window. "We're going to get out of this alive."

His eyes crinkling in amusement, he said, "Whatever you say, darlin'," then his eyes drifted shut, his head dipped, and he slept.

Afraid to leave him, she propped herself against the arm of the chair McLean was tied to and tried to rest. Where was Hannah? Was she really safe? If she managed to escape, did she try to summon help? Would she be able to ask for help given that she couldn't speak.

The questions rolled around and around in her brain until her vision clouded.

The lack of sleep must be catching up with her. The kitchen had a white, hazy look to it, like it was draped in a winter fog. Her head wobbling on her neck, her eyes burning from lack of sleep. She frowned and watched smoky ropes curl lazily around the stove pipe then dissipate into thin white threads spreading across the ceiling.

What? She blinked, clearing her vision, thinking it was exhaustion making her see things. Nope, still there. Glancing down she saw more ropes of white issuing from the cracks around the stove door. How strange. It looked like smoke. But it couldn't be smoke, there hadn't been a fire in the stove since yesterday, when she'd cooked dinner for the outlaws.

She looked over at the kitchen door, cocking her head to follow the tendrils drifting across the floor. More white clouds billowed out from underneath the door. Glancing over at Fox, she could see him still staring out the window at the darkness outside, muttering and fidgeting, while smoke continued to wisp into the kitchen.

She swayed, falling asleep on her feet.

Something tickled her throat. She coughed, jerked awake. Her eyes popped open and she realized the white wisps were definitely smoke.

"Fire," she screamed. "Fire, fire." Jumping up and down, she pointed at the smoke gathered like a thick woolen blanket on the ceiling.

Fox whipped around, taking in the smoke-filled room in an instant. "Shit," he yelled, alarm filling his face. "The goddammed house is on fire. We're gonna fry. I gotta get outta here." Shoving his Bowie knife back into his boot, he snatched up his hat and slammed it on his head. He rushed to the back door, threw it open and bolted outside.

"Wait," she yelled. "Help me get McLean loose."

"Fuck you," Fox screamed.

"Wait," Gracie yelled, but of course, Fox was gone. "Dirty rotten jackass," she muttered.

"Gracie. Never mind him," Mac ordered, frantically pulling at the ropes around his wrists. "Get a knife or something and cut me loose."

A scream came from outside. "Son of a— Shit!" Scuffling noises filled the air, then a loud thud echoed, followed by lots of cursing and more screams.

Ignoring the noise, she raced to the cupboard and rooted around for a sharp knife but found nothing sharper than a dull table knife. Why, oh why wasn't she more organized? She whimpered in frustration and fear.

From out of the mist, an amused voice said, "Relax, Miss Gracie. Nothing to worry about," making her jump.

The large form of Sheriff Rheingold materialized, looking pale and unearthly surrounded by the haze of smoke. "It's only smoke from wet straw we lit and stuffed into the stovepipe and under the kitchen door. There's no fire." He chuckled and patted her on the shoulder, hoping to allay her fear. "And we caught Fox. He's outside in handcuffs, spitting mad."

Relief swept through Gracie. The blood left her head with a rush and for the first time in her life—and wouldn't her stiff-backed, corset-bound, society-bred mother finally be proud of her—she fainted.

"WELL, MCLEAN, YOU GOT yourself in quite a pickle here," Oskar smirked, cutting the ropes binding Mac after opening the door and all the windows to air out the room.

Mac quickly untangled his arms from the ropes, his eyes not leaving the still form of Gracie on the floor. The ropes finally fell away. He jumped out of his chair, knelt next to Gracie and pulled her into his arms.

"Gracie, come on, sweetheart. Wake up," he crooned, brushing her hair out of her pale face. When she didn't stir, he tapped her cheek and was rewarded with a small gasp and a sigh.

Her eyes opened, unfocused at first before zeroing in on his face. He'd never seen anything so welcome in his life.

One of her arms snaked around his neck. "Oh good. You're all right," she said. "I was worried." Her voice teetered.

He pulled Gracie against his chest. "Gracie. Sweetheart," he whispered, his chest squeezing around his heart until he was sure it would implode from the pressure. "I was so afraid for you. I was so afraid those bastards would hurt you." He clutched her until she squeaked and then held her away so he could see for himself she was unhurt. "I don't know what I'd do if something happened to you." He couldn't stop looking at her beautiful face.

Still bleary, she smiled muzzily. "Oh, that's so sweet. You really care about me."

His hands clamped down on her arms. "Woman, you scared the ever-loving be-jaysus out of me," he yelled, his hands trembling. "Care about you? Of course, I care about you. I love you." His voice shook.

"Oh. Oh. Oh my," she whispered. Sitting up in his arms, she ran her fingers through his hair. "I love you too. More than you know."

He grinned a lopsided, wobbly grin at her, wincing when the cut on the side of his mouth split open again.

"Love?" he asked. His voice cracked and he cleared his throat to disguise it.

In response, she threw her arms around his neck, and locked her lips with his. The kiss was so intense, he expected smoke to start steaming from his ears like the stovepipe.

She slid her tongue along the seam of his mouth and he moaned.

"God help me, you shouldn't love me," he murmured against her cheek.

"Too late," she mumbled and kissed him harder. "You're mine, and I'm never going to let you get away ever again." Kisses landed on his lips ears, chin, throat. It all seemed fair game in her assault on his supposed virtue.

Rheingold cleared his throat. "Ahem, people."

Mac ignored the man. Why stop doing something he'd wanted to do for hours, days, weeks. Gripping the back of Gracie's head, he slanted his mouth over hers and let his kiss tell her how he felt.

The sheriff cleared his throat again, accompanied this time by a tap on Mac's shoulder. Occupied with more important matters, Mac shrugged and changed the angle of his kiss.

"Break it up, you two," the sheriff finally yelled.

They jumped apart.

"Enough, for Pete's sake," Rheingold grumbled. "If this is what love does to a man, I'm glad I'm not young anymore."

Mac grinned ruefully. Rising to his feet, every muscle protesting, he held a hand out for Gracie who seemed less than happy at being interrupted. After a few more grumbles, she took his hand and let him help her up. He tucked her under his arm where she leaned against his side.

Now that Fox was captured and Gracie was safe, Mac had a lot of questions. "Oskar, I can assume, since you're here and you didn't walk in blind, that somehow Hannah found you and figured out some way to tell you what was going on. She's not hurt or anything is she? She's all right?"

Oskar slapped his hat back on his head, smiling slyly and led the way to the back door. "Oh, I guess you could say so," he answered and pushed both of them out onto the porch where a group of men stood, Fox held captive in the middle. Off to one side, looking green with fear, Cletus cowered behind the men from the posse, shielding himself from Fox's view.

Mac ignored them all in favor of his daughter, a small figure who looked lost and forlorn until she saw her father. She yanked her hand from the man who held it and raced across the grass towards her father. "Daddy," she sobbed, and threw herself into his arms. "Daddy, Daddy, I was scared so I ran and ran and ran until I found Mr. Oskar."

Stunned, Mac could only catch her and pull her up against his chest. His arms tightened, and for the second time that night tears stung his eyes, hearing over and over in his mind the words his daughter spoke for the first time.

"Hannah," he groaned finally, his voice catching on the tears clogging his throat. "Ahhh, sweet heaven. Hannah... baby.... How..." His voice failed him, and he ground to a halt, unable to say more.

Gracie joined him. Her slim arms circled his waist, holding him, and all he could do was stand and shake and weep. He wasn't ashamed of the tears trickling down his check.

Hannah patted his cheek. "Don't cry, Daddy. Everything's all right. I told Mr. Oskar he had to save you and he did." Over her shoulder she beamed at the moist-eyed sheriff who flushed and wiggled his eyebrows comically.

Meeting the sheriff's eyes Mac flexed his jaw and swallowed several times, needing to regain control over his voice. "How...? I don't understand..." He shrugged helplessly, not having the words to ask the questions.

"I dunno, McLean," Rheingold answered, spreading his hands wide in confusion. "She came bursting into my office, all outa breath—I think she musta run the whole way into town—and opened her mouth and a regular flood of words came out." He rolled his eyes. "Coulda knocked me over with a feather, but I paid attention anyhow. When I heard what she had to say, it didn't take but thirty minutes or so to get a posse together and head on out here." He stuck his thumbs in the armholes of his vest and puffed his chest out.

Listening to his story, Gracie frowned. "Why did you try to smoke us out. Jupiter, we were sure we were going to die in a fire," she asked.

"Cletus," everyone yelled.

Oskar grinned. "Cletus told us Fox almost died when his house burned down when he was a kid so he's terrified of fire," he said, filling in the gaps. "Once we wormed that out of him, it didn't take much to come up with a plan."

A roar of fury came from the middle of the group. "Cletus, you stupid piss ant," Fox shouted, trying to break free and get at the shivering little man who had hidden behind the wall of men. "I'm gonna kill you when I get my hands on you."

Anger making his body cold, Mac set Hannah down and detached himself from Gracie. "Stay here," he ordered them both in a tone that said he meant it. He stalked over to face Fox.

"Dexter," he gritted.

Fox took one look at Mac and erupted, kicking and fighting the hands holding him prisoner. "You bastard. You goddammed sonofabitch. I'll git you for this. I got you once and I can git you again." He was spitting in his fury, nearly pulling the two men who held him off their feet when he threw his weight at Mac. "I shoulda killed you when I had the chance, you bastard. You sent me to prison for three fuckin' long years and I figured I'd give you a taste of your own medicine but I shoulda killed you instead. Next time I won't fool around with settin' you up. Next time I'll cut your throat, you bastard. Just you wait, you sonofabitch. I'll escape again, like last time and when I do, I won't settle for railroading you into prison. I shoulda killed you where you sat during that holdup. Instead, like an idiot, I let you live."

"Shut your mouth, Fox," one of the men holding him said. "Or we'll gag you."

Fox subsided but his gaze was still on Mac, filled with rage. "At least I had the pleasure of making sure you went to prison. Best idea I ever had, making you rob that train. At least it was some payback. But I won't make the same mistake again. Next time I'll kill you, and I'll kill the bitch next to you," he said in a low, threatening voice, still struggling to free himself from the three men who now had hold of him.

"Taken him to jail," Oskar said.

The men holding him hauled him towards the horses. He continued to scream and curse as they dragged him away.

Mac took a deep breath. It was over at last. Wanting nothing more than an end to the drama, he started to walk back to his family.

"McLean," Rheingold said.

Mac turned.

"Did y'all listen to what he said?"

Mac shook his head, his mind on other things,

His mustache lifting in a crooked smile, the sheriff said, "Well, you shoulda. 'Cause it was important," he stated, coming up to Mac and putting an arm over his shoulder. "He just admitted he railroaded you into prison. I think you and the state of Texas might have a few things to talk about."

Epilogue

The altar was a mass of pink and white flowers piled in tall spires towering over the smoking candles, draped in long colorful blankets spilling off the edge of the altar onto the floor, all courtesy of the Ladies Garden Club of Los Marcos, Texas. The sweet scent of roses made him dizzy so he shifted his weight from his right foot to his left for the tenth time and peered over his shoulder down the candlelit aisle of the church, searching for some sign—any sign—of Gracie.

Where was the woman? She was already twenty minutes late and he was beginning to worry she'd changed her mind. A lot of rustling and low murmuring came from the pews, an indication the crowd of people who came out to see them get married wondered the same thing.

Craning his neck in the other direction, he searched the pews for Oskar, finding him in the third row. The sheriff grinned at Mac's anxiousness. With a grimace, Mac looked away to find Gracie's mother staring at him from the front row. The woman frowned, her delicately arched eyebrows meeting over her nose, a question in his eyes. Where's my daughter?

He squirmed, shrugged and gave her a wan smile. Not ready to answer any more unspoken questions, he allowed his gaze to drift on to the next person in the pew, recognizing the man with a familiar jolt, followed by an uncontrollable desire to flee. The governor of Texas smiled a benign politician's smile and waved his pudgy hand.

Taking a deep breath to calm himself, he reminded himself he had no reason for nervousness. The man had personally seen to it Mac received a pardon and then with a jovial belly laugh, had invited himself to Mac and Gracie's wedding, a wedding which started out small, only him and Gracie and Hannah but rapidly grew out of control. But he guessed when the governor personally pardoned you and reinstated your license to practice law, you didn't argue with him when he wanted to come to your wedding.

But that was no excuse for the rest of these people. Looking around the crowded church, it seemed like most of Texas had shown up to see them get married. Hell, he didn't even know half of the attendees, and of the ones he did know, most of them he didn't like.

Furtively, he pulled his watch out of his vest pocket and snapped the lid open. Twenty-five minutes late. Sweat trickled down the middle of his back and his breathing grew labored. He still had time to back out, one tiny cowardly corner of his mind reminding him he was no great prize.

A crescendo of music filled the chapel. He whipped around with a deep breath to stare down the aisle, all thought of not getting married evaporating from his mind forever at the sight.

Walking carefully down the aisle and balancing her bouquet of pink roses in her tiny hands, Hannah beamed at her father. He watched her, dazzled by how pretty she looked in her rose-colored ruffled dress, still amazed by her recovery. They shared a joyful smile.

Then his gaze traveled over her head and locked on Gracie.

Air filled his lungs with a painful rush, and he forgot to breath. Her beauty nearly overwhelmed him. In later years he would have to look at their wedding picture in order to describe her dress, but now—today—he was only aware of a vision in white, her hair piled in a soft cloud on top of her head. Her cheeks glowed apricot in the warm light of the candles and her eyes sparkled with love when they held his. Her mouth was stretch in a smile of pure bliss. He swallowed, his chest inexplicably tight. Stepping forward to meet her, he took the hand her father passed to him allowing the man to retreat to his seat next to Gracie's mother.

"Mac," his love, soon to be his wife, protested, a hint of amusement in her voice. "You're holding me too tight."

He shook his head no and kept right on holding her hand. He was never letting her go so she simply would have to get used to it. She giggled, then everyone turned to face the minister, Hannah standing between them because it wasn't just the two of them getting married, all three of them were in this marriage together.

The minister cleared his throat and lifted his bible. "Dearly beloved," he preached, raising his voice so it reached even the back pews, "We are gathered together here in the sight of God, and in the face of this company, to join together this Man and this Woman in holy Matrimony." He rambled on for a bit, reminding them of the seriousness of marriage and getting the objections out of the way.

THE RUMBLE OF HIS VOICE blurred and receded into the back of her consciousness. Gracie barely heard the ceremony. Her eyes and attention were focused on the man she loved. Everything about him was perfect. His sense of humor, his sense of honor, the love he had for her and Hannah, his tall, strong body, his handsome face—even the scar was perfect, perfect for her, at any rate.

And the most important day in their lives was perfect too. Everyone she loved was here, Hannah, her mother, father and brother. Oskar Rheingold. Even the funny little rancher, Tom Gruber and his wife Rosie, had come. And the day was made more perfect by the fact the governor pardoned Mac, not that she wouldn't have married him anyway, but she was aware he'd be much happier if he could provide for his family more securely being an attorney. And happier if he never had to touch another strand of barbed wire the rest of his life if he didn't want to.

With a little thrill of excitement, she listened to the minister start the vows. He turned to Mac and said, "Repeat after me: I, Harold Franklin McLean,

"I, Harold Franklin McLean," Mac said.

"Stop," Gracie yelped.

Mac jumped. "What?"

"Harold?" she exclaimed, aghast. "Harold!"

"What?" he asked again, looking puzzled.

Her gaze dropped to his belt level and popped back up to look at her soon-to-be-husband with a twinkle in her eye. "Your first name is Harold?" She giggled. Seeing Mac's face redden, she laughed harder until she was bent over, holding her stomach while the wedding guests talked and tittered, wondering what was so funny.

The minister stammered, protesting her behavior. "Sir," he appealed.

Mac sighed. He got it. Yes, it was funny. He probably should have told her but... too late now. Eventually she'd wind down. Staring at the congregation, he tapped a foot and smiled apologetically, while Gracie continued to laugh uproariously.

Her raucous laughter eventually wound down to a giggle, then a titter and a snort or two. She hiccupped and finally stopped all together but the twinkle in her eye remained.

Shaking his head, he turned back to the minister. "Continue," he ordered.

"B-b-but sir," the man stuttered, eyeing Gracie like any second as if he expected her to start frothing at the mouth and biting people.

Waving his hand in a hurry-up motion, Mac glowered at the man of God. The minister cleared his throat. "Yes, of course. Uh, do you, Harold Franklin..."

"We did that part," he interrupted, looking at a breathless Gracie from the corner of his eye when a snicker escaped. Holding her ribs, she wiped tears from her eyes and attempted to straighten up. "And yes, I do. So hurry up. Get to the rest."

Resembling a scared rabbit more than ever, the man rushed to the next part. "Do you, Grace Elizabeth Hart, take this man, Harold..."

She gave a loud bark of laughter and dropped her bouquet. "I'm sorry but... Harold."

Mac rolled his eyes. "Oh, for heaven's sake. She does. Just get on with it, man," he growled, cocking an eye over his shoulder at the wedding guests, most of whom chuckled.

Seeing Mac's inquiring look, the governor roared with laughter and shouted, "She does, you ninny. Now, come on, Pastor, pronounce them man and wife." Laughter rolled through the chapel.

"I now pronounce you man and wife," the pastor blurted out and slammed his book shut. "Put the ring on her finger. Please."

Mac turned to his left and held his hand out to the best man. Digging into his vest pocket, Mayor Potter pulled out a slim gold ring and handed it over, beaming like he was personally responsible for today's wedding.

Shaking his head in resignation, Mac took the ring. Potter. Of course, it would be Potter, right? Well, why not? Potter's insistence on being best man in spite of his protests was all of a piece with the rest of the day. He grabbed Gracie's hand, slipped the ring onto her trembling finger and yanked her into his arms.

And kissed her.

ALL INCLINATION TO laugh was gone in an instant. His kiss trailed from her lips to her toes and back again, hitting all points in between like multiple bee stings. Gracie forgot they were in church in front of a hundred people, in front of her parents, in front of the governor of the state of Texas. Her eyelids slid shut and she rose up on her toes and leaned her eager body against the hard length of Mac's. The heat of his lips locked over hers was so enticing, she stopped breathing, not wanting to lose a single sensation. His heart thrummed in his chest...or perhaps it was hers thrumming. It didn't matter. She had forty or fifty years to figure it out.

She grew light-headed, her ears rang but then he separated his mouth from hers and stepped away. Gradually the dizziness receded. Staring at the wedding guests, she realized the ringing in her ears was their overwhelmingly enthusiastic response to the kiss.

Oh dear. She met the basilisk-like stare of her mother and shrugged. Unable to help herself, she flicked a glance up and down her husband's well-built frame and smiled at her mother. *I guess she's figured out that I didn't need her mother-daughter talk last night.*

Her mother winced, then smiled back at her daughter, albeit it seemed a little forced.

Quiet up till now, Hannah poked her head around her skirt and asked, "Are we married now, Daddy?"

Reaching down, Mac grabbed her up into his arms. "We sure are, dumpling. Forever and ever."

"Oh, good," Hannah stated. Reaching her arm out, she wrapped it around Gracie's neck and kissed her on the cheek. "We're married, Gracie," she exclaimed and then transferred her grip back to her father so he could carry her.

"Come on, Mrs. McLean," he said from the corner of his mouth. They started down the aisle together.

"Oh, heavens. Let's not be formal. You can call me Gracie," she answered with a sly look. "And I'm going to call you *Harold*. After all, we *are* old friends."

Returning the sly look, he replied, "Hmmm. Does this mean you'll invite Harold to bed every night for the rest of our lives?"

Walking into the sunshine, Gracie threw her head back and laughed.

THE END

If you enjoyed **Tangled Up in Texas**, check out **A Wild and Wooly Texan** available now.

Chapter One

London, February 1891

It was the smell of roses and unwashed feet that woke him. Dragging open one sleep-encrusted eye, Lord Algernon Grey stared up at the ruby-colored canopy draped overhead before carefully tilting his head to the right to gaze blearily at the wall. The familiar blue eyes of the third Duke of Stonebridge, the poor sod who lost his head under Cromwell, glared back from his portrait, seemingly critical of his descendant even after two centuries.

Ah, yes. Home, thank God, when he could as easily have awakened in any one of a dozen married ladies' beds, a whore's crib, or even a filthy gutter. Satisfied he was where he belonged, Algernon relaxed and swiveled his head in the other direction, toward the smell of feet.

One slender foot, complete with five dainty toes, rested on the pillow next to his head. He frowned as he dredged through his cloudy memory, trying to match a face to the foot. After minutes of painfully sluggish mental thrashing, Algernon admitted defeat, lifted the edge of the duvet, and allowed his gaze to trail along the length of the slim leg until it joined its owner.

Well, well, well. Deirdre Holmes. Deirdre of the scandalous reputation and even more scandalously clever mouth. Deirdre, whom he tried to lure into his bed for months but she always spurned him in favor of Lord Falkner.

Yet it seemed somehow, in some fashion, he had succeeded. He looked at the view, vaguely aware the room hung heavy with the scent of roses and sex, pleased because it meant he hadn't been too drunk to perform, always a concern when one couldn't remember entire evenings.

But, Algernon reminded himself, a man's performance shouldn't matter. Not when one possessed a handsome face, an ancient and sought-after name, and a great deal of parental wealth to support his needs, a happy state of affairs requiring nothing in the way of effort or thought on his part. Indeed, he couldn't imagine anything better than being the third son of the wealthy and generous Duke of Stonebridge.

Closing his eyes, Algernon rested his head back onto his pillow and basked in a sea of self-satisfaction. Alas, his contentment was not to last. With a crash, his bedroom door flew open. The sharp crack of heavy oak on plaster sent a shaft of blinding pain through his brain, making him want to howl. Howling, however, required entirely too much effort, so he moaned instead, and pressed the heels of his hands to his temples in a vain attempt to secure his reeling head to the rest of his body.

The heavy curtains covering the window were thrown back, sending a burst of yellow sunshine into his eyes.

He slammed his eyes shut and held a hand up to block the sunlight. "Bloody hell! Close the demmed drapes."

"Algernon. Be. Silent," his father growled.

He cracked open one eye, biting back his retort as experience with his father's tirades had taught him speaking would only make his parent angrier. Instead, he'd do as he customarily did, pretend to listen and then, the moment the lecture was over, go about his business as usual. Focusing his bleary vision on the dark silhouette of his father, he leaned back against his pillows, counting the minutes until he could return to the contentment of his own life.

Instead of the usual lecture, a bulging carpet bag dropped onto the middle of Algernon's stomach. He grunted from the weight. "Good God. What...?"

His father held up a hand and smiled a crafty smile which made Algernon swallow the rest of what he intended to say.

"Get dressed, my boy, and come down to the library," the duke said, his smile growing more devious, his thick, bushy eyebrows cocked in wicked satisfaction over his eyes. "I wish to tell you about the trip you are taking."

Texas, April 1891

"Molly Yeager, are you playing with those foolish chemicals again?" The outer door of the pharmacy slammed open.

Molly jumped as the sound of her mother's voice penetrated through the closed door of the small storage room she'd made into her laboratory.

"Oh no!" Grabbing a large cotton towel from her work table, she used it to cover all her precious beakers and glass tubes she scrimped and saved to buy. After a last distracted look, she scrambled off her stool and reached for the door leading out into her shop in order to lock it, but before she could reach it, the laboratory door flew open, banging against the wall so hard the glass beakers rattled on their metal stands.

A dark silhouette, short and round as a Texas tumbleweed, filled the doorway.

"Momma!" Molly smiled weakly and sidled backward until she stood in front of the cotton-draped mountain of glass vials, copper tubing, and Bunsen burners, and prayed Ethel Yeager didn't destroy all of her hard work.

"You *have*," her mother accused, her doughy face splotched purple with anger. She poked a pudgy finger into Molly's breastbone. "How could you? You know I've forbidden you to spend any more of our money on those foolish chemicals when we're barely making enough to get by."

Molly rubbed her sore chest and counted to ten before answering. "I know, Momma. I promise I'm not doing anything you wouldn't approve of." It was a lie but so what. She was the one who taught school all day then worked all evening in the pharmacy she'd inherited from her father to make a few extra dollars, and if she chose to spend a few pennies to accomplish her dream, she would. She just didn't want her mother to find out. "Anyway, the chemicals I buy only cost a few cents."

"I don't care how cheap the chemicals are. It's a waste of time and money. Why don't you just stick to making headache powders and Bromo-seltzers?"

"Because I'm better than that," she mumbled, distracted as she became aware of a faint acrid odor. She forced herself not to turn and look, but she knew darned well something was burning. "I'm a good chemist and I want to do something important." Something like create a new kind of fertilizer to help the local ranchers improve their grazing land. Though so far without much success.

It wasn't her fault things never went as planned. Her equipment was outdated, and her chemicals were either ten years old, left over from her father's day, or of the cheapest manufacture.

"You're just like your father," her mother huffed. "Determined to make me a laughingstock in this town. And for what?" Her lip curled. "You're a woman. Do you think you'll get paid to work as a chemist?"

Molly dug her fingers into the edge of the lab table, her nose starting to twitch from the chemical smell. "No, Momma. I guess not." But she didn't see why not. Marie Curie did.

"Hmmph. You better not. Because that's not what men want in a wife," her mother sneered. "Maybe if you weren't so smart, someone would have already asked you to be his wife."

"I'm sure you're right, Momma," Molly gritted. The acrid smell got stronger and she tilted her head to peer over her shoulder. She stifled a gasp. A thin curl of black smoke rose in the air as orange flames consumed the towel she'd thrown over her experiment.

Whirling back around, she grabbed her mother by the shoulders and pushed her through the narrow doorway of her lab then propelled her across the wooden floors of the shop to the front door.

She yanked it open. "Bye, Momma," she gasped, and pushed her mother out onto the boardwalk. Slamming the door behind her mother, she locked it.

"Molly Yeager!"

Her mother's bellow followed her as Molly ran through the door into her laboratory and out the back door leading into the alleyway. Grabbing up several tin pails, she dipped them both into the rain barrel and staggered back inside, sloshing water behind her.

She threw a pail full of water over the flames.

Instead of extinguishing it, the fire erupted into an orange ball of fire that billowed over the table, scorching everything in its path, including Molly's eyebrows. She shrieked and grabbed a heavy gunny sack from the pile she kept under the table. Swinging it wildly, she beat at the flames until the fireball flickered and went out, leaving Molly to glower at the broken beakers and bent brass pipes of her experiment.

"Mith Molly. Are you all right?"

Molly yelped and spun around to see a gap-toothed grin beaming up at her from a freckled face. "Tommy. How did you get in here?"

"I camed in with your mother and hid behind the counter."

"Oh." Molly smiled down at him as she absentmindedly licked a finger and slicked down the cowlick on the back of his head. "Yes, but I've told you not to come into my laboratory when I'm working."

"But, Mith Molly," the young boy lisped, ignoring her admonition. "I had to tell you." He pointed a dirty finger at his mouth, which he opened even wider. "See! I lost a tooth."

Molly peered into his mouth. "Good heavens. I do believe you're right. You did lose a tooth. Do you still have it?"

"Nope," he answered, sticking his thumbs into the straps of his overalls and puffing out his chest. "I swallered it." His grin faded to be replaced by a frown. "Do you suppose it'll come out the other end?"

Molly shook her head, regarding his round face with two parts exasperation and three parts affection. Not the sharpest tool in the shed, she smiled to herself, but of all her students, eight-year-old Tommy Brady was the most lovable, as if God blessed him with an unlimited amount of sweetness in exchange for the brains He hadn't given him.

Her student grinned up at her, pleased with his question. Gazing back, a tiny ache unfurled in Molly's chest. She may have given up on being married, but it didn't mean she didn't want to have children. Unfortunately, God seemed to have other plans for her. Her hope was God's plans might get her out of Briar, Texas, and away from her mother.

"What should I do if it comes out the other end, Mith Yeager?" the youngster asked, interrupting Molly's thoughts with his fixation on one particular topic as was often the case.

Molly grabbed him in a big hug. "Well, I'm sure it won't, but if it does, you probably won't know about it."

He frowned as he seemed to consider the possibility. Finally, he nodded his head. "Oh. Okay, but I was kind of hoping I could show it to Joey Clump."

After ruffling his hair, which made his cowlick pop up again, she turned back to her work table and surveyed the damage. Over a week's wages up in flames.

She sighed, because she knew her mother would somehow find out and—she glanced down and saw her charred bodice—make her pay for the cost to replace her dress. The material, old and worn, had almost disintegrated under the heat. Gaping holes rimmed with blackened fabric decorated the front of her dress like giant polka dots. In a few spots, the material had given way and hung in long tatters around her waist, exposing her chemise.

Oh dear. And her mother would know Molly lied. With a grimace, she yanked up the long shreds and tucked them into the top of her chemise to anchor them. She'd find pins to secure the pieces later, before she went home.

"Tommy, find me an empty bucket for this mess." Eager to help, he raced out the door as Molly scraped the soggy ashes and the shards of glass into a pile. Conscious of the recent disaster, she carefully picked up the last remaining beaker filled with chemicals, intending to put it safely on a shelf.

"Hey, Miss Yeager!" a different voice shouted behind her.

She jerked, startled, and dropped the beaker. The chemicals spilled out and mingled with the mess still on the table.

Whoomp! A ball of fire flared up.

"Oh my gosh. Help me!" Molly grabbed up her gunny sack again and lifted it over her head. Without warning, a wall of water hit her, soaking Molly, and leaving behind damp, tattered strands of blue cotton and lots of stringy brown hair dripping onto her chest. With a furious look at the water flinger, she walloped the flames until they were out, hopefully for the last time.

"Morty Adams!" she yelled, swinging around to face the older boy. "I've told you not to come in when the back door is closed."

The twelve-year-old bridled at her tone and dropped the empty bucket at his feet with a clang. His pugnacious jaw thrust out and his short nose rose in the air as he scowled at her from beneath shaggy blond bangs. "I ain't a dope, you know. If the cotton-picking door was locked, I wouldn't have been able come in. The door was wide open."

"Don't say 'ain't,'" Molly said as she turned to check the veracity of his statement. Sure enough, Tommy stood in the open doorway leading out to the alleyway, bucket in hand, guilt written all over his face.

Oh dear. "I'm sorry, Morty," Molly offered.

The boy grunted and stuck his hands in the pockets of his faded denim pants, sulking. Then he brightened. "Miss Yeager, you've got to come see what come in on the stage. You ain't gonna believe it."

Grabbing her hand, he dragged her out the front door of her pharmacy, ignoring the fact Molly wore only half a dress, the other half lying somewhere on the floor in the form of ashes. Moving at his slow, thoughtful pace, Tommy followed in the rear.

Morty stopped on the boardwalk and pointed at the stage depot across the street. A mountain of luggage accumulated on the ground as the stagecoach driver threw more suitcases from the top of the stagecoach. Next to the dozen or so valises stood two men, the likes of which Molly had never seen in her twenty-eight years of life.

The closest one—a prissy little man—was short and skinny, with thin legs that disappeared under a jacket too large for his short torso, making him appear to be a child clad in adult clothing. His proper little mustache twitched under his beaky nose as he hopped around, shouting at Ike, the stagecoach driver, to be more careful with the luggage.

Every time a valise hit the ground, the little man wrung his hands and moaned to the other man, "Oh dear. Please forgive him, my lord. He doesn't know what he is doing."

Molly blinked. The Lord? Had God come to town? Unlikely, although the other man seemed to believe he was God as he stood on the boardwalk twiddling his thumbs, nose in the air, while everyone else did the work.

Tall and lean and long-legged, "my lord" wore a black velvet jacket fitting his trim waist and broad shoulders to perfection, a waistcoat of scarlet-and-black embroidered silk, and a matching red-and-black ascot tied in an intricate knot under his firm chin.

Three gold fobs hung from the pockets and an umbrella—an umbrella?—in Texas?—hung over one forearm by the hooked handle.

As she stared, he removed his high crowned hat to reveal a glorious mass of pale-golden curls that sprang to life and curled beguiling about his lean face. Beating the dust off his hat on his thigh, the Lord turned to survey the long dusty street.

"Good heavens," Molly exclaimed. "Who *is* that?"

Standing next to her on the boardwalk, unconsciously echoing Molly's earlier thoughts, Tommy answered in reverent tones, "I think it'th God."

LOOKING AT THE DUSTY street of the dismal little town that was to be his home for the next year, or until he could make his father's cattle ranch profitable, whichever came first, Algernon's heart sank in his chest and collided sickeningly with his stomach. Never a good carriage passenger, the trip to Briar, Texas, had been hellacious. He was nauseous almost every mile of the way and staring at the dusty, dingy, brown town he felt doubly ill.

The wide main street was a mere block long. A number of scraggly houses peeked out from behind the dozen or so single-storied businesses lining the dirt street. All poorly constructed, with the paint beginning to peel in long strips from the cracked and splintered wood. Most of the buildings wore some sort of crude hand-painted sign over the door, indicating the nature of the business.

A quick glance told Algernon more than half the establishments were saloons.

Well, good, because he would need every one of them since he intended to stay drunk for at least the next month of his life. Drunk was better than having to deal with this town and the louts who seemed to inhabit it. The way the yokels stared and whispered, one would think they never saw a civilized man before.

Narrowing his eyes in annoyance at their rudeness, Algernon swept a gaze in a one hundred eighty-degree radius around the street, making sure he included everyone.

His eyes focused on—someone—something—he wasn't sure what, across the street. Tall, very tall. Large brown eyes blinked back at him from within a sooty-black oval. Dark-brown hair hung lank onto square shoulders. Underneath the face, he saw some sort of raggedy dress with the front removed to expose a grimy chemise. As he stared in shock, the black oval split and white teeth suddenly gleamed.

Damnation. It smiled at me. He winced and poked Martin, his valet, in the back.

"Yes, Lord Algernon?" Martin responded, turning and bowing.

Algernon pointed with distaste. "There. What is that?" he asked, wondering what kind of place allowed creatures to blacken their faces and run about, half dressed, in public.

Martin glanced across the street in the direction Algernon pointed, pausing in his attempts to make order out of chaos. "I'm sure I don't know, my lord. Shall I find out for you?"

Algernon shook his head, deciding he had no desire to examine the creature any closer. In truth, he only needed one thing: a quick and easy profit from the ranch his father sentenced him to, after which he would leave this sorry excuse for a town and return to London, where he belonged.

"No. No, thank you, Martin, I don't believe I wish to know. Just rent a conveyance and let us remove ourselves to Crossroads Ranch as quickly as possible." He sighed with exhaustion. "I'm sure you are as fatigued as I."

With a nod, Martin scurried off to look for the town livery stable. Algernon waited for his return, standing hot and itchy on the boardwalk as sweat ran down the middle of his back into the top of his trousers, feeling more and more irritable as he tried to ignore the sly smiles, stares, and whispers of the crowd who stood nearby. He took his hat off again and wiped the thin trickles of sweat from his brow.

"Godforsaken place," he muttered to himself, and jammed his hat back on. From behind, something hard poked him in the back. He turned and raised an inquiring eyebrow.

"Oh, I do beg yer pardon, ma'am," the man, one of those Western cowboys from the look of him, said. The cowboy grinned while behind him a crowd of men snickered.

"Quite all right," Algernon answered through gritted teeth, revolted as he viewed the filth-encrusted denim pants, the manure-covered high-heeled Western boots, and the greasy blond hair of the cowboy. A sour smell drifted up to his nostrils, a disgusting combination of unwashed human and liquor.

And the acrid animal smell of cow.

Algernon shuddered, the memory of cloven hooves thundering at his back and the feel of sharp horns flinging his eight-year-old self still vivid even after twenty years.

"Ooooh, did you hear that, fellas?" The rude cowboy thrust out his lower lip in a pout and placed his hand on his hip, simpering. "The lady said it was all right. I just hope I didn't hurt the poor little thing's feelings." His equally uncouth friends roared with laughter and slapped their legs with their bedraggled hats, raising a cloud of dust.

Algernon stiffened at the insult.

"Hey, Slim," another dirty ruffian said, smirking at his unwashed friend. "Would you look at all them pretty yellow curls; just like one of them high society ladies back East."

Slim chuckled. "Well shucks, Frank, I think your right, but I can't see them so good with that there fancy hat hiding them." He knocked the hat from Algernon's head with a sly grin. Then he deliberately laid his foot on top of it, smashing the crown.

"Go on, sweet thing," he smirked. "Pick it up."

His churning stomach, the unexpected attack from the cowboy, and the burning sense of being ill-used by his father all served to bring Algernon's blood to a furious boil. But...no reason to cause a fight. It wouldn't do, his first day here. Teeth clenched, he bent down to pick up his hat. He clasped the brim. And a foot smashed down on his knuckles.

Bloody...hell! He clenched his teeth against the pain and waited a moment for the foot to be removed but, of course, it wasn't.

Well, something must be done about that. "Terribly sorry, old chap," he said and surged upward, yanking his fingers free as he made a fist and caught the cowboy square on the nose with a squishy splat.

A suspended instant of consternation hung in the air while the cowboy blinked at Algernon in surprise. Then his eyes rolled back in his head and he hit the boardwalk with a crash. Silence reigned as the crowd of men stared in astonishment at the fallen Slim, arms and legs sprawled, eyes closed, and mouth opened inelegantly, a thread of saliva dribbling from his mouth.

Puzzled eyes swung back up to stare at Algernon before dipping back toward the prone man. Then there was a collective howl from the group and they all rushed at him at once.

"FIGHT!" MORTY YELLED, his eyes gleaming in masculine glee, and leapt off the boardwalk heading toward the melee.

"They're beating up God," Tommy howled and raced after Morty.

"Tommy, stop," Molly called after him, picking up her skirts. She sprinted across the street after the boys. Grunts, groans, moans, and shouts of pain filled the air as she approached. Fists flew, feet kicked, and bodies rolled in the dust. Spectators stood around them, laughing and cheering as they incited their friends to further murder and mayhem.

She forced herself through the cheering crowd of men gathered around the brawling men and stopped next to the younger boy.

"They're hurting Him, Mith Molly," the boy yelled, grabbing hold of Molly's skirt. "They're hurting God. Make them stop."

The simmering violence in the air sent a chill up Molly's spine. She gripped the boy's shoulder and pushed him toward the back of the crowd. "Tommy, get back before..."

Bang! The stagecoach horses squealed and lunged in their traces at the sound of the gunshot. The nearest horse bucked and a thrashing hoof smacked into Molly and threw her to the ground with a bone-jarring crash. The back of her head hit the packed-dirt street with a hard whack. Steel-shod feet flashed over her head. A heavy hoof thudded on the ground then another. With a gasp, she threw her arms over her head to protect herself, her heart thundering in her ears.

God help me!

Suddenly someone grabbed her collar, yanked her to her feet, and shoved her out of the way. She staggered, her head still reeling from the impact with the hard ground. After a moment, she caught her balance, and blinked at the cowboys who'd stopped their fighting and stood around her, mute and red-faced with shame.

"Oh geez. We're real sorry, Miss Molly," one of the cowboys muttered, twisting his hat in his hand.

"Yeah. We didn't mean no harm," another chimed in.

"Any harm," Molly corrected, her voice still shaky.

"That's what I said," he agreed, nodding eagerly. "We didn't mean nothing. It was that Slim Muldoon what started it and we just kind of got caught up in the fun. We wasn't thinking you might get hurt." The rest of the men added their own apologies.

Tommy sidled up to Molly's side and gripped her skirt in a small hand. Molly wrapped an arm around his shoulder. "Well, you should have been thinking," she responded sharply. "Someone could have been injured."

The men stared at the ground, looking embarrassed.

She softened her next words. "But you pulled me out from under the horse and saved my life, so I guess I have to forgive you."

The men looked at each other, shame written on their faces, and scuffled their feet like small boys.

"That weren't one of us, Miss Molly," one admitted in a low voice.

Molly frowned. "Then who did?"

As one, the men pointed behind her. "He did," they chorused.

"Who did?" she asked, frowning as she turned.

And blinked as she stared at the closest thing to perfection she'd ever seen. Even bruised and bleeding, everything about him was mind-boggling, from his large, sleepy gray eyes, slashing cheekbones and strong chin to his chiseled nose and perfectly sculpted lips, never mind the long legs, broad shoulders and tapered waistline, which didn't bear repeating since she'd already admired them more than once from across the street.

"You did?" she whispered.

"Are you unhurt?" he asked. One blond brow rose in question.

Molly blinked, taken aback by the movement. How did he do that? "Oh. Yes, I'm fine. I guess thanks to you, mister."

"My lord," he replied. The eyebrow went higher and disappeared into the shiny blond curls falling over his wide forehead.

The thought of running her fingers through those curls stopped the breath in Molly's chest. She swallowed, realizing she'd let the silence drag on in her admiration as he stared at her, his eyebrow still cocked. She pulled herself together with difficulty. "Well...er, I don't approve of taking the Lord's name in vain, however I suppose it's forgivable under these circumstances."

"No," he corrected. "That is how you should address me. 'My lord.'" He brushed at the dirt on his jacket sleeve while eyeing her from under his long lashes.

Next to her, Tommy jerked in excitement. "Thee, Miss Molly," he whispered in awestruck tones. "He is God."

God? He certainly wasn't God. She grimaced, all thoughts of his good looks and his good deed erased by his rudeness and the fact he was staring at her breasts, barely concealed by what was left of her chemise.

She jerked the bits and pieces of her charred dress up as far as the strands would reach and held them to her chest. "Hah! I don't call anyone 'My Lord' except God." Just to make sure he understood, she added, "And you aren't him."

His mouth fell open. She glowered at him for a moment, her nose raised in the air then spun on her heel and stalked away.

STUNNED AT HER TEMERITY—AND the fact she could actually speak English—Algernon watched the woman march across the dirt road, her back stiff and her skirts swishing like an angry cat's tail.

He sucked in a breath. In spite of the tatters and the dirt, there was something beguiling about the sway of her backside. He watched, fascinated, his head cocked, until she disappeared inside one of the dilapidated buildings across the street, and slammed the door behind her. The view gone, he turned to glare at the spectators who still remained on the boardwalk, eyeing him with amusement. Bloody hell, what kind of country was this where the residents mocked a man simply because he chose to dress like a gentleman? In England, no one ever questioned his manhood; in fact, everyone who mattered admired him for being a bruising rider, a better than average tennis player, and a first-rate pugilist able to best his opponent as long as it was a fair fight.

The problem was these country bumpkins didn't obey the Marquess of Queensbury rules. His pride still smarting, Algernon pulled his handkerchief from his pocket to dab at the blood trickling down his chin and sent the bystanders another glare. With a smirk, they all drifted away, leaving him standing alone on the boardwalk. Except for the young boy, who still stood and stared at him, his mouth agape.

"I try really hard, God, honest I do, but sometimes I can't help myself and I just do bad things. Am I going to go to hell?" the boy asked.

Algernon blinked. The boy continued to stare, waiting for an answer, his eyes large and worried.

"Go away, child."

The boy's lower lip went out. "Wath I bad? I'm thorry."

Oh, dear God. Why were little boys so appealing? And why was he such a sucker? Heaving a sigh, he reached into his waistcoat pocket and pulled out a small paper sack filled with horehound candies, his favorite. He'd eked them out for the last month of travel, not sure when, if ever, he'd be able to find more. He stared at the sack for a moment, his mouth watering then thrust it at the child.

"Don't worry...Tommy," he added at the end, at last remembering the boy's name. "God loves all little boys." Tommy stared, his eyes huge. Algernon shook the sack, causing a papery rattle. "Well, go ahead. Take it. You've been forgiven."

His mouth open in awe, the boy slowly reached out and took the sack. His eyes widened when he opened it and saw what was inside. "Thank you, God," he whispered in awe.

"Yes, yes," Algernon answered. "Now go and sin no more." *Damnation.* Had he just said that?

With a quick smile, the boy spun around and raced back across the street while Algernon patted his empty pocket, already missing the comfort he got from his favorite treat. Still, he'd enjoyed the small thrill of pleasure he'd felt at the sight of the boy's excitement, so perhaps it was worth it.

However, time was wasting. It was hot and dusty here on the street, and he was exhausted. Seeing the crowd gathered for the fight had dispersed, he gave a passing thought to locating Martin, because, after all, without Martin, his plans would come to nothing. Upon further consideration, he decided his current needs were far more pressing.

Entering the closest saloon, he extracted a hundred-dollar bill from his wallet, delighting the saloon owner, and bought a case of fine Kentucky whiskey. If he was to live in Texas for the next year, he may as well enjoy it.

Coming May 2025

Knight Time in Texas

www.ingramcontent.com/pod-product-compliance
Lightning Source LLC
LaVergne TN
LVHW010603100826
845148LV00014B/2826

* 9 7 9 8 9 8 8 1 0 0 7 7 5 *